Warning Signs

An Alexis Parker novel

G.K. Parks

Copyright © 2021 G.K. Parks

A Modus Operandi imprint

ISBN:
ISBN-13: 978-1-942710-27-1

For the readers I've met along the way, who have turned into friends and love the characters as much as I do, this one's for you.

BOOKS IN THE LIV DEMARCO SERIES:

Dangerous Stakes
Operation Stakeout
Unforeseen Danger
Deadly Dealings
High Risk
Fatal Mistake

BOOKS IN THE ALEXIS PARKER SERIES:

Likely Suspects
The Warhol Incident
Mimicry of Banshees
Suspicion of Murder
Racing Through Darkness
Camels and Corpses
Lack of Jurisdiction
Dying for a Fix
Intended Target
Muffled Echoes
Crisis of Conscience
Misplaced Trust
Whitewashed Lies
On Tilt
Purview of Flashbulbs
The Long Game
Burning Embers
Thick Fog
Warning Signs
Past Crimes

BOOKS IN THE JULIAN MERCER SERIES:

Condemned
Betrayal
Subversion
Reparation
Retaliation
Hunting Grounds

BOOKS IN THE CROSS SECURITY INVESTIGATIONS SERIES:

Fallen Angel
Calculated Risk

ONE

"You killed him." His hot breath danced along my neck, clinging to my skin. "Steve Cooper's dead because of you."

It wasn't true. I knew it. I just didn't believe it. "No."

He laughed. The sound made my skin crawl, and I shuddered. Images flashed behind my closed eyelids. The crime scene. The barely recognizable body. So much gore. Flesh and bone painted a sinister red. My friend dead, drowned in his own blood. Tears sprang to my eyes, and I swallowed a whimper.

I tried to jerk away when he nibbled on my earlobe, so he grabbed my wrists and held them above my head. My chest heaved. He already had my legs pinned. Now he had my arms too.

He settled his body on top of mine, pressing me into the ground with his weight. "I bet you enjoyed it. You wanted me to do it. You let me do it. You wanted to see me work, Alex. You wanted to see the lengths I'd go to for you. Doesn't this make you happy?" He kissed along my neck.

"No, please."

"Just like Jablonsky. The only thing better would have been killing him. But I got Lucca instead. You can't keep your partners alive, can you? As soon as someone helps you, cares about you, he has to suffer the consequences. You killed them all."

"That was you. You did that."

"You wanted me to. You let me escape. Isn't this what you wanted, chica?" He peered over his shoulder, and I followed his gaze, spotting Agent Eddie Lucca on the floor, the knife lying beside him as blood seeped out of the wound in his chest.

Lucca coughed and trembled. I had to get to him. I had to save him, but this bastard had me pinned. If only I'd been stronger or faster. Why didn't I shoot him when I had the chance? Why didn't I stop this?

The fear took over. I couldn't move. I couldn't think. *Dammit, Alex, focus.* Despite my better judgment, I rotated my thighs and spread my legs, easing my limbs out from beneath his weight. He settled more firmly against me, pleased by the invitation, but at least my legs were free. Now I could fight back.

I locked one heel behind his knee, but I wasn't at a good angle to flip him off of me. Repositioning, I tried to worm my way out from beneath him, but he didn't seem to notice. And no matter how hard I tried, I couldn't make him budge.

He interlocked his fingers with mine and skimmed his nose along the side of my face. The bile rose in the back of my throat. His lips brushed my temple, and I gasped. I'd never felt so powerless.

My breath grew shallow, frantic, and I couldn't stop shivering. Any minute, I was going to be sick. Not that it mattered. That was the least of my worries. "Stop," I said as forcefully as possible, though the command could barely be heard on account of how severely I was hyperventilating. Maybe I'd pass out. I didn't want to be around for what was to come. At least he'd kill me. That was the only positive in this fucked up situation. Not that I deserved to live. I couldn't save Cooper. And now, it looked like I couldn't save Lucca. I couldn't save anyone. My friends were dead because of me.

For what felt like an eternity, all I could hear were my own gasps. And then he spoke, except it wasn't his voice.

This voice was familiar and comforting, not the gravelly sound I expected to hear from the sadistic killer.

"Alexis, open your eyes and look at me." He released my hands and lifted off of me. "What's wrong, sweetheart? Are you okay?"

I forced my eyes open, finding James Martin kneeling at the end of the bed. He ran a hand through his dark brown hair. His lips pressed into a thin line. His green eyes remained fixed on my face as I scrambled toward the headboard.

"What just happened?" he asked. "Did I hurt you? What did I do wrong?"

"Nothing." I shook my head, still unable to breathe. Lucca wasn't dead. At least, I didn't think he was, but I couldn't be sure. I wasn't sure of anything. It had to have been a dream. A terrible nightmare. It wasn't real. Except I didn't dream that crime scene. Cooper had been violently killed by a man hell-bent on getting my attention. It was my fault.

A salty, metallic taste filled my mouth. Darting out of bed, I dashed across the room and slammed the bathroom door behind me.

I hugged the porcelain throne, but my stomach was empty. When was the last time I ate? I couldn't remember, and now wasn't the time to worry about such things. I wiped my eyes with the back of my hand, unsure how far I'd get before I had to heave again.

"Hey," Martin knocked softly on the door, "are you okay?"

I stayed silent, unsure what to say.

"Sweetheart, answer me." The knob twisted, but the door didn't open. "May I come in?"

"Your house," I muttered.

He cracked the door open a few inches. "Are you okay? Do you think it was the crab rolls? I knew I should have thrown them out this morning."

"I didn't eat the crab." I heaved again, my body determined to rid itself of the panic-inducing images through any means necessary. Though, this had no effect other than making my ribs ache and my throat burn. No matter what I did, I couldn't assuage the fear and guilt.

Martin knelt beside me and stroked my back.

"Don't touch me." I didn't deserve to be comforted.

He withdrew his hands and stepped away. A few seconds later, he pressed a cool, damp cloth against the back of my neck. For whatever the reason, it eased the panic and nausea, and my body gave up trying to purge my memories by emptying my stomach.

Taking a steadying breath, I pushed away from the toilet and curled up on the bathroom rug, too exhausted and broken to do anything else. Martin looked down at me, gently rubbing the washcloth over my cheek.

"We've talked about this. You have to let it out."

"I don't think there's anything left to let out."

"I'll get you some ginger ale and crackers."

"I don't want anything."

But he ignored me, as usual. I stared at the base of the toilet. I didn't remember falling asleep. The last thing I remembered was kissing Martin, but I must have zonked out. How else would I have ended up in the midst of that horrible nightmare? What if it was more than just a nightmare?

I pulled myself off the floor and went back into the bedroom. The digital clock said 1:32. Was that too late to call? Federal agents worked strange hours. Eddie Lucca might still be awake. Or Mark Jablonsky. I could call Mark. He already knew I was crazy. A call at this time of night wouldn't be out of the ordinary. I picked up the phone just as Martin returned with a can of soda and a sleeve of saltines.

"Work?" he asked.

I shook my head. "I have to talk to Mark."

"It's the middle of the night. Can't it wait? He needs his rest. It's only been four weeks since his surgery. Did you know he's already back at work?" Martin tugged the phone out of my hand and exchanged it for the can of soda.

"So is Lucca." But my thoughts jumbled. I wasn't sure of anything. "Lucca's alive, right? I haven't spoken to him in days. Not since he dropped by Cross Security to see me. Maybe something happened to him. I don't know. I need to find out." I reached for the phone, but Martin intercepted me and eased me onto the bed.

He stared at me like I had lost my mind, a look I'd grown accustomed to seeing. "He's fine, Alex. You told me he's settling back in at the OIO. While he recovers, he's manning a desk until medical clears him. Don't you remember?"

"He shouldn't be here." I sipped the soda. The bubbles tickled my nose, but I forced the fizzy liquid down my throat. For a moment, I feared I might spew it everywhere, but I kept it down. "He should have stayed in D.C. I never meant to convince Director Kendall to transfer him. That wasn't my intention. I don't want him here. It's too close. He could get hurt again. So could Mark, or you, or anyone." I gasped, my frantic ramblings bringing me to the brink of another panic attack.

Martin touched my arm, but I jerked away like I'd been burned. He sat on the edge of the bed and rubbed his eyes. He reached for his t-shirt and pulled it over his head. "You can't keep doing this. I've been giving you time and space, but dammit, Alex, this isn't getting any better. You're spiraling. You have to let this out. Let it go. Whatever. Please."

"There's nothing to let out. No matter what I do, I can't fix this. I just have to make sure it can't happen again."

He stared at me with an intensity that made me think he moved mountains in his spare time. "Let me help you. Let me in, sweetheart. Talk to me. What can I do?"

I swallowed another sip. The cool bubbles soothed my throat and stomach. "Do you know how to go back in time?"

"Alexis—"

"No?" I took a breath, angry at the world and myself. "Then you can't help me. There's nothing left to say. No reason to talk about it. Lucca shot the man who killed Cooper. And like you said, he and Mark are recovering from surgery. They're already back at work. That's why I can't let this happen again."

"Bullshit. You didn't let this happen in the first place. This isn't your fault."

"It sure as hell feels like it." I opened the crackers, tucked my legs beneath me, and nibbled on one. "I don't want to talk about this."

Exasperated, Martin let out a huff. "Fine, let's not talk about that. Let's talk about us." He gestured at the rumpled covers. "Do you want to explain to me what the hell just happened here?"

"I had a nightmare. You should recognize them by now."

"But you weren't asleep."

"I must have been." Even I wasn't sure what had happened, but that was the only logical explanation.

"In the middle of foreplay? If that's true, something is seriously wrong with me. We might need to go to the emergency room or visit a gypsy. My pre-game should not put you to sleep, and if it did, then the world as I know it has officially come to an end. I was a sex god. Now I'm," his features contorted in utter horror, "a mere mortal."

I washed the cracker down with another swig of ginger ale. "Glad to see your priorities are in order and your humility's still intact."

"That was me being humble." He held his palms up and studied his hands. "Look at me. Where did my powers of seduction and ecstasy-inducing abilities go? At this moment, shouldn't you be trying to rip my clothes off? That's normally how things escalate between us."

My heart rate hadn't calmed down yet, but my body had decided instead of ridding itself of food, it would prefer to be fed. After all, I hadn't eaten in a day or two. It just hadn't fit into my schedule, but now my stomach growled, ravenous, even though my mind had yet to get on the same page. Those thoughts competed with the conversation, and I looked up from my snack, confused. "What?"

"My sexual prowess has turned into a chore. Something mundane. Boring. Worthy of putting you to sleep." Despite the dramatics, his eyes held a challenge. "Right? That's what you're saying?"

"We're not talking about this either."

"I should hire a sexual consultant or do some research. I have to find my mojo, figure out where I went wrong." He wouldn't let this go. "Is there a directory for gypsies?

Maybe someone cursed me. Don't they lift curses?"

"Only in movies. But if you find one who's legit, let me know. I've been cursed my entire life."

"Sweetheart, you're not cursed."

I sighed and glared at him, unwilling to let his theatrics distract me. "Go watch porn and jerk off like everyone else. I don't care. Just leave me alone."

"I have been leaving you alone. And I'm sick of it. Fine, forget the gypsies. We should look into sexual surrogates since I'm not cutting it for you anymore."

"That's not true."

"Then why did you have a panic attack?" He didn't buy that I was asleep or my panic attack had been induced by one of my nightmares. "What did I do to trigger you? I need to know so I don't do it again."

"Nothing. You didn't do anything." I took a deep breath. The crackers and soda threatened to make a reappearance. "It was a bad dream. Just drop it."

"You're sure?"

"Yes."

"Okay, I'll check into sleep clinics in the morning. I know I used to tease you about being narcoleptic, but to go from a willing participant to sound asleep like that," he snapped his fingers, "makes me think that was more than just a bad joke."

"All your jokes are bad, especially this one."

Fire burned in his eyes. "I'm worried about you."

"Don't be." I folded the wrapper around the remaining crackers. "I'm fine. You're just off your game. Stop putting me to sleep and this won't be a problem."

"You're not fine. You haven't been since Cooper died."

"He didn't die. He was murdered."

"It wasn't your fault."

"No? What about Mark? He almost bled to death. So did Lucca. And Lawson nearly suffocated. So don't you dare tell me those weren't my fault either because they were." The killer's words reverberated in my brain. I bit my lip to stop my chin from quivering and stormed out of the bedroom.

"Alex," Martin called after me, but I couldn't do this

anymore. And he knew it.

By the time I reached the second floor, I felt trapped. Even if I escaped the house, I couldn't escape myself. Sure, I could go to our apartment, but what good would that do? I'd still be there, along with my guilt and memories. Frankly, I was too tired and shaky to drive. I'd probably crash into something or kill someone. That seemed to be the story of my life. Maybe I should carve notches in my belt to keep up with the body count.

Instead, I flopped onto the sofa and turned on the TV. I found a cartoon, something with lots of bright colors and happy melodies. When that ended, I aimlessly flipped channels until I came to a cooking competition. On the bright side, I was no longer hungry or nauseous, just numb.

I was nearly asleep when Martin came down the steps and slid onto the couch beside me. He wrapped his arms around me, which brought tears to my eyes. So much for being numb.

"I love you. I don't want to see you hurting."

I snorted, recalling something similar an FBI psychiatrist had said to me once. "You can't fix this."

"Maybe not, but I'm sure as hell going to try."

TWO

I clicked off the TV when the news came on. I didn't want to hear about any more tragedies. At least there'd be early morning cartoons starting soon. That would get me through the next hour or two, until Martin left for work.

He kissed me and climbed off the couch. Even though he'd sworn couches weren't meant for sleeping, we'd spent almost half of our nights down here on account of my insomnia. "You should stay home today. You didn't get any sleep last night."

"I'm fine."

"The hell you are. You promised you wouldn't shut me out, so we ought to talk about this." He gestured around the living room. "What are you doing?"

"The same thing I do every day."

"That's it. I'm cutting you off."

"You should have a long time ago."

My comment irritated him. "I meant from the cartoons."

"That's not what I meant," I mumbled. "Plus, someone needs to make sure your cable subscription doesn't go to waste. Have you seen what they charge every month? It's a good thing I've been putting it to use these last few weeks. It makes great background noise while I work out of my home office." I thought for a moment. "Or is it your home office?"

"Don't start that. One argument at a time, sweetheart. You can't distract me."

"Ten bucks says if I take off my shirt I can." I grinned at him, but he appeared to be impervious to my flirtation.

Instead, he ran his hand over my thigh, the bullet wound still tender beneath his touch. "Aren't you supposed to go to physical therapy?"

"I'm fine."

He gave me that look that said he knew better. "Does it still hurt?"

"Only when you do that."

"Sorry." He retracted his hand. "Did I hurt you last night? Is that what set you off?"

"No."

"Care to tell me what did?"

"Nothing. It was a nightmare. Plain and simple."

"What was it about?"

Flashes from Mark's bedroom and Cooper's apartment jolted me upright. "Crime scenes." I took an unsteady breath. "You know what happened. You were there for the aftermath. You saw what that bastard did to Mark."

"He's okay."

"Cooper isn't." I gagged on my words. "It should have been me."

He brushed my hair behind my ear. "Don't ever say that. I don't know what I'd do if I lost you."

"Then drop it. I don't want to think about it. I have too much to do. Too much to focus on."

He kissed my hair. "What are you doing? You've been so secretive lately. I didn't think Lucien assigned you any new cases. So what are you working on?"

"Personal matters, research and threat assessments."

"You're making sure this can't happen again." Martin took my hand and kissed my knuckles. "I would move heaven and earth for you. This," he laced his fingers with mine, making sure I could see the ring on his finger, "means something. We might not be married, but you are my other half. You complete me. When you're broken, so am I. So we're going to find a way to fix this. I told you before I won't let you stay lost. And I meant it."

"Then let me deal with it my way. I'm handling it, so back off."

"You're handling it? How? By not eating? By not sleeping? The nightmares are worse, and now you're having PTSD episodes while awake. This can't go on. You can't go on like this."

"That's not what that was." I pulled my hand free.

"Yes, it is." He licked his lips. "I know you don't want to talk to a professional, and unless you're willing to make the effort, it won't help anyway. But you have to do something. You can talk to me. Yell at me. Fight with me. Whatever it takes. Whatever you need. I'm here."

"What I need is to finish my assessments."

"And once that's done, then what? Things aren't just going to magically return to normal."

"Things have never been normal for us."

"Well, it's about damn time we try for some normal, don't you think? Why not multitask? While you're performing background checks or whatever," he waved his hand in the direction of the second floor office, "you can rehab your leg and talk about some of these issues."

I scowled at him. "The more you push, the more it hurts. Don't you understand that? When did you become so sadistic?"

"Then push back." He shook his head. "But you've given up, and that scares me. At first, I thought you'd bounce back. You always had that determination, but it faded. It burned out. Ever since Lucca told you he transferred back to the city, you've been paralyzed. C'mon, sweetheart, let me see that fire. Wake up. Fight."

"Screw you." I climbed off the couch and went into the kitchen. He better be careful, or he'd regret those words.

"Obviously not."

Shoving a coffee filter into the machine and scooping the coffee into it, I said, "You're going to be late for work."

"Fine." But from the look in his eyes, this was far from over. "Do I need to come home for lunch to make sure you eat something? Or do I have to ask Bruiser to force-feed you?"

"Leave your bodyguard out of this. I can fend for myself. Don't worry about it."

"That's precisely the problem, Alex. I am worried." He went up the stairs, returning a few minutes later in workout gear. Between last night's coitus interruptus and this morning's argument, he had a lot of pent-up aggression to work out. He went down the steps to the first floor and blasted rock music while he ran on the treadmill. When he finished his run, he pummeled the heavy bag for the next thirty minutes. Finally, he came up the steps, drenched in sweat.

He stripped off his shirt and used it to wipe his face. I watched the way his abdominal muscles rippled and flexed as he moved his arms. Bastard.

He caught me staring and chuckled. "Guess I haven't lost my god-like qualities after all. Maybe my mojo's coming back."

"If you expect me to drop to my knees and worship you, you'd better stop acting like such an asshole."

Amusement and lust danced in his eyes. "It's nice to know feisty Alex is still in there somewhere. When she wants to come out and play, tell her where to find me. I'll be in the shower."

I raised my middle finger, but before I could shoot back a proper retort, my phone rang. The sound made my blood run cold. *Not another one,* I thought. Swallowing, I reached for it, squeezing my eyes closed and hoping someone else I loved wasn't dead.

Martin's playful expression dropped. "Who is it?"

"Nick O'Connell."

He nodded at the ringing phone in my hand. "You should probably find out what the detective wants." He waited until I answered to make sure everything was okay before disappearing up the steps.

THREE

I lingered in the doorway to the hotel room. O'Connell didn't normally invite me to crime scenes. This was new. And I didn't like it. Frankly, this was the last thing I needed this morning.

"As you can see, we have one victim. No signs of a struggle. Nothing to indicate a break-in," O'Connell said.

I peered into the room. Dizziness washed over me, and for just a moment, the sheets appeared to be smeared in blood. But on second glance, they were basic white. I rubbed my eyes. Damn, I was losing it. And what made matters even worse was that meant Martin might be right. "Shit."

O'Connell turned to look at me. "You planning on joining us, Parker?"

"Not if I can help it." I sucked in some air. "I can see more than enough from out here."

"Don't be ridiculous." He waited for me to step into the hotel room. "Any thoughts?"

"Just one. Why did you call me?"

"You've been a police consultant in the past, and this," he gestured at the lavish hotel suite, "seems like it might be in your wheelhouse."

"Are you even sure it's a homicide?" I approached the

bed, but nothing indicated this was murder. "Plus, you know homicides aren't my thing."

"I didn't realize consultants could be this picky. Do you remember the good old days when you used to beg me to let you help on a case? You didn't even care what kind of case it was. You just wanted something to work on."

"That's before I found a permanent gig."

"Cross Security has spoiled you," O'Connell teased.

In the trashcan were six used condoms and several tiny liquor bottles from the mini bar. "When do you think he died?"

"Sometime yesterday."

"Martin has an alibi."

"What?" O'Connell moved beside me and peered into the garbage. He chuckled. "Good for him." He glanced at me. "And you."

"It could have been a heart attack." I moved away from the trashcan, toward the window.

The medical examiner lifted the sheet, letting out a snort. "I'd say we're looking at multiple sex partners."

"At least three," I said, not bothering to turn around. I had no interest in seeing the dead guy's junk. Three wine glasses sat on the table, each with a different shade of lipstick. "Those lipstick stains probably match whatever you're seeing." Another wine glass sat on the bedside table. I moved into the attached bathroom and found another two glasses. "Looks like the dead guy hosted a sex party." I returned to the main room. The walls were covered in arterial spray. But I blinked, and it was gone. Okay, I was definitely losing it. "You don't need me here, Nick. Frankly, I'm not even sure why you're here. This may not even be a homicide, but even if it is, what does this have to do with major crimes?"

O'Connell followed me out of the room. "Do you recognize the victim?"

"No, why would I?"

"I just thought you might know him."

"Am I supposed to know everyone who ends up dead in this city? Because lately, it feels like it."

"I know you've been going through a tough time. I

figured you could use the work. This case is perfect for you, and I need your help."

"Perfect? Are you kidding me?" I swallowed and leaned against the wall, putting my hands on my knees and inhaling. "You know how to work a case, and if you've forgotten, you have no business possessing a badge. You don't need a consultant. Pull hotel records and surveillance footage, and find out what happened, if it's even murder, which I doubt."

"Martin thought—"

My head shot up. "Don't finish that sentence, unless you want to solve an actual homicide." Martin ran a multimillion dollar corporation, so he was used to making unilateral decisions. We'd fought over his tendency to overstep several times in the past, but now it looked like he needed a reminder why he shouldn't meddle in my life. "I can't believe you'd let him dictate the terms of your investigation."

"That's not what happened. And for the record, we're all worried about you." He reached into his jacket and pulled out an evidence bag. "This is the reason I called you." Inside the bag was a Cross Security business card. "We've always been straight with one another. Was this guy your client?"

"No." I forced my mind to stay on point and peered into the hotel room. "I've never seen him before. Do you know his name?"

"Victor Landau." He read the victim's address off his license, but that meant even less to me than the guy's name. "Any idea why he might have gone to Cross Security or which investigator was working a case for him?"

I examined the card through the evidence bag. "No."

"Do you think you could find out?"

"That's why you asked me to consult. You just wanted someone to perform your due diligence."

O'Connell took back the evidence bag. "You have to admit, it's pretty damn brilliant."

"Maybe for you." I glanced back into the room. "But this is the last thing I need right now."

"Why, what's going on?"

"Nothing. I'm fine," I snapped.

O'Connell held up his palms. "Okay, I just stepped in something that I'm guessing has nothing to do with me. Did you wake up on the wrong side of the bed?" He searched my face for a moment. "Jesus, Parker, when's the last time you even slept?"

"I gave it up for Lent."

"Did you give up returning favors too?"

"No, but if Martin pulled strings to force the PD to offer me a consulting gig, I don't want it."

O'Connell glanced around to make sure no one was close enough to overhear our conversation. "He didn't. But when he called Jen to cancel our plans last weekend, he said you weren't doing well. I know you and exactly what that means. I thought this would be mutually beneficial. Your boss hates cooperating with the police. But you don't. I thought you might be able to get me more reliable answers without dragging in high-powered attorneys, who will demand warrants and subpoenas. And it'll keep you busy so you stay out of trouble."

"Fine, but you don't even know if it's murder yet." I narrowed my eyes. "And you still haven't explained why major crimes is investigating this. If you want my help, I need to know what's going on."

"This isn't the first crime scene I've seen like this. Once the tox screen comes back, I'll know for certain if it's connected, but until then, I want to get a jump on this."

"A jump on what? From where I'm standing, this guy probably died from too much sex."

"In that case, you should cut Martin off."

"Oh, believe me, after this morning, he's cut off."

O'Connell cringed. "Okay, I know I started it, but let's reinstate that moratorium on sharing info about our sex lives."

"Great."

O'Connell tilted his head toward the dead man. "So you'll find out what Cross Security knows about Victor Landau?"

"Sure, just tell me what you expect the tox to reveal."

"Poison."

"How many of these scenes have you been to?"

"Four, so far. I'm going over old cases, anything with a suspicious death and similar staging, to see if there might be more."

"Shit." I ran a hand down my face. Last night should have tipped me off that today would be brutal. "Don't you have to question Lucien about this anyway? And shouldn't I be a suspect? I work at Cross Security. That could be my business card in Mr. Landau's wallet. Maybe I killed him and three other guys."

"Did you?"

"Not that I remember."

"I take it since you randomly volunteered an alibi for Martin that means he could vouch for your whereabouts too."

"Either him or Bruiser."

"Oh, so now you have a ménage," O'Connell teased.

"Didn't you just say we weren't sharing that kind of personal information?"

"Yeah, sorry." O'Connell gestured into the room. "It's called gallows humor. It's how cops deal. You used to have a wicked sense of it."

"Try me after I've slept." I winked at him and cracked a smile.

"Okay, that's good enough for me. Plus, I've seen your business cards. You have your name on yours, and a little bird told me you haven't worked any cases in the last four weeks. That means this guy can't be your client."

"I've still stopped by the Cross Security offices on occasion."

"In that case, take another look. Maybe you passed Landau in the hallway or remember Cross mentioning him during one of his infamous morning meetings."

"I haven't been attending those lately, and your dead guy doesn't look familiar. But I've been too busy to pay attention to pretty much anything else."

"Busy doing what?"

"Threat assessments."

"You're still working on those? I thought by now you'd be finished."

"I was a federal agent for almost five years before going private, and then I went back to the OIO for a while, and then back to the private sector. You know all of this, Nick. Needless to say, I've made a lot of enemies, so I need to know who might come after the people I love. I should have done it before, but I didn't. And you know what happened."

"Look, I get it. But I could use your help on this. It's not a mugging. Landau still has his cash, credit cards, and watch. The girls could have been hired, but nothing indicates they did him in. Well, not intentionally. If they were pay-to-play, middle management might have stepped in to force Landau to pay up, but someone in the hotel would have heard an altercation like that."

"And the vic wouldn't still be in possession of his wallet." I went back into the room for another quick walkthrough. "You shouldn't assume the only other people in the room were women. The two wine glasses in the bathroom don't have lipstick smears."

"We'll see what the DNA shows. We have plenty of samples to test."

"Who's the room registered to?"

"Victor Landau, single occupant. He checked in two days ago. He requested a late checkout for yesterday afternoon but never left. When maid service came to clean the room, they found him." O'Connell glanced at the security camera posted at the end of the hallway. "I should know more once I get a chance to check the footage."

"What about defensive wounds?" I hadn't seen any, but I might not have been paying enough attention.

"None."

"What about puncture marks?"

"ME will let us know."

"But you suspect poison." I eyed the wine glasses. "That's different, especially since nothing indicates he vomited or seized." I stared out the window, anything to avoid looking at the body. I already had enough nightmares. It was overcast today. Gloomy. With a cold breeze. Bruiser, Martin's bodyguard, was waiting outside in the car. Hopefully, he had the heat on.

"I'll be dropping by Cross Security after your boss returns from lunch. In the meantime, find out everything you can on this guy and why he hired a private investigator."

"Maybe he didn't. The Cross Security card doesn't have a name on it. That means it could have come directly from Lucien Cross or reception. All of Cross's investigators have their names on their business cards, but it's possible this guy just grabbed a card on his way out. It's also possible he didn't hire a private investigator." I eyed O'Connell. "After all, it is called Cross Security for a reason."

"You think he hired a bodyguard or protection detail?"

"He might have needed one. After all, he's dead."

"All right, see what you can dig up. I'll catch up with you in a couple of hours. Try to stay out of trouble until then."

"Easier said than done. You know my boss won't be happy about this."

"Since when do you care what Lucien thinks?"

"I never said I did."

FOUR

Victor Landau wasn't listed anywhere in the Cross Security client database. I searched the servers for any hits on his name. Again, nothing. This wasn't getting me anywhere. I swiveled back and forth in my chair. "Dammit."

Reluctantly, I got up and went across the hall. Kellan Dey was another of Cross's investigators, and one whom I personally despised. We started out as friends, but that was short-lived on account of Cross recruiting Kellan to spy on me.

"Let me ask you a question," I said.

Kellan looked up from the research he was conducting. "What's up, Alex?" He glanced down at my leg but didn't ask how I was.

"Victor Landau, does that name ring any bells? I need to know if he's a client."

"I don't know." He reached for his keyboard. "You checked the database, right?"

"Yes."

"Did you check billing?"

"I checked everywhere."

Despite my answer, he typed in the name and waited for the results to populate. Then he picked up his phone. "Hey,

Cindy, can you check the appointment schedule? I'm looking for Victor Landau." He waited. "No, he's not one of mine."

I crossed my arms over my chest and waited.

"Okay, thanks." Kellan put the phone down. "He had a meeting with Lucien two months ago. No follow-up and nothing on the books. Why the sudden interest?"

"No reason." I'd have to check with legal and see if Cross requested contracts be drafted.

"Bullshit. What's going on?"

"Don't worry about it. I'm sure you'll find out soon enough, if Cross wants you to know."

"Ooh, intrigue." Kellan cracked a smile. "Anything else I can do for you?"

"Nope." And now I felt like an idiot for not contacting reception myself.

"Well, if that ever changes, my door's always open. Remember that."

"Yep."

I returned to my office, closed my door, and phoned legal. They didn't know anything about Victor Landau or the services he might have requested. So why was O'Connell's latest DB carrying around a Cross Security business card for the last two months? When I couldn't come up with any logical explanation other than he liked the cardstock and font or just never bothered to clean out his wallet, I considered going directly to the source. But Cross was currently out of the office.

So I did the next best thing. I ran a background check on Victor Landau, which turned up nothing. Then I searched for details on O'Connell's other three murders, but I didn't have access to current police investigations, at least not legally.

Shifting gears, I decided to make the most of my time in the office and finished running my latest list of currently incarcerated offenders to make sure they remained behind bars. Then I checked into recent criminal activity regarding their known associates, noted their release dates, pending appeals, and parole board hearings, and turned off the computer.

I was too tired to stay in the office and wait for Cross or O'Connell to show up. So after phoning the detective and updating him on my lack of helpfulness, I took the elevator back to the lobby. Bruiser brought Martin's newest sports car around front, and I climbed into the passenger seat.

"Where to?" he asked.

"Home."

Once we got back to Martin's compound, I changed clothes and did some basic stretches before climbing onto the treadmill. Even though I was tired, I had to exercise. My thigh was stiff and sore. I needed to get it back in working order, especially since O'Connell expected me to do all this running around for him.

Over the last few days, I'd experimented with different workouts. Two days ago, I tried lunges, which cramped my leg and forced me into a quivering ball. Yesterday, I switched to squats, and after about a hundred, I toppled over. Today, I would learn from my mistakes and take it easier.

I'd been walking around for over a week without the crutches, so I should be able to handle the treadmill. The sooner I could get back into the swing of things, the sooner I could rebuild. The voice in the back of my head said I had to be at the top of my game. Better than I'd ever been. I couldn't let my guard down, not even for a second. And this stupid bullet wound was taking too damn long to heal.

A threat could come from anywhere. The crime scene today proved it. I didn't think Victor Landau had any idea his number was up, but at least he went out with a bang. Maybe that's how he'd want to go out. I thought about it, but dying didn't seem like a great plan, regardless of the events leading up to it. On the bright side, that meant I wasn't suicidal, even if I'd been accused of having a death wish on several occasions. Those were the joys of survivor's guilt, I suppose. But I had to be prepared for what was to come. If history had taught me anything, danger lurked just around the corner.

After a few minutes of walking, I turned the dial and started jogging. My thigh ached, but I ignored it. Pain was a state of mind, weakness leaving the body, or some other fortune cookie saying. Instead, I ran faster and faster until my leg gave out, and the treadmill ejected me off the back.

I landed in a heap at the end of the track. The emergency shutoff engaged, and the machine came to a stop. Martin's bodyguard opened the door at the top of the steps and peered down at me.

"How's the leg?" Bruiser asked. He hadn't said much on the drive to and from the office.

"Wonderful." I pushed myself onto all fours, crawled up the steps, and flopped onto the couch, exhausted. Tomorrow was another day. Perhaps, by then, I'd learn my lesson.

"Is that what you call it? I might need to buy you a dictionary." He quirked an eyebrow, which I pretended to ignore. "Earlier, you didn't put up much of a fight when Martin told me to drive you to work. That's not like you. I figured maybe you weren't supposed to drive, which probably means you shouldn't be trying to place in the five hundred meter dash either."

"I'm fine, and I can drive, if I have to. I just thought you didn't have anything better to do. Plus, you've been itching to take Martin's new car for a spin. So driving was solely for your benefit."

"You're a terrible liar."

"Did Martin tell you to be a pain in my ass?" My beloved probably contracted out the task just to save himself some time and energy.

"No, but he told me to make sure you ate something." Bruiser went into the kitchen and opened the refrigerator.

"I'm not hungry."

"He said you'd say that. He also said something about force-feeding you." He pulled a container from the top shelf and reached into the cupboard for a soup cup. He filled the oversized mug, popped it into the microwave for two minutes, and proceeded to pull out sandwich ingredients. When the microwave beeped, he removed the mug and brought it to me. "Careful, it's hot."

Obediently, I took the mug from him and readjusted on the couch, so I could sit up and stretch my legs out. On autopilot, I blew on the rising steam and took a sip. Bruiser grinned and went back into the kitchen to make himself lunch.

"What else did Martin say?" I asked.

Bruiser made two double-decker sandwiches and found a container of salad. "That was about it." He unfolded a paper napkin and tucked it into the collar of his shirt. Then he took a bite of his sandwich. Mustard dribbled out from the corner, but it landed on top of the other sandwich. "You know I don't stick my nose in your business. But I know something's wrong. I've seen that look before. In case you ever need to unload, I got your back."

"Thanks, Jones." I graced him with a smile and used his actual name instead of the affectionate nickname I'd given him. "But I'm good."

He watched me sip the soup, chuckling again. "It's scary how well he knows you."

"Who?"

"Mr. Martin." He jerked his chin at the mug. "He told me if I made you a sandwich it'd sit on the coffee table all day. But you'd eat the soup, if I handed you the mug."

I growled and put the cup down. "What else did he ask you to do besides babysit and feed me? Are you going to burp me and put me down for a nap too?"

"No, but now that you mention it, you look like you could use some sleep."

"Thank you, Captain Obvious." I limped into the kitchen and rinsed the mug before placing it in the dishwasher. I didn't want Bruiser to have to clean up after me too. "Do you want something to drink?" I opened the fridge, wondering if any of my actions were my own free will or if they'd all been orchestrated by Martin. He knew I didn't like people waiting on me. He probably arranged this entire scenario, just so I'd get up and do something.

"Water," Bruiser said around a mouthful.

By the time I turned around to hand him the glass, he had inhaled both sandwiches and most of the salad. I sat down beside him, hugged my knees to my chest, and rested my chin on top of them. "When you were in the Navy, did you ever work black ops?"

"No, why?"

"You've got that need-to-know thing down pat. I'd hate to be stuck in an interrogation room with you."

"I answered all your questions, didn't I?"

"Hardly."

He stifled a laugh. "Martin tells me what he wants handled, and I don't ask why. My mission objectives today – chauffeur you around, make sure you eat something, and keep you alive. Unless there's an airstrike or raid I don't know about, I'd say mission accomplished, so long as you don't make another ill-advised attempt at trying out for the Olympic track team."

"Maybe tomorrow."

"Didn't they give you a list of exercises to work on in physical therapy?"

"I haven't gone yet."

"Why not?"

"It's not a priority. I can do this myself."

"It doesn't look that way from where I'm sitting."

"Injury or not, I'm just off my game. Truthfully, I have been for a while. I've grown complacent." I looked around the opulent room. "Soft. I have to get my edge back." I narrowed my eyes as a thought came to mind. "I could use some help training. Do you mind?"

"Not at all, but you can't go from zero to sixty overnight. You'll have to build back up first."

"Yeah." But I didn't like the idea of waiting.

Bruiser laughed. "You and Martin are a match made in heaven. You're the most impatient and stubborn people I've ever met."

"Save the smack talk for the ring."

He held up his palms. "Those weren't meant to be fighting words. However, since you're at a clear disadvantage, I might actually kick your ass this time."

"You wish." Truthfully, Bruiser could kick my ass, even on my best day.

"When do you want to start?"

"Just as soon as I can isolate on my right leg without falling on my face."

"Weren't you classically trained?"

"Ballet," I said. "Why?"

"Injuries are common for dancers. The recovery routines might get you back to where you want to be if you don't go to PT."

I smiled. "Has anyone ever told you you're brilliant?"

"No, ma'am. I'm just hired muscle. I don't get paid to think. Point me at a target, and I'll take care of it. That's what I'm good at."

"You're so full of shit."

"I learned from the best." He bowed down, rolling his hand a few times in my direction. "After all, you trained me. You were Mr. Martin's original bodyguard. Isn't being full of shit part of the job description?"

"Only when dealing with the boss man, not me." Getting up, I returned to the living room and settled onto the sofa. My leg ached, and the exhaustion from being up all night hit me like a ton of bricks. I just needed to get some rest, and then I'd devise an appropriate training schedule and finish up the threat assessments. But at the moment, I couldn't think about any of that or O'Connell's case. I just needed a few hours of sleep.

I flipped on the TV. At least my outing had lasted through the soap operas. More cartoons had just started, and Martin wasn't around to give me grief for watching them. I lowered the volume and closed my eyes. My mind wandered, and before I fell asleep, I pondered how O'Connell's meeting with Lucien Cross went.

FIVE

The phone rang, jolting me awake and sending a shiver down my spine. Now what? Reluctantly, I turned off the TV and peered into the kitchen. Maybe it was a telemarketer. I waited, giving careful consideration to letting the machine get it. It could be Martin, but I wasn't sure I wanted to speak to him. It rang another two times. When the machine answered, the caller hung up. *Problem solved*, I thought.

And then the phone rang again.

I climbed off the couch and grabbed the receiver. "What do you want?"

"For starters, I'd like to know why you haven't answered your phone or replied to any of my texts."

I tugged the phone away from my ear and regarded the caller ID. *Cross Security.* "Lucien?" I patted my pockets and searched the kitchen counter, realizing I must have left my cell phone downstairs when I changed clothes.

"Yes, Alex. It's your boss. Remember me?"

"Vaguely."

"Let me refresh your memory. I sign your paychecks."

"I thought I had direct deposit."

"Details."

"How'd you get this number?"

"Cross Security's the best."

"Martin gave you the number."

"Oddly, no. But when you didn't answer the dozen calls and texts I made to your cell phone, I had the techs ping your location. Given your track record, I was afraid something terrible happened to you. Once I got the address, I realized you must be at home and looked up the number. I'm relieved to find you are safe and well."

"The number's unlisted."

"Really? That's good to know."

"What do you want, Cross?"

"We need to talk. How quickly can you get to the office?"

"How's tomorrow morning?"

"How about now?"

I grunted, stretching my leg as I checked the time. "This can't wait?"

"No." He hesitated. "How are you feeling?"

"I've been better."

"All right. Medical will check you out once you get here, and I'll brief you on what's going on. Then we'll take it from there." He paused. "I heard you stopped by earlier today asking for information on someone. Strangely enough, Detective O'Connell just left my office. He had questions concerning the same someone. Care to elaborate?"

"You first."

"Again, do I need to remind you who's in charge? In case you're confused, you work for me."

"Victor Landau's dead. He had your card in his wallet. O'Connell wanted to know if he was a client."

"What did you tell him?"

"That I didn't know and couldn't find anything on the servers, so he should ask you."

"Good call, Alex. I knew I hired you for a reason. Liaising between Cross Security and the police department is a big part of what made you so appealing. That and I'm in desperate need of more investigators. With you on sick leave, I'm short again, so unless your injury makes you a liability, I need you back at work. I have a case for you."

"What kind of case?"

"The usual cheater check."

"Divorce case?" I asked.

"No, the opposite."

"What's the opposite of a divorce case?"

"Our client wants to make sure his wife-to-be is as she appears and isn't stepping out on him before they tie the knot."

"Did he ask for a pre-nup?"

"He wants to avoid that, unless we give him a reason not to. With the right lawyers and judge, even the most airtight pre-nups can be tossed. You know that."

I sighed. I hated these types of cases. Thankfully, Cross Security rarely dealt with them. Lucien was in the big leagues. He prided himself on privatizing policing. Cheating spouses or soon-to-be spouses weren't a security issue. So I wondered why he suddenly had a change of heart. Was this my punishment for helping the police? "Who's the client?"

"Andre North." The name meant nothing to me, but from the way Cross said it, North must be someone important.

I looked down at my cropped t-shirt and running shorts. "Fine. I'll see you in thirty minutes."

"Make it less."

*   *   *

"Have you gone to physical therapy yet?" the medic asked.

"If I had a nickel for every time I've heard that today." I winced while he held my ankle and straightened my leg. "No."

"You're coming up on four weeks. You should schedule an appointment."

"I'll get right on that."

"When did you stop using the crutches?"

"I'm not sure. Ten days ago, maybe."

His brows knit together. "I see. What about painkillers?"

"I don't want any."

"Should I assume that means you stopped taking them?"

"I never started."

He turned to consult my records, and I resisted the urge to tell him I wasn't an addict. Several of Cross's employees had fallen down that rabbit hole, which is what ended their government careers and landed them here, in the land of broken toys.

Cross cleared his throat from where he stood in the doorway. "How is she?"

"Her muscles are weak and her tendons are stiff. Several of the muscle tears are still rather prominent, but I don't see anything that would prevent her from carrying on normal day-to-day activities or rehabbing." The medic closed my file and looked at me. "Does your leg get sore when you walk around?"

"I don't pay attention."

Before he could inquire further, Cross interrupted, "Thanks, Doc. That's all I needed to hear." He met my eyes. "Come along, Alex. We're wasting daylight."

I hopped off the table and followed Cross out of the medical wing and to the elevator. Even though I'd seen most of the nifty toys and gadgets before, the thirty-first floor still impressed me. Instead of conference rooms and offices, like downstairs, this floor was broken into sectors, each with state-of-the-art equipment designed to process evidence, run computer analyses, provide medical care, recreate crime scenes, and conduct ballistics tests. It wasn't the Office of International Operations or any other division of the FBI, but in some ways, it was better. I'd just have to remember not to say that to Jablonsky or Lucca.

The elevator closed, and Cross scrutinized my reflection in the mirrored doors. "I heard Jablonsky's set to make a full recovery."

"Yes. Thank you."

"No need for thanks. You work for me. James Martin is my newest business partner. Providing a safe house and medical team for your friend was my pleasure." He turned to face me. "Speaking of which, I had a meeting with James this morning. He's set to move to a new phase in research.

He hopes to have an efficient way to develop the biotextiles within the next few months. Depending on how the preliminary trials go, it looks like we might have that new line of body armor sooner rather than later."

"Is that why you called me?" Martin needed to stay out of my business.

"No, but when we need volunteers to act as test dummies, I'll let you know."

"That's not what I'm asking." I stared at my boss. As usual, I couldn't get a read on him. "Did Martin ask you to assign me a case?"

"No, and for the record, Cross Security operates autonomously from Martin Technologies and vice versa. We're not crossing the streams." Cross's eyes twinkled. "At least not yet."

"Bullshit. You hired me to get to Martin. Don't tell me you wouldn't grant him a favor like this."

"True, but James didn't ask me to assign you a case." Cross's gaze dropped to my throat, but I hadn't worn the necklace Martin had given me with the GPS tracker since Cross found it and returned it to me. "Why do you think he would do that?"

"It doesn't matter."

Cross turned back to the doors, just as they opened, and led the way to his office. "The reason you're here is because Mr. North requested we look into his fiancée. Her name's Eve Wyndham. She's an event planner. High-end. We're talking massive parties. She used to work for Elite before going freelance. She has tons of contacts and spends most of her days and nights in clubs. She caters to celebrities and powerful people. Her friends are famous. If she wants to lunch in Hawaii, she catches an early morning flight. Dinner in Paris, she hops on someone's private jet."

"That'll make surveillance difficult."

"You'll have to get creative."

"What about Andre North? What's his deal? Is he old? Ugly? Violent?"

Cross gestured to the sofa, and I took a seat. He went to the locked cabinet behind his desk, opened the top drawer, removed a file, and handed it to me. "That's our preliminary research on the couple."

I pulled out a photograph. The man in the photo was probably in his early forties. He wore sunglasses, which made it difficult to see most of his face, but he had a healthy tan and a toned physique. His thighs and shoulders were thick, like a body-builder. His freshly shaved head gleamed in the sunlight. His jaw had a dusting of stubble, and the woman beside him rubbed his cheek with perfectly manicured fingernails. She had movie star curls, designer sunglasses, and a see-through coverup that left little to the imagination. A large diamond stud sparkled from her belly button, and another glittery rock weighed down her left hand.

I flipped the photo around, checking for a caption. "This is the happy couple?"

"That's Andre and Eve."

"So he's not old or ugly."

"Beauty's in the eye of the beholder. But no, I don't imagine most women would find him unappealing."

"Obviously. So why does he think his fiancée is stepping out on him?"

"I don't know."

"He must have some kind of flaw or quirk. Does he snore?" I flipped through the rest of the information in the file but found next to nothing on Andre North. Most of the details contained inside were about Eve Wyndham. "Does he have a record? History of violence? Alcohol or drug abuse? Some other kind of vice?" I looked up. "Is he faithful? A lot of people who accuse their partners of cheating are cheaters themselves. Unless he's just a control freak. Any allegations of stalking or complaints by former lovers?"

Cross snickered. "You're already blaming our client for his fiancée's bad behavior."

"No, I just want to get the facts straight."

"That is important, but you're jumping the gun. We don't even know if his fears can be substantiated." Cross leaned back in his chair. "I haven't dug too deeply yet. North asked me to investigate this matter just a few hours ago. Everything I've collected thus far is basic. Most of that is what he brought to us. But it's a start. You'll need to do a full workup on them and figure out a strategy to keep an eye on Eve."

The last page in the file contained a copy of the signed contract. I checked the deadline. We had a month to prove her infidelity. If she was cheating, it probably wouldn't take a month, but if she wasn't, that would take longer to prove. "Do you think she's stepping out on him?" I asked.

"That's what I need you to find out."

I glanced at the contract again. No maximum had been set on billables or expenses. "Is North a regular client?"

"No, he's brand new. I met with him for the first time this morning."

"But you're personally invested in his case, so he must be someone important." The ring on her finger told me as much. "Let me guess. He owns a national chain of gyms or he's a famous skier."

"Neither."

"Really?"

"Cross Security caters to more than just the wealthy."

"Not often."

"Maybe that's why I hired you. To protect the poor and downtrodden. But I have been known to take on my fair share of pro bono cases in the past."

"I hadn't noticed."

"Oh, so you think I'm just another money-grubbing dictator?"

"The jury's still out."

"Let me know the verdict." Cross tapped his phone. "I have a dinner date. Justin will get you whatever information you require. Occasionally, people who travel in Eve's circles use multiple aliases to ensure their privacy. If you have any trouble accessing her work records, extracurriculars, or details on her clients, I'll get someone to help you with that. But I'm guessing you can handle it," he examined my thigh, "even with your current impediment. However, if you find it to be too much legwork, let me know so I can assign someone else."

"I should be fine. I hope. I have done this before." But I didn't move to stand.

"So what's the problem?" Cross focused on me, but he itched to look at the time again.

"What does any of this have to do with Victor Landau and the police investigation?"

"Absolutely nothing."

I narrowed my eyes. Cross was hiding something. "I thought you called me down here to discuss that."

"There's nothing to discuss. I met with Mr. Landau once, eight weeks ago. He showed up, took a phone call, and left five minutes later. I don't even remember what he wanted. He said he'd call to reschedule when he had time, but he never did." Cross stared at me. "I told Detective O'Connell the same thing. I would have offered to show him my records, but I'm sure you already gave him everything he wanted."

"I didn't find anything."

"I know. You looked and told him there was nothing. It saved me and the police department a lot of time and unnecessary paperwork. It's nice to have someone on the payroll they trust. I doubt the detective would have taken my word at face value."

"You understand he asked me to assist in any way possible."

"Have you signed a consulting contract with the PD?"

"Not yet."

Cross rubbed his hands together. "I guess that means you have a choice to make. You made me strike the moonlighting clause from your contract, so you're free to do as you please." He stared into my eyes. "Just remember, Cross Security should be your primary focus. This case will require a lot of time. I'm not sure you can do both, and even though you are free to work for outside clients, mine take priority."

"Is that why you gave me Andre North's case? Is it supposed to be a reward or punishment for speaking to O'Connell?"

"It's just a job, Alex." He fought to keep his annoyance in check. "Andre North didn't want us to set up the usual honey trap. He wants someone who can go where Eve goes. Only a woman can handle that. And the other women who work here are already busy with other assignments. You're the next logical choice. My only choice."

"Sounds like Andre's insecure. That could be why he thinks she's stepping out on him. There might not be anything here."

"Or that could be the reason Eve would step out on him. Insecurity is unattractive."

"Fine. I'll see what I can do. But if you're already short-staffed, a month long surveillance gig won't help matters. Maybe you should refer Mr. North to another firm." My boss always had an agenda. This time, I was certain he wanted to keep me away from the police investigation. I just didn't know why.

"Leave the scheduling and administrative work to me. It's my company. My call." He looked pointedly at the clock. "You should probably get to work. I told him we'd start surveillance as soon as Eve returns from the UAE on Monday. You'll need to be well-versed on her life and routine by then." He tapped his pen against my knee. "I suggest you put a rush on the rehabbing. You should speak to the doctors again. They can schedule your physical therapy sessions."

"That won't be necessary."

Cross studied me for a moment. "You're not ready to come back, are you?"

"It's not like you've given me a choice."

SIX

My gaze drifted to the clock on the wall. It was late, probably on account of the nap I took in the middle of the day. But I was still tired, and performing background checks and scouring social media pages hadn't helped. This was a waste of time.

After turning off my computer, I took my notes and went downstairs. Bruiser was waiting in the lobby, reading a magazine.

"I'm sorry. You shouldn't have waited."

"It's fine, Ms. Parker." He put the magazine down. "Need I remind you again that my assignment for today is to chauffeur you around?"

"No." I glimpsed the article he'd been reading. "Did you determine your ideal sexual position or figure out what color lipstick is perfect for spring?"

"You'd be surprised."

"I bet I would."

He led the way to the front door, holding it open for me to exit. "Mr. Martin called about twenty minutes ago and said he was on his way home."

"He could have called me." But Martin probably knew better. "Did he ask Cross to assign me a case?"

"Why would Martin do that?"

"I don't know, but the timing is awfully suspicious."

Bruiser handed me his cell phone. "You can read our messages, if you like."

"That won't be necessary." I waited for the car doors to unlock before I lifted the door up so I could slip inside. "I don't need a driver anymore. The doctor said I'm fine. You can go back to guarding the boss man full-time."

He ran his palms along the steering wheel. "Off the record, this is more fun."

I chuckled. "I knew you were dying to drive this car."

"Boys and their toys," Bruiser said.

That thought made me wonder what types of activities Andre North enjoyed. His fiancée's life was nothing but a nonstop party. From what I'd seen on social media, he attended a lot of her events. Almost all of them, but what did he do? What did he like?

Cross made it clear. Andre wasn't the priority. Eve was. I'd spent the last two hours checking to see if either of them had a criminal record or a history of violence. But I didn't find anything. Despite Eve's very active social life, I couldn't find much about her that didn't relate to parties and work. What did they do in private? Did they stay home and play board games and take cooking classes? Or did Andre stay home watching sports while Eve stayed out all day and night?

I tried to schedule a meeting with Andre to discuss these things, but he wouldn't be available until the middle of next week. When we spoke on the phone, he explained his concerns were based on Eve's career. She was always around alcohol and celebrities. He wouldn't blame her for cheating. She had ample opportunities, and that mix didn't lend itself to the soundest decision making, especially given her profession. She made her money by pleasing clients, possibly in more ways than one. He just didn't want her mistakes to bite him in the ass.

"I'm mad about her," he had said. "But if she decides in a few months that she'd rather hitch her wagon to some sexy celeb and be tabloid fodder, I don't want to pay for it."

Apparently, they'd only been together for a year, which

made the engagement seem rushed. When I asked what he did for a living, he'd told me in vague terms asset management. My checks on him didn't turn up much of anything. He filed his taxes and kept out of trouble, but little was known about the man or even what assets he managed. He had several holdings and LLCs, so I'd have to dig deeper.

"We're here," Bruiser said.

I blinked, realizing I'd zoned out during the drive. Martin's town car wasn't parked at the end of the row, which meant we beat him home. That gave me a few minutes to get some work done before World War III started. Except before I even made it up the steps, my phone rang.

"Damn, you're popular today." Bruiser disappeared into Martin's second floor office to check the estate's security logs while I checked the display and answered the call.

"Hey, Nick," I said.

"You sound much friendlier now than you did earlier. Did you get lucky?"

"I thought we agreed not to discuss our sex lives."

"Sorry, that's just what happens when I spend my day elbow deep in a den of hedonism. You didn't happen to find anything else out about Victor Landau, did you?"

"No, but Cross wants me to stay away from it. Or maybe just you."

"Cross hates the cops. We all know that." The silence dragged on before O'Connell finally said, "Landau was poisoned. ME found a puncture mark between his toes."

"What kind of poison?"

"They're still narrowing down the properties." He read off a list of names. The only one I recognized was scopolamine.

"How much? Are we talking a remedy to motion sickness or Devil's Breath?"

"Probably the latter, but the details are still being analyzed."

"Huh." I thought for a moment. "As far as I know, Devil's Breath isn't normally injected. It's usually used to spike someone's drink and make them compliant and forgetful or blown into their faces, as the name would suggest."

"That's what I thought. ME didn't find any traces of it in the vic's nasal passages, so CSU's testing the wine glasses and the empty liquor bottles to see if that might be the source. I hate to think someone wanted to convince Landau to hand over his PIN and account numbers while someone else thought shoving a needle between his toes and killing him seemed like a much better idea."

"And I thought I was having a rough day. Have you identified anyone else who entered or left the room yet?"

"No, the surveillance footage shows two couples arriving around four yesterday afternoon and leaving around eleven. They arrived separately and left separately, within forty-five minutes of one another, but we found six different DNA samples in the room. One of them belongs to Landau."

"So you have five potential suspects or possible witnesses."

"Yeah, two male, three female. But we only caught sight of four people entering the room. That leaves one woman unaccounted for."

"Could the fifth sample have come from the housekeeper who found him?"

"I'm checking into that."

"How many samples did you find on Landau's body?"

"Four."

"That goes along with my maid theory. The two couples came to play."

"That seems obvious."

"Was Landau still alive when they left the room?"

"It appears that way, but with poisons, they aren't always fast-acting."

"So if the fifth wasn't an active participant in the bedroom, she could be our killer."

"Or the maid. Unfortunately, we're not sure how or when the lone individual entered or left the room. Like I said, two couples. That's four people. Not five."

"Wow, you're a detective and good at math. Wonders never cease."

"You're just jealous," O'Connell teased.

"Did you get any hits on the DNA samples?"

"Not yet. It's too early for that. Forensics has only finished the preliminary analysis. That's how I determined the boy, girl designation. But the reason I called is because you know Cross. You know how he operates and what goes on in his office."

"I don't know anything about Landau. I'd tell you if I did." I gnawed on my bottom lip. "I'd go out on a limb and say Landau must have been worth something. After all, he paid for that hotel room, and those suites aren't cheap. Plus, Cross doesn't typically entertain clients that won't add to his prestige or bottom line."

"According to Cross, he barely even took the meeting."

"That's the same story I heard, but..."

"What is it, Parker?"

"I don't know. It may be nothing."

"Tell me anyway."

"Cross knew I didn't find anything in our database on Landau. He even said he offered to give you his records, but you declined."

"Well, he said he'd be happy to help as soon as I came back with a court order," O'Connell corrected. "I will if I have to, but I'm guessing it'll be a dead end."

"Regardless, I didn't like the way he said it."

"You think he's covering something up?"

"I don't know. I don't believe Cross was involved in Landau's murder. It'd be easy enough for me to check to see if he has an alibi once you get the TOD window narrowed. But Lucien's not a killer, not like this anyway. He definitely wouldn't waste his time with poison. I just wonder if he might remember more about his meeting with Victor Landau than what he shared."

"How are you going to find out?"

"Me?"

"I thought you were helping out on this," O'Connell said. "Don't you owe me for something?"

"I'll always owe you. I'll see if any of the receptionists or assistants remember making notes regarding Landau's reason for the appointment. I'll let you know what I find, but in the meantime, Cross reminded me his case takes priority. He wants me to keep busy, so I can't assist you."

"He doesn't want you helping the police department on this murder spree. Big surprise."

"Spree? Oh right, this is the fourth. That makes it serial."

"No shit." He let out a sigh. "I already contacted the Bureau when we found the last one. They don't know anything."

I rubbed my eyes. The last thing I needed was to piss off another deranged killer. "I'll search Cross's database for clues, but I'll need everything you have on the other three victims, the locations where they were found, the evidence lists from the crime scenes, and the names of any witnesses or suspects you questioned. I'll let you know if anything pops. But I doubt it. You're probably on your own."

"All right, I'll get everything together and drop it by in the morning."

"Actually, I'll pick it up. I have to sign some paperwork, don't I?"

"You do. I just wasn't sure if you were still on board. You didn't seem particularly enthused this morning."

"I'm not, but turning a blind eye while some psycho murders people isn't going to help me sleep any easier. I don't want anyone else to die because of me."

"That's a good goal to have."

I snorted. "Isn't it?"

"On the bright side, you get to put the screws to Cross by helping me out with this."

"True, but I don't necessarily want him to know I'm multitasking until I'm certain he's not hiding something."

"All right. Get some rest. I'll see you in the morning. And Parker, it won't happen again. Lightning doesn't strike twice."

"Are you sure?"

We disconnected, and I dropped onto the couch and put my face in my hands. Now I had even more to worry about. Why me?

The overwhelming urge to hide under the bed and never surface again beckoned. But that would involve going upstairs, and despite what I'd said to everyone who asked, my leg hurt. Stairs might have been my greatest foe. Instead, I took the throw off the couch and put it over my head. The world would never find me under here.

"Hey, Parker." Bruiser put his jacket on and reached for the holster he'd left on the coffee table. He nudged the blanket, having deduced the Alex Parker shaped lump beneath it had to be me. "Are you sure you don't need someone to drive you around tomorrow?"

"No, I'm okay."

He laughed. "That's not what I would call hiding under a blanket."

I pulled it off my head. "I'm not hiding. I'm keeping warm."

"Anyway, I'm taking off. If something changes, let me know."

"You can stick around."

"Nah, the boss man's home. I'll get out of the way."

"What time is it?"

"A quarter to eight."

"You might want to stick around. He might need a bodyguard."

Bruiser held up his palms. "I'm not stepping into the middle of this, or you might take your revenge out on me when we spar." He tapped his temple. "I haven't forgotten." He patted my shoulder. "Try to go easy, slugger. He loves you."

Bruiser went down the steps. I could hear the two of them conversing, but I couldn't make out their words. A few moments later, Martin emerged. He'd already undone his tie and the top few buttons of his shirt.

"Hey, beautiful, how was your day? I heard you went to work."

"Was that your doing?"

His brow furrowed. "Why would you think that?"

"Call it gut instinct."

Martin pulled a bouquet of purple and white flowers from behind his back. "It wasn't me, but I brought you something."

"Is that supposed to be an apology?"

"No." He grabbed a crystal vase from the shelf and put the flowers inside. "Why would I apologize?"

"I can think of a few reasons."

He put the arrangement down on the coffee table and adjusted the irises and white roses. "They're silk. I didn't want to trigger your allergies too." He turned back and looked at me. "I thought they might cheer you up."

"I spoke to O'Connell. What did you say to him?"

Martin ignored me. "So you don't like the flowers?" He picked up the vase and moved it to the end table. "In that case, I hope you like your other surprise better."

"I don't want gifts. I just want to know what you did. You've been orchestrating my entire life lately."

"What are you talking about?"

"What you said to Jen and Nick about me, telling Bruiser how to feed me so I'd actually eat, and who knows what kinds of favors you asked Lucien for. How many times are we going to have this fight? It's my life, my career, my business."

He tugged on his collar, opening another button. "Yes, I spoke to Nick's wife. She's a nurse, and the O'Connells are our friends. She wanted to know how you were doing. So I told her. Big deal. As for Bruiser, I warned you this morning I'd have him force-feed you. So don't even start. Aside from the crackers last night, when's the last time you ate?"

"And Cross?"

"Oh for fuck's sake. You really think I'd go to him for something?"

"You already have."

Anger burned in his eyes. "Mark doesn't count."

"Not Mark, the necklace with the GPS tracker you gave me. You got that from him."

"So? I told you about that."

"You only told me because I found out."

"Well, it saved someone's life, didn't it?"

"That's not the point."

"Actually, sweetheart, that's precisely the point."

"Ugh." I let out a growl, wishing I'd stayed underneath the blanket. "You're the reason I got hired at Cross Security in the first place. For all I know, you're the reason for everything."

"I can live with that." A smirk tugged at his lips. "Blame me," he said with such sincerity I nearly slapped the look off his face.

"Don't say that. If that's what you want, we can't be together." I climbed off the couch, needing to be in motion and away from him. Unfortunately, he followed me into the second floor suite which I'd made into my office.

He leaned against the doorjamb with his arms folded across his chest, watching as I reorganized the papers I'd taken home from work. "You're hurt and sad. I get that. But in case you've forgotten, I told you to stay home today."

I glared at him. "Once again, you were right. Does that make you happy?"

"No, it doesn't. You're the love of my life, so anything that hurts you or makes you sad isn't something from which I take joy."

"You have no problem pissing me off. I'm pretty sure you enjoy that."

"Only because I love you. And it's fun."

"You're insane."

He laughed. "Truly, madly, deeply." He pulled himself away from the wall and nudged me. "I'm trying here, but you're not making it easy on me. Cut a guy some slack. It's bad enough I've already lost my mojo. Are you going to take my pride and my balls too?"

"Martin, tell me the truth. Did you convince anyone at the police department to offer me a consulting gig or suggest to Lucien that I needed to be assigned a case?"

"No. I won't interfere in your career like that." He held up three fingers. "I promise. Cross my heart."

"But you told Bruiser to make me soup."

"You like soup."

I pinched the skin along his ribs, making him wince.

"Hey, I was transparent about my intentions and threats. I wouldn't have to resort to such extremes if you weren't always so difficult."

"I told you I'm not easy."

"Good thing I love a challenge. That must be why I love

you." He ran his thumb across my cheek, waiting for permission before he kissed me on the mouth. "All right, just give me a few minutes to change and then I'll get dinner ready."

"Don't we have leftovers?"

"We do, but I promised Jabber I'd grill steaks. Since you were so desperate to talk to him last night, I thought I'd do you one better."

"You invited Mark Jablonsky for dinner?" The idea eased the pressure in my chest I hadn't even realized was there.

Martin smiled, pleased he'd finally done something right. "The steaks shouldn't take that long. We could properly make-up before he arrives."

"No."

"Suit yourself," Martin headed for the stairs, "but you'll change your tune once I find someone to lift this curse."

SEVEN

I straightened up the living room. The last thing I needed was Mark giving me more grief. He made it his life's mission to irritate me ever since the first time I stepped foot in his office. So finding the cushions indented in the shape of my body and the throw still warm would only add more fuel to the fire.

Once everything was organized and the evidence of my depression and heartbreak were safely hidden away, I made a pot of coffee. Napping earlier should have made me feel better. Instead, it emphasized how exhausted I was.

Martin came down the stairs just as I poured the contents of the pot into a tumbler. He went to the pantry and returned with the sugar bowl and a handful of spices for the steak. Wordlessly, he put the sugar down beside me and continued to the fridge. "Cream or milk?"

"Milk."

He handed it to me before pulling the steaks out of the fridge. "Do you need more ice, or do you want it warm?"

"It's iced coffee."

"I know, but I've seen you drink it warm on several occasions. Sometimes, I think you only add the ice in order to drink it faster." He massaged the spices into the steaks and put them on a plate to rest.

"Why do you always have to act like you know everything?" I stirred until the cubes dissolved and took a sip.

"Because I do."

"For the record, smug is unattractive."

"Is that why you didn't want to have make-up sex?"

I ignored the question and took a seat at the kitchen table while Martin scrubbed a few potatoes. "How did your meeting with Cross go this morning?"

"It went."

A disturbing thought entered my mind. The only times Cross specifically asked me to work cases was when they connected to Martin. "Do you know Andre North?"

Martin finished poking holes in the potatoes and put them in the microwave. "I don't think so."

"What about Eve Wyndham?"

He went to the fridge in search of salad ingredients. "Do you want roasted Brussels sprouts or grilled asparagus?"

"I don't care."

He pulled out the asparagus spears and placed them beside the lettuce, tomato, cucumber, bell peppers, and onion already on the counter. "Marcal said he picked up some baby portobellos on his last trip to the market. Do you want them as a side dish or sauteed over the steaks?"

"Martin, it doesn't matter. You know I don't have much of an appetite."

He met my eyes and decided it was best not to argue. "Which would Mark prefer?"

"More steak, less veggies."

"You're probably right."

"So, Eve Wyndham?" I repeated.

"Name doesn't ring any bells."

"You're sure? She's an event planner."

Martin washed the produce in the sink and made the salad, expertly chopping each ingredient with chef-like precision. "What does she look like?"

"Hot. Gorgeous curls. Expert highlights. Decent boob job. Nice legs."

"Where does she work?"

"She's freelance now, but she used to work for Elite."

He absently ran a hand through his hair.

"Ah ha." I knew his nervous tics just as well as he knew mine. "You do know her."

"No. Well, maybe. I'm not sure. Martin Technologies uses Elite for most of its major events, and half the time, when I organize something for charity, I use them. They have high standards and contacts with some great PR firms and major media channels – online, television, newspapers, magazines. You get the point."

"So that's why Cross assigned me this case. I knew it." Letting out a sigh, I asked the inevitable. "Did you sleep with her?"

He missed the vegetable and nicked his finger with the knife.

"Are you okay?" I asked.

"My finger's still attached if that's what you mean." He went to the sink, rinsed it under water, and wrapped it in a piece of paper towel. "However, I don't appreciate you assuming I've slept with every hot woman in this city."

"It wasn't an assumption. It was a question."

"Bullshit. You always think I've had torrid affairs with these women. When are you going to give me the benefit of the doubt?" He held up the bloody paper towel. "I could have lost a finger."

I tried not to laugh. Like the loving girlfriend, I grabbed the bandages and went to the counter. Given how often we went through first aid supplies, I could probably invest and retire on the dividends. He removed the paper towel, and I snorted at the tiny cut.

"Men always think it's bigger than it is."

He tore open the wrapper and wound the band-aid around his finger. "No, sweetheart, it's been so long, you've forgotten just how big it is."

"Men always think it's longer too."

He narrowed his eyes at me. "It's nice to see you're having fun at my expense."

Except I wasn't. "Did you sleep with her? You never answered my question."

"Why do you always ask me that?"

"Because you've slept with half the women in this city, and you're the self-proclaimed god of sex and ecstasy or some nonsense like that. Doesn't that mean every woman who crosses your path throws herself at you?"

"You didn't."

"We live together. Your point is moot. Plus, Cross handpicked me for this case. He only does that when it involves you."

"What?"

"He's obsessed with you. He probably wants me to keep your name out of the investigation. Maybe that's why he wanted me to handle it."

"To protect me?" Martin asked.

"Only if you're currently having an affair with her."

"Alex–"

I held up my hand. "I know you're not. You wouldn't do that to me. But Lucien has an agenda, and every case he's personally asked me to investigate connects back to you. I don't want to get blindsided again. I need to know how you connect to Andre or Eve."

He put away the bandages. "I didn't sleep with her. If I had, I would remember her name, but it's possible we've crossed paths. When did she leave Elite?"

"I don't know."

"Tell me what you do know, and we'll take it from there." He kissed my forehead. "In the meantime, I better finish making dinner. If you have any more insane questions to ask, give me the heads up before I lose a finger or worse." While Martin finished cooking, I brought my files into the kitchen. "Is that her?" He examined the photograph of Eve and Andre.

"Yep."

He tilted his head from side to side. "I've never seen her before."

"Are you sure you'd remember?"

"Not really, but I don't think we crossed paths. And for the record, she's not that hot. You have better legs."

"I used to."

"You still do," he insisted.

"She has a nicer rack."

"That could double as a flotation device." He reached for his phone and made a note. "I'll have someone from MT check and see who we've worked with from Elite. Someone must remember. I'll give you the name once I get it."

"What about Andre?"

He shook his head. "What would their pending nuptials or extra-marital affairs have to do with me?"

"That's why I asked if you slept with her."

He scoffed and rolled his eyes. Before he could say anything else, the security system alerted us to activity. "Jabber's here. Would you mind letting him in while I throw the steaks and asparagus on the grill?"

"No problem."

I opened the front door just as Mark reached for the doorbell. He'd lost a few pounds since the last time I'd seen him. His color had improved, and he looked healthy.

"You look like shit," he said. "When's the last time you slept?"

I looked at my watch. "About five hours ago. Thanks for the compliment. It's just what a girl wants to hear. I was going to say you look good, but you can forget it now."

Mark gave me that concerned look of his as he entered the living room. "Have you been working?"

"I caught a case today. Two, actually."

"While you were sleeping?"

"No. One before and one after."

He studied the sofa cushions for a moment. "I'd ask how you are, but you'll say fine even though you're not. So we'll skip that part. Marty said you almost called me last night. What's going on?"

"Nothing much. I finished the threat assessments. I just need you to double-check my work and make sure I didn't miss anything."

"That was quick. You went through every case you've ever worked in less than a month. That's—"

"Good work," I volunteered.

"Insane."

"No reason to wait." I led Mark into the kitchen.

He put the six-pack of beer down on the counter and

flipped through the file I left on the table. "What does Cross have you doing now?"

"Possible cheating fiancée. When I talked to the groom-to-be, he didn't sound suspicious, just cautious. I'm not really sure why he hired us or why Cross asked me to look into it."

"You specifically?"

"Yeah."

"Do you think it has something to do with Marty?" Mark asked.

"See," I said for Martin's benefit as he stepped out of the pantry, "I'm not the only one who assumes these things."

Mark nodded hello to Martin and snagged one of the longnecks from the carrier. He popped the top using the edge of the counter and took a seat at the table, making himself at home. "So, Marty, who are Andre North and Eve Wyndham?" Mark read their names off the page.

"Like I told Alex," Martin put the rest of the beers in the fridge and went back to slicing the mushrooms, "I don't know either of them, but it's possible Eve did some work for MT when she worked at Elite."

"That's it?" Mark asked.

Martin let out a frustrated growl. "That's it."

Mark and I exchanged a look. "Whatever you say." Mark flipped through the intel and pulled out his phone, performing an abbreviated version of the social media checks I'd spent far too many hours conducting. "Nothing indicates she's stepping out on her intended."

"Even he didn't seem convinced she was. He just wants to make sure. He's afraid if they divorce she'll take him for everything he's worth."

"Smart man." Mark leaned back, taking a long pull from his beer.

I stared at the bottle. "Should you be drinking?"

He waved a dismissive hand in my direction. "Should you be walking around without your crutches?"

"Medical cleared me today. I'm fine. I just need to build back my strength."

"Really?" Martin asked. "That's wonderful. When does PT start?"

"I'm trying something else instead." I gave him a look, and Martin dropped the subject.

EIGHT

"This is a mess." I grabbed my mug and took a sip. O'Connell had crime scene photos from the four poisonings pinned to a corkboard. "When did this first happen?"

"Eight months ago." O'Connell rocked back in his chair. "Homicide ruled the first case an accidental overdose. The autopsy was inconclusive. They didn't know to check for anything else."

"A puncture wouldn't be uncommon."

"Not with those track marks." O'Connell pushed the crime scene report toward me. "All four were poisoned."

"Did the ME decide what poison was used to kill Landau?"

"Yeah." O'Connell highlighted the scientific name. "Don't ask me for the pronunciation, but that's the fancy way of saying something derived from oleander."

"Was it the same poison used on the other three victims?"

O'Connell shook his head and pointed to the second and third victims. "Hemlock and deadly nightshade. We can't be certain what was used on the first. We didn't run enough tests at the time."

"What made you run them on these? Poison isn't something commonly tested for, and it's even harder to recognize."

"At the second crime scene, we found vomit and indications the victim suffered a seizure prior to death. We tested for everything."

"That's how you knew to check the third and fourth." I blew out a breath. "Different poisons could mean different killers, but all these scenes look the same to me. They feel the same. Nice private suite, untraceable group sex, and one victim. Anything ritualistic?"

"Not that I noticed," O'Connell said. "What are you thinking?"

"I'm not sure."

"Have you seen anything like this before?"

"No, but you know I didn't work murders or serial killings. At least not intentionally." I reexamined the toxicology reports from the four different crime scenes. "I'm having conflicting opinions. Serial killers tend to be male."

"But poison is usually a woman's preferred method of killing." O'Connell spread the photos from the hotel's security cameras out on the desk. "Our unknown fifth is female."

I examined the photos of the two couples who entered the hotel. They wore long trench coats with the collars pulled up. The two women had scarves wrapped around their heads, as a throwback to the 1960s spy flicks, and large sunglasses. One of the men wore a motorcycle helmet. The other had a cowboy hat with wraparound sunglasses.

"Facial rec can't get a hit. I spoke to the hotel staff, but these people weren't registered guests. They didn't even use valet parking. They arrived by cab and left the same way. They entered, went straight to the elevator, and straight to the room. No looking around. No distractions. They knocked and entered."

"Did you get the cab numbers?" I asked. "The drivers might be able to ID them."

"Nothing yet, but I'm guessing that's a bust."

Based on his expression, there was something he wasn't saying. "What is it, Nick?"

"You saw the scene. It's a fuckfest. With the previous

three murders, we never IDed any of the other parties. It was just like this. Always couples showing up to play. Maybe they're into swapping or group activities. I don't know, and I don't care. But none of the vics were part of a couple. They checked into the hotel alone, and as far as we can tell, they were all single."

"But there were six people in Landau's room, five not including the vic. So even though the vic was single, he might have invited a date, who somehow snuck into the room without us noticing." I stared at the stills from the security cam footage. "Was Victor Landau seeing anyone?"

"Not that we know of. IT found several dating profiles. It looks like he's been seeking his soulmate for the last four years but didn't have any luck. His dating profiles are still active."

"Any idea how he got involved in this scene?" I gestured at the photo. "Do you think the women who showed up were previous lovers? Or previous dates?"

"I don't know. We've tried contacting a few of the more recent hits he's gotten on the dating sites, but the women claim to know nothing about this. They even alibied out."

"Who are these people, and how did they know to show up at his hotel room?"

"I dunno. That's what I've been trying to figure out ever since major crimes took over the investigation. I'd say this reads like one of those underground sex clubs. The kind with anonymous high-profile members who get random texts with locations and times for the next event."

"Have you been reading Jen's trashy romance novels again?" I teased.

O'Connell's expression hardened. "How does this read to you?"

"The same." I sighed. "Do you have an actual lead?"

"Just some whispers from vice. Nothing's panned out yet. If we can identify at least one other person, we might have something."

"Have you tried flashing the surveillance photos around inside biker bars or those line-dancing places?"

"Hardy har. Any other suggestions?"

But I didn't have anything. "You still don't know when

or how the fifth person entered the room?" The autopsy helped narrow time of death to a four-hour window. Eleven to three a.m. It was possible the killer administered the poison and left the hotel before Landau expired, which could implicate either couple as the guilty party or accomplices to murder, but that didn't explain how the fifth DNA sample got inside the room. "Have you finished comparing the sample to the hotel staff?"

"The third woman in Landau's room doesn't work at the hotel. Forensics determined no one from the hotel laid a hand or anything else on Landau's body or on any of the wine glasses or prophylactics found at the scene."

"Where did you find the fifth DNA sample?" I asked.

"On one of the wine glasses and on the outside of one of the discarded condoms."

"Landau's condom?"

"No."

"So whoever the fifth person is, she didn't have sex with Landau. Is that the consensus?"

"It appears that way."

I flipped back to the printed stills from the security footage. "I don't remember an adjoining room to that suite."

"That's because it doesn't have one."

"Are these the only security photos you have?"

"I watched the footage. This was the extent of the suspicious activity in and out after Landau's arrival."

"What about before?"

O'Connell tapped his pen on the desk a few times. "Hey, Thompson," he called to his partner, "did the techs run the footage prior to Landau's check-in?"

"Yeah."

"And?"

"And what?" Thompson grabbed a stack of papers off the printer and headed toward us. He glared at me. "Parker, why do you always sit in my chair?"

"It helps me think."

"Move." He pointed to the folding chair beside O'Connell's desk. "The techs didn't find anything else. Just usual hotel operation."

"Meaning?" I asked before O'Connell could.

Thompson glanced in my direction. "Meaning maid service cleaned the room, changed the linens, restocked the mini bar and locked the room until Landau arrived."

"And no one else came in or out?" O'Connell asked.

"Only the room service Landau ordered." Thompson scooted my cup to O'Connell's desk and centered his keyboard. "I sent CSU back to check the balcony. It's the only place someone could hide without anyone noticing."

"Good call." O'Connell turned to me. "They'll get back to us when they finish. In the meantime, any insights you care to share?"

"Murder scenes aren't my thing."

"Besides that," O'Connell said.

"What is your thing?" Thompson asked.

"Not this." I reached for Landau's financial statement. He had money. Not as much as most of Cross Security's clientele, but enough to live comfortably. "Any 9-1-1 calls from his home, cell, or office in the last few months?"

"Nothing," O'Connell said.

"What about threats? He's an architect for a prestigious firm. Have they received any threats?"

"We're working on it." O'Connell gave me a look. "You were hired to consult, not micromanage or pretend to be Lt. Moretti."

Eyeing the lieutenant's office, I imagined how I'd look behind his desk. "What does he have to say about this?"

O'Connell glowered at me. "Seriously, Parker, do you have anything to add? Any reason why someone would want to kill Landau or who the killer might be? For some reason, Landau had Cross's card in his wallet. That has to mean something. I wouldn't put it past your boss to get his rocks off at some secret swingers' event. He looks like the type who'd enjoy an orgy."

"At least a quadruple," Thompson said.

"Again, I wouldn't know, but I'll see what I can find out. In the meantime, do some actual police work. I can't consult if you don't have anything for me to consult on."

"Ballbuster," Thompson muttered.

I smiled. "Be nice and I'll bring you donuts the next time

I stop by."

"Jelly," Thompson said.

"And sprinkles for Nick." I collected a copy of the intel and headed for the door. "Maybe I'll run this by the federal building and see if I can get someone from behavioral sciences to weigh in. Any objections?"

"None. Consult away," O'Connell called after me. "And don't forget to bring coffee with those donuts."

"No problem." Too bad I had no idea how I could help. The police had this situation handled. They had the evidence, the tools, and two topnotch detectives working on the case. They didn't need me. Frankly, I still wasn't convinced O'Connell hadn't used his phone-a-friend just because Martin asked. But that was another fight for another day.

Landau had a Cross Security business card on his person when he died, so my first stop was the architecture firm where Landau worked. After speaking to the woman at reception, who mistakenly believed I was a ditzy personal assistant who failed to write down my boss's meeting or even the architect's name, I left the firm. It was only nine a.m., but I'd already determined Lucien hadn't tried to hire Landau or his associates to design a new office building for him.

Perhaps I should take my boss at face value. He said he didn't know Landau or why the man contacted us. Maybe that was true. But I made a mental note to chat up every receptionist I found before cornering Justin, Lucien's righthand man, and interrogating him.

However, I had other fish to fry, or a full plate, or some other food-related metaphor that would probably make me queasy if I spent too long thinking about it. So I headed to the federal building, parked in a visitor space, left my gun and other hardware in the car, went through the metal detectors, and filled out the paperwork. With a visitor's pass clipped to my jacket, I followed the junior agent to the elevator and up to the OIO level.

Before heading to Mark's office, I detoured to Agent Eddie Lucca's desk. His back was to me, so he didn't notice when I snuck up behind him. The junior agent cleared her throat, causing Eddie to look up from the pile of paperwork. At least he was alive.

"Sir, you have a visitor," the agent said.

"That's not a visitor. That's Parker," Lucca said. "She doesn't count."

"Hey." I tried to sound offended.

He nodded to the agent. "Thanks. I'll take it from here."

The agent disappeared down the hall.

"Back so soon?" Lucca asked. "Agent Davis said he saw you lurking in the corridors two weeks ago."

"I wasn't lurking. I was doing research." I patted the stack of files I brought with me that Mark had forgotten to grab on his way out the door last night. "Jablonsky and I have been working on some threat assessments."

"So I heard." Lucca tried to hide his amusement. "Admit it. You just wanted to see me."

"Guilty," I teased, even if it might have been true. "Since you dropped in on me at work, I thought I'd return the favor."

"I'm surprised anyone let you in here. Aren't you banned?"

"You wish."

"If you keep showing up like this, Agent Nayyar's going to think you're vying to get your old spot back. And I don't think he wants to give up his desk."

"It was mine first." I glanced at the empty chair where I used to spend most of my days and nights. "But he has nothing to worry about."

"Are you sure? You've been spending more time in the federal building these last few weeks than most active agents."

"What's your excuse?"

"I'm just trying to catch up on the current caseload." He lowered his voice. "What are you doing here, Parker? I don't believe this is just about threat assessments? Is there some kind of top secret op you're working with Jablonsky? Or are you planning to make another comeback?"

"There's not a chance in hell that could ever happen, nor would I want it to." I swallowed. "I just need to find some peace of mind."

"You think going over every single one of our cases will help?" He stared at me. "Yes, Alex, I know what you've been doing. Jablonsky had me run the last set of names you brought him."

I froze, like a deer caught in headlights.

Lucca grinned. "I don't blame you. I've been doing the same thing. After what happened, none of us can be too careful. Especially since I have Kelly and Grace to think about." He studied my expression for a moment. "How's the leg? You seem steadier today than you did the last time I saw you."

"It's getting there."

"Good. Kelly wants to know when you're available for dinner. My wife is under the impression you're a normal human being who knows how to interact with other normal human beings."

"You haven't dissuaded her of this notion yet?"

"Believe me, I've tried." Lucca leaned back in his chair, wincing slightly from the shift in position. "It's no big deal. She just wants to thank you. Actually, *we* want to thank you. You didn't have to come back for me. You could have called it in. He wanted you dead. Showing up was suicide. It was stupid."

"It's my fault you were there. If I hadn't called to ask for your help, none of this would have happened." I gestured at his mid-section, a lump forming in my throat. "You saved the day, Lucca. I should be thanking you."

"In that case, when are you inviting us to dinner?"

I swallowed, feeling the blood drain from my face.

"Jeez. I forgot how difficult you can be. It was a joke. You need to lighten up."

"I've said it before, Eddie. You need to stay away from me, especially now."

"This is my desk."

"Right. I'm gonna go."

"What do you mean by especially now?"

"Nothing. The police want me to consult on something. It could blow up. I don't want you to get hit by shrapnel."

"I don't want that either."

"Good, we're in agreement. Take it easy, and feel

better."

"Yeah, you too."

I backed away from his desk, nearly tripping over Agent Davis in the process. Davis nodded at me. He didn't ask why I was here, and I didn't offer an explanation. Instead, I knocked on Mark's open office door and entered without waiting for him to acknowledge me.

"I finished the last set of prison checks. I'm surprised you can't get this done yourself with all the resources available at Cross Security," Mark said, not even bothering to glance up. I wondered how he knew it was me. Perhaps he'd seen me talking to Lucca.

"I can, but it wouldn't exactly be legal. And I didn't want to breach the prison database while the current investigation is under way."

"At least you still have some sense of self-preservation," Mark said. "I was beginning to wonder about that." He stared at the files in my hand. "I was halfway home last night when I realized I forgot to grab those. I guess I was too busy thinking about everything else going on in your life. Have you figured out Marty's connection to Andre and Eve?"

"Not yet."

"I'm sure you will eventually." Mark pulled a thick manila file out from his middle drawer and slapped it down on the desk in front of me. "I came in early and did some digging. You're gonna want to see this."

"Is it about Martin?"

"No, this is about your other case."

NINE

"Damn. If you're right, this is serial."

"It looks that way." Mark watched me read the files. "These aren't local or recent, but it could be the same guy."

"Or girl."

"These were violent suffocations. A show of dominance. I'd say this unsub is male."

I studied the files on the five unsolved murders. The first one occurred three years ago with the others taking place over the course of eighteen months. The scenes were up and down the PCH, hundreds of miles from one to the other. The method of killing was different from what was happening here, but the staging was eerily similar. Expensive hotel room registered to the victim, multiple DNA samples, multiple sex partners, and not a single witness or suspect ever identified. "I don't know. Why would this guy jump coasts and change his method of killing?"

"Things could have gotten too hot in California, so he came here."

"Or these aren't connected. Fingerprints and DNA found at these scenes should be in the system. O'Connell would have gotten a ping."

"Maybe, maybe not." Mark flipped open one of Interpol's files. "What about these? Similar thing happened in Mexico, six months after the PCH killings. Five more victims. These men were killed over the course of ten months in Cabo, San Lucas. That gives the killer enough time to jump coasts and start up over here."

I examined the report. "Knife to the heart?"

"Not just the heart. The victims' genitals were removed." Mark cringed, even though none of the files contained photos. "The Mexican police thought the cartel was behind it."

"In that part of the world, I can understand why." I closed the file. "Mutilations are different though. Killings are bad enough, but that's a whole other level. If this is the same killer, why would he suddenly turn down the violence and switch to poison?" I wasn't convinced they were connected.

"These are the only serial killings I found involving orgies."

"What about serial killers operating in the region who prefer using poisons, specifically those derived from plants and flowers?"

"I didn't find anything."

"Neither did O'Connell." I chewed on my bottom lip. "I told him I'd see if BSU could build a profile. We have four scenes to compare. That should be enough."

"Leave that to me. I'll make the request and have them run a comparison to these two other killing sprees and see what they think." Mark rocked back in his chair. "I hate to break it to you, Alex, but a request coming from a private investigator will probably be denied. However, since it's you, they might help out anyway, but it won't take top priority. If I ask, it'll go straight to the top since they owe me a favor."

"Great." But it wasn't.

"All right, I didn't ask last night, but I'm asking now, how are you?"

"Fine."

"Don't feed me that shit. I know this is the last thing in the world you want to be working on. Why didn't you tell

O'Connell to shove it?"

"I tried, but the killer's out there whether I search for her or not. I have to do something. People die because of me. They die because they know me or because they help me or because I can't save them. If I don't try to assist the police and someone else dies, that's on me. I don't want to wonder if I could have done something to stop it. But if someone else dies and I am helping, that's on me too because I didn't stop it."

"You realize you're not god, right? You don't control anything."

"I'm a control freak, so I don't accept that. But if this bitch targets someone I love because I'm assisting on the investigation, I'll probably jump off a bridge."

Mark gave me the look that I hated, the one that said he knew what was best for me even though I was too stubborn to admit it. "You can't bury this, Alex. Do not internalize the things that psychopath said to you. Cooper's death isn't on you. This," he patted his gut, "isn't your fault either. I assisted you on the arrest. I make my own enemies. Every single one of us knows what we signed up for when we joined the Bureau. Let it go or it will eat you alive. And quite frankly, I don't have the time or energy to deal with depressed, TV-watching Alex again. So talk or don't talk. Work, don't work, whatever. Just get through this and come out on the other side in one piece."

"That's the plan."

"Working a serial killer case with the police department isn't going to get you through this. It's going to make you crazy. Let me help out. After next week, I'll be back at full capacity, which means I won't have the time to do you any more favors and you can jump back in head first. But until then, I have nothing else to do except paperwork. Take this time to get your ducks in a row and your head on straight, okay?" He nodded at my leg. "You need to finish rehabbing, or you won't be good to anyone."

"No way. I'm not passing this off to you."

"Stop being such a pain in the ass."

"So you can paint another target on your back? Absolutely not."

"It's paperwork. Research. I'll stay behind my desk. Fair enough?"

"No."

"That's too bad because I'm going to do it anyway. Don't you have your hands full with Cross Security and Marty?"

"Don't remind me."

He sighed. "You can't carry this burden. You aren't in charge of anything. You don't have control. Shit happens. Shit will always happen. That's not on you." Mark reached into his desk drawer and slid a card across to me. "In case you need someone to help you put things into perspective."

"That's why I have you and Martin."

"Marty's not a miracle worker, and even I need help on occasion. Just think about it." Mark knew it was time to change the subject. "So you still think the killer's a woman?"

Arguing wouldn't get me anywhere. "The only DNA sample not found on Victor Landau's body belonged to a woman. The only person who entered and left the room undetected was female, and women like poison. That's three for three, and you always say there's no such thing as a coincidence."

"Only seven percent of killers are women. You're betting against the house on this one. Has the PD compared the samples from all four crime scenes yet? Once they do, you'll know for sure."

"O'Connell said they're working on it. We should know something soon." I cracked a smile. "Are you sure you want to bet against my gut instincts?"

"I'm telling you, the killer's male." Mark grabbed a sticky note and wrote *Check DNA*. "I'll see if any of the samples from these other cases match our local crimes. You're right. They should have been flagged if they matched, so I'm guessing they don't. Still, you have to admit, the scenes are very similar. There's overlap here. I know it."

"You sound certain."

"I am." He dug a twenty out of his wallet and slapped it down on his desk. "You gonna put your money where your mouth is, Parker? Twenty bucks says the killer's male."

"Fine." I matched his bet. "That'll just mean a bigger payday for me when you're wrong." I noticed the time. "Speaking of paydays, I better get back to my actual day job." I stared at the files on Mark's desk. "All joking aside, do you promise to be careful?"

"Nothing's going to happen to me, Alex."

"It better not. I can't spend any more time crying over you in a hospital, understand?"

"You won't have to."

"One last thing. Do you have any idea how a Cross Security business card got inside Victor Landau's wallet?"

"Just Landau's? Not the other three victims in the spree?"

"Not that I know of."

"You should ask Cross."

"He didn't have much to say on the subject. Apparently, Landau met with him two months ago, left a few minutes into their meeting, and never said what he wanted." I pointed at the two files from the other similar serial killings. "I guess I'll have to see if anyone else connects to Lucien or Cross Security."

"Cross won't be happy you're investigating him."

"He should be. More than likely, this will clear his name and remove any remaining suspicion."

"Cross is a bastard, but he's no serial killer. I doubt this connects."

"Well, there's that." I tapped the edge of the desk. "Be careful, Mark. I don't know what I'd do without you."

*   *   *

"Ms. Parker," the receptionist said the moment I stepped out of the elevator, "Mr. North is here to see you. He's waiting in your office."

"Thanks." Confused why North showed up today when he told me he was busy until the middle of next week, I went down the hall and pushed open my office door.

The overhead lights cast a reflection on North's freshly shaved scalp. The large man sat on one side of the sofa with a tiny teacup and saucer in his hands. The sight was almost comical. He wore a dress shirt with no tie. He'd taken off the jacket and folded it over the arm of the couch. His jeans were tucked into a pair of expensive work boots.

"Mr. North," I wondered if he'd been bored enough to search my office, "I didn't realize we were meeting today. If I had known you were coming, I wouldn't have kept you waiting."

He turned with a bright, friendly smile. "Don't worry about it. To be honest, I've been enjoying the quiet."

"I can go, so I don't disturb you." I jerked my thumb back toward the door.

He laughed, the creases deepening around his eyes and mouth. My research told me he was in his early forties, but I wouldn't have guessed it just by looking at him. He had a youthful glow. "After we spoke last night, I thought you probably had a sense of humor. I just didn't realize how funny you are." He turned the full wattage of the smile on me. "I hope my appearance isn't an inconvenience. If you're too busy, I can reschedule. I told that to Cindy, but she said your day was wide open."

"No, you're fine." I tucked the OIO file into my drawer, scribbled a note to call O'Connell, and grabbed a blank legal pad. "Can I get you another cup of tea or something to eat?"

He took a final sip before placing the cup gently on the glass coffee table. "I don't want you to go to any trouble."

"It isn't."

"I'm okay for now."

I took a seat on the other end of the l-shaped sofa. "As you've probably guessed, I'm Alex Parker. The name on the door should have given it away."

He chuckled again. "Yes, indeed." Finally, someone who appreciated my wit. But his smile faded. "After we spoke last night, I thought it would be best to meet in person." He took a deep breath. "Maybe I'm making a mistake."

"By marrying Ms. Wyndham? I haven't done much digging yet, but the background check didn't find anything suspicious. If she's a con artist or gold-digger, most of the time, the background checks spit out some type of red flag."

"No, not about that. What I'm not sure about is having you spy on Eve." He looked embarrassed. "I love her. I should trust her completely."

"Do you?"

He thought for a moment, letting out a sigh. "What does that say about me?"

"There's no reason not to be cautious, Mr. North."

"I'm afraid what will happen to us, to our relationship, if she finds out."

Leaning back in the chair, I crossed my legs and uncapped my pen. "I'm sure you went over most of this with Mr. Cross, but would you mind starting at the beginning?"

"Sure, no problem." He checked his watch. "I have plenty of time. My meetings for today got canceled on account of flooding."

"Flooding?"

"I was supposed to be golfing with clients. Something happened with the water hazard, and it turned a good chunk of the course into wetlands."

"What exactly is it that you do for work? You said something about asset management."

"I wouldn't exactly say that I work." North's cheeks flushed a little. "I started out flipping houses when I was in my early twenties. Me and some buddies from college saved up and bought this fixer upper, and in our spare time, we fixed it, sold it for ten times what we paid for it, and did it again. And again. Our entire goal was to retire by the time we turned thirty-five."

"Did you?"

"Kind of. We actually buy vacation properties now. Cabins, beach houses, chalets. If they need work, we put it in, but most of the time, the bones are good. We just spruce up the place, splurge on the amenities, and put it up for sale or rent."

"Like AirBnB?"

"Sort of." He relaxed against the cushions. "It's fun. I like to get my hands dirty, and I like to play with the cool toys before anyone else visits the place." His eyes twinkled. "Eve loves it. Every time I finish a project, we go on a romantic getaway. A weekend here. Two weeks there. It's amazing."

"It sounds wonderful."

"It is, but I'm away a lot when I'm painting or installing new floors. My buddies and I do most of the work ourselves. Eve keeps busy. She's always flying here, there, and everywhere. We don't get to spend enough time together."

"Is that why you think she might be having an affair?"

"I don't think that," North insisted. "At least, I don't want to think that. I just don't know. She receives late night calls and texts. She giggles on the phone the way she used to giggle with me when we first started dating. I asked her about it, but she won't tell me who she's talking to. She says she's working on a surprise for me, for our wedding. But it's been like this for months now."

I wrote a note to check her phone records and internet activity. "Has anything else been weird between you two lately?"

North carefully considered the question. "I don't know. She hasn't been around as much, but it's a busy season for her. She's planning a million weddings, not to mention ours. I just miss her. I don't want to lose her over this."

"Over what?"

"Hiring you," he said, as if it should have been obvious. "Be honest, Ms. Parker. If your husband or fiancé hired someone to follow you around, wouldn't you kick him to the curb?"

I resisted the urge to laugh. *Try a GPS tracker hidden in a heart pendant*, I thought. "I wouldn't be too happy about it, but if I gave him reason to worry, I might understand what drove him to do it."

North sighed. "Is it too late to call this off?"

"No, sir. That's up to you." I had barely cracked into their financial statements yesterday. I hadn't put in that much work yet and would prefer to have this off my plate.

"I don't know what I should do." North reached for the teacup, placing it gently back on the table when he realized it was empty. "My college buddies and I started the business together. We're partners. We split the work and the profits. That's only fair. I want it that way. I wouldn't be where I am without them and vice versa. I'm afraid by giving Eve half of everything she'll get half of that too if things go south between us."

"Have you spoken to a lawyer?"

"Yes, there are things he can do, but he recommended I hire an investigator to tail Eve."

"Again, it's your decision. I'll do whatever you want."

"Mr. Cross promised me this wouldn't be like those cheater shows on TV, where Eve gets catfished or hit on at a bar. I don't want anything like that to happen. I don't want other men to flirt with her or trick her. I just want to know if she loves me as much as I love her. That she's faithful. That this will be forever."

It sounded like he hired Cross Security because he was afraid of getting his heart broken, and now he came to the realization that depending on what we found, we might cause him that heartbreak even sooner. "Do you think she loves you?"

He stared at the floor, a bashful smile tugging at his lips. "I hope so."

"Then you probably don't have anything to worry about."

While he considered my words, I refilled his tea and poured myself a cup of coffee. I'd just handed him the cup when his phone buzzed. He apologized, showing me the display like a kid who just won a first place ribbon. *Eve.*

"Hey, babe, how are you? I miss you." He listened for a few moments. "Really?"

I sipped my coffee and moved behind my desk, sending a request upstairs for someone to pull Eve Wyndham's phone records and internet history, and then I did a quick search on the LLC registered to Andre North and his pals. Each one had their own separate business or two. One for rentals, one for sales. Depending on the country and region, they might have created other corporate entities, probably to address the tax or business laws for that region. Once I found Andre's main business, I brought up property records. Before I had a chance to scan the dozen entries, North and Eve exchanged their 'I love you's, and

North hung up.

"Is everything okay?" I asked.

"She said her trip might get extended." He swallowed the tea. "You know, I might be an asshole for doing this, but I'll always wonder if I don't. Eve deserves better from me. She deserves to be trusted completely and utterly. I'm thinking this is my problem, my neuroses, but I have to be sure. Do you think she'll forgive me?"

"Would you forgive her?"

"I'd forgive her for anything, even if she is cheating."

"Okay then, let's go over some details so I have some idea of where to start."

TEN

My interview with Andre North saved me a lot of time. He told me everything there was to know about Eve from her work schedule to her pilates classes to the grocery store where she picked up her favorite flavor of ice cream, mint chocolate chip. Based on the pages and pages of detailed notes, I'd say Andre North knew his fiancée well, which made me think his fears might not be entirely unfounded. Anyone who paid that much attention, who was so hopelessly head over heels for his partner, would pick up on little cues or subconsciously note any changes.

I dug through the drawer to find my colored pens since the purple one I'd been using had run out of ink. Then I continued detailing Eve's schedule in a blank planner so I'd know every place she'd be and when she'd be there. The color coding made it easier to depict work activities from Eve's personal activities. The grocery store wasn't a given, except on Thursdays. She always stopped by on Thursday nights after work to get supplies for whatever weekend work event she had planned and for movie night with Andre. Even if they went to the theater, they liked to sneak junk food into the movie since they didn't like the limited options available at the concession stand.

When I finished writing down Eve's schedule, I checked

my dropbox to see if the records I requested had been delivered yet. I found details on Andre North's business but nothing on Eve Wyndham. After putting my computer to sleep and locking the sensitive materials in my drawer, just in case any inquisitive clients or coworkers wandered in, I headed for the elevator. This was my chance to do some digging into Cross's meeting with Victor Landau, all while working on my current Cross-approved case. Soon, I'd be named the queen of multitasking.

While IT pulled Eve's records, I asked about Victor Landau and his firm, but they'd never run his records. Aside from asking for a copy of Cross's phone logs, this wouldn't get me anywhere, so I took the information packet they handed me and went upstairs to update Cross on the situation.

When I arrived, Justin told me he was on the phone. "Is there something I can do or a message I can pass along?"

"Actually," I leaned closer, tucking a strand of hair behind my ear, "I just had IT run Eve Wyndham's phone and browser history for me. I have her daily routine and weekly meetings noted, so I don't think surveilling her is going to be a problem. As far as her fiancé knows, she doesn't have any trips planned until after they get back from their honeymoon."

"Okay."

"So just let Lucien know I have a plan and most things are taken care of. I am curious about a few things, though." I frowned and bit my lip while performing a hair flip. However, Justin didn't seem the type to have much interest in the damsel in distress routine, or I'd already shown my true colors by barging into Lucien's office on more than one occasion.

"What?" He'd mastered almost the same level of dread as everyone else who knew me, and this was probably the first actual conversation the two of us ever had.

"I'm sure you're aware the police asked me to consult on a case."

Justin busied himself with something on the computer screen. "Uh-huh."

"Right, so I was hoping you could shed some light on

Victor Landau or what he may have wanted."

"I don't know."

"Are you sure? Didn't you schedule the meeting?"

He stopped typing and wheeled his chair backward. Opening a cabinet, he pulled out a large leather portfolio. "That was two months ago. The meeting was scheduled for the seventh." He held the book out for me to read. *New client consultation.* "Anything else I can help you with?"

"Do you remember meeting Mr. Landau?"

"Vaguely."

"Did he seem distressed?"

"Compared to everyone else we meet?"

"Fair point."

"Look, Ms. Parker, I understand you're in a pickle, but you put yourself in this position. Lucien spoke to the police. You've checked our records. There's nothing here. Nothing to find. I'm sorry Mr. Landau was killed, but I don't know why it happened. Landau never explained why he wanted a meeting with Lucien. He didn't tell me anything on the phone when I made the appointment, and he didn't stay long enough to share his problem with the boss."

"Do the phone calls get recorded?" I asked.

"No, ma'am."

"Fine. I just have one final request."

"I'll help if I can."

Yeah, right, I thought. "I want to know how Andre North or Eve Wyndham connects to James Martin."

"Why would you think—"

"Don't even," I interrupted. "Just answer the damn question."

Justin fought to keep the amused look off his face. "Check the records you requested on Mr. North's business. I'm sure you'll find the answer there."

Before I could say anything else, the door to Cross's office opened. Lucien didn't appear surprised to see me. "Justin, I need you to deliver this to Mr. Almeada right away. I don't have time to wait for the courier."

"Yes, sir."

"On your way back, stop by city hall and pick up the

copies of the records I requested. For some reason, their website is being finnicky today." Cross rubbed his eyes. "That's the last thing we need right now."

"On my way, boss." Justin slid out from behind his desk, took the manila envelope from Cross's hand, and disappeared into the elevator.

"What do you want?" Cross asked as he headed for the espresso maker in the rear of the room. This might have been the first time I'd ever seen him get his own coffee. Until now, I wasn't even sure he was capable of such a feat. He waited for the steam to stop shooting up from the spout before he pulled the first tiny mug away and placed a second one beneath it. He pushed the button again, waited for it to finish brewing, and handed me one of them. "Besides coffee."

I inhaled deeply. "Andre North just left."

"Odd." Cross led the way back into his office and gestured at the sofa. "What did he want?" After I filled in the boss on everything that happened in my meeting, he cleared his throat. "It sounds like you'll have your hands full for the next few weeks."

"Once Eve gets back. Until Monday, I'll do some recon, ask around, get the lay of the land, so to speak."

"Good idea."

"Uh-huh. And that'll give me a few more days to assist the PD in their hunt to catch a killer."

He put the cup down. "That's not Cross Security business. I don't care."

"You should." I took a deep breath. "You're not a suspect. Your fingerprints and DNA are on file with the police department. They know you weren't in the room."

"Hurrah," he deadpanned, growing irritated the longer I dragged this out.

"But I have questions."

"You or the police?"

"Me. But if I've come up with them, they will eventually."

"Again, I believe you give them far too much credit." He eyed the open door and then his watch. "Well, spit them out. I don't have the time or patience for you to prolong this."

"Did Victor Landau tell you his life was in danger or try to hire a security detail?"

"No. If he'd stayed longer, maybe. But I'm not a mind reader, and neither are you."

"You run backgrounds on everyone."

"That's not a question."

"What do you know about Landau?"

"You give me too much credit. I don't waste my time on potential clients."

"We both know that's not true. You vet everyone. Employees. Clients. The window washers."

He worked his jaw for a moment, at a loss for words. "Not always, but I try."

"What turned up?"

Cross sighed again. "You should let this go. It's not our problem. It's definitely not my problem, but you're making it my problem. And I don't like it. I've already spoken to Mr. Almeada about this situation. Cross Security need not be involved."

"Cross Security is uninvolved, just the way you like it. I'm a private contractor and a current consultant to the police department. I don't count."

"If you're questioning me in that capacity, I want my attorney present."

"Dammit, Lucien, what are you so afraid of?"

"Nothing, but I've learned it's best to mind my own business. It would serve you well to take that lesson to heart."

"Don't you dare."

He narrowed his eyes at me, and the staring contest began. Given how little sleep I'd had in the last month, I was positive I could probably stay here all day and fall asleep with my eyes open. Cross didn't have that kind of time. He had a company to run. Finally, he relented, "Victor Landau is a partner at an architecture firm. He's been featured in various nationwide publications for his design skills. In professional circles, he's considered a rock star, but that's his public persona."

"He sounds like your kind of client."

"Yes, well, he approached me. Not the other way around. After Justin scheduled the meeting, I did some preliminary research. I didn't find any threats. No police reports filed. Nothing." His cheek twitched. "His business is sound and solvent as well. I'm not sure what he wanted to discuss, but if I had to guess, I'd say it might have been the usual corporate security package. Employee background checks, upgraded security systems, internet security and privacy improvements."

"Wouldn't someone from the firm have contacted you about that when Landau failed to follow up?"

"They could have gotten a better deal elsewhere."

"Did they?" I knew Cross would have had his ear to the ground on this.

"No."

"So it probably wasn't that." I studied Cross carefully. "What do you suspect?"

"Off the record?"

"Yes."

"Victor Landau was a member of an exclusive underground club. The location changes weekly. The private events are invite only. Identities are supposed to be kept anonymous. Each member contributes on a rotating basis, providing the room and," Cross searched for the proper word, "favors. There's nothing illegal about it. All parties must consent before participating. They are all of legal age. No illicit substances are to be on the premises."

"You're talking about a sex club."

"I'm talking about a secret that could destroy a man's reputation and decimate his career if such things ever came to light."

"He's an architect, not a politician."

"In this day in age, do you think it makes much of a difference? It doesn't matter what our opinions are. It's up to the media and the masses to pass judgment. And they will."

"Even if it's perfectly legal?"

"This isn't about legality. It's about morality, and everyone has a different definition of the word."

"Do you think someone was blackmailing Landau?" I

asked.

"I never found any indication of it, but that's the only blemish I discovered."

"That would mean one of the members is a killer." I thought about the first murder in the recent spree. The police had found various narcotics beside the body, and based on the track marks, the first victim was obviously an addict. Had that been a test run?

"Let the police handle it, Alex."

"Landau wasn't the first victim." O'Connell would kill me for sharing this. "He's the fourth."

Cross cleared his throat again, a sure sign of his discomfort. "It doesn't matter."

"You know a lot about this underground club." I didn't want to ask the question, but I had to know. "Are you a member?"

"No."

"So what's the problem?"

"Some of Cross Security's clients are."

ELEVEN

"IIey, Thompson," I held up the grease-stained brown paper bag and shook it at him, "I didn't forget."

He eyed me suspiciously as he exited the precinct. He crossed the parking lot and took the bag from my outstretched hand. "Donuts are better during shift, not after."

"Fine, give it back."

"Hell no."

I picked up the large paper cup from where it sat beside me on the hood of O'Connell's car and took a sip. Another brown paper sack sat beside it, along with a drink carrier with two other coffee cups.

"Did you bring me a mocha?"

"You're off shift. Why would you need coffee?"

"To go with the donut." He read the side of the cup, making sure to select the one that didn't have the check mark next to latte. "Does Nick know you're out here?"

"Nope." I leaned back, resting my elbows against his windshield. "I thought I'd surprise him."

"He won't like you sitting on top of his car."

"Should I sit on top of yours instead?" *Dirty*, my mind retorted, nearly making me laugh. That was a sure sign I'd had too much sugar and caffeine today and not enough sleep.

He gave me a look. "Night, Parker."

I watched him cross to his car and drive away. Several detectives and other police personnel eventually wandered out of the precinct. Ten minutes later, O'Connell exited from the rear door. As usual, he was the last one out. No wonder we got along so well.

As soon as he spotted me, he snickered. "What are you doing here?"

"You mean you didn't place an order for a sprinkled donut and vanilla latte? I could have sworn that was you. Guess it must have been another one of my favorite detectives."

He took a seat beside me on the hood of the car and dug into the bag. "Jen wouldn't want me eating this."

"So don't eat it."

"I can't just not eat it." He nudged the brown paper bag toward me. "What kind did you get?"

"Chocolate crème."

He took a bite while I took my donut out of the bag. Perhaps I should have gotten a dozen to take home. Apparently, I had an appetite for sugary fried dough filled with chocolate. It was just one of those days.

"Jablonsky stopped by earlier." He wiped his mouth and tossed the napkin into the bag and balled it up. "The DNA comparison came back. The female DNA was a match to the other three murder scenes."

"She was at all four?"

"Yep, but we still don't know if she's the killer."

"Hell of a coincidence if she's not."

"It is."

"Jablonsky doesn't believe in coincidences."

O'Connell reached for the vanilla latte. "He shared the other two killing sprees he discovered with me, along with his theory that it's a man. Apparently, you two have some money riding on this."

"I hope you didn't bet against me."

"I'd never bet against you." He waited for me to finish my donut before taking our trash and tossing it into the bin. "Jablonsky's going to get the FBI labs to compare the DNA samples from our crime scenes to the ones he discovered, but since the original investigators never found a consistent match connecting those scenes, I don't think we'll get a match now. All of that should be logged in the database anyway. We should have gotten an automatic hit."

"Mark's just being thorough. He's bored." My eyelid twitched. "I don't like this. I didn't ask for his help. I didn't want him to get involved. That wasn't what last night was about. But as usual, he stuck his nose in where it doesn't belong."

"That must be where you get it from."

I narrowed my eyes at him.

"Don't worry. He has no jurisdiction, and his leads are crap. It'll be fine," O'Connell insisted.

"Nothing about this is fine."

O'Connell crossed his arms over his chest and gave me his patented expert interrogator stare. "You came here for a reason, and it wasn't because the donut place had a two for one deal."

"It's three for two."

"Parker."

"I need to tell you something, possibly off the record." I glanced around, but we were alone. "Victor Landau was a member of Priapus, the underground sex club. Their membership requirements are ridiculous. Secrecy is a must. It's my understanding their clients sign NDAs, possibly blood oaths."

"I've never heard of them."

"They're that exclusive, and they don't have a location. The party bounces around. The members sometimes have private gatherings, one-on-one sessions, or giant free-for-alls. It varies. From what I understand, they receive a private notification, probably a text, and whoever's in shows up. The groups rotate. It varies every week or however often they gather. One of the members books the room. Others join him or her. They aren't doing anything illegal, so they've managed to stay off police radar."

"I'll still check with vice." He dug out his phone and

typed out a reminder. "So that's what was going on when Landau was murdered?"

"That'd be my guess, but it's possible this could have been a separate social gathering and had nothing to do with Priapus."

O'Connell snorted. "Nice spin."

"The only problem with this theory is the first murder doesn't fit Priapus's strict policy restrictions. They don't allow drugs at club events."

"All right," O'Connell rubbed his palms on his pants, "it looks like I've got my first solid lead. See, this is why I asked you to consult." He saw the expression on my face "What is it? Don't tell me you and Martin are members?"

I slapped his arm. "You know me better than that."

"Okay, so what's the problem?"

"Priapus has some powerful and wealthy members. I don't have a list of names. Cross explicitly forbade me from using company resources to find out any details, but some of our clients are on that list. I'm guessing you might find some city officials on there too. I'm not sure how easily you'll be able to investigate."

"I'll find a way." O'Connell glanced back at the police station. "I just hope none of the brass is involved. It'll make for some awkward conversations in the break room."

After parting ways with O'Connell, I headed home. The thought of working out held no appeal, a sure sign all was not right in my world, but I ignored it and changed clothes. After removing the plates from the side of Martin's weight bench, I sat on the floor and stretched. The doctor had been right about my leg being stiff.

Climbing to my feet, I used the bench press bar to steady myself while I worked my way through an old barre routine I probably hadn't done in a decade. When I finished, I turned to find Martin sitting at the top of the steps, watching me. I'd rarely seen that look on his face. It was a combination of loss mixed with lust.

"What's wrong?" I asked.

"Nothing. You're beautiful." He came down the steps as I stretched out on the floor. "Is that one of your old ballet routines?"

"Just a beginner's warm-up. My leg would probably snap in half if I tried to get on pointe at this point." I hoped he'd smile at the play on words, but he didn't.

"I've never seen you dance before."

"That wasn't dancing. I'm sure someone with your upbringing has seen an actual ballet with actual ballet dancers."

"Several." He searched my eyes, knowing how much ballet had cost me. "Is this the proper rehab?"

"Bruiser suggested it, but I think he's right. It should get me back where I want to be. Right now, running and strength training are too much on my leg. Pilates would probably be good too. The floor exercises anyway." My mind drifted back to Eve Wyndham's daily activities.

"Pilates was originally designed for injured dancers."

I dropped onto my back and raised my leg straight in the air. "Help me stretch my hamstrings."

Martin put one hand behind my ankle and the other behind my thigh and gently pushed my leg back. I grunted. "Too much?" he asked.

"No." I took a breath. "Just wait." I exhaled. "A little bit more."

He knelt down, supporting my leg against his chest and shoulder as he leaned over me. "Is this better?"

"What do you think?"

He cracked a smile. "Weren't we in a similar position a few nights ago?"

"Were we?"

"As I recall, I rather enjoyed having your legs thrown over my shoulders."

I ran a hand through his hair. "I'm sorry, handsome. I've been terrible to you lately. I don't mean it. I just..."

"I know." He released the pressure and lowered my leg to the ground before offering me a hand up. "I'm not taking it personally." He pulled me against his chest and kissed me, sending tingles throughout my body. Martin was electric. He could set my world on fire. He pulled back, licking the corner of his mouth. "Powdered sugar?"

I wiped the side of my mouth, flushing with embarrassment. "I had a donut with O'Connell before coming home."

"That would explain it." He grabbed my bag and the files I'd left on the floor beside it. "I'll put these in your office for you. You should soak your leg in a hot bath. You don't want your muscles to cramp."

"Thanks."

TWELVE

I stared at the data on the screen. Martin had sold his ski chalet to Andre North. He probably didn't even realize it since someone brokered the deal for him. All he had to do was sign the papers. Andre's name didn't appear anywhere on the contract, just his LLC. They weren't connected, not really. But Cross had failed to make a connection once before when it came to Martin and real estate holdings. My boss wouldn't make the same mistake twice.

"That explains it." I rubbed the grit out of the corners of my eyes and blinked a few times. I got up to tell Martin what I'd found, but he wasn't in the kitchen. A glance at the clock told me he'd probably gone to bed. Deciding I should do the same, I turned off the lights and went up the stairs.

A cone of light cut across the fourth floor hallway from where Martin had left his office door cracked open. At least I wasn't the only one who had to work late. Peering into the room, I found him behind his desk, clicking away at the computer while he spoke to someone over the phone.

"Are you sure these are the right projections?" Martin sighed and ran a hand through his hair. "These are for next quarter?" I backed out of the room and headed to bed, determined not to have any more nightmares.

For a couple of hours, I managed a light sleep while my

brain processed the dynamics of Andre and Eve's relationship while also considering Victor Landau's lifestyle and ways to infiltrate Priapus. I was in the midst of a quasi-dream, not entirely sure if I was awake or asleep, when the covers shifted. That was enough to fully rouse me.

Martin settled on the bed beside me. He kept his distance, which wasn't typical for us, but he didn't want to spook me. I remained facing the wall, listening to his breathing and waiting for it to slow and deepen. After an hour, I knew he couldn't sleep either, so I asked, "What do you know about Priapus?"

"According to Greek mythology, he's the god of intercourse and hard-ons. Have you seen the paintings and sculptures? He's the reason ED pills have warning labels about four hour erections."

"Is that the sex god you claimed to be embodying?"

"I don't have a perpetual hard-on, except when you look at me the way you do, or you let out that little sigh, or when you smile or laugh. Don't even get me started on what happens when you kiss me or wear my shirts. Yet despite all that, I still contain my urges and maintain some sense of decency." He shifted beside me, slipping an arm beneath my pillow. "A nonstop erection would be an accident waiting to happen. One slip and someone could lose an eye. You'd have noticed by now if I were *that* sex god. Just imagine what my tailor would think every time I got fitted for a new suit."

"He'd think you liked him."

Martin laughed. "Then there'd be the inevitable unwanted sexual advances lawsuits I'd face at work. No, I'm more of a Himeros."

"Unrequited love?" I reached behind me until I found his other hand and wrapped his arm around my waist.

"No, just the desire part."

"You don't get to pick and choose which aspects of mythology apply."

"Why not? It's my game. I make the rules. Plus, it all depends on which myth you're reading." He brushed his lips against my ear. "Did I walk into the wrong room? I thought this was our bedroom, not the Mythology 101 classroom."

"Technically, you started it."

"How? You asked me about Priapus."

"Not the myth. The club."

"I'm surprised you didn't ask if I was a member." He laughed, finding that particularly funny given the double meaning.

"How do you know what it is?"

"I've been around."

"Oh, really?"

"Not like that. I just happen to know things."

"So now you're all-knowing?"

"It's just another of my god-like qualities." The laugh rattled around in his chest, but he didn't make a sound. He was enjoying teasing me.

"I hate to break it to you, but if you're a god, you're probably Narcissus."

He nuzzled my neck and kissed me. "You're just saying that because I'm incredibly handsome."

"You're missing the point."

"I'm ignoring the point." His breath danced across my skin. "Mythology aside, what's going on?"

"A member of Priapus was killed inside a hotel room after possibly hosting a sex party. This is the fourth murder that's occurred under similar circumstances. O'Connell thinks they're connected. We've matched the same female DNA to all four scenes. The killer could be part of Priapus or has some way of finding out about these events, shows up, and poisons the host."

"Shit."

I laced my fingers with his and held his hand against my chest, my heart beating against the side of his fist. "Any idea who runs Priapus?"

"No." He kissed the nape of my neck. "Someone I dated belonged to the club. She invited me to join. According to her, that's how membership spreads, from person to person."

"The same as herpes."

He chuckled. "She thought it'd be fun to hook up on

occasion, trade off, add a third or fourth, whatever. That was never my thing." He wrapped both arms around me. "I don't believe in sharing."

"Good. Neither do I."

He pressed his lips to my cheek.

"I'm going to need her name, Martin. Actually, I don't, but O'Connell does. Text him in the morning. You can let him know it's an anonymous tip, so no one will know it came from you."

"But if I text him—"

"It's Nick. He'll say he got a tip. He won't say it came from you. Hence, anonymous."

"You want me to give him a tip?" Martin snickered.

"Are you twelve?" But I laughed anyway. Then I went on to tell him how he sold his ski chalet to Andre North, who now made a hefty sum of profit by using it as a rental property.

"That reminds me, I found out MT's contact from Elite is Poppy Rosewood. She's always been our rep. From what I gather, Eve Wyndham never had anything to do with any of the events I hosted. I doubt we've ever crossed paths."

"Probably not. The Andre connection is big enough for Cross to have noticed. He would have seen the paper trail as soon as he looked into Andre's business ventures. That explains why he assigned me this case. Though, I'm not sure what he expected me to find or why it would matter." My gut said it had everything to do with Cross's desperate attempts to keep me away from the police investigation, which only irked me more.

"Lucien's wonderful at causing problems."

"What's wrong?"

"He won't listen to reason." Martin shook his head. "The projections aren't anywhere near where they need to be for his undertaking. He wants access to a reliable source of biotextiles. I've read his proposal, and I understand why he needs the amount he does. I just don't think we'll have enough raw material stockpiled for the timetable he set forth. When I told him this, he told me I'd find a way. If this works, it could do a lot of good, but I just don't see it working."

"It could also cause a lot of harm."

"I know, sweetheart, but the good outweighs the bad in this instance. The only reason I agreed to partner with him was to keep you safe."

"It's body armor, Martin. The bad guys will get their hands on it too. Pair it with automatic weapons, and a lot of people may get hurt."

"I know. That's why I'm not looking to sell the technology."

"You might not have a choice. The government could impress their point on you."

But he ignored my objection. "Like I told Lucien, the technology isn't there. It can't be mass produced to scale, which is why I'm not worried about military applications. If we're lucky, and that's a big if, we might be able to produce enough to outfit Cross Security. That's it. And that will be over the course of a year or more, once we go into production."

"That doesn't sound profitable."

"It's not, which is why I need to find a way to make it profitable without selling the research."

"Why were you screwing around with biotextiles in the first place?"

"For their strength and elasticity. I needed something with those attributes for another project and thought this might work, assuming they could be produced cleanly and the process was cost-effective. I'm still thinking the research could be applied to my original plan, but it'll come down to how quickly the silk is produced. I just have to find a way to make it feasible and figure out how to convert it or the byproducts for other applications. That's the only way this will work, and even if it does, I don't know if it'll work for Cross's purposes. We still don't know how durable it'll be."

"Is that why you can't sleep?"

"Probably. Though, now it might be because I'm debating the merits of different myths and thinking I might have to resort to rereading Aesop's fables."

"Nerd."

He laughed. "I'm sure they would put me to sleep."

I leaned back against his chest and tilted my head so I could look at him. "Have you made any progress on removing the curse?"

"You tell me." He kissed me and didn't stop until the alarm clock sounded a few hours later.

Blindly, he reached for it, shutting it off while we remained tangled together. He flopped onto his back, and I nestled against his chest. His skin felt scorching hot against mine, but I enjoyed the contact. "Are you sure you're not Priapus?"

Grinning, he brushed my hair out of my face. "Only with you."

"Good answer."

"Ready to go another round?"

"Don't you have to get ready for work?"

"What if we work from home today?" He checked his calendar. "I have a conference call scheduled at noon, but I can take that in the other room."

This might be the last opportunity I had to spend the day with Martin. Once Monday rolled around, I'd be tailing Eve. O'Connell and Thompson could manage without me for one day. "Text O'Connell. He can do the research and conduct interviews without me."

While Martin searched through his little black book for a name and number, I closed my eyes. Now that it was morning, the only thing I wanted to do was sleep. We'd survived another night without any three a.m. phone calls. Everything seemed safer in the light of day, even though I knew it wasn't. The sunlight eased the tension in my body, or maybe that had been Martin. He sent the text, put his phone on the nightstand, and tucked my hair behind my ear. And then I fell asleep.

I was in the midst of another nightmare. This time, Jablonsky was bleeding out, and there was nothing I could do to save him. Luckily, when Martin returned to the bedroom after making his conference call, I woke up. To distract myself from the horrors of my subconscious, we made love a few more times until O'Connell called with questions I couldn't answer.

"Nick, come on," I begged, "I don't even want Mark

involved. I sure as hell don't want Martin anywhere near this."

"Trust me."

Reluctantly, I handed Martin the phone. Aside from one name, Martin knew even less about Priapus than I did. Unfortunately, O'Connell still needed answers. Unless the woman Martin hooked up with gave O'Connell sensitive details and violated NDAs and whatever other legal protections the sex club had in place, the police would have a hell of a time identifying the five people who'd been inside Victor Landau's hotel room and an even harder time stopping the killer. That meant I had to convince Cross to help.

THIRTEEN

The best way to convince the boss to play ball was to do what he wanted. Lucien loved a good quid pro quo, so I'd give him one. I researched everything I could on Eve Wyndham. Andre had told me what he could, which had been more than I expected, but if she was having an affair, it would involve the little things he didn't know about. So I put in the work.

In four days, Eve would return home after helping an influencer throw the biggest party known to humankind, or something along those lines. That didn't matter. That was work. I needed to know how she played, with who, and where.

The thought made me feel sleazy, but it was a job. And it would make Cross happy, so I gritted my teeth and reminded myself if Eve was cheating, Andre should know. Frankly, I wasn't sure it mattered one way or the other. He was hopelessly in love with her. I just didn't want to be the one to break his heart.

Snorting at the notion, I couldn't help but wonder when I became such a romantic. Martin probably had something to do with it. Damn him.

The best way to figure out Eve was to take a walk in her

shoes, and while my Jimmy Choos might have been a match for her Manolo Blahniks, I stuck with a pair of sensible flats. The stilettos would have to wait until I finished more than a couple workout routines.

According to my research, Eve would spend the morning and afternoon at the office. So I drove to Elegant Events and performed some recon. Even though she'd gone freelance, Eve had several assistants. Two of them manned the phones while the other two worked on something in a large portfolio and examined fabric swatches. Without going inside, I couldn't be sure what they were doing, but they appeared busy.

Around lunchtime, one of the two phone operators put the handset down on the desk, grabbed her purse, and went out the door. As soon as she was half a block away, I got out of my car and followed her. Two blocks later, she stopped at a smoothie bar. While she waited in line to place an order, she grabbed two containers of premade salad from the cooler, a bottled iced coffee, and two wraps.

I slid into line behind her, decided the coffee looked safe, and grabbed a bottle labeled coffee and almond milk. The smoothies didn't look bad, but they'd take too long to make, and I might lose sight of my mark. I wasn't sure about the tiny green sprouts poking out from the end of the wraps. And the salads looked like they'd been left out in the sun too long.

We inched ahead in line. The impatient part of me wanted to make conversation, but it was too soon. *Patience, grasshopper.* I glanced down at the sandwich selection, but they were vegan. And I had no desire to consume tofu. On the bright side, vegan meant there wasn't an insect in sight, at least not intentionally.

After she paid, she slid everything to the end of the counter to make room for me. While I handed the cashier my credit card to pay for my bottled coffee, the woman put her wallet away, slid the salads and wraps into a reusable bag, slung it over her arm, and lifted the drink carrier. She took a few steps before her heel snagged on a crack in the sidewalk.

She stumbled but kept a firm grasp on the drinks. The

mango berry smoothie sloshed a little too far to the right. She tried to wipe the dripping liquid off her fingertips while she held the carrier as far from her body as possible.

"Do you need some help?" I came up behind her with a napkin. "That looks like it'll stain."

"Did I get it on me?" She looked down at her dress and pantyhose.

"No, but that'd be a terrible thing to have happen to your beautiful dress."

"Thanks."

"Sure, no problem."

She eyed my outfit. "I like your leather jacket."

I had come up with a plan. Now I had to decide if I should commit to it. This was supposed to be recon, but I'd never been particularly patient. "My boyfriend, well, I guess he's my fiancé, got it for me when we were in Milan." I toyed with the engagement ring hooked to the chain around my neck. It was the first time I'd worn it in a month, but I knew it'd come in handy today. My subconscious must have had this plan all along and hadn't bothered to share it with my conscious mind. One of these days, I'd have to get the two together for a chat.

"Wow, he has nice taste."

"Yes, he does." I giggled. "Here, let me help you with that." I took the leaky smoothie out of the holder while she wiped it off, but it continued to drip from the bottom of the lid. "These sidewalks are such a mess. What's taking the city so long to fix them? Are they waiting for someone to fall and break her neck?"

The woman laughed.

"I'm Alex, by the way."

"Samantha."

"Where are you heading, Samantha?"

"To Elegant Events." She nodded in the direction of her office. "But I can manage. I don't want to put you out."

"It's not a problem. I was heading in that direction anyway, but I needed a caffeine fix first." I wrapped a napkin around the smoothie cup and carried it in one hand and my bottle of iced coffee in the other.

We walked in companionable silence for half a block

before she said, "When's the big day?"

"We haven't set one yet. The venues we've looked at are booked so far in advance we'll probably pick a date after we pick a location. Isn't that crazy?"

"Tell me about it."

"Are you wedding planning too?"

"No, I work at Elegant Events."

"Elegant Events," I repeated the name as if I'd never heard of it and hadn't paid attention when she mentioned it a few minutes ago, "is that a bridal shop or something?"

"We're event planners. Eve Wyndham runs it. Have you heard of her?"

"I haven't."

"She's amazing. Topnotch. All the celebrities are crazy about her. Did you see that spread in *People* magazine of you know who's big day?"

"Yes."

"That was Eve."

"Wow. How have I not heard of her?"

"Don't worry about it. She's this city's best kept secret." She leaned in closer. "Can I ask you a personal question?"

"You can, but I might not answer."

Her eyes burned like a predator toying with its prey. "Who's your wedding planner?"

"We haven't hired anyone yet. We've just been looking on our own."

"That's a mistake." We crossed the street and approached the front of the building. "Eve's out of the office this week, but I can show you her portfolio. She's done so many parties and weddings. We do business with tons of vendors. I bet I can help you pick a venue and get a reasonable date set, if you want to check them out."

"I'd love to, but I'm actually meeting some friends." I handed her the smoothie wrapped in a soppy purple napkin. "Do you think I could stop by another day to discuss it?"

"Sure. Let me get you a card."

"No, that's okay." I looked at the sign. "Elegant Events by Eve Wyndham. I assume you're online."

"Absolutely."

"Great, I'll be in touch."

"Check out our social media page. We have albums of photos for everything from linens to centerpieces to venues."

"That sounds great."

"It was nice meeting you, Alex." She paused, waiting for me to offer my last name, but I pretended not to notice.

"Shoot, I'm late. It was nice meeting you too. We'll talk soon, I'm sure."

I hurried down the street, ducking into the first boutique I found before turning around to make sure she wasn't watching. I wasn't entirely sure what that accomplished, but it gave me an excuse to return to Elegant Events if need be.

I returned to my car and continued my recon, but everyone that came and went looked like they belonged. I didn't spot Eve, which bode well for Andre. She was supposed to be in Dubai working an event. I had no reason to doubt that's where she was, but that would be a great excuse to lock herself away with another lover for a week or two without her fiancé getting suspicious.

"Hey, this is Alex Parker," I said when one of the Cross Security techs answered the phone. "When's the last time Eve Wyndham used her credit card?"

"Six hours ago."

"Where did she use it?" I'd reviewed her financials, but given her job, most of her charges looked out of place – hotels, bars, florists, chocolatiers. But those were all part of her business.

He read off the name and address of a restaurant located in Dubai. "That's on her business card," he clarified.

"And her personal credit card?"

"The last charge on here was four months ago at a burger joint."

He offered the name, but it didn't matter. Eve must expense everything, or Andre picked up the tab. "What about her debit card?"

"No activity in the last month."

"Okay, thanks." I hung up, a sinking feeling growing in

the pit of my stomach.

Andre said Eve shopped for groceries every week, but she picked up things for work. Would she expense those too? Did this woman pay for anything? Perhaps I'd been doing it wrong all these years.

When I grew bored, I went by Eve's gym and signed up for a monthly membership and saved the receipt. I'd give it to Cross, who would pass it off to the client, along with the bottled coffee I bought at lunch. Apparently, Eve wasn't the only one who could get Andre to pay for things.

After a brief tour and introduction to the trainers, I checked the class schedule and sign-up sheet for personal training sessions. Lance had been Eve's personal trainer, but she had stopped the training sessions when she started pilates classes.

To be thorough, I took a seat at the juice bar and watched the patrons mill about. Most of the people at the juice bar were fifty-somethings who looked like they should be playing tennis at the club. Instead, they used the gym to socialize while catching up on the latest gossip, power walking on the treadmills, or drinking liquified celery. The gym rats were more my speed, with the cropped tanks and baggy muscle tees. Several men near the free weights were rather attractive. If they all shaved their heads, they could probably be Andre's body doubles.

Could Eve be having an affair with someone at the gym? Pulling out my phone, I took a few surreptitious photos of the men I spotted. I'd have to come back during Eve's normal gym time to see who was around. But if she was having an affair, this might be where she found her side piece.

Giving the green juice a final evil look, I left the gym. Since I'd already blundered into an encounter with someone from Eve's business, I decided to keep my distance from any other work related locations for the day. On my way back to the office, I stopped by Eve's preferred grocery store. None of the employees looked like Andre or were in the right age range for Eve to be having an affair, unless she had a thing for septuagenarians or high school seniors. One would land her in jail, and the other was old enough to be her father or grandfather. They did have a plentiful stock of mint chocolate chip ice cream, though.

By the time I made it back to the office, most of my fellow investigators were in the midst of calling it quits for the night. I ran into Bennett Renner, one of my colleagues, in the elevator. He looked like he'd been burning the midnight oil for the last month, and since I hadn't been around much or paying attention, I wasn't sure that hadn't happened.

"Hey, Renner."

"Parker," he pressed the button for the thirtieth floor, "how are you doing?"

"I'm okay."

"Getting shot sucks."

"Yep."

"Just getting in?"

"Recon," I said. "Potential cheater. You?"

"Insurance fraud investigation."

"Fun."

Renner snorted. "If you say so. Hey, is she hot?"

"Who?"

"The girlfriend or mistress. Because if she is, I'll trade you. She might need a shoulder to cry on."

"Actually, the groom-to-be hired us."

"Oh." Renner thought for a moment. "But is she hot?"

"Bennett."

He held up his palms. "I'm joking." He waited for the accountants from the seventeenth floor to file out before he said, "I heard something about O'Connell dropping by to ask about a murder. What's going on with that? Rumor has it you're consulting with the police." Before coming to Cross Security, Renner had been a homicide detective.

"You can't believe everything you hear." But Renner didn't believe me. "I have a question for you, and keep in mind, you owe me for helping you out on Chef Easton's case."

"What is it?"

"Lucien took a meeting with Victor Landau two months ago. Do you know anything about that?"

"The architect?"

"Yep."

Renner pressed his lips together and thought for a moment. "Not much. You know how Lucien gets when he thinks he has a whale coming in. He was excited. He brought it up during one of the morning meetings. Don't you remember?"

"I don't think I was there."

"You're supposed to go to those."

"I'll remember that in the future."

Renner rolled his eyes. "That's the only thing I ever heard. I'm guessing the consultation didn't go well because that was that."

The elevator stopped on the twenty sixth floor, but no one was waiting to enter. At this time of day, most people were going down, not up. "What about Priapus?"

"What?"

"Priapus," I repeated, fearing asking a colleague about this would get me into deep trouble with Cross, but my gut said I could trust Renner. My head said there was a fifty-fifty chance he'd tattle to our boss. That gave me three to one odds this wouldn't bite me in the ass. Then again, math wasn't my strong suit.

"What is that?"

"Never mind."

Renner gave me an odd look as the doors closed. "Are you going to tell me what's going on, or do I have to guess?"

"Just forget I said anything. I am helping O'Connell. At least, I'm trying to."

"Cross won't like it. He doesn't like us getting involved in murders. Those are solely within police jurisdiction. There's no grey area for us to maneuver."

"I'll keep that in mind." The doors opened, and Renner gestured that I go ahead of him. We parted ways at his office, and I continued to mine.

Cross stood in Kellan's doorway. At the sound of my footfalls, he turned. "Alex, we need to talk." He nodded to Kellan and followed me inside.

FOURTEEN

"Is there something I can do for you?"

Cross cleared his throat and circled my office. Since I didn't have any exterior facing windows, he couldn't look outside. Instead, he closed the blinds and shut my door. "The police are poking around into Priapus."

"Good."

"How did they find out about it?"

"Dedication and dogged investigative techniques."

"What did you tell them?"

"Nothing."

He stared at me. "You're lying."

"Prove it."

He let out an unhappy growl. "How much do they know?"

"Why? Afraid someone else is going to replace you as number one on the suspect list?"

"Am I?" He didn't sound like he was concerned or even that he believed me, but I couldn't be sure.

"No, you should have been cleared by now. You have an alibi, and according to what you told me, you're not a member of a secret underground sex club."

"At least not that one."

"Oh really?"

The corner of his mouth twitched. "Another time, perhaps." He took a seat in the client chair across from my desk. "They believe the killer is a Priapus member?"

Spinning in my chair, I pressed my palm over my mouth. Martin's dirty jokes had filled my mind. After taking a few deep breaths to regain my composure, I opened and closed one of the cabinet drawers to conceal my momentary insanity. "It makes sense. This string of murders occurred in similar settings and under similar conditions to those established by the underground sex club."

"The police have identified a common DNA sample."

I turned back around to face him. "How do you know that?"

"I have my ways."

"The DNA isn't on file. The police don't know who it belongs to."

"Which is why they want to find out who belongs to the club."

"Do you want to offer your assistance? It'll earn you some brownie points with the PD and make their jobs easier."

"I have no interest in either of those things."

"Then why are we having this conversation?"

Cross took a folded sheet of paper from inside his breast pocket and placed it on my desk. "You'll make my life difficult and jeopardize the integrity of my firm until you get what you want." He stabbed the paper with his pointer finger. "I don't reward that type of behavior, and I don't enjoy being manipulated into compliance. But just this once, I believe it might be for the greater good. If any of our clients are exposing themselves to dangerous situations and possibly putting themselves in the crosshairs of a serial killer, it's my duty as their security consultant to stop it." He removed his finger from the paper. "Don't do it again."

"No, sir." But I would if the situation warranted it, and he knew it.

Cross slammed the door behind him, and I reached for the paper. Centered in the middle of the page was a single typed name: Ritch Summers, attorney at law. I couldn't be sure what that meant, but Summers had to be involved with the sex club somehow. Obviously, it wasn't his DNA we'd found, but he might know who it belonged to.

On my way out of the building, I called O'Connell to tell him I had a lead. Then I called Martin and told him not to wait on dinner. I had a long night ahead of me.

*   *   *

"How do you want to do this?" O'Connell asked. "He's your lead."

"It's your case."

"Yes, but a name on a sheet of paper doesn't do much for me. Legally, I have no ground to stand on, and this guy's some shyster attorney. He'll shut down my questions before we even get started."

"So you want me to ask the questions?"

"No." O'Connell opened the car door. "Just back me up."

"Always." I stared up at the law office, wondering how exactly Ritch Summers, corporate attorney, fit into the salacious world of underground sex clubs.

Since it was after hours, the law offices weren't expecting any random walk-ins. The receptionist had gone home for the night, but one of the paralegals pointed us in the direction of Summers's office. The glass and chrome interior made me wonder who designed the place, which brought me back to Victor Landau.

"Ask about Landau," I whispered.

O'Connell gave me a funny look. "No shit."

"Hey, you asked how I wanted to do it."

He snorted. "When the interview goes south, you should ask Summers that. It might get us back on track."

"Bite me."

"Another wonderful suggestion."

Before I could offer a retort, O'Connell knocked against the open door. He rested one hand on his hip, revealing his badge. "Mr. Summers?"

The attorney looked up from the research on his desk, removed his reading glasses, and blinked a few times.

"Yes? What is it?"

"I'm Detective O'Connell. This is Alex Parker. May we have a few minutes of your time?"

"What is this about?" Summers asked.

We took that as an invitation to enter, and I pulled the glass door closed behind me. Summers stretched back in his chair, making the hinges squeak. O'Connell looked around the office before taking a seat in one of the client chairs. I went to the bookcase against the wall and scanned the volumes for anything that might be out of place.

"Sir, do you know Victor Landau?" O'Connell asked.

"I don't discuss my clients," Summers said.

"So he's a client?" I asked.

Summers glanced in my direction. "He designed this building."

"So he's your architect?" O'Connell pulled out his notepad and pen. He'd already checked this information before we arrived, but it still didn't explain their connection or if Summers had anything to do with the sex club.

"Yes." Summers watched O'Connell jot down the note, more for show than anything else, but the attorney didn't know that.

"I hate to be the bearer of bad news, but Mr. Landau is dead." O'Connell looked up from his notepad. "When's the last time you saw him?"

"Dead?" Summers appeared shocked. I just didn't know if that was due to the news or because we'd connected the two men. "I don't know. A few days ago."

"What is the nature of your relationship?" O'Connell asked.

Summers bit his lip. "I told you. Victor designed this building."

"According to building records, construction finished on this office building eighteen months ago," I said.

"So?" Summers did his best to keep his cool. He had that arrogant mentality that came from too many years of practicing law, but he wasn't used to dealing with law enforcement. He went head to head with other attorneys and administrative agencies, like the IRS. He didn't deal with local law enforcement, but he tried to apply the same principles in order to make the problem go away. "We could have been discussing plans to expand."

"Sure." O'Connell shrugged. "Don't you want to know what killed him?"

"I don't see what that has to do with me." Summers's gaze shifted to the door. "You can show yourselves out."

O'Connell stood. "Thanks for your time, Mr. Summers. Just one quick question before we go. Do the senior partners know about your involvement with Priapus?"

Summers blanched.

"It'd be a shame if that information got out," I said, "but then again, it's just a matter of time. Landau was killed because of his involvement with the sex club. And murder trumps NDAs." I put the law book down that I'd been examining. "I'm sure you're well aware of that."

O'Connell and I made it to the door before Summers shouted, "Wait. Let's not be hasty. How did Victor die?"

"The same way at least three other people have died in the last few months. They were poisoned during or soon after partaking in group sex."

"Jesus." Summers ran a hand down his face and put his reading glasses back on. "Tell me it wasn't that night."

"What night?" I asked.

Summers spun his wedding band on his finger. I noted the tell, as did O'Connell. "Sunday."

"What time did you last see him?"

"I should call my attorney," Summers said.

"You're well within your rights to do so," O'Connell said. "But at the moment, you aren't under arrest. Do you think it's necessary to get more people involved, given the sensitive nature of this situation?"

Summers eyed the detective. "It was around eleven."

"Where did you meet?" I asked.

Summers blinked a few times, determined to take control of the situation. He inhaled and stood up. "What's it going to take to make this go away? I can't have the senior partners find out about this. The firm won't tolerate this kind of embarrassment."

O'Connell pretended to consider Summers's proposal

for a few moments. "Did you kill Victor Landau?"

"No, sir. He was still alive when I left."

"What time was that?" O'Connell asked.

"Around eleven. It could have been 10:30. I'm not sure. I wasn't alone. I have an alibi."

"What's her name?" I asked.

He spun his ring a few more times. "Buffy."

"Is she your wife?"

Summers stared at a spot on the floor. "No."

"Last name," O'Connell said.

"I don't know. Buffy isn't her real name. That's just what she told me to call her. We hooked up around lunchtime for a one-on-one session before joining the group. Priapus is based on anonymous sex. They allow for single hookups, threesomes, whatever, in addition to group activities."

"But you knew Victor," O'Connell said.

"Yeah, we became acquainted when the firm hired him to build our new offices."

"Did you invite him to join Priapus?" I asked. According to Martin's story, membership was by invitation only.

"Victor was attractive and smart. He fit in perfectly, and he liked to play. He didn't have anyone steady, and we needed to add some more singles, especially ones who didn't have hang-ups about being with men and women."

"Was Victor Landau bisexual?" O'Connell asked.

Summers made a buzzing sound almost like a bee. "He didn't have intercourse with men if that's what you mean, but he didn't mind sharing or participating with other men either. He was open to all sorts of possibilities. That's why he made an ideal candidate and why he'd been so popular at so many events."

"Someone in the room with you that night killed Victor Landau." O'Connell clicked his pen a few times. "I need to know who was there."

"I don't know. What part of anonymous don't you understand?"

"Had you ever encountered any of them before?" I asked.

"Just Victor."

"How many people were in the room?" O'Connell asked.

But the attorney didn't want to fan the flames. Whatever we didn't already know for certain, he didn't want to tell us.

"We have DNA samples from three men and three women," I said, causing O'Connell to tense beside me. He didn't like it when I gave up valuable information to potential suspects, but this was the only way to get Summers to open up. "Is our count wrong?"

"No, that's correct. Buffy and I were the last to arrive and the first to leave."

"So when you got there, two couples were already there?" O'Connell asked.

"Yes."

"Two women, a man, and Victor?"

"Yes."

"And no one else arrived or left afterward?"

"That's what I said."

"Not even room service?"

"No."

"What about the maid bringing extra towels?"

"We didn't need extra towels."

"What about clean sheets?" I asked, earning a glare from the attorney.

"We need names," O'Connell said.

"Aside from Victor, I don't know. The only reason I know him is because I invited him."

"Is that why you were invited to his private party?" I asked.

Summers went back to staring at the floor. "We have similar tastes. We like to party together. I've never encountered any of the others before that night or since."

"Not even Buffy?" O'Connell asked.

"No." Summers dropped back into his chair. "Priapus is run by an app that one of the members designed. It's not like the other hookup apps. It has a posting feature, so if someone wants to host an event, he or she lists their preferences and plans for the evening, and the first however many who want to join can do so. Once the slots fill up, the event is deleted. There's also a private message feature if you want to have a repeat hookup or invite a special someone, but you'd have to know his or her handle.

No real names or photos are listed anywhere. Partners use that a lot so they can play together."

"Can I see the app?" O'Connell asked.

Reluctantly, Summers took out his cell phone and handed it to O'Connell. "As you can see, it's anonymous. No one uses their real names. No personal information is ever entered or stored. The location tracking is turned off. It's untraceable."

"I doubt that," I mumbled.

"Is there any way to view profiles?" O'Connell asked.

"No. The profile is a handle and nothing else. No photos. No real names. Nothing that could lead to embarrassment or discovery. Even if you get a court order, you won't find anything that will conclusively link to a person."

"What about IP addresses or phone numbers?" I asked.

"It's self-sustaining and routed through an internet site and various servers. Everything gets bounced. It's the only truly secure piece of software I've ever seen." Summers was in awe, but I didn't have nearly as much faith in the technology as he did. Then again, he probably hadn't seen CIA or NSA black sites firsthand either.

"How did you know you and Buffy would be an ideal match?" O'Connell asked, handing me the phone to study more carefully. "For all you know, she could have been a dog."

"Attractiveness is a requirement for membership."

"Beauty's in the eye of the beholder." I scanned the various functions for something useful.

"Think of this as ordering off a menu. You might not know what the dish will look like, but you still know what you're getting." As Summers said that, he licked his lips, making the words sound even slimier.

I fought to contain my cringe. O'Connell asked a few more questions, but it did nothing but lead us in a circle.

"Describe everyone who attended Victor's party," O'Connell finally said.

After taking copious notes, he sighed. This outing might not have gotten us any closer to identifying the killer, but we now had descriptions of everyone in the room. We just needed to get a roster of everyone from Priapus. Except nothing about Priapus was centralized. As far as I could determine, no one person knew everyone else in the club. The descriptions Summers provided were general enough that they wouldn't be easy to pin to an individual. Frankly, I wasn't even sure he bothered to look a single person in the eye or study a face, but that might have been intentional.

"What about the NDAs?" I asked.

"What?"

"Come on, Ritch," I gave him a look, like I might be a member, "I know how this works. My boyfriend got invited to join by a rando from his past. She said everything was confidential. People had to sign NDAs when they joined. You're a lawyer. Are you in charge of the paperwork?"

"You'd know the answer to that if he'd joined." Summers looked me up and down. "It's a pity. You would have made a fine addition. Doesn't he like to play?"

"He doesn't like to share." I locked eyes with the lawyer. "But we got your name easy enough. I'm guessing you're in charge of the paperwork and protecting people's privacy."

"Like I said, I don't discuss my clients or business. That's privileged." Ritch had access to everyone's signed documents, or so I imagined. He probably couldn't link the legal names back to faces or the aliases used when signing in to the app or at events, but he possessed the member list. He had to. Why else would Cross have given me Ritch's name?

"We need to see your records," O'Connell said.

"You can't prove I have anything. And even if I do, you'd still have to convince a judge to grant you access. Good luck with that."

FIFTEEN

"That smug son of a bitch." O'Connell gripped the steering wheel to stop himself from slamming his fist against it. "Doesn't he realize he was inches away from a serial killer?"

"Maybe he's into that. It gives new meaning to the term lady killer."

O'Connell ignored me and called for a surveillance unit to sit on Ritch Summers. Once they arrived, O'Connell put the car in gear. "Do you think he's involved? He could be Priapus's recruiter, poster boy, or CEO."

"I'm not sure about recruitment, since it is invite only. As for poster boy, Priapus is a secret society. As a rule, they don't have poster boys." I considered O'Connell's final suggestion. "And as far as we know, Priapus doesn't charge fees, so that rules out CEO."

"Fees would make this easier. We'd be able to trace them and ID the members."

"They wouldn't want that. There'd be paperwork and tax forms, and we'd know precisely who's involved."

"God forbid." O'Connell sighed.

"They only target wealthy professionals."

"No shit."

"It could be a barter system. Summers provides legal advice in exchange for his admission."

"Was Landau invited to join because he could design their playrooms?" O'Connell asked.

"Possibly."

"So what you're saying is Summers was recruited because he has a firm grasp of the law and could keep everything legal, airtight, and below the radar?"

"Pretty much, or they wanted him for nothing more than his firm grasp."

"Anyway," O'Connell resisted the urge to roll his eyes, "that might explain it. You said other Cross Security clients are members, possibly city officials and judges. Priapus could have members everywhere."

I chuckled. "As we observed from the crime scene."

"Are you done making jokes?"

"No, but I'll do my best to stop." I stared out the window. "They aren't a cult. Membership is voluntary and recreational. The club is catering to desires which these individuals would be less likely to pursue given their public personas and business reputations."

"So instead of finding a family values politician in a public restroom with another man, the two make arrangements for clandestine meetups, where everyone involved has something to lose."

"Mutually assured destruction is a great way to keep a secret. That or murder."

O'Connell turned to look at me. "You think Landau tried to blackmail the killer?"

"I don't know. We have yet to come up with a motive, but serial killers rarely need incentive to kill. They have their own reasons. But since everyone is determined to keep their activities secret, no one's willing to come forward, even if they were around when Landau died."

"Poisoning isn't bloody or brutal. In the second victim's case, it probably looked like a seizure. In Landau's case, a heart attack. Someone could have picked up the hotel phone and called 9-1-1."

"We'd have their voice on a recording. That's too risky," I said. "Like Cross said, reputations are on the line. They stand to lose everything."

O'Connell ran a hand over his mouth. "They could have called down to the desk, reported a problem, and left. Hell, they could have asked for towels and let housekeeping deal with it."

"People panic. Self-preservation kicks in. Fight or flight. Unless," I swallowed, unhappy with the thought but unable to shake it, "killing someone is why they went to the hotel in the first place."

"Like a snuff film?"

"Something along those lines, only less bloody."

"Do you think Landau was suicidal?" O'Connell asked, surprising me with the question. "He could have wanted to kill himself and figured he'd go out with a bang. We have no way of knowing what he listed on the event profile. According to Summers, those automatically delete."

"You need a warrant for the app."

"That won't be a problem." O'Connell pulled to a stop outside my office building. "Do you think the woman's DNA we've found at every scene could belong to a nurse? Maybe this is something like physician-assisted suicide."

"That's a stretch." But I didn't have any better ideas. "Have you gotten Landau's medical records yet?"

"The coroner did a full autopsy. He didn't find anything wrong."

"So no tumors or terminal maladies?"

"None."

"Try to get access to Landau's mental health records. This still reads like a serial killer to me, but you're the detective. Maybe this is some depraved suicide-sex thing."

"Or a murder-sex thing." O'Connell ran a hand down his face. He was halfway through a double shift with no end in sight. "Summers must know what happened in that room. He admitted to having similar proclivities to the victim. He could be next, or he could be the killer."

"He's not the killer, unless you go with Jablonsky's theory."

"Or every person who entered that hotel room played a part in murdering Victor Landau." O'Connell glanced at me from the corner of his eye. "Don't forget about the scopolamine."

"Shit, that's right. Did CSU identify the source?"

"It wasn't in any of the glasses or bottles. At the moment, we're assuming it was injected, along with the poison, but without the syringe, we have no way of knowing."

"That's not helpful." The more I learned about this case, the less I liked it.

"Don't worry. I'm getting a court order for Summers's DNA. He said he was there. So let's prove it. The more painful we make this for him, the more likely he'll be to cooperate."

"Even if he doesn't, placing him in the room will support your request to open his records."

"I'm going to get those NDAs if it's the last thing I do. Any idea how Cross got Ritch's name? Is he a client?"

"Nope."

"Attorney?"

"Cross uses Almeada's firm for everything. The Priapus app looks like the kind of thing Cross Security would evaluate or develop, but there's no record of any interaction with Ritch Summers in the Cross Security database. Ritch isn't one of ours. Obviously, we share clients since we're assuming Ritch has NDAs for everyone involved with Priapus. Someone might have mentioned him to Cross or had their attorney look over the contracts before signing with our firm."

"And their attorney was Ritch, so your boss kept that in mind for a rainy day?"

"Or blackmail."

O'Connell glanced at me again. "I don't want to know the kinds of things you people do."

"I don't do anything."

"Uh-huh." But the detective didn't sound particularly convinced. "I'll question Martin's friend again. If she'll verify the attorney's name, specifically her attorney's name regarding this matter, I'll have Summers inside an interrogation room by morning."

"Good idea."

O'Connell handed me his notebook where he'd written

down the descriptions of Victor Landau's sex partners. "Read those again and let me know if you have any idea who they might be."

After rereading the descriptions, I stared out the windshield. "I'm going with an updated, X-rated version of the *Village People.*"

"Parker."

"No, listen to this." I read from the page. "Male, tall, athletic, wore a cowboy hat the entire time. Eye color unknown. Height unknown. Weight, likely average. So we're looking for a cowboy." I read the description of one of the women. "Brunette, D-cups, and a mole on her left ass cheek." I glanced at O'Connell. "I don't know about you, but when I meet with clients, they're usually wearing pants or skirts, something to cover up their ass cheeks."

"Fine, I get your point."

"Maybe Landau dressed like a construction worker. Ooh, and we saw the footage of Summers and Buffy entering the hotel room. Maybe he was supposed to be dressed like a cop. A motorcycle cop, of course."

"Forget I asked." A strange look came over O'Connell's face. "At least they weren't dressed as vampire slayers."

"What?"

"You get every other TV and movie reference and not that one. Wonders never cease."

I stopped reading. "The descriptions are worthless until you narrow down suspects. Then you'll be in business. But for the record, you hired me to consult. I'm not doing any mole checks, so don't even ask. Now what are you going to do with this?"

"I'll put the descriptions together with the hotel surveillance footage and have a sketch artist sit down with both of them and see what he can come up with while I convince a judge Summers is a suspect and we should be allowed to search his business records."

"Good luck." I opened the car door and stepped onto the sidewalk. "Anything else you need from me?"

"Are you sure you don't want to meet me at the precinct? You can watch how a real detective works."

"Where would I find one of those?" I smiled. "Actually, I

have some work to get done on another case. Cross didn't give us that intel for free. He expects me to sing for my supper." Another thought occurred to me. "Hey, while you're at it, you should request a search warrant for Summers's house, car, and office, just to make sure he doesn't have any poisonous plants or syringes stockpiled."

"Already done."

"Okay, that's my two cents. Call if you need anything else, and if something shakes loose on my end, I'll let you know."

"Do you need help on whatever it is you're doing?" O'Connell asked, concern in his voice.

"Not yet, but if I get arrested, I'll have the officers call you to bail me out."

"Be careful and don't do anything stupid. Try to stay on the right side of the law, please."

"Always. Night, Nick." I closed the car door and headed upstairs to my office.

SIXTEEN

"How'd it go?" Cross asked, startling me. Automatically, I pulled my gun and aimed. My vision blurred, zeroing in on the target. *Not a target*, I realized. He eyed the weapon curiously. "Gunfire will attract building security."

"I'm not going to shoot you this time." I shoved the gun back into my shoulder holster, annoyed and embarrassed. "But stop sneaking up on me. This is my office. The door was closed. Do I need to add a second lock?"

"You're jumpy. I suppose you have every reason to be. I apologize for the intrusion. But even if you add another lock, I'd still have the master key. That would defeat the purpose."

"What happened to allowing me to operate autonomously?"

"I don't know, Alex. You came to me for help. Did Detective O'Connell hurry home to bake my brownies?"

"How did you get Ritch Summers's name?"

"I have my ways."

"Which are?"

"Trade secrets." He glanced into the corridor. "I don't know how helpful he'll be to the police investigation. He's an attorney, so I'm sure he's more than capable of protecting his secrets."

"He was there. Did you know that?"

"Where?"

"In the room where Victor Landau was killed."

Something flickered across my boss's face. "I did not know that, but that's wonderful news. The police now have a valuable person of interest. They should be able to handle the case without further assistance from us."

"You mean me."

"I mean us." Cross approached my desk and put down a file folder. "Andre North phoned again while you were out with the information on Eve's current workload and clients. He e-mailed you copies of her work details. I took the liberty of having someone determine the venues she'll be visiting and the vendors she's been contacting. I also analyzed her phone records and browser history. No dating sites. No unknown numbers or suggestive text or voice messages."

"Thanks."

"You sound surprised."

"I didn't expect you to do my work for me."

Cross snorted. "That's all I've done today." He headed for the door. "Andre mentioned Eve might be returning home sooner than expected. Originally, she thought her trip would be extended. Now it appears it may be shortened. Assuming you plan to search her apartment, I'd make that a priority."

"Thanks for the heads up."

He nodded. "Good night, Alex. Try to stay on track tomorrow."

Grumbling to myself, I went into the break room and made some coffee while I searched the fridge and cabinets for something to eat. When I found several boxes of leftover pizza in the employee fridge with Cross's name on the order, I knew those had been for everyone. So I grabbed two slices and my coffee and went back to finish updating my Eve Wyndham itinerary.

Afterward, I set out to visit a few of the clubs and hotspots on her list of locations. The high-end nightclubs wouldn't have let me inside dressed like I was, but my business card got me in the door. Scouting locations for potential security issues for our clients made my presence welcomed, and since Cross Security was known to protect celebrities, none of this seemed out of the ordinary. But I didn't know what I hoped to find.

With Eve out of the country, I had no way of knowing much of anything. For all I knew, she could have found a lover while walking down the street. So why had I started my recon here?

While I pondered that question, I finished scouting a few other venues and drove to Eve Wyndham's apartment. She and Andre spent most of their time together at his house, but she had kept her place. According to Andre, she planned to sell it once they were married, but he was hoping she'd let him convert it into a rental.

Even though the city was more than just a vacation hotspot, plenty of tourists visited every week. However, the cynical part of my mind thought she might have kept the apartment to conceal her adulterous ways. Then again, I'd kept my apartment as long as possible, and if it hadn't burned to the ground, I might still have it. But that wasn't about cheating. Honestly, that was fear and insecurity. Mine, not Martin's. Of course, Martin had gotten us an apartment in addition to his estate, thinking that'd be a good compromise. But that was different. It wasn't mine. Instead, I had to get used to the idea that he was mine.

I found a parking spot three blocks from Eve's apartment. After a few minutes of scoping out the neighborhood, I slipped into the hooded sweatshirt I kept in the back seat, pulled up the hood, put my leather jacket on over it, made sure my lock picks were easily accessible, and set out down the street. *Don't get arrested or O'Connell will kill you*, I reminded myself.

Eve's building had a doorman, so I ducked my head and kept walking. If nothing else, the exercise loosened my sore muscles. Unfortunately, I didn't know how I'd get inside the building undetected.

At the end of the block, I turned the corner and found an alleyway that ran directly behind the apartment building. It was just wide enough to fit a garbage truck.

Since this is where the dumpsters were kept, there had to be a rear door. I just had to find it.

Except it was locked. A security camera posted near the door told me picking it would be frowned upon by building security who'd likely call the authorities. So sneaking in through the back was no longer an option. I opened the dumpster lid and pretended to toss something from my pocket into the garbage. Sure, that made walking down a dark alley seem reasonable.

I continued back the way I came, considering methods of short circuiting the camera, but this wasn't a secret spy mission. If it was, I'd have one of those masks that perfectly mimicked someone else's face. Then I wouldn't have to worry about the cameras or getting caught.

I considered my options. The building didn't have a fire escape. It might have roof access, but again, I wasn't a spy with all the cool tech toys. Perhaps, I'd talk to Lucien about that in the morning, but for tonight, I'd have to come up with a better plan.

Andre North could probably get inside the building, but since he already had concerns about surveilling his bride-to-be, asking the client for assistance was a bad idea. From the way he'd talked about Eve's apartment, it sounded like he didn't spend that much time here. Did he even have a key?

"Think, Parker." I'd broken into plenty of apartments. This was no different. Maneuvering to the side of the building that allowed me to watch the front door, I kept my eyes peeled for movement. As the minutes ticked by, I knew my chances of making a stealthy entrance were diminishing.

I was reconsidering trying my luck with the back door when a man stepped out of the building. He spun his keychain around his finger and whistled. He didn't speak to the doorman, but leaving wouldn't require an exchange or answering any questions. Only arriving would draw unwanted scrutiny.

With no better plan in mind, I headed down the street in the same direction as the man. Except I was ahead of him, and following someone from the front took skills, willpower, and great visual acuity. At the moment, I lacked all three.

Instead, I played up my limp, hobbling slowly along the sidewalk. The man passed me within a few minutes, unaware of my presence. If he'd been the chivalrous type, that would have complicated matters. Thankfully, he wasn't.

Picking up the pace, I followed him another two blocks to a twenty-four hour pharmacy. Once inside, I took off my hood, fluffed my hair, and kept an eye on him. He picked up a bag of cheese doodles and a box of microwave popcorn before heading to the checkout. Beside the register was a cooler with drinks. He grabbed a twenty ounce soda.

I came up beside him with a bag of nacho cheese tortilla chips and a package of chocolate candies. "Leave that open, please." I used my shoulder to hold the cooler door while I shuffled the chocolates to the other hand and reached for a cherry cola.

He turned when I spoke and smiled. "I'm glad I'm not the only one on a junk food run."

I laughed. "Movie night?"

"Nah, I just needed to grab some snacks."

"Me too. I'm binge watching one of those cooking competitions, and they make me hungry."

"You must live nearby."

"Yep." I squinted at him. "Haven't I seen you in the building?"

"Maybe?" He rattled off the street address.

"Guess that must be why you look so familiar."

"14J." He patted his chest after placing the items on the counter.

"17C." That was Eve Wyndham's apartment. I just hoped he didn't know her.

He didn't act like the apartment number meant anything to him. "Do you live with your husband?"

I held up my naked hand, relieved that I had left Martin's ring at the office. "Nope."

"Partner?"

"No. What about you? Wife? Girlfriend?"

"Daisy." But that didn't stop him from flirting. Too bad

he wasn't my mark. I'd have this assignment completed in no time.

"Ah, lucky girl."

"She'll think so when I come home with cheese doodles."

"That is the way to a woman's heart."

He continued to smile as he paid the cashier and grabbed his bag. "She thinks so. She'll probably sit up and beg."

I gave him a strange look. "Okay."

"She's a French bulldog."

"I bet she's adorable. I'd love to meet her sometime." I made my purchases and picked up my bag.

"What are you doing right now?"

"Nothing."

"Want to come over, watch some TV, and chow down on junk food? Or is that too forward? Since we live in the same building, you can go home at any time. I'm not trying to pick you up or anything."

"Good, because after eating all this crap, I'm probably too heavy."

His eyes swept up and down my body. "You don't look that heavy. Can I at least walk you home? After all, we're going to the same place."

"Only if you introduce me to Daisy."

"Deal."

We were half a block from the apartment when he said, "I'm TJ, by the way."

"Allison." If he pushed me on the apartment number, I'd stick with the same story, but I regretted giving him Eve's address. I could always say I was staying with my cousin or housesitting while she was away, but I hoped it wouldn't come down to that. The fewer lies I had to tell, the better.

"It's nice to meet you."

"Likewise."

We made it to the apartment building, and the doorman pushed open the door. He spotted the FOB in TJ's hand and nodded to him, probably recalling he had only left twenty minutes ago.

"Ladies first," TJ said, gesturing that I enter.

I gave him my most flirtatious smile, hoping the doorman wouldn't inquire as to who the gentleman's guest was for the evening, and I stepped into the lobby. TJ followed at my heels. Now that I was inside, I asked TJ how he and Daisy met, hoping to distract him while I noted the security cameras and exits.

The hard part was over. All I had to do was follow TJ to his place, come up with an excuse to leave, and continue on to Eve's apartment. What could be easier?

TJ pressed the button for the elevator, filling me in on how he found Daisy in a cardboard box at the side of the road. It could have been true, but something told me it wasn't. I made the appropriate aww sounds.

Once we were alone in the elevator, TJ moved a little closer. "Do you have any pets?"

"No, I'm not great at feeding myself." I held up the bag. "I always have this fear they'd starve."

"You look like you might be starving."

"That's why I have junk food."

"Which apartment did you say was yours? I could bring you dinner sometime. I have this terrible habit of ordering too much food. Was it 17E?"

"You do that too? No wonder the delivery guys always give me that look. It's not because I order too much. It's because they're probably tired of both of us ordering." I didn't want to answer the apartment question. I hoped he thought I had said E because the last thing I needed was him knocking on Eve's door, especially if I was in the midst of snooping.

The elevator opened on the fourteenth floor. "Here we are." He stepped out, and I followed. The stairs were at the end of the hallway. Security cameras caught sight of me since I had to lose the hood when I approached TJ inside the pharmacy, but that wouldn't matter. It wasn't illegal to go home with a strange man, though it typically wasn't the best plan either.

He unlocked the door but didn't turn the knob. "Be warned, you're about to be attacked by twenty-two pounds of pure bulldog with separation anxiety issues. If it gets too intense, I'll intervene with the cheese doodles."

"Thanks."

He opened the door and a tiny short-haired mass raced toward him. It made whimpering noises before jumping up and down and pawing at his leg. He knelt down to pet her, and she shook her butt and spun in circles. Mid-turn, she spotted me, let out an excited bark, and ran headfirst into my leg.

At least she didn't knock me to the ground. "Hey, Daisy." I squatted down, afraid I might not have the strength to get back up unassisted. I tried to pet her, but she was too excited to do much but let out snorting gasps and lick my hand.

"This is the lady in my life." TJ pointed at a dog bed on the floor. "Daisy, go lie down."

She ran to her bed, circled it, and turned to stare at TJ to make sure he entered the apartment. I grabbed the doorjamb and hoisted myself up while his back was to me. I definitely needed to work out more. Daisy raced back across the room, circling TJ's legs as he put the bag down on a snack tray. He took off his jacket and plopped onto the couch. He patted the cushion beside him. "Sit down. We can hang out for a while."

Daisy took that as her cue and hopped onto the couch and crawled onto his lap.

"I guess I can stay for a few minutes." I checked my phone, working out excuses in my head. Not that I needed one, but I didn't want to give this guy the wrong idea or risk having him follow me or report me to building security. So I could play along for a little while.

Twelve minutes later, the alarm I set on my phone when TJ went into the bathroom went off. It sounded like my ringer, and I apologized, said it was my mother, and told him this would be a long conversation. "She never shuts up, and she'll keep calling until I talk to her. I'm sorry. I'm sure we'll run into each other again sometime soon."

"I hope so," TJ said. "We should do this again. Maybe make plans. Can I have your number?"

The chime on my phone sounded again. "I'll drop by tomorrow night and hand deliver it, okay?" I tucked the hair behind my ear, implying that I might be open to other possibilities.

"I'm looking forward to it."

"See ya." I waved to TJ and spotted Daisy cuddled up beside him, stretching her neck as far as she could to try to get her nose into the opened bag of cheese doodles. "Night, Daisy."

At the sound of her name, she cocked her head, causing her tongue to loll out the side of her mouth.

I went out the door and dashed toward the stairwell, afraid if I waited too long TJ might follow me out. I regretted telling him the floor number, but once I made the trek up the three flights of stairs with a little help from the handrail, I knew the coast was clear. Now it was time to get to work.

SEVENTEEN

I put my hood up before stepping foot on to the seventeenth floor. With the lockpicks in my jacket pocket and the plastic bag slung over my arm, I made my way down the hall. No one would think anything of a woman coming home with a bag of snacks. I stopped in front of 17C and knocked. The last thing I needed was to break in only to find Eve's side piece inside. When no one came to the door, I withdrew the picks in one fluid motion and used my body to shield what I was doing from the security cameras.

The door had two deadbolts in addition to the basic lock. I started with the bottom lock, hoping she hadn't bothered with the deadbolts. When the knob twisted and the door didn't give, I went to work on the top lock. It took me a good two minutes to get inside. I pushed the door open, tucked my hand into my sleeve, and blindly reached for the light switch. No reason to leave prints, if I could avoid it.

Once I was certain no one was home, I shut the door and slid the locks back into place. After slipping on a pair of gloves, I dropped the plastic bag on the floor beside the door and took out my phone. Before I did anything, I checked for a security system. I didn't find any record of one in her financials or on the building schematics, but it never hurt to double-check. Once I was positive Eve didn't have any cameras hidden in her apartment, I took out my phone and snapped a few photos, so I could put everything back the way it was. I didn't want Eve to know anyone had been inside. Andre wouldn't like that, and at Cross Security, we were all about pleasing the clients.

All right, Parker, where to begin? The first thing that caught my eye was a large flower arrangement on the dining room table. Eve had left the blinds open so the flowers would get sunlight, but they were starting to wilt. I examined the large red bow around the ornate glass vase. A card stuck out from the middle of the arrangement. I removed it and read: *Something beautiful for my beauty. Love, Andre.*

So much for finding a smoking gun. I tucked the card back where it was. Why would Andre send flowers when he knew Eve was going out of town? Maybe he didn't know or sent flowers every week. He could have a standing order with the florist. I could picture Martin doing something like that, except I wasn't a flower and jewelry kind of girl.

Moving away from the arrangement, I examined the rest of the dining room. Then I moved on to the kitchen. The cabinets were adequately stocked with cookware and pantry staples. The notepad on the counter had a grocery list: lettuce, bread, sparkling water, marshmallows. Nothing particularly romantic or sneaky about that. No mention of caramel, chocolate, or whipped cream.

Continuing on, I examined the exterior of her fridge. Eve had a few magnetic frames. One was the same photo of her and Andre that Andre had brought to Cross. Another was a picture of Eve with her assistants and coworkers. The last two were taken at parties and events. I snapped a photo of her photos, just in case, but those looked like events she'd planned. The woman worked hard. She had a right to be proud.

When I didn't find anything damning in her fridge or freezer, aside from a few too many bottles of wine, I moved into the living room. More photos on the walls and end tables caught my attention. Most were of Eve at various locations. From the different backgrounds, I wondered if these were the places Andre had taken her on vacation.

I snapped shots of those too and searched beneath the furniture and in between the couch cushions, but I didn't find any misplaced cufflinks or forgotten thongs, just lint and a dime. The broom closet didn't conceal anything of interest. Neither did the linen closet. In the coat closet, I found a man's raincoat. The pockets were empty, but I pulled it out, checked the label, and took a snapshot. My gut said it belonged to Andre. Still, it'd be best to ask. Assumptions were detrimental in my line of work.

Entering the bedroom, I froze in the doorway. My heart hammered against my ribs. Blood pooled in the center of the mattress, streaks ran along the edges of the sheets and pillowcases. I gripped the doorframe, forced air into my tightening chest, and blinked. The blood was gone. "You're cracking up, Parker." I ran a gloved hand down my mouth and took in the room. Concentrate on what's real, not what's in your head.

The bedding was bright white with accents of red. The floors were hardwood, and the walls were white with monochrome art. It was the red on white. That must have been what triggered that macabre memory. I took a few more photos with my camera before stepping foot inside the room.

Every cell in my body wanted to run out the door, but I resisted. "It's in your head. It's all in your head." Going to the bedside table, I noticed a corded telephone. That brought back images of a swinging receiver, and I gulped. Sinking to the ground, I put my head between my knees, closed my eyes, and waited for the panic to ebb.

I could barely breathe. I knew how irrational it was, but I couldn't shake it. With trembling fingers, I dialed Mark. "Talk to me."

"Alex?" He could hear the panic. "What's wrong? Where are you?"

"I can't tell you. I just need you to talk to me."

"Yeah. Okay. Are you okay?"

I forced the lump down my throat. "Uh-huh."

"Where's Marty? Is he with you?"

"I'm working."

"But you're okay? You're safe?"

"Uh-huh." I gulped again. "Are you?"

"Yes, I'm fine." Though he had rarely witnessed one of my panic attacks, he knew about them. He just liked to pretend they didn't exist, much the same way I did. "Take a deep breath and tell me what you see."

"A bedroom." I described Eve's room to a T. By the time I finished describing the last piece of art on the wall, my chest no longer heaved with the force of my beating heart.

"What are you looking for?"

I grabbed the side of the bed and hoisted myself off the ground with a grunt. "Signs she's having an affair."

"Don't forget to check the trash."

"I'm saving that for the end." I went to the closet and opened the door. Eve Wyndham had more clothes and shoes than I'd ever seen in one person's closet. And I lived with Martin, who had a walk-in devoted entirely to his suits.

"Good plan." He waited to make sure the moment had passed before asking, "Are you good now?"

"Yeah, I just needed to hear your voice."

"You know you can call anytime, but Alex, talking to me isn't going to solve this."

"I know. I have it under control."

"It doesn't seem like it. Do you want me to meet you?"

"No, I have to get this done, and you don't need to know about it. You already know too much."

"My lips are sealed. Just be careful."

"Always." I tucked the phone back into my pocket. I didn't have time to lose it now. I had to get this done. Once this case was over and O'Connell didn't ask me to help on anything else, I'd deal with my shit or find something else to distract from it until it went away. That's usually how I dealt with things, and for the most part, it worked okay.

This was still fresh. That's what's wrong, I decided. That and who in their right mind decorates their bedroom in white, red, and black. Wasn't that a riddle about a newspaper or zebra or something? I couldn't think how it went. Instead, I took more photos and searched every nook and cranny inside Eve's closet.

A leather and lace outfit hung in the back corner. On the floor beside it was a leather collar, riding crop, and some oversized feathers. The last thing I wanted to do was question Andre about their sex life, but if Eve had a kinky streak that Andre didn't share, she might go elsewhere to scratch that itch.

After closing the closet door, I checked her dresser. Her lingerie drawer was brimming with a typical selection and a few lace masks. Nothing too odd. Perhaps Eve had gone through an experimental period. That would explain the leather in the closet.

Searching her bedside table made me feel icky. She had several items for solo play, condoms, and lube. I took another few snapshots and closed the drawer. This was the worst violation of a woman's privacy I could think of, and yet, here I was. I'd be lucky if I could look myself in the mirror in the morning. Then again, with the things I'd done, this shouldn't even register. But it did. And it bothered me.

I checked under the bed, behind the furniture, and beneath the mattress. She had a sex life, but she was also engaged to an attractive and physically fit man. I had no reason to assume this wasn't part of that. But Andre thought there was something wrong between them, so I kept digging.

Her bathroom contained the usual items. She had a few prescription pill bottles in her cabinet, so I checked the labels. Nothing sinister, just some leftover antibiotics from a dental procedure, prescription ibuprofen from the same procedure, and some anti-anxiety medication. I snorted, laughing at the ludicrous notion that I should pocket them.

After closing the cabinet, I spotted a sticky note that had fallen from the corner of her mirror. *Have a great day. You're gonna knock them dead.* It wasn't signed, but the writing looked like Andre's. Again, I took a photo. Cross's experts could compare handwriting samples, or I'd just ask Andre about it when we had our next chat. This next one wouldn't be nearly as comfortable as our last.

Before leaving, I checked the garbage, but Eve had taken it out before leaving on her trip. I made sure nothing appeared disturbed, turned off all the lights, grabbed my snacks, and let myself out. I left the deadbolts unlocked. This was a safe building. Eve wouldn't notice. She'd put the key in and twist. It'd be fine. I was too drained to entertain any other possibilities.

But I didn't go home after leaving the apartment building. I went back to the office, took a shower, and put my clothes back on. They weren't dirty or disgusting. I was. Settling in behind my desk, I examined the photos I'd taken and jotted down notes and follow-up questions while I worked my way through the bag of chips.

By the time I looked at the clock, it was nearly five a.m. Cross would be in soon. I'd tell him what I found and ask how he wanted me to proceed. Given Andre's hesitance to move ahead with our investigation, I'd let Cross decide my next course of action. Frankly, I didn't care one way or the other. I didn't want to pry into intimate matters or inadvertently break someone's heart.

I settled onto the longer part of the l-shaped sofa and stretched out my legs, folding forward as far as I could. On my injured side, I couldn't even touch my toes. This wasn't good, but I didn't have it in me to work out. Instead, I settled against the cushion and thought about O'Connell's case. A killer had already struck four times. For all I knew, she or he was a client. There had to be a way to figure this out.

I tried to picture the hotel footage, but the disguises would prevent an easy ID. How did the third woman get inside the room? Summers said she was already there. The footage didn't show anyone else. Did someone inside the hotel tamper with it?

I reached for the notepad and made a list of possibilities, one more farfetched than the other. "Think, Parker. You just broke into a woman's apartment. How would you sneak into a hotel suite?"

My eyelids grew heavy, and my thoughts went back to spy movies. Ziplines and rappelling gear. A firetruck and ladder. A wing suit. My mind wandered farther and farther from reality until I was back in my own personal hell.

"Alex." I jumped, unsure where I was. Kellan Dey stood on the other side of the glass coffee table. "Is everything all right?" he asked.

"Why?" I sat up and rubbed my eyes.

"You were screaming."

"Shit." I tried to make sense of the world. "Are you going to tell Cross?"

"Tell Cross what?" Kellan stared at me for a long time. "I don't get my kicks gossiping to the boss. I was just doing my job. Forgive me or don't. That's up to you." He nodded at my leg. "Are you okay?"

I rubbed a hand over my thigh. That's not why I was screaming. I just didn't know how long it had been going on or what he might have heard. And I didn't want to ask. "Yes."

"At least you didn't have the daylights knocked out of you like the last time I found you asleep in your office."

"You mean when you accused me of being an alcoholic?"

"I didn't realize what had happened." He scrutinized my expression, taking in every minute detail and flinch. "I don't really know what's happening now either, but I'm here."

"I don't need your help."

"Too bad. Scream again, and I will run across the hall, prepared to fight to the death. That's just how it is."

Brushing my hair out of my face, I stared up at him. "What time is it?"

"It's almost seven."

"Great." I climbed off the couch, grabbing the arm for support.

Kellan stepped closer to assist. "You sure you got it?"

"I'm fine."

"Glad to hear it," a voice said from the doorway. Thankfully, it wasn't Cross. Though, in this instance, I would have preferred an unwanted appearance by the boss. Martin strode across the room and extended his hand to Kellan. "James Martin."

Kellan shook his hand. "Kellan Dey."

Martin's back stiffened, but he held that professional

smile. He knew who Kellan was. He'd listened to me bitch and moan about the wolf in sheep's clothing. "Would you mind giving us a minute?"

"Not a problem." Kellan glanced back at me. "I'll save you a seat in the conference room, Alex."

I almost told him not to bother, but I didn't want word of Martin's appearance getting back to Cross. So I mumbled thanks and waited for my office door to close.

Martin put a travel cup on the desk. "I snuck past the lady at reception. This place could use better security. Too bad they didn't hire a consultant I know."

"What are you doing here?"

"I brought you coffee. I wanted to bring you breakfast, but you always sound so enamored with the way Cross stocks the break room, especially in the mornings. I didn't feel like competing."

"I'm sorry I didn't come home last night. By the time I finished what I was working on, it was already morning. I should have called."

"At least you called to tell me not to wait on dinner. When you didn't come home, I tracked your location. According to the data, you've been here all night."

"Sure." The charm with the tracker had been here all night. I'd been breaking and entering, but I suppose that gave me an alibi.

"I wasn't invading your privacy, sweetheart. I just had to make sure you were safe."

"I told you I was working."

"That doesn't mean you're safe. It doesn't even come remotely close." He ran his thumb across my cheek. I tried to look away, but he caught my chin and forced me to look at him. "You've been bogged down these last few days. I get it. I just want to make sure that's all it is."

"Afraid you're still cursed?"

"You did run out on me and haven't come back since." He kissed me gently. "Is Kellan still giving you shit?"

"No."

"You sure?"

"What are you going to do? Kick his ass?"

Martin shrugged. "Whatever it takes."

"Don't treat me like the damsel in distress."

He searched my eyes for a moment. "Then I need you to stop being in distress." He pressed his lips to my forehead. "Will I see you tonight?"

"Probably. I have to speak to Cross about the case he assigned, and then I'm heading to the precinct to see how O'Connell's doing. After that, I think I'll go home and crash."

"All right. You might hear some noise outside. A delivery is scheduled for early this afternoon. Marcal will handle it, but I just wanted to give you the heads up so you don't shoot the delivery guys or my valet."

"I'll try to resist. What's getting delivered?"

He ran his fingers through my hair, brushing out the tangles. His eyes were dull, not their usual lively green. "Something for you."

"Martin, I told you I don't like surprises."

"I know."

EIGHTEEN

After attending the morning meeting and speaking to Andre North, I headed to the precinct to see if O'Connell had made any progress.

"Are you stalking me?" Mark Jablonsky asked when I appeared next to him.

"Don't flatter yourself."

"What are you doing here?" O'Connell asked. "I didn't call you." He glanced at his partner, but he knew Thompson wouldn't call unless it was an emergency.

"I had some free time."

"I thought Cross had you paying your dues." O'Connell got out of his seat and brought another folding chair over and placed it on the other side of his desk. "Did you decide you wanted to learn investigative techniques from a real detective?"

"She already learned them from an FBI agent," Jablonsky said. "Then threw it all away to work for a schmuck like Lucien."

I ignored the dig. "It's cute how you boys fight over me. I just had some time and thought I'd drop by to see how you're doing."

"That's code for she's making sure you didn't screw

anything up," Jablonsky said.

"I'm aware," O'Connell said. "Just give me a few minutes. I have to get a person of interest settled, and then I'll come back to update you." O'Connell clicked a tab on the computer, leaving it open for us to read while he and Thompson headed toward booking.

"I told you I'd take care of this," Jablonsky said. "You should be taking care of you."

"Says the man missing a few inches of intestine."

"Do you want to compare battle scars? I'm sure you win. And in this case, that means you lose."

"Don't fight with me, Mark. I'm not in the mood. I spent the last hour on the phone with a client asking about the nitty gritty of his sex life."

I'd shrouded the questions in general terms, but once Andre opened up about how he and Eve had been broadening their horizons, my questions became more specific. I also learned he had bought the flowers after Eve scored a new client and had sent them to the office. She must have brought them home, out of force of habit, not thinking they wouldn't survive her trip. He also admitted to owning a raincoat that matched the one in her closet. When he asked why I wanted to know, I'd fudged on the details and said I'd seen a photo of a man dressed in that attire and wanted to make sure it was him. That appeased him long enough for me to change the subject. So far, Eve appeared to be faithful, but for all I knew, she could be in a foreign country rocking some celebrity's world.

"Is that related to this?" Jablonsky asked.

"No, that's my other case."

"So why are you here?" He stared at the dark circles beneath my eyes. "What happened after you called me?"

"I finished what I was doing and returned to the office."

"You didn't go home?"

"This isn't twenty questions."

"So you worked all night and now you're here."

"You told me it'd be good for me to work. I'm working. What more do you want from me?"

He bit his tongue, but from the look on his face, I knew this was far from over. "You were right. The other two killing sprees I found don't appear to be connected to whatever's going on here. The DNA profiles aren't a match. The method of killing is different. BSU and the PD believe we're looking at three separate killers."

"Great, as if one psycho isn't bad enough."

"Since the other two sprees came to an abrupt end, BSU believes those killers have gone dormant. Nothing has surfaced to indicate either is back in play. They might have been caught committing another crime, killed, or satisfied their cravings for now."

"Different coast. Different country. Not our problem," I said.

"You mean to tell me there's something in this world that isn't your problem? That you don't have to fix everything?"

"Screw you." When I got in these funks, Jablonsky liked to push. His entire goal in life was to make me push back, usually to emphasize some kind of point. But I was too tired and aggravated to deal with it today. "That's different. What happened to you and Coop—," his name caught in my throat, "Lucca," I swallowed, "that's on me."

"The hell it is. We were all FBI agents at the time. We were all involved in making that arrest. You got shot in the leg for fuck's sake. He wanted to kill you too. The only reason you weren't the first one he attacked was because he couldn't find you."

"It's because he was infatuated with me. He said he was saving me for last."

Jablonsky scoffed. "That wasn't infatuation. That was obsession. He got off on the killing and the torture. What he did to the rest of us tortured you. And you're still letting him win because you won't let it go. You won't deal with it."

I slammed my palm against the desk. "Shut up." Several sets of eyes turned to look at me. Violence in a police station was generally frowned upon. "I came here to help O'Connell on his case. He asked me to consult. We can discuss that, but that's it."

"What about last night?"

"You told me if I ever needed you, you'd be there. Are you going to take that away from me too?"

The compassion in his eyes nearly broke me. Mark always knew where my breaking point was, so he backed down and slid into O'Connell's chair. "Ritch Summers was brought in this morning as a person of interest after a known member of Priapus named him as a contact person for the underground club. Officers are searching his apartment and office as we speak. Since he admitted to you and O'Connell that he recruited Landau and was in the room where Landau was killed, the police have enough to hold him on suspicion of murder. But without hard evidence, he'll be released."

"What about convincing Ritch to give up the Priapus member list or the NDAs?"

"The PD's still working on it. The judge doesn't want to release Summers's files. That would be an egregious violation of attorney-client privilege."

"What about narrowing the scope to only Priapus members? NDAs can't be enforced to conceal illegal activities or prevent witnesses from reporting a murder."

"You're trying to reverse engineer this. I don't think it'll fly."

"It should. It stands to reason someone who signed an NDA with the sex club witnessed Landau's final moments. They must have seen the murderer. Hell, one of them probably is the murderer."

"The police have to prove it, and before Landau's murder, they never even heard about the underground sex club. Priapus isn't a business. It doesn't charge fees, so no tax forms. It'll be hard to prove the club is doing anything wrong when we can't prove it does anything at all."

"What about the things Summers admitted last night?"

"The state isn't going to pursue adultery charges."

"It's a class B misdemeanor. It's in the penal code."

"When's the last time someone was arrested for adultery? You'd need evidence besides participant testimony, and even then, the prosecutor's office wouldn't pursue it. It's another one of those antiquated laws that needs to be repealed. Guaranteed, it was unfairly applied with a sexist slant, like in the days of Hawthorne. Didn't you learn anything from high school English class?"

"Do you have a better idea? I'm grasping at straws."

"O'Connell's hoping to convince Summers to cooperate. He's an officer of the court. An arrest, along with morally and ethically questionable behavior, could result in losing his license to practice law."

"Assuming anyone on the review board cares." But it was worth a shot. "What else?"

"What else is there?" Jablonsky scrolled down the page. "O'Connell and Thompson haven't questioned Summers yet. They want him to sweat first. Based on the TODs, it's unlikely Summers was present for the other three murders, which makes it unlikely he's our killer."

But I saw the flicker in Jablonsky's eye. "You're starting to buy into my theory the killer is female."

"Only one DNA sample was found at all four scenes. It's XX. It has to be female."

"I told you that. Do we know how she got inside Landau's hotel room?"

"Did you watch the hotel security footage?"

"Yes, but it didn't help."

Jablonsky ran his fingers over O'Connell's keyboard. "Landau checked in before the party got started. He had room service brought to his room. It came on one of those fancy carts with the tablecloth."

"You think she pulled a Lucy Ricardo?"

Jablonsky laughed. "I hadn't considered that."

"So what's your point?"

"The cart was rolled into the room. O'Connell questioned the hotel staff. Room service didn't recall seeing anyone inside the room with Landau. Sure, she could have been hiding in the bathroom, but it looks like he was still alone at that time. Summers and his date arrived ninety minutes later. So she had to have shown up somewhere during that window."

"The other couple showed up first."

"They didn't have a third with them."

"What did CSU find on the balcony?" I asked.

"Dirt, dust, and a few footprints. However, it's inconclusive."

"Dammit. What about fingerprints?"

"Three different sets on the balcony door handle. They're too badly smudged to be used in a comparison. However, the prints found on the wine glass match prints found on the exterior railing."

"So she could have gained entry from outside." I just wasn't sure how likely that was since they were a few floors up.

"Or she stepped out to get some air." Jablonsky stared at the data. "Is Summers positive she was there when he arrived and remained after he left?"

"Yes. He said the event was for three couples. Six people. He and Buffy were two. The cowboy and his date made four. Landau hosted, so that leaves one woman. We don't know if her DNA's the one we found at the other three crime scenes, but since she went to great lengths to get in and out of the room without being detected, it makes the most sense that she's our killer."

"Are you sure Summers's date isn't the woman you're looking for? He could have made up the rest to cover for her."

"Buffy?" I shook my head. "No, I don't think so. Summers had a thing for Landau. He would have noticed if his date didn't participate in their group tryst. What is that? A ménage à cinq?"

"Glad to see your foreign language skills aren't suffering." Jablonsky clicked the mouse once he found the footage, and we watched it play on fast-forward. "Landau checked in alone. An hour later, couple number one shows up. Thirty minutes later, couple number two arrives."

"That's Summers and his date." I searched the top of O'Connell's desk for any intel on Buffy. "Has she been identified?"

"Not yet," Jablonsky said.

O'Connell returned and placed a cup of coffee on the desk beside me. "The judge is reluctant to give us access to Summers's phone. However, since Summers voluntarily showed us the app last night and told us its purpose, the paperwork's processing on accessing it." O'Connell leaned over Jablonsky's shoulder to watch the footage again.

"Talk about splitting hairs." I inhaled the scent of the

burnt sludge the precinct brewed. It didn't matter if it was mud mixed with battery acid; I'd still drink it.

"I'll take whatever I can get," O'Connell said.

Thompson snorted as he came around the desk and took a seat in his chair. "Have you told your wife that?"

O'Connell glanced at him. "She knows."

Thompson snickered. "You're whipped, dude."

"That's the key to a happy marriage."

Jablonsky pointed to Thompson. "You should listen to your partner. He knows what he's talking about."

"Are there wedding bells in the air, Thompson?" The last I heard, he and Detective Sparrow had been taking some time apart. O'Connell didn't think they'd last, but I'd been so consumed these last few months, I might have missed something important.

"Hell no." Thompson eyed me. "I'll take the plunge just as soon as you do, Parker."

"Careful," Jablonsky warned, "Alex has an engagement ring. On occasion, she even wears it."

"Yeah, but not on her finger," Thompson said, "so it doesn't count."

"I don't know," O'Connell added. "I've seen two rings on that chain." He'd also been on enough double dates with Martin and me to know we had a private commitment ceremony, even if it wasn't legally binding like a marriage. "You should be careful before you jump to any conclusions about this one." O'Connell nudged me. "She might surprise you."

No one told me it was pick on Parker day, but I didn't feel like fighting. I stared at Jablonsky, waiting to see if he would add more fuel to the fire or get us back on track. Luckily, he read my expression.

Meeting my eyes, he nodded. "Back to the matter at hand, we still don't know how the unknown woman got inside the room."

"What about after the fact?" Thompson said. "How'd she get out undetected?"

"Summers puts her in the room before Landau was killed," O'Connell said, "and said she was still there when he left."

"He could be lying," Thompson said.

I studied the photos taken of the hotel suite and the balcony. "Since she didn't enter through the front door, this is the only way she could have gotten inside. Jablonsky said you checked for prints. Did you find any on the balcony door?"

"Inside, not outside," O'Connell said.

"She could have wiped them."

"Landau's suite was on the fourth floor. How did she get up there? And wouldn't the door have been locked?" Thompson asked.

"I don't know." I examined the photos again. "The balconies connect from room to room with just the railing separating them. She could have climbed over. That might explain the prints on the rail."

"Let's get a list of guests who stayed on that floor. Parker might be on to something." O'Connell picked up the phone and made the request before phoning the techs and asking them to rewatch the hotel's security footage for the entire weekend and compare it to the mockups the sketch artist had made based on the descriptions Summers had given us.

"Wouldn't Landau have questioned his date's odd entry into the room?" Jablonsky asked.

"It's a secret sex club. She might have said she wanted to take extra precautions to keep her identity a secret," I suggested. "For all we know, she could be a politician or something."

"Great, now we're looking for a high-profile serial killer. This just gets better and better," Thompson mumbled.

"That could be how the scopolamine fits into this," O'Connell said. "Her strange entry might have required a little bit of forgetful compliance."

"How'd she get it in his system?" I asked. "It wasn't in his nasal passages."

"The autopsy revealed trace amounts in his stomach contents, so it was ingested. Maybe she knocked on the door, said she locked herself out of the room, slipped it into his drink, and stayed for the festivities," O'Connell said. "Maybe it was supposed to be a party of five, not six. That would explain why he didn't object when she didn't have sex with him."

"With four other people actively involved, I'm not sure he'd even notice," Jablonsky said.

"I thought you didn't find scopolamine in any of the wine glasses." No matter how I thought about it, the facts just didn't make much sense.

"It wasn't, but if she came from another room, she could have dosed one of the mini liquor bottles and offered it to him as thanks for allowing her into his room," O'Connell said. "Or she brought drinks or snacks with her which were already dosed."

"And took the empty bottle with her when she left?" Jablonsky looked skeptical.

O'Connell shrugged. "Do you have a better idea?"

"I would if I could make heads or tails out of this." Jablonsky slid the folder toward O'Connell. "The evidence might be right here, but with this mess, who knows."

Thompson pushed away from his desk. "Give me the case numbers, Nick."

O'Connell rattled them off while Thompson scribbled them down on a notepad. "What are you going to do?"

"Find out why we haven't made more progress." Thompson tore off the sheet of paper. "I'll be back in a sec." He pointed at me. "Don't steal my chair."

NINETEEN

"We found Madam X's DNA at the other scenes but not on any of the other victims or on any discarded rubbers. She might have gotten sloppy this time, or this is the first time anyone struck her fancy. As far as we can tell, this is the first sex party where she actually had sex, just not with the vic." Thompson dissected the file on his desk. "The DNA evidence places her at every scene. She was there when all four murders were committed. Her DNA's always been found on the rim of a wine glass. Nowhere else, except on that one used condom."

"And we don't have an ID for her sex partner." I read the details. His DNA wasn't in the system either. But unlike Madam X, the evidence didn't place him at the other three crime scenes.

"Madam X? That's what we're calling her now?" O'Connell asked.

Thompson shrugged. "That's what forensics named her."

"What kind of wine is it?" I asked.

Thompson looked up. "Does it matter?"

"At this point, everything does," Jablonsky said.

Thompson ran his finger along the file as he read.

"Different wines. Always white. No rhyme or reason for them, I don't think. Chardonnay, Reisling, Pinot, and Spumante." Thompson handed me the room service charges from Landau's room. He'd ordered the Spumante, along with a few other bottles of wine and spirits. That's what room service had delivered. "Maybe she thought the alcohol content would eradicate the DNA evidence."

"Or she drank to get up the nerve to inject these men with poison," O'Connell said.

"She's like a black widow." I tried to think of a motive, but I didn't know enough about the victims or the killer.

"Wouldn't that require her to be married to them?" Thompson asked.

"No," O'Connell said, "but it would require her to have sex with them, and nothing indicates that ever happened."

"At least not at the crime scenes," I said, "but they might have had a history. Are we looking into that?"

"We're searching for any commonality we can find among the victims," Thompson said. "So far, we have nothing."

"Except Priapus," I said.

"Assuming that pans out. The first scene makes me think it might not," O'Connell said.

"So we got nothing," Thompson muttered.

"Not nothing. Our killer's a white wine drinker who likes to use plant-based poisons. Let's start canvassing the suburbs and bring in every bored housewife with a garden." Jablonsky's phone buzzed, and he checked his message. "I have to get going. Think you can manage without me?"

"It's not like you were that helpful, anyway," Thompson teased, earning himself a searing look. "Lighten up. I'm just kidding."

Jablonsky gave me a look. "You gonna be okay?"

"Yep."

"Call if you're not." He picked up his coat and nodded to the detectives. "Let me know if you need anything else."

"Watch your back out there," O'Connell said.

"I'll do my best." Jablonsky headed for the double doors, stopping momentarily to talk to Lt. Moretti. The lieutenant followed him out of the bullpen and down the stairs. They'd been friends for a long time, but something told me the conversation wasn't about Jablonsky's recovery or O'Connell's case. Then again, I might have been paranoid. Not everything was about me. But when Moretti returned and asked to have a word in private, I was pretty sure that conversation had been about me.

"If I'm not out in ten minutes, one of you better interrupt with an urgent matter," I whispered to O'Connell and Thompson.

"Not a chance in hell," Thompson said.

"Fine. It's all on you, Nick. Don't let me down." I walked away before O'Connell could also refuse my request.

"Have a seat." Moretti shut the door and rested his hips on the edge of the desk. "How are you doing, Parker?"

"Fine."

"Really? Why do you look like shit?" Moretti held up his hand before I could say something snarky. "Jablonsky's worried about you. The reason he subbed in today was because he thought you were taking a step back. O'Connell was under the same impression."

"That was before I got a handle on my Cross Security case, but I'm more than capable of dealing with both matters. Frankly, I haven't been able to stop thinking about O'Connell's case. I wanted to see how much progress had been made."

"Summers is a good lead. From what my detectives have said, they don't believe he's involved in the murders, but he was there when Landau was poisoned. He should be able to ID the killer."

"Let's hope so."

"You know, we hired you to consult since that seemed easier than the alternative, but we can take it from here. I don't want you to overextend yourself."

"I'm fine."

"Jablonsky said you haven't been to physical therapy yet. If you were a cop or agent, you'd have to pass the physical before going out in the field."

"I'm not a cop or agent. I'm a consultant. The work's not nearly as grueling."

"I've heard about several of your recent cases. We both know that's not true."

"I'm fine."

"The hell you are." He pressed his lips together. "Look, go home. Get some sleep. Go to physical therapy. Do whatever it is you do over at Cross Security. If something pops, let us know. Otherwise, this is a police matter. We appreciate your insight and assistance. We wouldn't have gotten this far without you."

"Unbelievable." I got out of the chair. "Jablonsky used to beg me to go back to the OIO. He wanted me to work cases until I dropped, and now, he asked you to remove me from a consulting gig. That bastard."

"Go easy, Parker. I make the decisions here. But we all have a different perspective after recent events."

"You don't think I can hack it?" I inhaled through my nose, my eyes stinging. "You think I pose a danger to the cops out there." I shook my head. "I get it. I've put Detective Heathcliff's life in danger more times than I want to think about. O'Connell's too."

"It's not that. No one think's you're a liability. You're more than capable, but we don't need you. If that changes, we'll call."

Biting my lip, I stormed out of the office, grabbed my jacket off the chair, and headed for the door. O'Connell caught up to me before the door swung closed.

"What happened?"

"Moretti fired me."

"Parker," he tried to soften the blow, but I couldn't think straight, "I'm sorry."

"It's not your fault, Nick. Jablonsky offered up his two cents, but he's right. I shouldn't be here. It's not safe." I swallowed. "Whatever. I'm done."

"Alex—"

"Just nail this bitch. I don't want to find out more people died. Save them, Nick."

"I will." He gave my upper arm a squeeze, but I pulled away from him and headed down the stairs, too angry and hurt to notice much of anything.

I drove home with the radio blasting, hoping to keep the

destructive thoughts out of my head. Lt. Moretti was right to ask me to leave. Jablonsky was right to tell him to do it, even if a part of me felt betrayed. Mark had his reasons. None of which I could argue with. I didn't even want to work on that stupid case. I wasn't ready. I didn't want to go up against another killer, let alone some psycho serial killer with a flower fetish. But damn if it didn't hurt to be asked to leave. God, I was more screwed up than even I realized.

"Ms. Parker," Marcal, Martin's driver and valet, stopped me in the driveway, "you'll have to go through the front door. The garage and connected areas are under construction."

"Of course, they are." The only thing I wanted to do was work out until I collapsed, and now I couldn't even use the home gym.

"Leave your car here. I'll park it for you."

"What's Martin doing?"

"I'm sorry. He gave me specific instructions not to tell you."

Reminding myself it wasn't Marcal's fault and lashing out at him wouldn't be very nice, I let out a lengthy exhale, wanting nothing more than to scream until my throat hurt. "Does whatever this is require a building permit?"

"No."

"Are they painting?"

Marcal gave me an odd look, almost as if he suspected I might know what was going on inside. At least someone was willing to give me more credit than I deserved. "No." A man with a saw and hardhat stepped out of the rear of a panel van carrying what looked like lumber. "Please, Ms. Parker."

"Fine. It's not like I have any control over my life anyway. Why should this be any different?" I handed him my car keys and trudged up the steps to the front door.

The smart thing to do would be call the medical staff on Cross's payroll, ask if they could get me an appointment for physical therapy, and do something safe and productive. Instead, I went upstairs, changed into some compression leggings, running shoes, and a cut-off tank top, stretched, and turned on Martin's ridiculously powerful stereo system. Then I ran stairs. Up and down, from the second to the fourth floor, over and over. My leg hurt, but not nearly as much as my insides. Anger kept my legs pumping. My lungs burned until I found a steady rhythm. I hadn't done much cardio in the last month, but the muscle memory and breathing techniques came naturally. I wasn't looking to find my stride. This was punishment, self-inflicted. So I pushed harder.

I tripped and stumbled, but I kept going. Second floor. Third floor. Fourth floor. Whenever my leg gave out, I wouldn't have far to crawl. At least I planned ahead. How could Moretti approve me to consult only to take it away from me? This wasn't the first time I'd been taken off a case. It probably wouldn't be the last. For everyone's sake, even my own, this was for the best. So why did it bother me so much? I didn't even want it.

"Fuck." My thigh cramped, and I banged my knee against the edge of the step. I took a minute to rub it out, turned, and ran down the steps. I'd lost count of how many times I'd gone up and down. At least fifteen. Maybe more. In our apartment, Martin and I would occasionally race on the stairs. That was twenty-one flights. It didn't take us more than a few minutes. This was different.

After three more trips, up and down, the cramp returned. I crawled up the last few steps and struggled to get back on my feet. I couldn't breathe, and with my heart beating this fast, I thought the sudden stop might kill me. Probably not, but that'd just be the icing on the cake.

With the help of the wall, I got back on my feet, relying solely on my left leg, which burned and ached almost as much as my right. I swung my arms a little, stretching my back and shoulders. Just keep moving. I gasped for air as I hopped down the hall and into the bedroom. By then, my heart rate had come down enough. I grabbed the dresser and eased onto the floor. Sore and drenched in sweat, I army-crawled into the bathroom, turned on the water in the tub, and drank from the faucet. Talk about classy. I had no business being here or anywhere for that matter.

Despite my best efforts, the self-loathing kicked into high gear. I filled the tub, stretched as best I could, stripped out of my clothes, and sunk into the water. The bathtub in the master suite doubled as a hot tub, with powerful massaging jets and various heat functions. I'd never bothered with any of it before, but I turned a few knobs to make sure the water would stay hot, lathered, and rinsed. After clipping my hair up, I settled back against the seat, letting the jets work on the sore spot near my shoulder blade where I liked to carry my stress. And then I let myself cry.

TWENTY

"Sweetheart," Martin took off his tie and cufflinks and placed them on the bathroom counter before rolling up his sleeves, "are you trying to drown yourself?"

"It might be an improvement." I closed my eyes again. This had been the only place I'd found enough peace to sleep. Maybe I was a shark. The *Jaws* theme played in my mind as I started to drift off.

"Should I join you?"

I didn't answer. I was too far gone and had little desire to return. He scooped me out of the water, wrapped me in a fluffy, oversized bath towel, and carried me to the bed. He lifted my hand, examining my pruned fingertips before gently kissing each of them.

Without a word, he pulled down the covers, laid me down, and slid in beside me. He knew something was wrong, but he didn't inquire. I hugged him hard and pressed my cheek against the exposed skin of his opened shirt. He nuzzled the top of my head and rubbed patterns on my back until I fell asleep.

When I woke up, the grief hit me hard. Every loss amplified. My own imperfection at the root of it. I'd been here before. A few times, actually. It wasn't pretty or rational, but it's where the darker parts of my psyche liked to go. I thought I'd already dealt with it, but being asked to step away from my consulting gig with the PD had brought everything to the forefront. Mark's involvement in that made the sting even worse. He almost died because of me. He didn't want others to face the same fate.

A part of me knew that wasn't true. It was ludicrous, but that's what the sadistic bitch in my head kept saying. And no matter how hard I tried not to listen to her, she wouldn't shut up.

Martin unclipped my hair and ran his fingers through the tangles. I clung to him as if my life depended on it. My throat so tight I couldn't find my voice. I buried my face against his chest.

"What's wrong, gorgeous?"

I swallowed. "Everything."

"Did you go downstairs?"

"No."

His chest rose, and he exhaled in relief. His fingers pressed against my ribs, working the soreness out of the surrounding muscles. "God, you're tense."

"Really? I feel like Jell-o. My legs anyway. The rest is just painful numbness."

He moved his hands to my neck and shoulders, working his nimble fingers gently over my flesh. I hissed when he brushed against the knot beneath my shoulder blades. "Do you want me to stop? I don't want to hurt you."

"Keep going. You can press harder."

But he knew that was my masochistic side talking and kept his touch feather light while he caressed my taut skin and coaxed the bunched muscles underneath to relax. I turned my head to face the other way, so I could hear his heartbeat. The steady rhythm soothed my inner turmoil.

"I hate this."

His hands stilled, waiting for an elaboration.

"I don't know what to do or how to deal. I just need to figure out what I'm supposed to do. At first, Mark tells me I should stay busy, work to keep my mind off of things. But that's going to blow up in my face. We all know it. So, now

I'm off the case. I was told I should take some time for me. What does that mean? I should do nothing?" I snorted. "Apparently. But now that I'm supposed to do nothing, I think I should do something. I do this all the time. What is wrong with me? I must be the most indecisive person on the planet. I'm fucking crazy. Why would you put up with this? I wouldn't put up with me if I didn't have to."

He laughed quietly. "Because I love you."

"You're more bat shit crazy than I am."

"Possibly." He went back to massaging my back. "What can I do?"

"Nothing. Mark had Moretti pull me off O'Connell's case. After the call I made last night, I understand why, but..."

"You didn't want the case, but now you're invested." His fingers brushed against the back of my thigh. "What did Moretti say?"

"I helped enough, and if the police need further assistance, he'll let me know."

"What did Mark say when you bitched him out?"

"I didn't, and I'm not going to." I sighed, turning to check the time. "Wow, it's almost nine."

"You were tired. You haven't slept more than three hours straight in over a month."

"Don't remind me." I rolled off Martin, wincing and letting out a groan. "Since my days and nights are flipped, I should probably do some more research and possibly run some surveillance on Andre North."

"That can wait." Martin brushed a strand of hair out of my face and kissed me. "You need to sleep, and the hour and a half nap you just took doesn't count."

"I slept in the tub before that."

"For what? Twenty minutes?"

I looked away.

"Alex, you're killing yourself. You have to stop this."

"If I stop, I'll die or everyone else will."

"Dammit, sweetheart." A single tear fell from my eye, and he caught it with his fingertip. "Fine, but you can't go anywhere on Jell-o legs." He sat up, pushing the covers away. The bath towel remained wrapped tightly around me, like a giant white dress. "God, you're beautiful."

"You're insane."

"I thought we already established that." He smiled. "Flip over." He lifted my leg and started at my ankle, running his thumbs against either side of my Achilles tendon before working his way up my sore calf to the back of my thigh. He repeated the process on the other leg, working out the stiffness and muscle soreness before telling me to flip over again. He rubbed my quads, getting a little brazen with his fingertips when it came to my inner thighs, but he backed off when I pressed my legs together. "Is that better?" he asked, but I had zoned out, back to crime scenes and dead friends. "Alex?"

"Yeah."

He cocked an eyebrow at me. "How'd you get so sore?" That wasn't the question he wanted to ask, but it was the safest one that came to mind.

"Running up and down the stairs."

"Do you think that's wise?"

"No, but I needed to do something."

"You mean you wanted to punish yourself." He climbed off the bed, unbuttoning his dress shirt and reaching for a t-shirt to put on. He hadn't even bothered to change out of his suit before fishing me out of the tub. "Is that how you got the bruise on your shin?" I looked down, surprised to find a purple welt just beneath my knee. "You do the same song and dance every time. Frankly, sweetheart, you need to learn some new moves. Next, you'll do everything in your power to sabotage us and push me away. So let me be clear right now. It won't work. I'd prefer if we just bypass that and move on to the next phase."

"What's that?"

"Compromise and acceptance."

"You sound like a self-help book."

"How would you know? You've never read one."

"Neither have you."

"Why would I?" He grabbed a pair of jeans and a t-shirt out of my dresser, along with a bra and underwear, and dropped them on the bed beside me. "Is that okay? Or do you need to wear something else to conduct recon? I'm partial to a catsuit with cutouts, but I doubt you'll let me go with you to enjoy the view."

"This is good." I moved to the edge of the bed, slipped on the underwear, and pulled on my jeans before pulling the bra on and lowering the towel. I stood up on wobbly legs, went into the bathroom, brushed my teeth and hair, finished getting ready, and put on my shirt. When I returned to the bedroom, Martin had a glass of water waiting for me.

"You're probably dehydrated after that catnap in the hot tub. Y'know they put a warning in big bold letters in the manual saying not to fall asleep."

"I guess that makes me a firebrand." Parched, I glugged down the water. "You worry too much."

"Or not enough." He gave me an exasperated look. "I just want to make sure you're okay."

"I'm not okay, Martin. I'm not even close. I guess I've accepted that." I smirked. "Isn't that one of those steps you wanted me to reach?"

"Not like that." A guilty look came over his face. "Shit."

"What?"

"Nothing."

I stared at him, knowing he'd done something he regretted. I just didn't know what it was, and I didn't have it in me to push. Not today. "Do you still love me?"

"Why would you ask me that?" His face contorted in confusion. "I love you with everything I have."

"You shouldn't, but you already said you don't want to fight about it. I should get some work done while I still have a job. If I don't, Cross will be the next one to fire me, and then I'll really be lost."

He grabbed me, taking the glass from my hand and placing it on the dresser. "I won't let that happen. You're here. With me. You're not lost. Let me be your port in the storm."

"I can't even see land right now."

"I'll send out a search party." He searched my eyes, but all I could see in his were fear and grief. I just didn't know if it was mine or his.

I laced my fingers behind his neck. "I love you.

Whatever you did won't change that."

He swallowed. "Marcal told you?"

"No."

He tilted his head and kissed me, wrapping both arms around me and practically lifting me off the floor just to give my legs a break. "Don't go downstairs. I'm going to fix it."

Deciding he must have broken something or taken a golf club to the walls again, I chose to save that discovery for another day when I wasn't already emotionally and physically drained. "Fine, but I need my car."

"You're going back to work?"

"I have to. It's what I need right now."

"Okay." He kissed me again, picked me up, carried me down the stairs, and left me to collect my things from the second floor while he pulled my car out of the garage.

TWENTY-ONE

This was a bad idea. The last thing I needed was to be alone with my thoughts. But here I was, parked outside Andre North's house with nothing to do but list all of my shortcomings. Every person I failed to save. Every life I'd taken. Every mistake I'd made. Every near miss and close call.

"Stop it." I reached for the bottle of water Martin had tucked into my cupholder.

Andre lived on a quiet street. He had a nice townhouse. He had a picture perfect front yard. The grass and shrubbery had been trimmed to the appropriate height to match his neighbors. I hadn't bothered to check around back, but it was probably equally perfect.

Andre hadn't been home when I arrived, but he showed up just after 10:15. It was late, but not too late. He could have gone out for dinner or drinks with prospective clients or his business partners. Martin worked late a lot, so I figured the same might be true for Andre. Perhaps, he'd been at a paint store debating swatch colors until they closed. I had no reason to think he was cheating on Eve. But since I'd be surveilling her, and she spent a lot of time here, I wanted to get the lay of the land. Plus, I wanted to be sure Andre was a good guy and everything he said hadn't been some elaborate ruse to convince me to help him stalk his girlfriend.

The television lights flickered through the cracks in the open blinds. I checked the time. It was eleven. He was probably watching the news. Twenty minutes later, he turned off the TV. I followed the light patterns through the windows. He must be going upstairs to the bedroom. The rest of my night was about to get even more boring.

I thought about calling it quits, but headlights in the rearview caught my attention. I hunkered down in my seat and peered out the back window. A woman stepped out of a car, leaned in to say something to the driver, and sprinted toward Andre's townhouse.

With the blinding headlights, I couldn't make out much except her form. She had something covering her head to keep the drizzling rain off of her. The driver remained in the car with the infernal lights pointed straight ahead, preventing me from seeing clearly.

The house lights turned on as Andre made his way down the stairs and opened the door. The light from behind cast them both in silhouette. I saw them embrace before the door closed. What just happened?

I turned to get a look at the car, but it was backing down the street. Dammit. I couldn't get the plate number, not even the make, model, or color. *Add this to your list of screw-ups*, the voice in my head whispered.

Annoyed, I peered out the window, hoping to catch a glimpse of the woman, but I couldn't see anything. Andre had the blinds closed. The lights remained on in the living room. They could be talking. Maybe she was his assistant, and there was some kind of emergency with one of his properties. She could be his sister, except he didn't have a sister. None of this made any sense.

Had my initial reaction been correct? Did Andre fear Eve was cheating because he was a cheater? When we spoke, he seemed so sweet, so sincere. I believed he loved her and would do anything for her, so why was he hugging some woman? Had I really been that wrong about him?

I reached for my camera and waited for the money shot.

Once I had that, I'd go to the office, ID the woman, and update Cross on the situation. I didn't want to work for a liar or cheat. If Cross wanted to keep the case, he could work it himself.

Less than ten minutes later, the lights in the living room turned off, and I followed the light pattern as Andre made his way back upstairs. Would she stay all night, or would she leave when they were finished? I hoped for the latter. I didn't want to stay here all night. I felt icky and a little heartbroken.

The lights remained on in the bedroom, but I couldn't see anything on account of the blinds. So I waited. Eventually, my mind wandered and my eyelids drooped. I shook it off and checked the time.

Seriously? Even the prescription pill bottles warned about activity lasting more than four hours. Maybe they'd fallen asleep with the lights on. I could fall asleep with the lights on. Actually, sometimes, I preferred it.

My thoughts scattered, and my head bobbed. I jerked myself upright. Stay awake. I reached for the water, thinking I should have a thermos with coffee instead, but I hadn't planned for this. My nap should have been enough to sustain me, but Martin was probably right. I'd been running on fumes for so long, the tank was empty. Two hours of sleep wouldn't get me far.

I'd just taken a final sip when something slammed up against Andre's bedroom window. The blinds pressed against the glass, askew and partially raised. Then they stepped back, and I could make out two human forms cast in shadow. The bottom half of the blinds remained halfway open. I reached for my camera, zooming in to see what was going on inside. The two figures, backlit by the interior lamps, stood close together in front of the window.

Suddenly, the larger one, which had to be Andre, grabbed the woman from behind, yanking her head back and up. The motion was quick. Too fast for me to be certain, but dark specks splattered against the closed slats of the blinds, making it appear spotted, like a dalmatian, where the few slats near the bottom remained open, I saw red.

Blood. I tried to snap a photo, but the lights went out, plunging the room into darkness. Only one thought came to mind.

He sliced her throat open. That must have been arterial spray. He killed her. Did he kill her? I shook myself, unsure what was real and what wasn't. Was I awake or dreaming? Shit.

Blinking, I stared at the window through the viewfinder, but I couldn't see anything. Surely, there would be movement inside. He'd have to dispose of the body. But all the lights remained off.

Without the back lighting, I couldn't see the spatter pattern on the bedroom blinds. I couldn't see anything. Should I enter the house? I had to find out what happened. If he sliced her throat the way it appeared, it was already too late. She would have bled out by now. With trembling fingers, I reached for my phone. I dialed 9-1-1 but didn't hit send. My gaze shifted from my phone to the row of townhouses.

Surely, she would have screamed. The neighbors would have heard. But no one had turned on their lights.

Did I hallucinate it or dream it? Flashes of a gory crime scene came to mind. My friend dead from multiple stab wounds. Another image, a nightmare I'd had with Martin's throat sliced open. More images flooded my mind. I gasped for air, fighting to stave off the panic attack. After the other night in Martin's bedroom, I didn't know what was real and what wasn't. The nightmares had permeated my waking life.

Deciding to err on the side of caution, I called and reported a woman screaming. The police would send a unit to check it out. I thanked them and hung up before they could ask my name, but my information had already popped up on their screens. I knew how this worked, so I turned off my phone, waited a few minutes, and turned it back on. At least that would make it more difficult for them to track me, not that they would, unless it was a homicide and I became a suspect or witness.

I hit the speed dial for Mark but stopped myself from calling. After last night, I didn't need to add more fuel to the fire if I was wrong, and if I was right, I didn't need to get him involved in this.

Perhaps I should call O'Connell. He was a cop. He'd send additional units. But I resisted, deciding to wait it out. A few minutes later, a patrol car turned down the street. I ducked down so they wouldn't see me and waited. The car double-parked in front of the townhouse, and two officers got out and rang the bell.

Andre didn't turn on the bedroom light and answered the door alone. He wasn't covered in blood. Could he have changed clothes? I didn't see what he was wearing earlier. The lead cop stepped into the doorway, turned on the living room light, looked around, shook hands with Andre, and rejoined his partner. It wasn't exactly the thorough walkthrough I hoped for, but the police seemed satisfied, which made me doubt myself even more. Had I imagined it?

The patrol car drove away. The cops didn't notice anything out of the ordinary, not even the suspicious woman casing the place. Since they missed me, they might have missed the body upstairs too. It's not like they'd done a thorough walkthrough. I had to be sure it wasn't real, but aside from breaking into Andre's house, I was out of options.

Dialing Cross, I waited. My fingers drummed a beat on the steering wheel, but he didn't answer. Who else could I call?

I glanced back at the townhouse. Still no movement. No lights. After the police came knocking, a killer would do something. Lack of movement wasn't typical behavior, which made me even less certain of what I witnessed or thought I witnessed. It couldn't have been real, but the little voice in my head wouldn't give up. If Andre North murdered someone, I couldn't let him get away with it, no matter how pleasant he had been when we met. Obviously, that must have been an act too since he was inside with a woman. Or was there even a woman?

My perception of reality was shot. I needed help. Someone sane and rational to figure this out because I couldn't.

I scrolled through my contacts. Bennett Renner. He answered on the second ring. "Parker, I'm sorry. I'm doing my own recon right now. Try calling the office. Someone might be on call."

"Yeah, okay." I hung up and searched for other coworkers. Unfortunately, I didn't know most of them well enough to have their numbers saved on my phone. The only other name I found was Kellan's. I didn't have a choice.

"Alex?" From the background noise, it sounded like he was at a club.

"You said you'd help if I needed it. I need it."

"Tell me where you are." He said something to someone in Spanish that I couldn't quite make out.

I gave him the address, relieved to have someone else take over, even if it was Kellan.

"I'll be there soon."

The wait felt interminable. I couldn't just sit here, so I got out of my car, crossed the street, and went around the row of townhouses. The backyards were fenced in, like Jablonsky's. Thoughts of the fight that resulted in me getting shot in the leg came to mind, causing my breath to hitch. I had to focus on the present. No more flashbacks. No more anything. I had to be here. I had to stay awake.

The backyard behind Andre's townhouse was just as ornate and maintained as the front. I didn't find a deranged man with a shovel digging a hole to hide a body. Everything appeared normal. I inspected the back door, but it was locked. And since Andre had a state-of-the-art security system, I didn't try to break in.

I went back to the car and checked the photos I'd taken. If I'd hallucinated or dreamt it, I wouldn't have any type of photographic proof. Except, I couldn't tell anything from the pictures. A woman entered the house. The two had been near the window. I couldn't see any blood. The suddenness of the pair knocking against the window or the spatter covering the blinds wasn't conveyed in the photos. I should have taken video.

Leaning down, I peered up at the window. The blinds remained askew. I didn't imagine that. Something happened up there. But what?

A knock sounded at the window, and I screamed. Kellan held up his palms. "It's me, Alexis." I hit the unlock. Another dose of adrenaline surged through my veins. Kellan slid into the passenger seat, took one look at me, and asked, "Are you okay?"

"No."

"Are you hurt?"

I shook my head and told him what I saw or thought I saw. "I might be having a *Rear Window* moment."

"Did you call the cops?"

"They performed a wellness check and left. They didn't go upstairs. They should have." I handed him the camera. "What do you think?"

"Has anyone been in or out since?"

"No."

"Cross performed a background on Andre North. Did anything turn up?"

"No, he's clean."

"What about solicitation charges or domestic disturbance calls?"

"Nothing like that." I thought for a moment. "Nothing at all. He has no record."

Kellan stared at the townhouse. "Did the neighbors notice anything?"

"If they did, they didn't act like it."

"And you can't identify the woman or the car that dropped her off."

"You've seen the photos." If I wasn't so freaked out, I would have been annoyed.

He turned to study me. "Take a deep breath. I'm glad you called me. However, I would have preferred if I hadn't been in the middle of a date."

"Did you finally ask out the waiter from the Mexican restaurant?" I hoped to distract myself from the pounding in my chest.

"Sí." He adjusted the passenger's seat. "I'll call him in the morning and apologize for running out. In the meantime, we have to figure out what's going on in there."

TWENTY-TWO

"Alex," Kellan nudged me, "is that the woman you saw last night?" Andre North stood in his doorway, kissing a beautiful woman.

"I don't know. I didn't get a look at her." I rubbed my eyes. The adrenaline crash had drained me, practically putting me in a comatose state. Kellan didn't bitch about it, which surprised me. "Can you zoom in?"

Kellan snapped a few photos and handed me the camera.

"That's Eve." That didn't make any sense either. "She's supposed to be out of the country. What is she doing here?"

"I'll go ask her."

"No." I grabbed his arm to stop him, and he laughed.

"I was just teasing. I know you're supposed to be surveilling her."

"What about the bedroom window?" I hunkered down in the seat to get a better look, but someone had fixed the blinds. They hung properly with no detectable stains or spatter.

"I don't know." Kellan took the camera from me when a town car pulled up. He snapped several shots of Eve getting into the back seat. After they drove away, he handed me the camera. "You said Andre was alone when the woman arrived. I'm guessing that was Eve who showed up on his doorstep last night. At least she's alive and well."

"That's his fiancée."

"Even better, right?"

"Right." Andre wasn't a cheater or killer. I should have been ecstatic. Instead, I was more confused now than I was last night.

Kellan eyed me. "This is a good thing. You should be relieved."

"I guess, but what is she doing here?"

"Isn't it obvious? She's been away for over a week and her soon-to-be husband looks like that. Do you really need me to spell it out for you? Because if that's the case, I'd be happy to take your boyfriend off your hands. That tall drink of water could use some TLC. And someone needs to have the birds and bees talk with you, missy."

"No, I..." I stopped, realizing Kellan was teasing me. "I need to figure out what's going on. Something isn't right."

"Are you heading back to the office now?"

I fixed my seat. "Yes."

"Do me a favor. Tell Cross I'll be a few hours late. I want to bring my date breakfast and make up for abandoning him at the club."

"No problem."

"Does this mean we're friends again?"

"Let's not rush into anything. I'm thinking we're friend adjacent."

"I'll take it." He gave me another uncertain look. "Whenever you finally decide you can trust me again, I want to know what's going on with you. Whatever went down last night had you freaked. Like put a bullet in someone's head freaked."

"That's why I called you."

Kellan didn't say anything. Instead, he climbed out of my car and headed for his own. I gave Andre's townhouse one final look. Did I imagine all of it? Was that another PTSD episode brought about by recent traumatic events and lack of sleep? Did I fall asleep and dream up the details that didn't quite coincide with the surveillance photos I'd taken? Pushing those thoughts aside, I headed to the office. Since Eve was back, I had work to do.

I went straight to Lucien's office. He stood behind Justin's desk, waiting for forms to print while he sipped his espresso.

"Do you live here?" I asked.

My boss looked up. "You're in early. From the looks of you, I'm not sure I want to know why. Come into my office, so we can talk." He waited for me to enter and shut the door. "You called last night. What's going on?"

"You didn't answer."

"I know that. What I don't know is why you called."

"I wanted to get a jump start on the surveillance and to check out our client."

"Andre North?"

"That's the only case you've assigned me."

Cross adjusted the sleeve on his jacket. "What about him?"

"I thought he killed someone."

Cross stopped fidgeting and stared at me. "What happened?"

"It was dark. A woman came to his door. I didn't get a good look at her, but he let her inside. They went up to his bedroom. I don't know what happened, but I thought he attacked her and cut her throat. The police did a wellness check, but they left quickly."

"You called the police?"

"What would you have had me do instead? It's not like you answered the phone."

"But they didn't find anything."

"They barely looked."

"Typical." Cross cleared his throat. "Go on."

"A woman emerged this morning." I held out the camera. "I'm assuming it's the same woman from last night."

He took it from my hand, powered it on, and studied the images. "That's Eve Wyndham."

"Yep."

"Huh." Cross went to his desk and hit the intercom. "Justin, find out when Eve Wyndham returned home.

Check her social media pages for any mention. If you can't find it there, see if you can get a hold of her travel itinerary or pull passport records."

"Yes, sir."

"Andre said she might be coming home sooner rather than later. Did you get a chance to check her apartment?" Cross asked.

"I didn't find anything conclusive. I also went by Elegant Events, but I didn't go inside. Her assistant said she was out of the office but didn't say when she'd be back."

Cross nodded a few times, as if agreeing with the voices in his head. Maybe I wasn't the only one suffering from that malady. "Where is she now?"

"I don't know."

"You didn't follow her?"

"I was preoccupied with the possibility her fiancé murdered someone."

"Do you still believe that?"

"No."

"Keep me abreast of the situation, if there is a situation." He opened the office door, holding it for me. "Should I assign someone else to handle this?"

I couldn't be taken off another case less than twenty-four hours after my first firing. "No, I'll take care of it."

"Find out what's going on from Andre. I want an update by lunchtime. Assuming nothing has changed, I want you to take the rest of the day. Go home. Get some sleep. Get changed. Tomorrow, dress like a professional and do whatever needs to be done."

"Sir?" I hated when my training kicked in for no apparent reason.

He cocked an eyebrow, surprised yet smug. "Did I not make myself clear?"

Recovering, I said, "Kellan came to assist me last night. He'll be in late because of it."

Cross collected the files off the corner of Justin's desk and led me to the elevator. "Glad to see you're finally getting along with your coworkers again. They aren't your enemies, Alex. And neither am I. That being said, whatever you're going through, I need you to get a handle on it. For your own good and mine. This company can't afford unnecessary lawsuits. Keep that in mind before you make any accusations or decide to phone the police department with anonymous tips."

"Yes, sir."

We parted ways at the conference room. Cross went inside to put the files down and prepare for the morning meeting while I continued down the hallway to my office. It was too early to start making phone calls. No one in their right mind would choose to be awake at this time of day, and if they were, they were busy getting ready for work. But I knew Andre was awake. At least he had been when he escorted Eve to the door.

Plugging in the memory card, I copied the data onto my computer and blew up the photos in question from last night. Even after some tinkering, I couldn't positively ID Eve or figure out what happened in the bedroom. So I sent the files upstairs for the techs to play with. They might find something I missed.

I examined the shots Kellan took this morning. That was Eve. I wrote down the plate number and traced it back to a car service. Eve owned her own car, but she'd charged the ride this morning on her corporate card. She also expensed a rideshare last night, but her financial activity didn't provide any additional details.

My phone rang, and I picked it up. "Hello?"

"According to Eve Wyndham's social media posts, she arrived home late last night," Justin said. "I'll send you the links."

"Thanks."

I hung up, opened the interoffice messenger, and clicked. Eve had posted a photo of the rainy sky over the jet's wing. *This is the opposite of an arid desert, but I'm glad to be home.* I scanned the rest of her page, but I didn't see any other new posts. Based on the timestamp, she posted that photo roughly an hour before arriving at Andre's.

Since he'd gone to bed, she must have surprised him. Didn't he follow her on social media? Shouldn't he have seen the alert? I checked her followers and friends list, but it was massive. He might have missed it, had his alerts turned off, or figured his fiancée would call or text him instead of expecting him to learn things the same way as her thousands of friends and clients.

A few minutes later, the phone rang again. "Hello. Cross Security."

"Good morning. This is Andre North."

"Yes, Mr. North. How can I help you?" If I were any more professional, someone might mistake me for one of the receptionists.

"I'm glad I caught you, Alex. You can call me Andre. No need to be so formal. Not when I've been airing my insecurities and dirty laundry for you to see." He laughed. I'd never heard him sound so giddy. "Eve came home last night and surprised me. She came straight from the airport. God, I missed her."

"That's wonderful."

"It is, isn't it? She left her overnight bag here. I told her I'd drop it off at her place." He hesitated. "I didn't know if you needed to see it. I'm not exactly sure what I'm supposed to do in this situation. I hired you to investigate my fiancée, so do I call you with these things?"

"What's wrong with her luggage? Did you find something troublesome inside?"

"No, not really. She brought this one bag straight from the airport. The rest she had delivered to her place. But this is her work bag. It has her day planner, notebook, and work binder. It's full of photos and brochures and other stuff from her trip."

"Have you looked inside?"

"I snooped a little," he admitted. "I don't feel right about it. My father always said I should never go through a woman's bag."

"All right, I'll take a look."

"I shouldn't worry, right?" he asked. "I mean she came straight here from the airport. She surprised me. If she were having an affair, wouldn't she have gone to see him instead?"

Last night, I thought Andre was a killer. Now, I thought he made Martin's clingier tendencies seem standoffish.

"I wouldn't recommend turning a blind eye, but so far, I haven't found anything indicating you should worry."

He sighed in relief. "That's wonderful to hear. I'll bring her bag to you in an hour."

"I could come to you," I offered, hoping to get a look inside his townhouse and put those nagging second-guesses to bed.

"No reason. I have to pass your office on my way to Eve's. I'll see you soon."

TWENTY-THREE

While I searched Eve's belongings, Andre went upstairs to speak to Lucien. He didn't want to watch me snoop through his bride-to-be's things. I didn't blame him. I wouldn't want to watch someone go through Martin's belongings either.

I scanned the pages and her notes for any indication she might have had a little too much fun while working, but I didn't find anything definitive. Everything appeared to be business-related. In the back of her notebook was a stack of receipts for catering and rentals. Those must be what she planned to expense to the client.

More importantly, what I didn't find in her bag spoke volumes. I didn't find any condoms or sexy lingerie. Eve considered this bag too valuable to allow someone to deliver it to her apartment, so she took it with her to Andre's. If she had any dirty little secrets, she wouldn't want a stranger to stumble upon them. Then again, she might not risk taking them to Andre's if she thought he didn't trust her. But if he didn't trust her, why would she leave her bag behind?

When I finished copying and photographing everything that could be relevant, I repacked her overnight bag and phoned Justin to tell him it was safe to send Andre back downstairs. The one thing I wanted was to go to his house with some Luminol and a blacklight, but that might have been my insanity talking.

After Andre collected Eve's bag, he thanked me again. "I want to trust her, but she's been acting odd these last few weeks. She's been working a lot more too. I just...I have to be smart about this. You understand, right?"

"Yes, sir."

"Do you think I should tell her?"

"You should probably wait and see what I find first."

He chuckled. "I guess that would be the smart way to do it."

"If nothing turns up, you don't have to tell her."

"How can we start our lives together with a secret hanging over us?" He rubbed his brow. "Hiring you could destroy us, but I'm not sure I could go through with it without knowing for sure that she loves me and only me."

I didn't have anything to say. We'd been over this before. It was his call. I just had to do my job without hallucinating any more murder scenes.

Once he was gone, I went into the break room to get some coffee. Kellan hadn't shown up for work yet, but unlike me, he might actually be at home sleeping. I bit my lip, considering my options. I had to do something. I couldn't go on like this. Martin knew it. Mark knew it. And based on my conversation with Lucien this morning, he knew it too.

Returning to my office with a fresh cup of coffee, I closed the door and took a seat behind my desk. I rummaged through my purse for the business card Jablonsky had given me, but I couldn't bring myself to call the number on the card. Therapy and I had never gotten along. The mandated counseling sessions and psych evals while I'd been a federal agent had only irritated me enough to force me to quit the first time. Now, I had other dangers to worry about, namely O'Connell's investigation. If the police consultant who supplied him with witnesses and suspects was declared unstable, the entire case could fall apart if the defense had a good enough attorney and a biased judge.

But last night proved I was a liability. Mark knew it before I did. I had to do something. Perhaps I could use a fake name or see if we could keep these records privileged. Mental health records had additional protections on top of those already afforded to other medical records.

"It'll be okay." I repeated this a few more times before digging out my cell phone and placing the call. The last thing I wanted was Cross to get wind of this, so I didn't dare use the company phone.

A woman answered on the third ring and asked how she could help.

"I...uh..." *Don't hang up, Parker.* I fought to keep myself from pressing the red disconnect. "I need to make an appointment."

"Are you a current client?"

Client, not patient. That gave me something else to think about besides the fear running through me. Why was I so afraid? I knew why. I knew how much the prying hurt, and I didn't want to go through that. I already hurt enough. I didn't want to hurt more.

"Ma'am, are you still there?" the woman on the other end of the line asked.

Of course she had to use that word. "Yes, sorry. I'm not. Is that a problem?"

"Not at all. I can schedule you for a consultation. Were you recommended to us?"

"Not by a medical professional."

"By whom?" she asked.

"Mark Jablonsky." I still didn't want to give my name. Maybe I shouldn't have given his, but the shrink would figure it out. We'd have the same trauma to discuss.

"Are you available this afternoon? I can fit you in at one."

I didn't want to go. "Okay." I hung up before she could ask anything else. It wouldn't matter if I didn't show. She didn't have my name. But something told me the doctor already knew more about me than I liked. Mark proved yesterday he had a big mouth. I doubted that was limited to what he shared with Lt. Moretti.

For the next two hours, I didn't do much but stretch and pace. My legs were stiff and sore from yesterday's workout and spending all night in the car. To kill time, I went upstairs and spoke to the medic about my workout regimen and supplemental things I could do to aid in speeding up my recovery.

"You're doing it. Stretch often. Switch up your exercises to make sure you're rebuilding your strength, mobility, and flexibility. Whatever you do on one side, do on the other. Your left leg is stronger than your right, but you want to even it out. So even if you can do more and stretch more on that side, don't."

"Okay."

He went to the cabinet and removed a bottle of prescription strength ibuprofen. "Just in case, but if you need to take one to get through the workout, you're working out too hard."

"Got it." I pocketed the bottle. "Thanks."

"Not yet." He handed me a stack of printed exercises. "Lucien asked me to prepare these for you. These are the exercises you'd be given in physical therapy."

I scanned the sheets. "I'm familiar with all of them."

"Good, if you have any other questions or change your mind, let me know."

"Will this really take six weeks?"

"Be patient. Rome wasn't built in a day."

"That was hundreds of years ago. I've seen fast food places get built in a week."

"Your leg isn't a fast food joint."

"It's not an empire either."

The medic rolled his eyes. "Good luck."

I tapped two fingers to my brow and gave him a mock salute before taking the elevator up to Cross's office.

After I updated him on the Andre and Eve situation, I grabbed my things and left the office. I stopped at the bank and withdrew a few hundred dollars to cover the cost of the appointment. I didn't want anything linking me back to the shrink's office. Again, I considered all the reasons why I shouldn't go and the one glaringly obvious reason why I had to.

Even as I parked in the garage, I fought the instinct to leave. Physical torture and pain were easier to deal with. I could handle those. This was something else.

I stood outside the door and stared at the address. Eventually, my leg started to shake from the pressure of supporting my weight for so long. "Here goes nothing."

Swallowing, I entered, finding the tremor had moved from my thigh all the way to my low back. The waiting room was empty. So I sat down. I'd just reached for a magazine when the door opened.

"Hi, are you my one o'clock?" a fresh-faced woman with auburn hair pulled back in a loose ponytail asked.

"Um," I looked around the empty room, "I guess so."

"Why don't you come inside?"

I put the magazine down and hoisted myself out of the chair using the arms for support. The tremor continued, growing more widespread as I stepped into her office. She pretended not to notice as she sat down in one of the oversized chairs.

She had a sofa, two oversized chairs, a straight-back chair, and one of those ergonomic things that would flip you on your ass if you didn't balance properly. "Sit wherever you like."

I wondered if this was a test, so I sat in the other oversized chair which might have been a miniature loveseat.

"Are you FBI?" she asked.

"I used to be."

"Me too."

I studied her, which she found amusing.

"You're wondering if I said that to build a rapport and earn trust."

"Oh, so you're a mind reader."

She laughed. "No, sorry, but didn't they pound interrogation techniques into our heads at Quantico?"

"They did." The walls were a boring slate grey with blue and silver borders. Not a single "hang in there" cat poster in sight.

"I'm Dr. Sarah Shelton, but you called me. I assume you already know that."

"Uh-huh." Her diploma hung on the back wall. I did the math in my head. She had to be in her late forties or early fifties, but she didn't look that old.

"And you are?"

I let out a breath. "Here."

"Okay." She waited me out. "Why are you here?"

"I need help."

"Okay." Again the pause, but I wasn't in a rush to fill the silence. "On the phone you said Mark Jablonsky recommended me."

"He did." I tucked my legs beneath me, hoping that would stop the shakes. "Last month he was shot. A former agent was killed, and two other agents were attacked."

"I'm aware." Her gaze drifted to my leg. "Were you injured by the same man who attacked Mark?"

"Yes."

She nodded. Mark had already told her the story. He probably told her about me. I wondered what he said. But Mark was a straight-shooter. I doubted he'd say anything to a stranger that he wouldn't say to my face.

"Have you been in therapy before?" she asked.

"Just what the job required and couples counseling."

"Are you divorced?"

"No."

"You're not wearing a ring."

"I'm not married."

"Oh." That caught her by surprise. "But you went to couples counseling, so you must have been in a serious relationship."

"Still am."

"So it worked."

"Not really."

She sat back in her chair, confused. "I'm just trying to establish a baseline of your experiences with therapy in the past. Why would you say it didn't work? Has there been no improvement to your relationship?"

"No, we're fine. We just didn't make it more than two sessions with any one therapist. It didn't help us."

"What did, if you don't mind me asking?"

"Talking and a shift in mindset." I studied her, but she

hadn't made a single note. "You know who I am, don't you?"

"Yes, Mark asked if I'd be willing to see you. He just didn't know if you'd call."

"Is he a patient?"

"More like a friend. I don't discuss my clients. Everything said in session remains confidential."

"Good because I'm afraid what the ramifications could be if this got out. I've been consulting on a murder case for the local police."

"You have no reason to be concerned, but given the nature of your career, I understand why you might be. There is no shame in seeking counseling. Why don't you tell me what's been going on lately?"

"Mark didn't tell you?"

"I'd like to hear it from you."

So I told her everything that happened over the last few days. She listened without interjecting or asking inane questions. Once I was finished, I took a deep breath. "Am I crazy?"

"That's not a clinical term, but no, I don't think you're crazy. How much have you been sleeping each week since the attack?"

"I'm lucky to get two or three hours a night."

"Okay," she glanced at the clock and went to her desk, "I think what you're experiencing are hallucinations brought on by lack of sleep and extreme stress. I'd wager your cortisol levels are through the roof. Your coffee drinking is only exacerbating the situation." She scribbled something down on a pad and went to a locked cabinet. "The reasons for your nightmares are something we can work to remedy through therapy, but in the meantime, I'm worried about you. Not sleeping can impair judgment, make it difficult to concentrate, hurt hand-eye coordination, and contribute to exaggerated stress responses. You mentioned having a lot more panic attacks recently. That could be why. Again, caffeine is not your friend in this instance. Not getting enough sleep over long periods of time is known to cause hallucinations. I think that's what's going on here. So the first thing we need to do is get you to sleep." She pulled out a sample pack and handed me the prescription.

"I don't want pills."

"I understand, but this isn't long-term. I just want to see if it helps. They're mild sedatives. They should help you relax and induce sleep. I'm hoping they'll take the edge off your nightmares." She returned to her desk and rummaged through the drawers for a box. She tossed it to me. "That's a sleep tracker. It should give us a general idea of how much sleep you're getting and if the pills are working."

"This will stop me from seeing crazy things?" I asked.

"It should, but once we get this sorted, we need to address the underlying causes. This isn't a quick fix. Grief and guilt are strong emotions."

"Tell me about it."

"Follow the directions. If you have any questions or problems, call me. If not, I'll make you an appointment for next week. You can let me know if the hallucinations have stopped and if you're still having frequent panic attacks. We can assess our next steps from there."

"Great."

"Asking for help doesn't make you weak, Alex. You recognize something is wrong, and you're strong enough to take steps to change it. Keep that in mind." She nodded at the bottle in my hand. "Give the pills a try. They might make you groggy for a few days until you adjust. If you can avoid early mornings or driving yourself to work, I'd recommend it."

"All right." I sighed. "What do I have to lose?"

TWENTY-FOUR

I went home, casting furtive looks at the bottle on the seat beside me. Pills bothered me. I'd seen so many people become addicted, and without knowing my family history, I didn't want to tempt fate. Plus, I was a control freak. Any substance that altered my perception or ability to function meant I wasn't in control. Unfortunately, these last few days proved that was already the case. How much worse could it get?

When I arrived at Martin's house, I didn't find any panel trucks or construction workers in the driveway. Marcal wasn't standing guard in front of the garage, so I entered the code and pulled the car inside, grabbed my bag, and went through the door.

The boxing ring Martin had in the center of the room had been moved to the left. The other equipment in our home gym had also been moved, expanding outward into the lounge area where Martin had his workbench and other gadgets with which he tinkered.

The entire back of the room had been cleared. Polished wood flooring spread across the padded tile. Floor to ceiling mirrors covered two of the walls, and a barre had been mounted along one side. Beside the treadmill sat a brand new reformer. I examined the pulleys and cables.

Martin built me a dance studio and bought pilates equipment to make my rehabbing easier. If I hadn't been so sore, I might have given it a try.

I ran my hand over the polished barre, recalling the hours wasted while I practiced. From the time I could walk until I turned thirteen, ballet had been my life. My adopted parents insisted on having a prima ballerina. They hated that I didn't live up to their expectations, and no matter how hard they tried, they just couldn't love a failure. That's when I decided I hated dance of any kind. I probably hated it before that, resented it for dictating every aspect of my life, but I'd been conditioned to believe life was about dance and training and nothing else. I didn't know any better until everything crumbled, and the two people who were supposed to love and protect me no matter what gave up on me. I'd learned an important lesson that day: I had to be the best, and if I wasn't, lives were destroyed. Apparently, I was still learning that same lesson.

"Alex," Martin startled me, "you weren't supposed to see this."

"Why aren't you at work?" I watched his reflection in the mirror.

"I took the afternoon off. I wanted to get rid of this before you got home. I didn't mean for you to see this."

I turned, resting both hands on the barre and leaning back to test its sturdiness. "You built me a ballet studio."

"It was a mistake."

"Why would you do this?"

"You wanted to use your dance training and pilates to recover from your injury. So I thought I'd help. But I didn't think it through all the way. I've been trying to get the construction crew back here to remove it, but that's a joke." He glanced at his workbench. "I figured I'd just grab a claw hammer and do it myself. I was upstairs changing when you came in. I thought you said you wouldn't come down here. You weren't supposed to see this. Go upstairs. I'll get rid of it. You won't have to lay eyes on it ever again."

"The hell you will." I stared at him, flabbergasted. "You built me a dance studio."

"I know. Bad idea. But I'm going to fix it."

"Martin, stop." I pushed away from the barre. "You're insane."

He wasn't listening. "You always bitch when I make unilateral decisions, but you've been so, y'know, I just wanted to do something to help. Shock you out of it. But after seeing you yesterday, I realized what a terrible idea this was." He moved toward the hammer, but I intercepted him.

"Step away from the tools."

He moved closer to me and ran his hands up and down my sides. "Let me fix this."

"You're not listening, handsome." I took his face in my hands. "I want to keep it." I stood on my tiptoes, keeping most of my weight on my left foot, and kissed him. "Right now, I'll do anything to get on top of my game. This will help me get there."

"At what cost?"

"Whatever it takes." I sunk back on my heels.

"We'll see." The wheels turned in his head. "If this makes things worse, it's gone. I will not be the cause of your pain."

"Is this the part where I make a comment about my ass hurting?"

"I wasn't joking."

"Neither was I." I headed up the steps, turning around halfway when I felt his unwavering gaze. "Stop staring at my butt."

"You said it hurt. I wondered if that was discernible to the casual observer." He smirked. "You'll be happy to know it is not."

"Bastard."

"Charmer." He waited until we were up the steps before enveloping me in his arms. He buried his nose in my hair, running the tip of it against my earlobe. "How was your night? I missed you."

"Not good." I told him what happened and about my consultation with the psychiatrist.

He lifted my hand away from his face and kissed my palm. "You'll be fine. You just need to sleep, preferably not in the bathtub."

"Yeah, I know."

He gave me a final reassuring kiss. "Have you eaten anything today?"

"Does coffee count?"

"No." He took my hand and led me into the kitchen. "You should probably eat before you take those pills. They're mild, but it's you."

"Are you calling me a lightweight?"

He grinned, grabbed my hips, and lifted me onto the counter. "I stopped by Giovanni's on my way home and had them wrap up some chicken parmigiana. I'd prefer to take you out to dinner, but I'm tired of hearing no. So I brought dinner to you."

"It's lunch."

"Close enough." He opened the fridge and took out two aluminum containers and removed the cardboard lids. "Unless you'd rather have the beef braciole."

"Giovanni's chicken parm is my favorite."

"I know." He put the containers in the oven and pulled out a large plastic container with fresh salad tossed with an Italian vinaigrette. On the other side of the counter was a paper bag with breadsticks. He put them in the warming tray and set the table. Then he lit the crystal candlesticks and dimmed the lights.

"Where's the accordion player? Are you going to roll a piece of braciole across the plate with your nose?"

"Only if we do the spaghetti kiss."

"No wonder I hallucinate things. I live with a madman."

"You need to relax. We haven't had a date night in weeks. You haven't taken any time for yourself."

"That's not true. I watched cartoons, remember? But you cut me off."

"I would say we should open a bottle of wine, but that's not advisable." He picked up the pill bottle and read the instructions and warning labels. "No alcohol."

"What about ibuprofen?"

"It doesn't say." He checked the facts on his phone. "No, that's fine. They don't interact."

"Good." I took one of the painkillers, so I wouldn't have to deal with the constant ache. Then Martin and I sat down for a romantic mid-afternoon meal. When we finished, I popped one of the sedatives, put on the sleep tracker, which looked like a defunct watch, and went upstairs to change for bed.

Martin had some work calls to make, but he brought in my tablet and propped the case on the bedside table so I could watch something from one of the streaming services. "I better not find you using this for work."

"Says the man with a list of calls to make."

He whispered some filthy promises in my ear of what he'd do once he was finished and disappeared out the door. Watching a movie didn't sound appealing. Truthfully, nothing appealed to me. I sunk into the pillow and stared up at the ceiling. A warmth slowly spread within me, and my muscles relaxed. Within an hour I was out, and I slept for the next sixteen.

8:53. I stared at the neon display, unsure if it was night or morning. Martin wasn't in bed, but he left a note on the pillow.

I love you. Take it easy today. Marcal's at your disposal. ~ JM

After stretching, I pulled the curtain away from the French doors. The morning sun shone brightly over the swimming pool. My head hurt from too much sleep or not enough sleep. It felt like a hangover but not as severe.

Finding my phone, I called the office to see if there had been any updates on the case. Since Andre hadn't phoned again, I'd stay the course and start surveilling Eve. I itched to hear from O'Connell, but I resisted the urge to call him for an update. He'd let me know once they made an arrest or if they needed my help. Hopefully, he'd gotten the hotel's complete guest list and was running down possible suspects and witnesses from the fourth floor. But that was no longer my problem, even if it continued to eat away at me. Instead, I focused on my other case.

According to Eve's planner, she'd be in the office until four today, so that gave me some time to exercise. I changed into a pair of leggings and an oversized t-shirt, put my hair into a sloppy bun, and grabbed a cup of coffee and a bottle of water before making my way to the ballet studio.

My ballet studio.

The coffee alleviated my headache, which might have been partially due to caffeine withdrawal. I started out on the reformer. It helped me stretch and strengthen while working everything from my arms and legs to my back and core. After a few reps in various positions, I slid off the machine.

I cycled through the exercises from the papers Cross's medic had given me and approached the barre. I did some pliés and variations on squats. Then I moved through a few of the positions. Halfway through my workout, the tremor returned, but I pushed on until my muscles completely gave out. I stretched again and crawled up the stairs, trying to figure out if ice or heat would be beneficial.

After a brief rest and shower, I changed into Cross-approved attire and went into the garage. Marcal was buffing one of Martin's sports cars.

"Going somewhere?" he asked. "Mr. Martin said to drive you wherever you need to go."

"I'm conducting surveillance. This is a solo mission. I'll be fine. Blame me. You can tell Martin I snuck past you."

Marcal didn't like it, but he knew better than to argue. "Please be careful, Ms. Parker."

"Always."

TWENTY-FIVE

Surveilling Eve wasn't as difficult as I imagined. Unlike me, she didn't lack focus. She stuck to her schedule with pinpoint accuracy. I knew every place she'd be and when she'd be there. It really took a lot of the guesswork out of my job. Of course, all this structure in her work life probably meant her home life was utterly unpredictable.

The first day, I tailed her from the office to a meeting at a venue. While she toured ballrooms and conference centers inside one of the hotels, I meandered from the hotel bar, to the lobby, to the restaurant in order to maintain eyes on her. She didn't disappear upstairs or lock herself into any room with a stranger, handsome or otherwise. At the end of the meeting, she signed a contract and waited at the valet stand for her car. From there, she made a few more stops before returning to Andre's.

Once they were settled for the night, I went to the office, checked the details I had, and went home. Despite sleeping more in one day than I had in the last week, I was even more exhausted. So I took another pill and went to bed.

This time, I didn't sleep sixteen hours, only eleven. I didn't bother working out. Eve had a pilates class, so I grabbed my gym bag and my membership card and waited for her to arrive. Since she spent the night at Andre's and this was her first stop the next morning, I didn't think she'd have time to rendezvous with anyone else. Given her punctual arrival, I decided my assumption was correct.

She entered the room and took a spot near the front. She had probably been a straight-A student. I'd been the same, but I wasn't the raise your hand to answer the question type. I preferred blending into the background. Eve wanted to stand out. Everything about her screamed it, from her neon pink leggings and sparkly black tank top to her perfectly applied makeup and stylish braid.

I scanned the surrounding area, wondering who she wanted to impress. Several men eyed her when she walked in. A few smiled when she glanced in their direction. Some even said good morning. They weren't bad looking. One of them added a few more plates to the bar while watching Eve in the mirror. She watched him perform a few squat lifts before turning to stretch on the other side.

Based on Andre's physical attributes, muscly men were right up her alley. I paid attention to see if anyone else caught her eye, but Eve had turned her entire focus to the instructor as she guided the class through some basic floor exercises to warm us up. I followed along while keeping an eye on the men working out on the nearby machines and lifting the free weights.

Forty-five minutes later, class ended. Eve spoke briefly to three other women, all brides-to-be, about their big days and how hard it was to stay in shape with so many showers and parties and tastings. I remained on the floor, stretching, while I waited for the chatter to die down. Once they left the room, I gathered my things and ventured out into the main gym area.

Two of the women had gone to the juice bar, carrying their own large thermoses filled with green sludge. The one with the pigtails pulled a binder out of her gym bag. It had lace around the edges. Weddings, ick. I shook off the horror and headed for the ellipticals.

Eve had gotten onto one of the treadmills, again near the front of the room. She picked the one directly beneath the television showing DIY decorating techniques. That probably counted as research for her business.

Ten minutes later, when my leg threatened to give out, I stepped off the elliptical and took a seat on one of the recumbent bikes. Instead of peddling, I pulled out my earphones and pretended to tinker with the controls. The weightlifter from earlier climbed onto the treadmill beside Eve. He smiled at her before turning the dial.

They ran side by side, racing, for the next five minutes. Eve spun the dial and stepped off the machine. She wiped her face on a towel. The man brought his machine to a stop and hopped off. He leaned against the railing.

I couldn't hear their conversation, but he looked friendly. Too friendly. From this angle, I couldn't see Eve's face, so I had no way of knowing if she was flirting back. Her body language remained neutral. Deciding it was too hard to tell what was going on from back here, I headed toward them.

Eve ran her hand against his bicep, giving it a little rub, before heading to the locker room. I lifted my phone, hit the camera, and snapped a shot of the guy before he had any idea what I was doing. Then I pretended to answer a call and followed Eve into the women's locker room.

While she showered, I changed into my street clothes. Other women came and went, but no man entered the locker room. I unbraided my hair, letting the brown waves cascade freely down my back. After Eve emerged from the shower stall, I pulled on my hooded sweatshirt, left the hood up to conceal my features, and knelt down to tie my shoe.

She dressed and primped in front of the mirror. When she was finished, she slung her gym bag over her shoulder. I stepped out of the locker room ahead of her and went to the juice bar. She emerged a few minutes later, stopping to speak to the two women from earlier. She oohed and ahhed over the photos in the binder.

"Where'd you get your linens?" Eve asked.

"From Gary." The lady with the binder flipped to the back. "Have you used him?"

"No, never." Eve examined his business card. "Do you mind?"

"Not at all."

Eve took out her phone and entered Gary the Linen Guy's information. "Thanks, Steff. Let me see what I can do. Vendors give me great discounts. I'm sure we can work something out."

"I hope so."

Eve bid them goodbye and left the gym. I caught sight of the guy she'd spoken to earlier. He was flexing in front of the mirror. I gave careful consideration to making an approach, but Eve was on the move. And Muscle Man didn't appear to be in any rush to leave. I'd catch up with him later.

After the gym, Eve picked up lunch for the office. Thankfully, she didn't go to the same place her assistant did. I left my hoodie in the car, put on a pair of oversized sunglasses, and waited for three other people to enter before I went into the café.

Eve sat at a table, tapping on her phone and furiously scribbling notes in her notepad. When I made it to the counter, I placed an order for a grilled chicken wrap and an Americana coffee with two pumps of white chocolate. The barista swirled some whipped cream on top and added chocolate sprinkles. I left a nice tip, which Andre would cover, and took my coffee to the nearest empty table to wait for my to-go order.

Eve didn't pay a bit of attention to me or anyone else. She kept her nose to the grindstone. When her order was ready, the server called out her number three times before spotting her and bringing her bag to the table. "Here you go, Eve," he said. "I threw in a few extra packets of salad dressing and that honey mustard you like."

"Thanks, Matt." She barely glanced in his direction. "Did you remember the extra napkins?"

"Yep." He turned and went back to the counter. Obviously, he was used to her by now.

She didn't grab the bag and head for the door. Instead, she continued to write notes in her book. Now I was getting curious. To write with that much vim and vigor, she could have been penning the next great novel. Then again, this was a coffee shop, so it would have to be a screenplay.

Instead, it looked like notes for work.

Ten minutes later, they called my number. I picked up my half empty coffee cup, grabbed my chicken wrap, and went outside to wait in my car. Wraps weren't the ideal food for a stakeout. I couldn't just shove it in my mouth if I suddenly had to engage in a high speed pursuit or I'd be covered in grilled chicken and melted cheese, but this wasn't that kind of assignment. Still, I didn't open the packaging. I waited.

A few minutes later, Eve left the café with her cell phone pressed to her ear. She carried the bag in one hand and her drink in the other. She made it to her car, put the cup on the roof, and unlocked the doors. After putting the bag inside, she tossed her purse in after it and reached up to grab her cup. She never let go of the phone, even as she put the car into gear and pulled into traffic. Didn't she know it was illegal to talk and drive?

I remained three car lengths behind her, but she didn't deviate from her path. She went straight to work. By then, her call had concluded. She carried the lunch bag in and put it on top of the big desk near the back corner.

While she and her assistants ate and worked, I sent the photo of Muscle Man to the techs at the office. Facial rec would get me an ID and address. I also gave Andre a call and asked what time Eve left his house this morning and when he expected to see her again. Then I settled back in the seat and ate my lunch.

After work, it was more of the same. I left Eve under Andre's watchful eye, deciding if she was with him I didn't need to worry where she was or if she was meeting other men, and went home.

This became the routine for the rest of the week. Eve never deviated from her schedule. Muscle Man turned out to be nobody special, just like Matt from the café. They were just people she interacted with on a regular basis. There was no heat, no clandestine meetings, and no trysts in hotel rooms with vendors or other contacts.

That meant this job would drag on. On the bright side, I came home every night, slept for ten hours, and made time for exercise, sometimes at Eve's gym, other times downstairs in my own ballet studio or sparring with Bruiser. My leg was getting stronger. I was doing better. I hadn't had any prolonged panic attacks or hallucinations either. I should have been relieved. Instead, I found myself thinking everything was just a little too perfect. I didn't like it.

This routine dragged on for days. Yet despite all the sleep I'd been getting, I found it exhausting. Or I was exhausted. I wasn't sure which. I suspected the pills had something to do with it. The only plus was they kept me from dreaming, which meant no nightmares. But I never felt rested.

Kellan was going to cover surveillance for me while I went to my doctor's appointment. He thought it had to do with my leg, and I didn't correct him. The last thing I wanted was to tell the office spy that I had to see the shrink again. Still, he came through when I needed him, which had been soon after he found me asleep in my office, screaming bloody murder. So he probably suspected the truth. He was familiar with don't ask, don't tell, and there was no reason not to apply that principle in this instance.

"I'll be back in time to pick up surveillance from the flower shop." I double-checked the schedule. "It's Wednesday. Eve has a meeting with her flower supplier at 2:15."

"Okay, I'll follow her from the office there. Once you arrive, I'll break off and get back to work. In the meantime, I'll see what I can dig up on her client." He nodded toward the window.

"Thanks."

I gave Elegant Events one final look. Eve was in the midst of a meeting. That should take up the next hour of her time. But just in case, Kellan would follow her if she left, especially if she left with her sexy new client.

I didn't know who he was. His name wasn't mentioned in her day planner or appointment books, which raised several red flags. Eve was meticulous. Leaving off a client's name didn't bode well.

With my mind preoccupied on the current development, I headed for the doctor's office. Since I was in a rush today and focused on my case, I didn't spend nearly as long fidgeting in front of the door. I went in before the tremor started. I'd just taken a seat when her office door opened and her previous patient stepped out.

TWENTY-SIX

"Lucca?" I swallowed the lump in my throat. "What are you doing here?"

He cocked an eyebrow at me. "You look like you've seen a ghost."

"Worse. You."

"Now that isn't very nice." He glanced back at the doctor who seemed far too amused by our interaction. "See what I mean?"

"Were you talking about me?" I didn't know why Lucca was here, but insane reasons came to mind.

"Relax. I'm just screwing with you, Parker." He folded the form Dr. Shelton handed him and put it in his breast pocket. "Thanks, Doc."

"Take care, Eddie," she said. "If you ever need to talk, just call."

"Will do."

She looked at me. "I'll be with you in a moment." The door to her office closed.

I glanced around the waiting room for surveillance cameras. Did she like to observe her patients in the wild? Did she plan this? This felt like a setup. Every instinct in my body said I should escape while I still could.

"What are you doing here?" Lucca asked.

"I asked you first."

He tapped his jacket. "Psych eval."

"She's not FBI."

"She's not active FBI, but she is FBI. It's my understanding Dr. Shelton's taking a hiatus, but since the regular OIO shrink is out, she's filling in. She has the security clearance and training. The director approved it."

"Oh." That would explain why Mark had her card and had been in contact with her recently.

"What are you doing here? You're not one to discuss feelings, and you're the farthest thing from an open book. Is this about one of your cases?"

"I'm crazy, remember? This is the kind of place crazy people go before the men with the butterfly nets take them away."

His brow furrowed. "That never seemed to mean much to you before. If anything, you thrived on the insanity. You wore it like a badge of honor."

"You're wrong."

"Am I? That's what made you a good agent. You take risks that no one else will. By definition, that's a little insane. It's also why you had problems following rules and staying out of trouble."

"Can't have that." I fought to keep my face and tone neutral. "After all, you're Mr. Rulebook. I hope your new partner's more of a stickler. You need someone who won't get you into trouble. It might tarnish the shine on your badge."

He held up his palms in surrender. "I'm not trying to bust your balls, Parker. I'm grateful. So is Jablonsky. Don't ever doubt that."

"That craziness, as you call it, that recklessness, that's what's gotten so many good agents killed." I looked away. "I don't want to talk about it, Eddie. I'm here because things need to change. You told me that, remember?"

"That was before."

"Maybe if I'd listened, this wouldn't be our after."

"You're seriously here to get your head examined? I never thought I'd see the day." He reached out to touch me, but I shrugged away. "Whatever's going on with you, I'm around. All right? I'm not saying you don't need to get help. Help's good. This is good. You should be here. If anything, you might need a few dozen experts and some electroshock therapy to get your head on straight."

"Whatever you say."

"Call me if there's anything I can do, okay? I'm serious."

"I'm good."

"Call me anyway. You still owe me dinner."

"Where do you want to go? I'll send you a gift card."

He rolled his eyes. "Take it easy."

"You too." I watched him leave. If this was his psych eval, that meant he was ready to return to active duty. No more working behind a desk. He either passed the physical or was on his way to take the physical. Either way, I didn't like it. It was too soon.

"Alex?" The doctor stood in the opened doorway. "Are you ready?"

"No." But I strode into her office anyway. Lucca would have sat in the straight-back chair. I touched the seat to see if it was warm, which it was, before sitting on the couch.

The doctor sat where she did the first time we met, and I handed her the sleep tracker she'd given me. "I'm sorry my previous appointment ran late," she said.

"Are you?"

"You think I set this up?"

"Eddie Lucca was my partner." I watched her, but her expression didn't change. "But you already know that. He also said you're still FBI. That's not what you said the last time I was here."

"I'm no longer with the FBI."

"So why are you performing mandatory psych evals?"

"Director Kendall asked if I'd do it."

"Uh-huh, so that's why Lucca was here and why he happened to be here right before I showed up."

"We weren't discussing you," she said.

"Sure, you were. You had to talk to him about the incident. I was part of it. I came up."

"Yes, but that was the extent of it."

"Even if it wasn't, you told me last time you don't

discuss clients or what goes on in these sessions. You can't tell me what you discussed. That's against doctor-patient confidentiality, or do you not take that seriously?"

"Alex, I'm a former FBI psychiatrist. This is my job. I take all of it seriously."

"You keep saying former, but Lucca said this is a hiatus. Which is it, Doc?"

"I'm not sure. I turned in my resignation, but the director convinced me to take a break before making any rash decisions."

"A lot of that going around."

She met my eyes. "I did not intentionally arrange for this to happen. You were early. My appointment ran late. It was bad timing. I assure you this wasn't planned, nor were you the topic of discussion in my last session. Regardless of what Agent Lucca might have implied."

"I'm sure I wasn't. I know Lucca. He said that to mess with me because he knew it would mess with me. He likes to freak me out." A flash of Lucca bleeding came to mind, but I dismissed it. "The problem is I don't know you or what kind of mind games you like to play. Perhaps this is how you get your kicks. I don't know what I'm supposed to believe."

"This was a coincidence."

"Fine. Let's just get this over with."

She took the tracker to the computer and downloaded the details. "How have you been feeling?"

"Tired."

"Have you been sleeping?"

"More than I have in the last few months combined."

Her expression remained neutral as she read the data on the screen. "Have you had any more panic attacks?"

"No, but coming here nearly triggered one."

She didn't like my tone. "You don't trust me."

"Why should I? Trust is earned."

"That may be, but it's an integral part of therapy. If you don't trust me, you won't be open to my help." She finished making a note of the readout and returned to the chair. "You came here last week because you recognized you had a problem. You wanted me to help you with it."

"Are the pills the reason I'm so tired?" I asked.

"Possibly. I want to wean you off of them."

"It's only been a week. I'm not sure weaning is necessary."

"Humor me." She met my eyes. "I know what I'm doing."

"Uh-huh." That was the problem.

"Okay. Good." She smiled. "Try cutting back to one every other day. The nightmares might return, but now that you're getting more rest, you should be able to handle the added stress." She crossed her legs and settled deeper into the chair. "Do these nightmares have a reoccurring theme?"

"Death."

"Yours?"

"No, mine doesn't keep me awake at night."

"Really? That thought would keep most people awake at night."

Wrong answer, the voice in my head said. I shouldn't have said that. "That's not what my nightmares are about," I clarified.

"Go on."

"I dream about the incident. The attack on Jablonsky and Lucca. And Cooper's murder."

"Were you at the crime scene?"

"Which one?"

"Any of them."

"I was at all of them." I blinked. I didn't trust her, but I wanted to get this over with. The sooner I did, the sooner I could leave. Then I'd never have to set foot in here again. "That's what I think about. That's what I've been hallucinating. Bits and pieces from those scenes. Like the bloody sheets or victims getting stabbed or their throats slashed."

"Can you tell what's real and what isn't?"

"I could until the night before I came here." Unless that hadn't been a hallucination. *Don't go down that rabbit hole,* my inner voice warned.

"Have you had any more of these disturbing occurrences this week?"

"No flashes or hallucinations until I saw Lucca."

"What did seeing him bring to mind?"

"Questions."

"What kinds of questions?" She leaned forward, as if I was on the verge of a breakthrough.

"Like how you might want to see what his appearance would do to my demeanor and what kinds of things it might trigger." I climbed out of the chair before she could tell me that was paranoia. "I think we're done for today."

"Time's not up yet."

"That wasn't a denial."

"Alex, please. I already told you that was unintentional, but now that it's happened, I'm curious as to the effect his presence has on you."

"Relief. Fear. Guilt. Agony. Pick one." I strode to the door. "I'll see myself out."

"You forgot the—"

But I slammed the door before she could finish her statement.

I don't know why I thought this was a good idea. Even Lucca thought the idea was ludicrous. Lack of sleep must have impaired my judgment. At least the doc had been right about one thing. As long as I got enough sleep, I'd be fine.

Fuming, I drove to Elegant Events. Eve remained inside with the man from earlier. He was seated at a table while she showed him her portfolio. Kellan got out of his car and sat in mine.

"You're back early," he said.

"Yep."

"Is everything okay?"

"Fabulous."

He pointed toward a parked car. "That's his car. While I was waiting, I ran the plates. His name's Colton Raine. He's a former Formula One race car driver. He now does stunt driving."

"That's a career?"

"Yep."

"Cool." I studied the Lotus. "Do you think Eve's hoping to go for a ride?"

"If she's not, I am." Kellan snickered. "Oh, you meant the car." He hoped that would get a smile out of me, but it didn't. "How fast do you think it goes?"

"It probably tops out near 200."

"You're into cars?"

"Only the sexy ones." Martin had one in the garage, but I didn't volunteer that piece of information. "Let's hope she doesn't go for a ride. We'd never be able to catch them if he's driving."

"That's why I have his home address. I'll text you a copy."

"Thanks. Anything else I should know?"

"That's all I managed to get. You weren't gone that long."

"I appreciate it." My phone dinged, and I checked the details of the forwarded text. "He's not married."

"Nope." Kellan opened the door. "A man who drives a car like that is trouble."

"Our boss drives a car like that."

"Yep." Kellan gave me a sly grin over his shoulder and returned to his car. He was right. Only two types of men drove cars like that. The ones who were compensating, and the ones who wanted to make a statement that they could have whatever they wanted. Martin and Cross fell into the second category, and so did Colton Raine.

TWENTY-SEVEN

Colton left at 1:45. He was punctual, just like Eve. I watched the white sports car drive away.

Eve remained inside. She put away the portfolios, spoke to her assistants, and made a few more calls while working on the computer. At 2:03, she got into her car. I followed her to the florist.

The shop stood in the middle of a row of upscale boutiques. Every meter on either side of the street was full, so I kept going. The narrow lanes wouldn't allow me to double-park, and trying that would undoubtedly draw her attention. So I parked in the nearest garage and hoofed it back to the flower shop. Unfortunately, the shop's windows were blocked by arrangements, so I went inside.

The bell above the door chimed, alerting everyone to my presence. I just had to hope Eve hadn't bothered to look up, and even if she did, she might not recognize me. I'd been doing my best to alter my appearance between the gym and the other locations where I'd followed her. Today, I wore my hair in a loose ponytail with two brown locks hanging down to frame my face. This was a new look on me she hadn't seen, but since I didn't spot her, I probably didn't have any reason to worry.

Ten other people were in the store, so I maneuvered around them and examined the bouquets in the coolers while searching for my quarry. Eve had to be here. I saw her come inside, so where was she? I started on one end of the store, listening carefully for her husky voice or signature laugh.

Near the back, I heard her, but I didn't see her. I looked around, spotting plastic flaps hanging in front of an open doorway. It was marked "staff only".

From the bits and pieces of conversation I could make out, it sounded like she was in the midst of a discussion about daisies and sunflowers. Neither were high-end enough for Elegant Events or Eve's personal taste. So what was she doing back there?

While I waited, I examined the various colors of water beads.

"May I help you?" a man asked. He wore an olive green apron with the name of the flower shop stenciled on the front pouch.

"I'm just browsing."

"Shopping for yourself or someone special?"

"My boyfriend."

He smiled. "Not a lot of women come in here to shop for the man in their lives. That's refreshing. Is it a special occasion? Birthday? Anniversary?"

"It's Wednesday."

He beamed. "Even better. What type of flower does he like?"

Although I'd been making this up as I went, I didn't actually know the answer to that question. Martin must like flowers. He'd given me plenty of them in the past. What was in the silk bouquet? I couldn't remember. It was purple and white and pretty, but he might have chosen those for the colors. "I'm not sure."

"That's not a problem. What's your favorite flower?"

"Something without a lot of pollen or a strong scent."

"You must really love him to brave stepping foot in this store."

"I guess." I kept an eye on the plastic flaps, straining to hear Eve's voice, but she spoke too quietly for me to make out the words. On the bright side, I didn't hear any banging around or cries of ecstasy, so she probably wasn't doing the nasty in the back room with an unknown stranger. However, if that changed, I had my camera phone at the ready. I'd dash in, snap a photo, and run out of the store. It was nice to have a plan.

"Does he have a favorite color?"

I spotted a display case of orchids close to the plastic flaps blocking the doorway. "What can you tell me about orchids? Are they difficult to maintain?"

"Not really. You can even use the water beads if you like." Another employee called to him from the register. "I'll let you browse. Let me know if you have any questions. I'm Ken."

"Thanks, Ken." But I'd rather speak to Event Planner Barbie, except she was hidden in the "staff only" part of the store.

With Ken distracted, I moved closer to the flaps, practically pressing myself against them as I examined the display case from the side.

"We'll need two dozen of the smaller ones for the bridesmaid's bouquets and the white roses dipped in gold for the boutonnieres," Eve said.

"A dozen?"

"Let's go with eighteen just to be on the safe side."

"Not a problem. Anything else?"

"That's it for the Leachman wedding." Eve stepped through the plastic flaps, nearly colliding with me. Luckily, I saw her coming and ducked down, opening the cooler door to examine a purple orchid near the bottom of the case. "Excuse me," she said to my back. "I almost stepped on you."

I leaned into the display case. "That's okay." But I didn't need to waste my breath because she had gone back to her conversation with the flower shop manager.

"How's it looking on the Morning Glories?" she asked.

"They should be in stock in time for the Bateman's reception."

"Excellent." Eve went to the counter.

"Have you decided on your flowers yet?" the manager

asked. "Your big day is nearly here."

"Ugh, don't remind me."

That made me pause. I grabbed a blue orchid and some beautiful green water beads from the shelf and headed toward the counter, so I could hear the rest of the conversation.

The manager laughed. "Don't tell me you're getting cold feet."

"No, Andre's wonderful." But her tone didn't sound nearly as convincing as her words. "I'm just overwhelmed. I do this for a living, so planning my own special day shouldn't be a problem."

"Maybe you should hire someone."

"Oh, that'd go over great on the gossip sites. Plus, we're a little over three weeks out. There isn't time."

"What are you doing for your wedding?"

"Something low-key and private. I picked up my dress the last time I was in Paris. Andre's been fitted for his tux. We have the venue and menu locked down. It's just the linens and the lighting and the centerpieces."

"You mean all the tiny details you specialize in?" The manager commandeered the register from Ken and entered the information on Eve's orders. Eve handed over her corporate card and signed the receipt. "Just let me know what you decide. You're my best customer. I'll get you whatever you want with plenty of time to spare."

"Thank you. I'll bring Andre in on Saturday, and we'll figure it out." Eve pulled the binder out of her extra large purse, flipped to the proper tab, and taped the receipt inside. "We'll probably do something classic. Roses or peonies. I'll have to consult my portfolio. The Toumlinson's had amazing flowers. I don't remember what went into the arrangements though."

"Give me a sec. I'll look it up for you."

While Eve waited, I put my items on the counter. Ken smiled at me. "Good choice. The Exotic Blue Phalaenopsis orchid is sure to brighten anyone's day. I like the green water beads with it. Very masculine. I'm sure he'll love it." Ken looked straight at me. "Hey, what do you know? The blue almost matches your eyes."

"Do you deliver?" I asked.

"Yep."

"Great." I eyed the decorative vases behind him while keeping an eye on Eve. "Which one would you recommend for the office?"

Ken pulled three choices from the back counter and placed them in front of me. "Any of these will do. If you want the green to stand out, I'd go with this one."

"I'll take it."

I filled out the card while he refreshed the beads with fertilized water, placed them in the bottom of the vase, put the orchid on top, and added the rest of the beads to hold it in place like shimmering green soil.

I slipped the card into the envelope, scribbled *James* on the outside, and wrote the delivery address and instructions on the form. I handed Ken my credit card just as the manager found the Toumlinson's flower order.

"They did white and pink," the manager said.

"Yes, but the reception was in their garden, so the place was brimming with all kinds of flowers and lots of colors." Eve edged around to the side of the counter to see the order form. "All right, order some calla lilies for me. No matter what we decide, I'll want those."

"Yes, ma'am." The manager smiled proudly. "I'm not sure if anyone's told you this yet, but you're going to make a beautiful bride."

"I hope so." Eve said her goodbyes and left the shop.

I took my receipt, thanked Ken, and followed after her. Eve remained inside her car, tapping away at her phone. By the time I pulled out of the garage and circled back around, she had left. "Dammit." I stopped at the first intersection and looked in every direction. Starting tomorrow, I'd put a GPS tracker on her car. However, that wouldn't solve my current problem.

Unsure where she'd gone, I returned to Elegant Events, but she wasn't there. Eve had another meeting in forty-five minutes, so she'd have to show up. I just wondered what she was doing or who she was doing in the meantime.

TWENTY-EIGHT

When Eve didn't arrive for her meeting, I called Cross Security and had one of the techs ping her phone. Eve had gone home. That didn't make any sense. This woman was on the ball. She never missed meetings or appointments. She was punctual to the point where she had bathroom breaks penciled into her schedule.

None of the women in Elegant Events appeared frazzled or concerned when the boss didn't show up. Did she call to say she wouldn't be in? Throwing caution to the wind, I squared my shoulders and entered the shop. Samantha recognized me almost immediately.

"Hi, how are you?" she asked. "I hope you've been avoiding clutzes carrying smoothies."

"Only the ones not wearing couture." Drinking in the room, I toyed with the engagement ring hanging from the chain around my neck. It didn't hurt to imply I was here on important bridal business. "Is Eve in?"

"No, I'm sorry. She keeps a busy schedule. Would you like to make an appointment?"

"I checked out your website and the photos online. I just wanted to get some information. Do you have any portfolios or price lists I could see?"

"Sure." Samantha went to the shelf and pulled out a four-inch binder. "Have you figured out the type of venue you want for your big day?"

"Not yet. I just wanted to get an estimate of what this could cost."

"So many factors go into it." Samantha looked uncomfortable. "We've done events for as little as ten grand, and others were well into six figures. Weddings tend to run a little higher because everything has to be perfect. How much were you looking to spend?"

"Money's not really an issue. Figuring out what we want is the problem."

"How can I help?"

"I'm not sure you can. We're having a clash of opinions. I want something small and intimate, just us and a few close family and friends. But the last time we discussed this, he made it sound like he wanted something worthy of *Page Six*."

"Eve could help you with either or a combination of the two."

"But she's not here?" I made a show of looking around. "I don't want to waste her time with an official meeting or appointment unless I can convince him to come with me. I just hoped to pop in and ask her a few questions. Will she be back later today?"

"I'm afraid not," Samantha said. "Let me check her schedule. She might have a few minutes to spare Friday afternoon." Samantha went to the computer and clicked the mouse. "Friday at 4:10. Can I pencil you in?"

"Friday doesn't work for me, but I'll call on Monday to get something official scheduled."

"That sounds great." Samantha handed me a business card. "If you have any questions, you can e-mail me directly. I'm not Eve, but I can help." She pointed to her contact info.

"Wonderful. I'll be in touch soon."

Eve was supposed to work until seven. This was the first time since I started tailing her that she deviated from her schedule. I had to find out why.

When I arrived at her apartment, the neighborhood was

quiet. Most people were still at work, so rush hour hadn't started. The lull gave me a chance to snoop around, but I already knew the building's layout. I couldn't exactly break in. Instead, I counted the windows until I found Eve's. Her blinds were open, but she was too far up for me to see inside.

However, I'd prepared for this possibility. The building across the street had a fire escape, and even though it was broad daylight, I decided to risk it. Grabbing my camera bag, I entered the alley, jumped up to pull down the ladder, and climbed up the stairs. Once I was high enough to get a look into Eve's apartment, I used the camera to zoom in.

The flowers on her table were now a brown, wilted mess, but she had yet to dispose of them. Since the flowers blocked my view of her living room, I pointed the camera at another one of her windows. Nope, she wasn't in the kitchen. I shifted to the corner window.

Seated on the end of the sofa with his arm spread out over the back and a drink in his other hand was Colton Raine. I knew the man was trouble. His car was just a warning sign.

I snapped a photo, even though Eve wasn't in the shot, and scanned the street beneath me, but I didn't spot the Lotus. Ten minutes later, Eve stepped into view. She had changed from her smart grey dress to leather pants and a glittery gold halter top that tied around her midriff, exposing her naval ring and tanned skin. Her hair looked even better than before, with soft ringlets falling in all directions.

Frantically, I clicked away. Colton put the glass on the coffee table, took her hands in his, and held her at arms' length. With a sexy grin, he released one of her hands and spun her around for the full effect. She giggled, falling into his chest. He winked at her, releasing her hand once she regained her balance.

As soon as they were out of frame, I tucked the camera into the bag and hurried down the fire escape. Thankfully, my leg didn't cramp. I made it to the bottom just as they passed me on the opposite side of the street. I jogged to my car, turning to make sure I didn't lose sight of them.

I waited to see where they were going, but they didn't stop. Instead, they turned at the intersection. Putting my car into gear, I backed out of the space, nearly taking off the nose of the car behind me in my haste. I zoomed around a slow moving hybrid and took the turn a little too fast, clipping my side mirror on the walk sign.

Colton and Eve climbed into the back of a waiting limo. I closed the space between us, memorized the plate number, and backed off, allowing several other cars to get in front of me. I didn't know where we were going, but things didn't bode well for Andre and Eve's upcoming nuptials.

The limo pulled to a stop in front of Spark, one of the city's most exclusive members only nightclubs. Colton stepped out of the back, offering a hand to Eve. This wasn't good. She let him help her out of the car, her shiny spike heels catching the light.

It was still early, just barely five. Was the club even open yet? I would have thought this was nothing more than a meeting to check out a venue, but the chauffeured car and Eve's costume change made me question everything. It looked like a date, so I'd treat it like one.

The bouncer nodded to Colton and held open the door. Now what was I supposed to do? Reaching for the phone, I called Cross.

"Eve's with a man. They went into Spark," I said.

"Does James have a membership?" Cross asked.

"If he did, I wouldn't call you."

"Fine, I'm on my way. Stay put and don't make a scene."

While I waited, I got out of the car and tried to fix the side mirror, which now hung at an odd angle. Cross wouldn't be pleased I'd damaged the company car, but I didn't have time to take it to an autobody shop or find a store that sold duct tape in the exact same shade of silver as the sedan. Deciding the mirror was the least of my worries, I sat behind the wheel and waited.

Spark didn't have any windows, at least none allowed me to see in, so I had no idea what Colton and Eve were doing. For ten minutes, no one else approached the club. Eventually, a silver-haired gentleman and his college-aged girlfriend roared down the street in a cherry red convertible. It screeched to a halt in the alley beside the club. They stepped out and went to the door.

The doorman, who looked more like a linebacker, checked something, glanced up at the surveillance camera posted above him, and let the couple enter. *Tight security,* I thought. Getting inside would not be easy, unless they had an application form at the window. For all I knew, it could be like getting a loyalty card at the grocery store, but I doubted it'd be that easy.

A few minutes later, a familiar Porsche slid into the empty space in front of me. With a garment bag in hand, Cross climbed out of the car and met me on the sidewalk. He thrust the bag into my arms. "Put this on."

"What? Why?"

"Spark has a dress code." He eyed my outfit. "Didn't we have a discussion last week about how I expect you to dress more professionally at work?"

"This is professional."

"Then I'll need to get you a dictionary. One with plenty of pictures."

I narrowed my eyes at him and unzipped the bag. "Where'd you get this? Off your bedroom floor?"

"Shut up and get changed."

"Into what?" I held the hanger up higher. "This is a napkin with straps."

"That's the top. Beneath it is a skirt. I had to guess on the size." He looked down at my feet.

"I can't wear heels."

He didn't like that answer, but there wasn't much he could do about it. "How long have they been inside?"

"Twenty-two minutes." I opened the back door, leaned in, and unbuttoned my shirt. I shrugged out of it and slipped the shimmering white square of fabric over my head. The top strap tied behind my neck. "What kind of club is Spark? I've heard rumors that it's gambling or gaming. What is it really? Strippers? Sex?" Thoughts of O'Connell's case came to mind. I hadn't heard from him in over a week. I wondered if he'd identified the killer yet.

"They host a poker game in the back every other

weekend and some other events on and off the premises. It's private. That's all you need to know." Lucien knotted the bottom strap on my top and gave it a tug.

"Isn't that illegal? Does the owner have a license or some kind of arrangement with the gaming commission?"

"Don't worry about it." Cross took a step back and tucked his hands into his pockets. "Lose the bra."

"Since you're so fond of dictionaries, you should look up the term sexual harassment." I glanced down, making sure the tiny white square covered my chest before unhooking the clasp on my bra and sliding one arm out before pulling it free from the other side. "Happy?"

"What about the skirt?"

"I'm not wearing it."

"Alex, Spark has certain expectations. You don't want to stick out."

"I will if I put that on and it falls to my ankles when I walk in." I gave him a withering stare. "Do you want me to tell you precisely what you can do with that skirt?"

He cleared his throat. "Fine, it wouldn't have gone with your shoes anyway. At least you're moderately presentable." He gestured toward my face. "Is this how you go out? Can't you do something about that?"

"What's with the costume change, Lucien? You better tell me what your plan is or I'm gonna start to think you want to pretty me up just to sell me into the skin trade."

He muttered something under his breath. "I'm trying to get you into the club, but that won't happen unless you look like you're out for a night on the town. George won't take kindly to the presence of another private eye. One of the stipulations of my membership is I don't spy on the other members. But you can. They just don't need to know you work for me, so you need to look like my date, not my employee."

"Private contractor."

"Do you think George will quibble over that distinction?"

"Who the hell's George?"

"The doorman."

"You're on a first name basis with the doorman? How

often do you come here?"

Cross looked like he wanted to strangle me. "Often enough. I'm a member."

I would have just called him a dick, but I didn't see any reason to quibble over that distinction either. "So why can't you go inside and find out what's going on? Eve Wyndham is in there with a famous race car driver. A swoon-worthy, accented man with sexy clothes and a sexy car. They looked comfy in her apartment. If you get one good snapshot, we can be done with this, and I won't have to parade around in a handkerchief."

"You think she's cheating on Andre?"

"I'm not sure, but Colton seems interested."

He cleared his throat, fighting to keep his temper in check. "It's against the rules."

"Since when do you play by anyone's rules but your own?"

"I could ask you the same thing." He glowered at me. "Please, Ms. Parker, we are wasting precious time."

"Fine." I got into the front seat and flipped down the vanity. I rummaged through my bag for the makeup I had stashed in there.

Cross drummed his fingers against the hood of the car while I applied the makeup. "Do you have anything concrete to base this assumption that Eve and Colton are an item?"

"She canceled the rest of her day, met him at her place, changed into something sexy, and came here. Isn't that enough?"

"Andre North wouldn't think so, and I promised him we'd be sure before we presented anything to him." He stopped tapping. "I don't see Colton Raine's car."

"He didn't drive here. He hired a limo."

"At least he's not competing for pink slips tonight."

"What?"

"Nothing for you to concern yourself with." Cross shook the thought away.

I tucked the makeup back in my bag and flipped up the mirror. "I'm carrying. Is that a problem?"

"Spark doesn't have metal detectors."

"Good." I zipped my nine millimeter into my purse and tugged the ponytail holder out of my hair. The soft brown strands tickled my naked shoulders and back. "Now what?"

"Let me do the talking." Cross offered me his arm, scowling at the side mirror as we crossed the street and went down the sidewalk toward the club.

The doorman looked up from his spot. "Lucien, I didn't expect to see you tonight, especially this early."

"Is Mr. Kincaid in?" Cross asked.

"No, he's preparing for the weekend."

"At the club?"

"No." George eyed me. "Who's this?"

"Alex, she's my plus one tonight."

George took a paper wristband off his clipboard and waited for me to hold out my arm. At least it was better than those stamps that only glow under blacklight and were a pain in the ass to wash off. He hooked it around my wrist. "It's not like you to show up on a Wednesday. Poker's usually on the weekends."

"I know, but we wanted to get a drink somewhere private to talk. I'm sure Mr. Kincaid won't mind if we discuss business in his club."

"Not at all."

Cross peered through the door. "Is there anything I should know about the Wednesday night crowd?"

George chuckled. "It's the same as your usual nights, except nothing's going on in the back room."

"That's probably why I don't come on Wednesdays." Lucien pressed his hand against my spine, urging me through the door.

I stepped past George and entered the club. It didn't look that different from any of the other fancy clubs I'd been to. The bar stood out, large and curving on three sides. Recessed lights in various colors illuminated different parts of the dark, glossy hardwood, casting it in cool hues. A large dance floor took up half of the lower level with elevated areas behind it with tables and private booths. A DJ stood on a fancy platform, but the music wasn't a hyper techno beat. And no one was dancing, except the women in the cages.

"Do they strip?" I asked.

"It's not that kind of club." Lucien led me to the bar and ordered a drink.

"And for the lady?" the bartender asked.

"Club soda and lime."

Cross cocked an eyebrow at me. His forearms rested against the bar while I leaned back against it, studying the tables and VIP section for any hint as to where Eve and Colton had disappeared. The room branched off in different directions. A staircase on the side led somewhere, which I was sure wasn't good.

"Drinking on the job in most professions is frowned upon, but in this one, it might be necessary for blending in." Cross handed me a glass. "Are you sure you wouldn't prefer a cocktail?"

"I can't." It wouldn't mix with the sleeping pills. The bartender put Cross's scotch down on the counter. My boss paid and left a twenty in the tip jar. "What's in that direction?" I asked, looking past Cross's shoulder where the main room branched off into a narrow hallway that took a sharp turn around the wall and behind the DJ's stage.

"Tables, chairs, private rooms. The manager's office. Things like that."

"How private? What exactly goes on here?"

"Gambling, mostly."

"What about parties or events? The doorman said something about an event." Before Cross could answer, I spotted Eve and Colton. They were seated beyond the velvet ropes in the VIP section. They had a private booth, concealed on two sides by heavy velvet drapes, but the front remained open so they could watch the dancers or DJ. "There she is."

A third man maneuvered around the curtain, stepping out of their private booth. He wore a suit but had lost the jacket and tie. His sleeves were rolled up to his forearms, and his collar was open. I wasn't sure who this mystery man was, but he looked a little dangerous.

"That's Fox. He's the manager," Cross said, reading my mind. "Stay here. I need a minute." He picked up his drink and headed straight for them. Cross caught up to Fox the moment the man cleared the velvet ropes. He spoke to the manager, holding a smile that I could only assume was phony, and gestured toward me. The suited man said something to one of the bouncers guarding the VIP area, and then Cross waved me over.

By the time I crossed the empty dance floor and made my way through the tables and up the few steps to the private area, Fox was gone. The bouncer unhooked the velvet rope, and Cross led me into the VIP area. He didn't clue me in as to what was going on, and I didn't ask.

We were led to our own private booth, diagonal from where Eve and Colton sat. A waitress appeared a moment later with a bottle of whatever Cross was drinking and placed it on the table beside us. Then she asked if we wanted our privacy.

"It's quiet enough. Leave it open," Cross said.

"Yes, sir." She smiled and headed to another table.

A few moments later, Eve laughed. "That's her," I whispered. "And that sounds like more than business, if you ask me."

"Shh." Cross held his finger to his lips and pressed the voice recorder on his phone. He shifted closer to the side so he could hear them better.

"You're so bad," Eve said in a teasing tone.

"You love it," Colton replied. "Admit it. You have more fun with me than anyone else."

She laughed. "Fine. You've got me. You're my favorite."

"Then why won't you run away with me, darling?"

TWENTY-NINE

"Run away with you?" Eve laughed. "What would Andre say?"

"Who cares?" Colton asked. I couldn't see them through the velvet curtains, but I imagined him running his fingers through her hair. "Have you seen my car? It's not like your fiancé would ever catch us."

"You sound so sure of yourself. Are you this sure about everything?"

"Absolutely."

"So this is what you want?" Eve asked. "You want to do it right here?"

"Damn straight." Colton laughed. "What? This isn't classy enough for you?"

"No, it's perfect. The space is great, and the manager said you could rent out the club for the entire weekend. That'll give us time to prep and get everything moved in before your launch party. We can even hold the luncheon and press conference here."

Cross tucked his phone into his pocket and picked up the bottle and his glass. "Stay here."

I pulled the velvet curtain back as far as it would go, but I could barely glimpse the cuff of Eve's leather pants and sparkly left heel. Cross went around the long way, stopping just outside their private booth.

"Excuse me," he said, "I ordered this for the table, but my friends had other ideas. I'm about to take off but didn't want it to go to waste. Any interest?" He held up the bottle.

"Sure," Colton said.

Cross took a step into their booth. "Aren't you Colton Raine, the F1 driver? I saw you race in Bahrain two years ago. You were amazing."

"I'm retired now, but I can't exactly give up racing altogether, now can I?" Colton winked at Eve. "Why don't you join us for a drink."

"I really should go," Cross said.

"You're giving us the bottle, at least have a sip, mister…" Colton waited.

"Lucien Cross. I own Cross Security. Have you heard of it?" My boss disappeared behind the curtain, and I cursed. That bastard had taken over surveillance and blew our cover all at the same time. What was he thinking? He couldn't possibly be trying to sign Colton Raine while spying on Andre North's fiancée. That would be preposterous, and yet, that appeared to be precisely what he was doing. Son of a bitch.

"Bahrain?" Eve asked. "I just returned from Dubai. I took a side trip to Sakhir, but I didn't see the racetrack. When did you say you were there?"

"Two years ago," Cross said. "Wasn't that your last race, Mr. Raine?"

"It was. I think that means I'm ready to start a new adventure. Right, Eve?"

She leaned over, peering through the privacy curtains. I ducked back behind my curtain, hoping she hadn't noticed me, but she was looking for someone else. "I promise I'll get you off to a wonderful start. This weekend will be epic. The press will eat it up, Colton."

"Eat what up?" Cross asked.

"Sorry, Lucien. It's a secret," Colton said, "but if you're not busy Friday, you should stop by. I'm having a party here. Fans are always welcome. Eve, can we get Lucien put on the guest list?"

"Whatever you want." She stepped out from behind the curtains. "Didn't Mr. Fox say he'd be back with the contracts?"

"That sounds like my cue to leave." Cross got up. "Enjoy the scotch. It sounds like you two have something to celebrate."

"Friday at ten," Colton said. "Don't forget."

"I won't." Cross left the liquor with them and returned to our booth. "Did you hear that?"

"Yep. Colton's planning a party, and you introduced yourself as a private eye."

"CEO of a security firm," Cross corrected. "I saw no reason to lie. That would make me look suspicious."

"Why didn't you just tell them Andre hired you?"

"You asked for my help, Alex. I know what I'm doing." He looked at his watch. "I got you this far. Don't screw it up."

"Where are you going?"

"I have other commitments. Stay on them and see where the night leads. Colton hired her for a job, but he's an athlete of sorts. He's used to getting anything he wants. You're right. Colton is flirting with her, but it might be harmless. Maybe he's just being friendly. I can't tell how interested he actually is in her. After he gets a few more drinks in him, it'll be easier to determine." He glanced up just as Fox returned to the VIP section with a leather portfolio. The club manager went straight to Colton's booth. "I spoke to him." Cross stood in front of me to get my attention. "Fox won't kick you out, even though it's against club policy to allow a guest to remain without the member who brought her. I told him you're a client with an issue, and you needed some privacy. I also implied you're thinking of joining. He knows the types of clientele Cross Security caters to. He didn't question it, but if someone asks you something, play along. When you're done for the night, leave the company car in the garage so I can have someone fix the mirror. Report your findings to me in the morning."

"Yes, sir."

"And dress appropriately."

"Sure thing, boss." The annoyance dripped from my words, but Cross ignored it and left me alone in the VIP section. Hopefully, he'd paid for the bottle service.

While I listened to Colton, Eve, and Fox go over the cost and what was included, I scoped out the rest of the club. A few business types had staggered in and were now at one of the tables near the cages. It was too early in the evening for people to want to party or dance. From what I could tell, the majority of the people who'd come to the club this early were in the midst of business negotiations. The only oddballs were the couple I'd seen arrive in the red convertible, who were drinking and laughing.

"What time can I get started on Friday?" Eve asked. The question jilted me from my reverie.

"You can start as early as seven a.m., if you'd like. The cleaning crew will be finished by then." Fox consulted the chart. "Someone will be here to let you in."

"That's perfect," Eve said. They finished going over the details. "All right, I should get going. I have a lot to get done in the next day and a half."

"Come on," Colton said, "it's early. Just one more drink."

"I can't. I'm sorry." She leaned in and gave him a peck on the cheek. "You hired me to make your launch perfect. I have to plan the party and press luncheon in the next two days. I'll be lucky if I find time to sleep."

"You're the best, Eve. Take the car. I'm going to hang around here and soak up the ambiance and finish this scotch." Colton topped off his glass.

"Thanks. Have fun." She grabbed her purse and excused herself while the two men remained in the booth.

I followed her out of the club and back to Elegant Events.

Settling into the driver's seat, I watched as Eve bustled around the office. From what I'd gathered, Colton Raine had hired Eve to throw a party and luncheon to announce his next venture. For whatever the reason, he wanted to have the party at Spark. This afternoon's meeting cemented the details. I just didn't know why Eve had to dress like that or why she canceled the rest of her schedule to appease one client.

While Eve worked, I researched Colton. He partied often and never appeared with the same woman twice. I couldn't figure out when he and Eve had crossed paths, but from their interactions, I had trouble believing they only met for the first time this morning. No matter how hard I tried, I couldn't find the connection. Perhaps Andre knew Colton.

Forty minutes later, I traced Colton's French riviera vacation home to Andre's company. Letting out a tired sigh, I reclined my seat and turned on my side to maintain eyes on Eve. Despite the flirting, Colton knew about Eve and Andre. I didn't find any photos of the three together or Colton with either of them. Since Colton knew Andre and wasn't wining and dining Eve, I had to assume that meant they weren't having an affair. That marked another possibility off the list.

The hours dragged on, and I fought to keep my eyes open. Shouldn't these stupid pills be out of my system by now? I adjusted my seat again and fiddled with the radio. I hated surveillance.

Around ten, a town car pulled up in front of Elegant Events. With the tinted rear windows, I couldn't tell if anyone was inside, but no one got out. Eve locked up the office and slid into the back. I readjusted my seat and slipped into traffic behind them. My gut said she was on her way to Andre's, but my gut was wrong.

The town car headed for the entertainment district and slowed to a crawl. Lines had already formed outside several clubs. The car put on its hazards and double-parked near Club Infinity. It was under new management now, but I recalled the layout perfectly from my time spent working there.

Luckily, Eve didn't enter Infinity. She walked half a block toward Olympus, another of the city's trendiest clubs. Bypassing the line, she went straight to the doorman. He checked something on his clipboard and unlatched the velvet rope. Within seconds, she disappeared from view.

"Dammit." I searched for parking, but there was none to be found. Who knew Wednesday nights were this popular?

Didn't anyone stay home and watch TV during the workweek?

Four blocks away, I found a garage and pulled inside. I circled twice before I found a space. Then I backtracked to the club. My leather jacket protected my naked back from the cold night air, but hopefully, the slutty top would be enough to convince the bouncer to let me in. I just worried Eve might recognize it, but I didn't have another appropriate outfit to change into.

Just like Eve, I went to the head of the line. The doorman spent a little too much time analyzing the parts of me he could see from beneath my unzipped jacket. "Are you on the list?"

"I'm not sure. Eve told me to meet her inside." I paused. "Eve Wyndham."

He scanned the clipboard. "All right, go on in."

That was easy enough. I flipped my hair back and walked in, doing my best imitation of a runway model.

Unlike Spark, Olympus felt more like your typical club. The music played so loud I couldn't hear my own thoughts. The dance floor was packed with people grinding against one another. The bar had standing room only, and the line was already three people deep. Locating Eve would be harder than finding a needle in a haystack. Forget sticking a tracker on her car. Tomorrow, I'd stick a tracker on her.

Working methodically, I made my way to the nearest corner and walked the grid. It took me almost an hour to find Eve. She and three other women, two of which I recognized from pilates class, were standing around a high-top table just to the side of the dance floor.

Eve picked up a martini glass that appeared blue due to the glowstick garnish and toasted the others. I tried to move closer, but unless I was standing right next to her, I wouldn't be able to hear anything. Instead, I made my way to the railing, found an empty spot beside a couple who looked more like they were mating than dancing, and waited to see what would happen.

Over the course of the next two hours, several men came to the table with drinks or asked the women to dance. Eve and her friends accepted the drinks and the offers, but the four of them remained in a group. She never broke away from her friends. Their dance partners would eventually grow tired or thirsty and disappear.

When the women were finished dancing, they found another table and clustered around it. Two of them went to the bar to get more drinks. When they returned, Eve took a sip and excused herself. It was the first time she'd gone anywhere alone, so I followed.

She got in line for the bathroom and pulled out her phone. Even though it was risky, I stepped into line behind her. Leaning against the wall, I tried to stretch out my leg muscles, which had begun to ache from standing in one place for so long. Eve didn't notice me, and I cautioned getting closer, hoping to read her texts over her shoulder.

From what I could tell, she had sent instructions to her assistants regarding changes to tomorrow's schedule and plans to get everything ready for Colton's party. Did this woman do anything besides work? She was out with friends. Shouldn't she have been concentrating on that?

I tried to recall Eve's original plans for tonight, but I didn't remember seeing this in her planner. The line moved forward, placing Eve at the front. She tucked her phone into her pocket, but a second later, it buzzed. She'd just finished responding when a woman exited the bathroom. Eve entered, and I waited for her to go into one of the stalls before I walked in and went to the sink.

For the first time in two hours, the music quieted. I washed my hands and thoroughly examined my lip gloss container while I waited for Eve. The toilet flushed, and I leaned closer to the mirror, slowly circling the applicator brush over my lips. She came out of the bathroom and went to the sink beside mine. She washed her hands and examined her face in the mirror.

Her phone buzzed again, and she looked at it before putting it down on the counter. She had just blotted her face with an oil remover sheet and was now reapplying her makeup when her phone went off again. In her haste, she knocked it off the counter.

"I got it." I knelt down to pick it up for her, hoping to see who was texting. But it was a chain message that didn't identify the other party by name or number.

"Thanks." She smiled at me. "Hey, don't I know you?"

Shit. "Um...," I bit my lip and took a page out of Cross's playbook, "do you go to the gym on Holbrook?"

She pointed a finger at me, and I realized she was inebriated. "You're in my pilates class," she said excitedly.

"Yeah, I think so." I turned back to the sink to wash my hands again.

"When's the big day?"

At first, I ignored her, thinking she was talking on the phone, but her gaze bore into the back of my neck. I turned, feeling the engagement ring bump against my bare chest. I'd put it on when I went to speak to Samantha and had forgotten to take it off when I stripped out of my top. Normally, I kept it concealed beneath my shirt, but Cross's outfit didn't leave me with enough shirt to conceal much of anything. "We haven't set a date yet." Had she seen me on surveillance footage from Elegant Events? Did the event planner have security cameras set up in the office that she watched when she wasn't at work?

I turned and looked down at her ring. "That's gorgeous. What is that? Three carats?"

She blushed but held out her hand for me to examine her ring more thoroughly. "We're getting married next month."

"Congratulations."

She let out a contented sigh, a sound one was only capable of making after too much alcohol or really good sex. And since she hadn't been in the bathroom stall that long, it had to be the first one. "Hey, do you want to come hang out with me and my friends? We're all getting married."

"Is this your bachelorette party?"

She made a face. "I hate bachelorette parties. This is more of a girls' night out thing. Y'know, our last chance to have fun without feeling guilty."

That caught my attention. "Oh really?"

"We get to be bad." She laughed. "Okay, not really bad, but like let guys buy us drinks and have fun dancing with other men bad."

"That's not that bad."

"I know," she shrugged, "but it's still bad."

"What if one of the guys gets the wrong idea?"

She hooked her hand around my arm and laughed. "You're so bad." I wondered if she and her friends had made a drinking game out of using the word bad, but I refrained from asking. "Come on, join us. Unless your guy's here." She had no intention of taking no for an answer.

"No, I came with some girlfriends, but they ditched me."

"Then you have to hang out with us." She teetered on her heels, using my arm to steady herself.

"I don't even know your name."

"I'm Eve."

"Alex," I said, wondering if I should have used an alias instead.

"Nice to meet you. Now come on." She practically dragged me out of the bathroom and back to the table. Once there, she made the introductions. Her phone buzzed again, and she reached for it.

"Who's blowing up your phone?" Steff asked.

"Work. I got roped into doing a major event this weekend. We'll barely have enough time to prep. Luckily, I have a DJ on standby. The club has the tables and linens, so that's not a problem. But getting good media coverage might be hard. I'm trying to get the word out on social media and start some buzz." Eve put her phone on the table face up and reached for her martini glass. On the screen was an icon I'd only seen once before. Priapus.

THIRTY

"Have you made any progress on your case, Detective?"

"We're still working on it. Why?" O'Connell knew I called for a reason.

"What about the Priapus app? Did you get a chance to examine it?"

"Yes."

"And?"

"We've spoken to the developer, but it isn't available on any of the app stores. It's sent from person to person. It doesn't have any tracking features or geolocators, so we have no way of knowing who has it and who doesn't. We downloaded a copy. Techs are going through the profiles now, but without photos, real names, or any other identifying features, we have no way of knowing who the club members are."

"What about hooking up with them in real life?"

"There are over three hundred app users. They don't even differentiate gender on the profiles. It's like Summers told us. It's basically a want ad that uses the honor system. You tell me what you want, and if I fit the bill, I respond."

"Have you tried asking for a woman with knowledge of poisons who's looking to party?"

"No, but I'll run that by Moretti," O'Connell said.

"What about the lawyer's files?"

"The judge won't allow us access. Without definitive proof a member of Priapus is responsible for the murders, the judge won't let us snoop through his records. He said that would be a violation of the very foundation of our legal system." O'Connell sounded disgusted.

"What about Martin's friend? She said she dealt with Summers."

"It's not enough. Summers claims this is privileged and asking someone to point out her attorney is in direct violation of said privilege and could violate any NDA, should one exist."

"That sounds like bullshit." I rocked back in my chair.

"You can say that again."

"I thought you had this handled."

O'Connell grunted. "Do you kick puppies too?"

"Sorry, I just thought you'd have made an arrest by now."

"Are those steel-toed boots you're wearing?"

"Nick," I glanced at the door, making sure Cross wasn't going to sneak up on me or barge into my office, "Eve Wyndham has the Priapus app on her phone."

"Who?"

I told him about my case. "Her fiancé fears she might be cheating, and given what we know about Priapus, I might agree."

"Where are you now?"

"At Cross Security. Eve's in party planner mode. I don't think she slept. I know I haven't. She partied until three a.m., went back to her apartment, worked on the computer until dawn, and went back to Elegant Events at 6:30. Kellan's keeping an eye on her while I update Cross, but I wanted to speak to you first."

"Do you think she's the killer?"

"She can't be. She was out of the country when Victor Landau was murdered. When I spoke to her at Olympus last night, she and her friends went on and on about having fun and doing all the things they wanted to before getting married. They never mentioned having flings or sowing their wild oats or whatever, but–"

"You think she'll attend a sex party or two before

committing herself to one man for the rest of her life."

"Maybe. Obviously, she must be into the lifestyle if she's a member." I thought about the items I'd found in her bedroom.

"What about her fiancé? Is he involved with Priapus?"

"That's a good question." I finished looking up the details on Spark and the social media buzz surrounding Colton Raine's party and pending announcement and press luncheon. Eve was good. All the cogs were lining up just the way she wanted. Whatever Colton was announcing must be huge. "Andre never let on either way."

"See what you can find out. The more we know about the sex club, the closer I'll get to that court order."

"I'll do my best."

"Where'd you say she works?"

"Elegant Events. She owns it and runs it." We disconnected, and I went upstairs to speak to Cross.

Like most other early mornings, my boss was already in his office. He didn't appear surprised to see me this early, just a little shocked I was still in the clothes from yesterday.

"Don't start. I haven't had time to change. I've been with Eve all night."

"Did Colton make a move?" Cross asked.

"No, I have no idea where he is or what he's doing. She left Spark a few minutes after you did. I tailed her back to the office then to a club. She partied with some girlfriends until three a.m. and then went back to work."

"Admirable."

"She's a real go-getter." I sunk onto the couch. "We have a problem. Two, actually. First, Eve made me, but unlike you, I didn't introduce myself and hand her a business card. She recognized me from her pilates class. She thinks I'm just another bride-to-be."

"That's close enough to the truth, isn't it?" Cross glanced down at my necklace.

I ignored the question, deciding it was rhetorical. "Second, while I was hanging out with her and her friends, I noticed something suspicious on her phone."

"You really love dragging out the suspense. What did

you find?"

"The Priapus app."

"That's a problem."

"How do we find out if she's an active participant? Is there any way to determine if she uses the app or how often?"

Cross went behind his desk and took a seat. "I'll look into it, but I don't expect to find anything useful for our purposes or the police department's." He entered commands into his computer. "I assume you already shared this tidbit with Detective O'Connell."

I didn't answer.

"All right. Resume surveillance. If Eve is an active member of the sex club, she'll lead you to a sex party at some point, but don't discount other possibilities either. Eve knows a lot of people who have too much power, money, and free time. Any one of her clients could have invited her to join Priapus. For all we know, Colton could have sent her a copy of the app yesterday."

"Is he a member?" I asked.

"I don't know, but the man has a reputation. I wouldn't doubt it."

"This would be easier if you told me how you know so much about the sex club."

"I've explained all of this to you before, but obviously, you weren't listening." Cross didn't look up from the screen. "It's simple. I run a security company which specializes in investigations and private policing. I've been doing this for years. I've dealt with everything from blackmailers to opposition research on politicians. Priapus is a skeleton in a lot of closets. Despite the level of secrecy and protections established to protect the club and its members, I've evaluated it on numerous occasions to make sure questionably moral activity remains hidden away from the public eye."

"What about Ritch Summers? Is he in charge?"

"I don't believe Priapus is run by a governing body, but if it is, Ritch would know who's pulling the strings."

"But you just said—"

"I know what I said." Cross glanced at me. "I don't

believe a hierarchy runs the club, but I have no way of knowing anything for certain. All I can tell you is what I've surmised, but it's just a guess."

"How did you stumble upon Ritch?" I asked.

"It doesn't matter."

"The hell it doesn't."

Cross glared at me. He wouldn't talk, and I had no way of convincing him otherwise.

"What happens to someone who doesn't follow the rules or violates the NDA? Considering what I know about Priapus, suing for breach would draw too much unwanted attention to the club and its members, so I don't see that happening."

"It wouldn't. No one's going to get sued, but the threat's enough." Cross stopped typing to search his desk drawer for something. "I believe what keeps everyone in line and following the rules is fear of the truth coming to light. It's about self-destruction, plain and simple. No one wants to get caught, so no one will do anything to risk it."

"So each person governs himself? That sounds like anarchy waiting to happen or a reason why someone would want to kill the other members of the underground sex club."

"That's why membership is anonymous. No one is supposed to know anyone else, at least not their real names."

"But Ritch Summers knew Victor Landau. He invited him to join Priapus. And if what you say is true about politicians and celebrities being a part of this, wouldn't they be recognizable?"

"I don't know. Perhaps they wear disguises."

"Like a motorcycle helmet and cowboy hat? That won't conceal their identities for long."

"A mask or body paint would."

"Summers didn't mention anything about that." But he'd failed to give us accurate descriptions of the people in attendance at Landau's party. That might have been why.

"Focus on Eve's involvement, and let the police worry about the rest. It's 7:30 in the morning. You should get changed and resume surveillance. Leave the top with someone at reception." He glanced up at me. "Alex, be careful. These are powerful people who won't take kindly to investigators sniffing around their secret club."

*　　*　　*

"What are you doing here?" I asked, getting into O'Connell's car.

"I thought I'd return the favor." He pointed to the drink carrier nestled in the center console. "Cappuccino and a chocolate crème donut."

"This is why you're my favorite detective."

He handed me a napkin off the dashboard. "You say that to all of us."

"But when I say it to you, I mean it."

We watched as Eve paced inside the shop. Samantha manned the computer, turning to look back at her boss every few seconds. We couldn't hear what was going on inside, but from what we could see, Eve was relaying details to her assistants while they made additional arrangements for Colton's party. Every few minutes, Eve would push one of them aside to handle it herself.

"Damn, she's bossy," O'Connell mused. "Her fiancé might be better off without her."

"I don't think Andre would see it that way." I finished the donut, licked the powdered sugar off my fingers, and wiped my hands on the napkin. "What are you really doing here, Nick?"

"Moretti said we need you back."

"Moretti said?" I didn't believe that for a second.

"Yeah, he likes you, remember?"

"It didn't feel like that a week and a half ago when he fired me. What do you think? I don't want to step on your toes."

"No, you just want to fish for compliments," O'Connell teased. "It's my investigation, and it's getting colder by the second. It's not my fault you keep stumbling into the middle of it with warm leads. Frankly, I'm fine without you, but since you want to help, I figure it's best to let you. This is why I asked you to consult in the first place. I knew it'd be right up your alley."

"No, you didn't."

"Do you think Cross knew about Eve's connection to Priapus when he assigned you to this case?"

"Maybe." I bit my lip, but I could never figure out what Cross was thinking. "My head hurts enough already without me thinking that Cross would actually do something to help the police instead of hinder them. He gave me this assignment to keep me away from you. To keep me too busy to do anything else. When I told him Eve had the app on her phone, he seemed genuinely shocked."

"Lucien Cross shocked? I'd have to see it to believe it."

"More annoyed than shocked, but shocked nonetheless." But now I wasn't so sure. My conversation with Cross replayed in my head. Blackmail, background checks, fear of being exposed, Landau could have come to Cross Security for any of those reasons or a million other ones. Cross claimed not to know Landau's reason for making an appointment, but that could be a lie. Still, I couldn't fathom how Cross would have known Eve Wyndham was also a member of Priapus when Cross Security had no history of her or Andre prior to that morning, unless Eve and Landau had a prior connection.

"Do you know why he gave us Ritch Summers?" O'Connell asked.

"He said it was to protect other Cross Security clients from a killer. He said if anyone were to know how Priapus operates, it'd be Ritch."

"Do you believe that?" O'Connell asked.

"At this point, I don't know what to believe."

We watched Eve for another twenty minutes before O'Connell grew bored. "Is this what you've been doing all week?"

"Basically."

"And you haven't gone stir crazy yet?"

"When I tail her to the gym, it's more interactive. At least I get to work on rebuilding leg strength while working. Although, I think I overdid it last night with all that standing around in the club."

"Spark?"

"No, Olympus. Colton Raine's launch party will be held at Spark tomorrow night. Colton even invited Cross, but Eve met friends at Olympus after leaving Spark."

"Is Cross going to the party?"

"I don't know."

"Are you?" O'Connell asked.

"I have to, especially now that I know Eve might jet off to have group sex at any moment. I just don't know how I'm going to get in, unless Cross invites me to be his plus one. But since it's a private event, I don't know if he's permitted a plus one."

"I doubt a giant blowout like the bash Eve is planning would deny guests from bringing a date."

"Who knows? Spark is a strange place. Lots of security. Lots of private areas and back rooms. I have no idea what goes on in there, but it's all very top secret."

"I've heard that about the club and the owner." We sat in silence, watching Eve bark orders while she grabbed one of the oversized portfolios and put the call on speaker. She was tired, irritable, and coming up on a hard deadline. O'Connell examined his hand for a moment before taking off his wedding ring. He put it in his pocket and turned to me. "The only way to know what Eve's doing and what she knows about Priapus is to find a way to get you invited to that party. Since you've built up this bride-to-be persona, let's milk it for all it's worth." He grinned. "Alex, will you marry me?"

THIRTY-ONE

Eve didn't even glance up as we entered, but Samantha did. She passed whatever she was doing off to the woman standing beside her and came to meet us at the door. "Alex, is this him?"

"Nick." O'Connell stuck out his hand, and they shook.

She smiled brightly. "Hi, I'm Samantha Benson. Welcome to Elegant Events." She glanced back at the chaos going on just a few feet away. "As you can see, we're in hardcore event planner mode. If you want to peruse the books, I can set you up in the corner. But today's really not a good day. Would you like to make an appointment instead?"

"Actually, I ran into Eve last night," I said. "When I got home, Nick and I had a long talk and decided it must be kismet. We don't want to cause any trouble. We'll just make an appointment and go."

"Now, sweetheart," O'Connell said, doing his best impression of Martin, "let's not be too hasty." He turned to face Samantha. "We'd love to make an appointment to discuss our wedding with Ms. Wyndham at her earliest convenience, but we still haven't nailed down a theme or venue idea."

"Theme?" I asked.

"See what I mean?" he said to Samantha. "I think looking through the books might help us come to a decision. We don't want to waste Ms. Wyndham's time or our first appointment by arguing."

"It's not a problem at all," Samantha said. "Let me check our schedule." She led us to a computer on the counter while Eve spoke to the caterers for Colton's party. "Eve has an opening two weeks from now. Wednesday at ten. Is that okay?"

"I'm not sure." O'Connell pulled out his phone and pretended to consult his calendar. "I'll have to move my morning meeting to after lunch and reschedule that conference call, but it should be feasible."

"That's fine," I said to Samantha while digging my nails into O'Connell's forearm. He was taking this act a little too seriously.

"Great." She asked for our names, so I gave her the names O'Connell and I decided on while in the car, Alexandra Peters and Nick James. Since I'd written James on the forms at the florist, it seemed the safest option. She reached beneath the desk and pulled out one of the oversized portfolios. "Here are photos from weddings we've planned, along with themes." She looked up at O'Connell when she said that. "Go get comfortable, and take your time. Make sure you note whatever might be of interest."

"Will do." I glanced at Eve who was now desperately trying to find a crew to help with setup on such short notice.

O'Connell took the book, and we went to the far corner of the room, near the front door where a table and chairs had been set up. We flipped the pages, and O'Connell pointed and pretended to make notes while we listened to Eve and her assistants frantically throw the party together.

"Do you think they usually let people do this?" I whispered.

"No, but they think we're whales. That's why they're bending the rules. Plus, Eve knows you. She spent last night drinking with you and airing her dirty secrets."

"Samantha doesn't know that."

"No, but she might have surmised. She probably knows her boss pretty damn well by now."

That's something I hadn't considered. I should have thought to go to Eve's friends sooner. One of them might have been able to shed some light on her extracurricular activities, except Cross told me Eve's friends were rich and famous. And Andre hadn't done anything to dispel that notion. In fact, that's probably where Cross had gotten the idea. The women I met at Olympus last night weren't Eve's close friends. They were just going through the same pre-wedding turmoil and taking the same fitness classes as part of the wedding frenzy. They'd bonded over that, but aside from talking about all the things they should do before getting married and the tiny details that went into the wedding, they hadn't mentioned anything on a deeper personal level.

Replaying the conversation I overheard in the flower shop, I wondered if Eve even had bridesmaids or a maid of honor. She hadn't made any mention about any of that. Just her dress and Andre's tux.

"What's wrong, sweetie?" O'Connell asked.

"What about the wedding party?"

He cocked a confused eyebrow at me. "What about it?"

"They would need flowers and dresses and dinner."

"That's how weddings work. Don't forget about the rehearsal. That requires more flowers and dresses and dinner."

I could be wrong, but Eve didn't seem concerned about any of that. She hadn't even mentioned it. Something wasn't right. I sent a text to Cross asking if he knew anything about Eve and Andre's wedding plans, who was officiating, or the names of the members of the wedding party. Obviously, Andre would want to include his college friends who were now his business partners, so there would be more prep. Did Eve hire someone to handle these things and just not tell anyone for fear it would harm her reputation? Last night, she said it was going to be a small private ceremony. I imagined it'd be something like the commitment ceremony Martin and I had, except that wasn't a wedding and no one had been there except us and

Marcal, who'd taken far too many candid photos which Martin had framed.

My phone buzzed, but as I suspected, Cross didn't have any of those details. I thought about the photos in Eve's apartment. Aside from a few shots of her with Andre or the group shot from work, there had been nothing else to find. I turned my chair a little so I could watch Eve work. The woman didn't have any friends. She had coworkers and clients. Her job was her life. The women in this room probably knew Eve better than anyone else, except for maybe family.

"Alex, what's wrong?" O'Connell asked.

I sent another text to Cross. "Nothing. I was just thinking my mother's going to want to have some say on the wedding."

"Yeah, that happens." O'Connell and his wife had been married for ten years, but Jen was still telling horror stories about her mom and her mother-in-law arguing over the seating arrangement and Jen's wedding dress.

The backgrounds on Eve and Andre had shown living relatives. They each had a mother and father, and Andre had two brothers. That didn't include grandparents, aunts, uncles, or cousins. I stared at the photo in front of me of a hotel ballroom decked out in white and rose gold with an ice sculpture of two swans, their necks forming a heart, which when paired with the expensive linens, exquisite place settings, and a beautiful layout didn't seem cheesy at all, and I couldn't help but think Andre and Eve had no plans to get married.

"Alex?" Eve's voice disrupted my blasphemous thoughts.

I turned in the chair. "Hi."

She tapped one of the assistants on the shoulder and pointed to the speakerphone which had been playing hold music for the last three minutes. "Handle that."

"Yes, ma'am," the assistant said.

Eve came toward us, brushing a stray hair out of her face. "What are you doing here?"

"This is Nick." I wrapped both of my arms around one of his. "I've been meaning to make an appointment ever since

I ran into Samantha at the smoothie bar a few weeks ago, but we haven't been able to agree on any details. I didn't realize this was your place. After all those pilates sessions, you'd think I would have put it together." I laughed. "I'm so dense sometimes."

"Aren't we all?" Eve asked.

"Needless to say, after I ran into you and the other girls at Olympus, I realized just how behind we are on this whole wedding thing. Nick said we had to do something or we'd end up having a long engagement with no ceremony in sight."

"Don't blame me. You're the one who was freaking out when you got home last night." O'Connell turned to Eve. "You probably see this a lot."

"See it?" Eve laughed. "I live it."

"I'm telling you, Alex, it's fate." He ran his thumb against my cheek, and I fought to keep from glaring at him. The detective was having a little too much fun with his impersonation.

"We booked an appointment." I pointed to the computer. "Samantha said you'd have time to meet with us in a couple of weeks, but we thought it'd be best to have some idea what we might want before the time comes."

"Excellent idea." Eve pulled out one of the chairs and sat beside me. "As you've probably noticed, I'm in the midst of making everything perfect for this spur of the moment event. Things aren't usually this crazy." She looked down at the book. "What were you considering?"

Before O'Connell could say anything, I spouted out a similar set of details to what Colton Raine had given Eve, including the size of the guest list and the features he wanted for his party. Eve flipped through the book and found a few photos from different indoor venues.

"It's so hard to decide from pictures," I said. "I can never tell how things are going to look unless I see them in person."

"That's because you have wonky depth perception," O'Connell said.

"I do not."

"You do too." He took my hand in his. "Don't you

remember the first time we went ice skating?"

"I'm telling you that wasn't my fault. The sun was really bright that day. The reflection off the ice was bothering me." I didn't know what to say, but O'Connell and I had spent enough time together to make it up as we went.

Eve bought it and laughed. "You should check out some of the events I'm hosting over the next couple of weeks. It'll give you an idea of how it all works. The things I do for celebrities and any private affairs are off limits, of course. But there are some receptions and parties you could swing by and check out."

"No, I totally understand," I said. "We don't want to intrude on someone's special day."

She chewed on her lip for a moment. "Colton Raine's having a launch party tomorrow. It's invitation only, but the media will be swarming all over the place. He wants the publicity. I don't think he'd mind having two more guests show up."

"Are you sure?" I asked.

"We don't want to be an imposition or get you in any trouble," O'Connell said.

"No, it's fine. I'll make sure you're added to the guest list." Eve reached for a notepad. "So you're thinking a guest list of three hundred?"

"Give or take," I said. "He wants three hundred. I was thinking something smaller and quieter." I cocked my head to the side. "You're getting married soon. How many people are going to your wedding?"

"Not many. We're just having a small gathering."

"How big's your bridal party?" I asked, hoping that seemed like something Steff or one of the other bridezillas would want to know.

"I'm not sure."

"Aren't you getting married next month?" I asked.

"That's the plan." Eve flipped through the portfolio, scribbling notes in shorthand. Before I could say anything else, the annoying hold music stopped. "I have to get back to work. Feel free to peruse the books as long as you like." She wrote down the info for the party and tore it off the bottom of her notepad. "Don't forget to check out the party tomorrow night. It's at ten. I hope you can make it."

"We'll be there," O'Connell said.

THIRTY-TWO

"Did you notice the photos in her book?" O'Connell asked.

"Lots of extravagant décor."

"Not that." He circled the block. "The venues."

"Mostly hotel ballrooms."

"Two of them I recognized from the poisonings." He slid into a parking space at the other end of the street.

"Makes sense, I guess. Eve Wyndham organizes events for the rich and famous. The members of the underground sex club are equally rich and possibly just as famous. There are only so many places that would live up to their standards."

"I didn't realize group sex required two thousand thread count Egyptian cotton sheets." O'Connell rested an elbow on the door while he drummed the fingers of his other hand against the steering wheel. "Those parties had an awful lot of flowers."

"Anything poisonous?"

"I wouldn't be surprised, but I'm no horticulturist. I can't identify toxic plants from photos." O'Connell stared at the Elegant Events sign. "You said Eve Wyndham was out of the country when Victor Landau was killed."

"As far as I know. What are you thinking?"

"I'm not sure yet."

"You're thinking the parties Eve throws and the murders are connected."

O'Connell glanced at me. "Is that what you're thinking?"

"I don't know. Eve's around the types of people who would belong to Priapus. They'd make ideal clients, and what better way to celebrate a special event than with an even more exclusive private after party."

"That's kind of what I was thinking."

"Eve might know the killer."

"I need to check dates and find out what types of events the hotels had going on when the killings occurred."

"Start with Landau's." I thought about everything we knew about the four murders. "Cross said Priapus is in favor of anonymous sex. He suspects the participants might wear masks or disguises to conceal their identities from one another."

"You saw the security cam footage from outside Landau's hotel room. Motorcycle helmet, cowboy hat, sunglasses, and scarves."

"Yes, but they might have had other disguises. Latex or lace masks. Body paint. Something they put on once they stepped foot in the suite to make themselves unrecognizable to the rest of the participants."

"What are you talking about, Parker? You saw Victor Landau, he was recognizable."

"He's also dead. The victims might have tried to blackmail other members of Priapus."

"That seems unlikely. Is that what Cross said?"

"Not in so many words." I stared out the window, wondering if Eve's life could be in danger too. "I'm just thinking that might explain why Ritch Summers couldn't give us better descriptions of his fellow fornicators."

"Body paint is out. We would have found transfer at the scene, like the lipstick on Landau's body."

"They could have worn masks instead."

"Sure, or they kept on their sunglasses and scarves. Or hey, a paper bag with a few strategic holes cut out would work too." He studied my expression. "Does it matter?"

"It might." I thought about the lace masquerade-esque

masks I'd found in Eve's drawer. If she participated in these events, that might have been what she wore to conceal her identity, especially if the people she planned to have group sex with turned out to be her clients.

"What are you thinking?"

"Andre's hopelessly in love with her, and she doesn't even know how many people are in the wedding party. She hasn't picked out her flowers or colors or anything. She has a dress and Andre has a suit. Though, come to think of it, I don't remember running across a wedding dress anywhere in her apartment."

"When were you in her apartment?"

"That's irrelevant."

"Her dress could be getting altered or at his place."

"I don't think she has any desire to marry him. She's careful though. She doesn't flirt or fool around, not really. She and Colton got a little friendly in her apartment, but she put an end to it quickly."

"Are we still talking about the murders, or have you switched topics?" O'Connell asked.

"I'm talking about how the perfect couple is far from perfect. Sadly, I don't think Andre has any idea."

"He must if he hired Cross Security to tail his bride."

"Good point." I reached for the door handle, but everything about the situation bothered me. "I better get back to keeping watch. It's Thursday. Eve rescheduled her entire day in order to get everything ready for Colton's party, but I'm guessing she'll still make a grocery store run for last minute items and to pick up snacks for movie night with Andre."

"Since she's so slammed, isn't movie night canceled?"

"I'll find out."

O'Connell gave me a strange look. "While you do that, I'll see if I can run down any more coincidences and catch a killer. Are you sure you wouldn't rather join me? Killers usually take priority over movie nights and cheating partners."

"You know what you're doing. You don't need me getting in the way."

He didn't buy it. "What are you planning on doing?"

"Nothing. I'm going to stick around here. If you need something, you know where I'll be." I stepped out of the car and closed the door.

I'd taken two steps away from the car when O'Connell rolled down the window. "Hey, Parker, is everything okay?"

"Yeah, fine."

"You don't look fine." His brow furrowed and his mouth quirked to the side. "You're on to something."

"I hope not."

"Don't do anything reckless. If you need backup, you better let me know before it's too late."

"Yep."

"All right." O'Connell didn't look convinced. "If I don't hear from you tonight, I expect to see you at the precinct by eight p.m. tomorrow. Make sure you're dressed and ready to party."

"If you make me dance, I'll shoot you."

O'Connell laughed. "Martin would make you dance."

"You're not Martin."

"I thought I did a decent job."

"Go away." I stepped onto the sidewalk and headed for my parked car.

Our trip inside Elegant Events brought a lot of thoughts to mind. O'Connell had asked plenty of questions which resulted in my psyche drawing even more things into question. Could the killer have attended Eve's events? The guest list would be radically different for each one, which meant someone Eve worked with or one of the companies or vendors she usually hired could be responsible for Landau's murder. For all I knew, I'd already met the serial killer face to face and hadn't realized it.

I sucked in a breath, fighting off the anxiety. I didn't know enough to jump to conclusions, but I couldn't ignore the connection. Then again, it could be a coincidence. Like I'd told O'Connell, the city had a limited number of upscale hotels, and the more upscale, the greater the privacy. It was a coincidence, plain and simple, except Jablonsky had hammered that notion out of me years ago.

Focus on the facts. What did I know? Not much. What didn't I know? Plenty.

Digging through my bag, I found a notepad and pen. What were the commonalities in the victims' profiles? Aside from being male, the victims didn't share any obvious physical attributes. We didn't even have proof all four were members of Priapus. Did we jump the gun with that assumption? They had different careers, but they all had money. Only one was an addict, the rest were otherwise upstanding citizens. They were all single, but that's all I could come up with.

Single. I took out my phone and searched dating sites. If they made the screen any tinier, I'd probably go blind. I needed a computer. That would make this easier. Since I wasn't in a position to do the research myself, I requested complete workups on the killer's other three victims. I also asked if we had any definitive proof they were also members of Priapus, but again, Cross stonewalled me.

"I don't know, Alex. I have no way of knowing that. None of us do. Shouldn't the police have figured a way around this by now?" he asked.

"How?"

"You tell me. You're the one who praises their mediocre investigative tactics."

"Just find out if any of the other vics were on dating sites and let me know."

"Again, shouldn't the police have done this?"

"I'm sure they did."

"Well, why don't you call them?"

"I'm calling you. You said I could use office resources for my side cases."

"Not this one."

"Lucien, please. I'm not asking for our records." I already checked, and we didn't have any on the other victims. "I'm asking for the usual profiles. The research department could put this together in their sleep."

"Fine, but you owe me."

"Whatever," I said, more annoyed than worried. "I also need additional details on Eve Wyndham's recent trip out of the country, profiles on her usual suppliers, the vendors, her contacts at the hotels and other venues she frequently uses, a list of her clients for the last eight months, and any friends or relatives you can locate."

"Shouldn't you have put that together already?"

"When did you expect me to have time? She came back early, remember?" I sighed. "I also need financials on her personal accounts and business accounts and on her employees too."

"What's wrong?"

"Eve doesn't seem particularly gung-ho about her upcoming nuptials. I just want to make sure it's nothing more than cold feet."

"All right, I'll put Justin on that since it is a priority, unlike your other request."

I didn't bother to mention the two were probably connected. Cross wouldn't like that. "While he's at it, can I get the same workup on Andre North?"

"Why? He's our client."

"It wouldn't hurt to be thorough, and since Eve has the Priapus app on her phone, we should probably try to figure out where it came from. I assume a lover or potential lover invited her into the secret sex club. For all we know, it might have been Andre. If not, it might give me some idea of how to prove her infidelity."

"The only way to find out if Andre is part of Priapus is by examining his phone. We've already been over this more times than I care to count," Cross said.

"Fine, but if he's buying her expensive lingerie or sexual paraphernalia, it might give me an idea of what her kinks are. Again, making it easier to determine if she's cheating and with whom."

"I'll have Justin look into it in conjunction with the info you've requested on Eve and her associates."

"Thanks." I stifled an unexpected yawn. "Is the GPS tracker I stuck beneath Eve's rear bumper transmitting?"

"Yes. Why?"

"In case I have to follow up, I don't want to lose track of the mark."

Cross wasn't thrilled by the idea that I wanted to use technology to keep an eye on Eve, but there was only one of me, and Kellan and the rest of Cross's investigators had other things to do today besides taking over my

assignment. "Let me know what you find."
"Will do."

THIRTY-THREE

I remained outside Elegant Events for an hour and a half, watching and waiting. Aside from Samantha making a coffee run, no one entered or left. They were too busy. Eve would work until at least their normal closing time before calling it quits, and I had my doubts she'd throw in the towel at five. She had a lot to accomplish and not much time to get it done. Everything had to be prepped and ready for Colton's launch party tomorrow.

Once Justin sent me a list of Eve's recent clients and events, I decided it was time to do some recon. With any luck, Eve would remain at work. She should be too focused on Colton's event to run off to have a quickie with someone, but just in case, I set my phone to alert me if the GPS tracker moved. I just hoped if Eve left, it'd be in her own car and not some chauffeured thing or Colton's Lotus. Then I drove to her apartment.

Again, I faced the issue of getting inside. After careful consideration, I stopped by the nearest Chinese restaurant for takeout and approached the building. When asked, I told the doorman I was delivering food to TJ in apartment 14J. The doorman didn't seem surprised by this. Instead, he called up to the apartment.

When the elevator opened, I smiled at TJ. "Hey, stranger. I thought I'd bring you lunch."

"What happened to you?" He put his hand against the elevator door. "Didn't we have plans?"

"I'm sorry. I came down with a terrible cold later that night. How are you? Any sniffles?"

"I feel fine."

"Good." I faked a cough. "The morning after we met, I woke up feeling absolutely awful. I didn't want to stop by again and make you sick, especially if I was already to blame, and I didn't want to leave a note on your door because I thought you might think that was a line."

The doorman watched our exchange, but TJ took the takeout from my hands and looked inside the bag. "I see you're still over-ordering."

"I'll never learn. Do you forgive me? I have egg rolls."

He laughed. "Only because I'm starving. I was in the middle of something. Do you mind coming back to my place?"

"That sounds great."

That satisfied the curious doorman, and I stepped into the elevator beside TJ.

"How'd you know I'd be home?" he asked.

"I didn't. I just hoped. I was in desperate need of soup, so either way, I'd win."

"Are you still sick?"

"I don't think I'm contagious anymore, but I'm not a hundred percent. It's lingering." I faked another cough and rubbed my chest. "The cough mostly." That should be enough to give me an opening to escape.

"That sounds bad." He studied my face. "You still look a little under the weather." He held up the bag. "You didn't have to do this."

"I wanted to, unless you don't want to be around Typhoid Mary. In which case, at least take some of the containers for yourself. As you can see, I have way too much."

"I'm not worried." The doors opened, and TJ waited for me to exit. "How'd you know I had a hankering for Chinese?"

"Just a guess. I've been craving egg drop soup for the last few days. I didn't know what you liked, so I got a little of everything." I laughed. "Actually, I always get a little of everything."

He unlocked the door, and Daisy ran in a circle, excited to see us. He put the bag on his kitchen table. "Just give me a second." He went to his computer, saved whatever he had been working on, and closed the program. He returned to the table and watched as I removed the containers from the bag. "I'll get plates."

"I don't need one. I'm sticking with soup and maybe a spring roll. I'm still not feeling that great." I picked up the pint-sized container of egg drop soup and the disposable utensils.

He took a plate from the cupboard and piled it high with rice, beef, chicken, and veggies, pulled out the chair, and sat down. "Y'know," he said around a mouthful, "I have a pizza coming in a few minutes if you want some of that."

"You're joking."

"Nope."

"I'm sorry. I should have asked. This was rude of me."

He waved the chopsticks at me. "No, it wasn't. It was sweet. You're sweet. Don't worry about the pizza. I can always reheat it in the oven for dinner or eat it cold for breakfast. Daisy doesn't mind either way, just as long as she gets some scraps."

I looked around the apartment, which was laid out in an almost identical manner to Eve's. Notebooks and an electronic drawing pad were piled on the desk beside the computer. "What do you do for a living?"

He scratched at a spot behind his ear, ducking his head down as if embarrassed. "Freelance graphic design."

"That's cool." I jerked my chin toward the computer. "What kind of stuff do you design?"

"Commercial art. Labels, logos, advertisements. I did a billboard once." He shrugged. "I get to make my own hours and get some use out of my art school training. It even pays the bills, much to my parents' astonishment."

"That's always a plus."

"What do you do, Allison?"

That's why I hadn't asked that question before. "Lunch delivery."

He laughed. "What do you do, really?"

"I'm a paralegal." I had no idea where that came from.

"Huh." He nodded a few times, finding the thought boring, which had been my intention. "Is that where you picked up the habit of over-ordering? Do you have to order lunch for the entire office?"

"No, they took that duty away from me, but when I'm really lucky, I get sent to pick it up or pass it out. Like I said, I do lunch delivery." I finished my soup, rested my head on top of my arm, and closed my eyes. Despite the fact that I hadn't slept, this was an act. With any luck, TJ would suggest I go home and get some rest.

He skewered a slice of beef and a piece of broccoli with the end of his chopstick and popped it into his mouth. The silence felt awkward. In the light of day, I wasn't nearly as appealing as I had been in the pharmacy. TJ cleaned his plate and put it in the dishwasher.

"You look tired."

"I am." I lifted my head off the table. "I'm not very good company today, and I interrupted your work. I'm sorry. I should go."

"Don't apologize. I wondered what happened to you. Plus, I needed a break and a lovely lunch companion who doesn't drool." He closed the containers and put them back in the bag. "Here, take these with you."

"No, keep them. I don't have much of an appetite. They'll just go to waste, and I hate wasting food."

"Okay," he said reluctantly. "How about I walk you home?"

Before I had to come up with an excuse why this wouldn't work, the intercom alerted TJ that his pizza had arrived. "Go take care of that. I'll survive the trek upstairs," I said.

"All right, but I better not hear rumors about a woman sleeping in the hallway."

We parted ways at the elevator. TJ got into the one going down, and I got into the one going up.

Inside, I put my jacket back on, tied my hair up, and

slipped on my sunglasses. When I stepped foot on the seventeenth floor, I hoped security wasn't paying too much attention since I wasn't nearly as prepared today as I had been last time. I didn't know why I wanted to revisit Eve's apartment, but something told me I should.

THIRTY-FOUR

The dead flower arrangement had been thrown out, replaced with a smaller assortment of African violets. This time, I didn't find a card, but I assumed they had come from Andre. I'd know for sure once I got a look at his financials.

The photos from last time remained where they'd been. Everything looked about the same. Eve hadn't gone shopping yet, but she spent every night at Andre's, with the exception of last night. I closed the fridge, gave the living room a cursory glance, and picked up one of Eve's many calendars.

She had girls' night out penned in pink ink with a circle around it. So that had already been on the books. No wonder she didn't reschedule. I wondered if she regretted it now that she'd been up for a day and a half. I know I did.

I couldn't find her day planner. She probably took that with her since she had to reschedule her meetings. I'd photographed the original pages, but I wanted to see what changes she'd made.

When I didn't find anything else of interest, I went into her bedroom with fresh eyes. She'd changed her sheets to a white set with black trim. For someone so feminine, it struck me as odd that those were her sheets, but they coordinated well with the room and didn't trigger any hallucinations or panic attacks, so I couldn't complain. Opening her closet, I checked every inch, but I didn't find a wedding dress, veil, or any obvious wedding accessories. I went through her dresser. Again, no indication this woman had plans to get married. She didn't even have one of those tops with "Bride" written in a fancy script.

I stopped at her lingerie drawer. Again, that icky feeling took hold, but I pushed it aside, removed my phone, snapped a shot so I'd get everything back into the drawer in the same order, and took everything out and laid it out on the bed. She had several masquerade masks that tied behind her head. The largest ran down both sides of her face, leaving only her mouth, chin, and eyes exposed. With that on, no one would recognize her.

After taking several shots of it and the other three masks, I carefully replaced everything in the drawer and searched the rest of her dresser. Moving on, I checked beneath the bed but found nothing. I went through her bedside table again. From what I could tell, the contents hadn't changed.

Returning to the closet, I did another pass, but aside from the one leather outfit and accessories, I didn't spot anything else. I took several more photographs. Eve had a series of bins in her closet. Aside from a quick glance, I hadn't wasted my time with these before, but today was different.

I laid out her scarves, photographing each of them. Near the bottom of the pile of Hermès, I stopped. The design had been one of the most popular, but I'd seen it before. I took a few more photos and carefully examined it for signs of damage. The delicate material appeared pristine. *It's a coincidence*, I repeated, fighting the urge to pocket it. I had to know for certain, but tampering with potential evidence wouldn't help matters.

Instead, I put everything back, checked the bathroom and hall closets, and left the apartment. Eve didn't have a wedding gown, veil, or shoes. No garters, at least not the kind that gets tossed into a crowd, or any bridal memorabilia. Not one ounce of taffeta or a single invitation or save the date card. Eve Wyndham might be the best event planner on the planet, but she hadn't done a damn thing when it came to her own special day.

After making sure Eve's car hadn't moved from its spot in front of Elegant Events, I headed to Cross Security. The side mirror remained lopsided, so I left the company car in one of the visitor spaces for Cross to fix and went to my office to conduct more research.

"Ms. Parker," one of the assistants said the moment I stepped foot into the break room to grab a cup of coffee, "Andre North phoned an hour ago."

"Did he leave a message?"

"No, he said he'd try back later."

"Thanks." With my cup in hand, I unlocked my door and turned on my computer. Additional background checks and profiles had been compiled and left in my dropbox concerning the women who worked so closely with Eve. I skimmed the details, but aside from two of the ladies having received DUIs and one count of indecent exposure, the rest of Eve's staff didn't have records. Samantha and Valerie, another of her assistants, remained in the clear.

Picking up the phone, I dialed Justin's extension and waited. He answered in his usual professional manner.

"This is Alex Parker," I said, though I was sure he already knew that. "How are we coming on Eve's client list?"

"Still working on compiling all the details."

I'd asked for everything imaginable. That would take time and patience. "What do you have so far?"

"The names of her clients and the list of locations where they held their events, dating back for the last six months."

"Go ahead and forward those to me. I'll get started while you continue to dig."

"Right away."

Clicking open the tab on my dropbox, I brought up the spreadsheet with the names, dates, and locations. It didn't give me much to go on, but it might be enough. The first thing I did was compare it to the list I'd already pulled from the data Andre had brought us. Everything matched, but there'd been several holes which were now filled. As I read, I recognized the names of three hotels.

"Shit." After checking the corresponding dates, I cursed again. This wasn't good. Grabbing the phone, I called upstairs. "How are we coming on those financial records I requested?"

"Still working on getting bank records and the corporate credit card charges. Ms. Wyndham has four authorized users on her corporate card, each with a separate expense account."

"Do your best to put a rush on it." I hung up, the unease growing in my gut.

I didn't have anything yet, but from what I could tell, Eve had hosted parties at three of the hotels where the killings occurred. The parties took place two or three months before each murder, but that didn't mean much. At least they didn't happen on the same day. What was going on? And what did an event planner have to do with a serial killer?

Opening a tab on the computer, I perused Eve's social media pages. According to this, she'd been out of the country when two of the murders occurred. I turned back to check the details I'd read on her assistants. One of them could have done it. The events would have given the party planners access to the hotel, the rooms, the layout, security, and all kinds of other things, which would have made sneaking in and out a lot easier.

"Hey, Nick," I said when he answered, "you need to check the hotel security footage prior to the killings. See if you spot anyone familiar. I'm sending you a photo. Let me know if this looks familiar." I forwarded the photo of Eve's scarf to O'Connell.

"Could be what the cowboy's date wore to Landau's poisoning," he said.

"That's what I was afraid of."

"Who does it belong to?"

"Eve Wyndham."

"You said she was out of the country."

"Yeah."

"Do you think she let someone borrow it?"

"I have no idea, but Elegant Events hosted events at those hotels prior to the murders. We know Eve has the Priapus app on her phone, and we saw the way she works in tight quarters. Her assistants have access to everything, including her phone and computer. Have you found anything concrete connecting Eve's business with the murders?"

"Elegant Events threw a wedding, a bat mitzvah, and an executive retreat at the hotels where our serial killer struck."

"How'd you get that so fast?" Even I didn't have those details.

"I called the hotels and asked. The ballrooms, conference halls, and catering were paid for by Elegant Events. I'm looking into Eve and her associates as we speak."

"So am I."

"I thought you were maintaining eyes on her."

"I got bored." Before I could say anything else, my desk phone rang. "I have another call. We'll finish this later." I hung up and answered. "Cross Security."

"This is Andre."

"What can I do for you?" I asked.

"Eve didn't come home last night. She told me she had plans with girlfriends. They were having some kind of bride squad thing. Normally, I wouldn't have thought much of it. Eve's entitled to blow off steam with her friends, but when I spoke to her this morning, she told me she promised to do a friend of ours a favor. I'm not sure how she could do both."

"Friend?"

"Colton Raine."

"How do you know him?" I asked.

Andre made a sound. "You saw her with him, so it's true. Shit."

"I'm not sure what's true. That's why I'm asking you what she told you."

"Colton's launching his own performance parts brand. He's holding a launch party tomorrow night and a press luncheon on Saturday to answer questions and make sure no one misses the press release. Eve's running herself ragged. I know her. She should have said no. She shouldn't be anywhere near that guy."

"Didn't you say Colton's a friend?"

"Mine, originally. He bought a vacation property from me, but he wanted some very specific things included. We worked closely together for three months while I did the renovations and decorating to make sure it was up to his standards."

"What did he want?"

"I shouldn't say."

"Andre, I don't know much, but I've seen Colton. I know several men who are a lot like Colton. Why does his presence have you so freaked out?"

"He's into alternative lifestyles."

"That encompasses a lot of things. Can you be more specific?"

"He wanted me to build him a sex dungeon. Bondage, hooks for chains and built in cases for whips, that sort of thing."

Flashes of the spiked collar and riding crop from Eve's closet came to mind. "Do you know anything else about his dating habits?"

"Dating?" Andre snorted. "Please. He'd bang anything that moves." He sighed. "I'm worried about Eve. He's a famous race car driver. He's attractive and wealthy. Was she with him last night? Is that why she didn't come home?"

"No, I followed them yesterday. Nothing happened. They visited a venue and made arrangements for his launch. Then Eve left to meet friends."

"Okay, so I shouldn't worry?"

"Not about Colton." Under different circumstances, I wouldn't have opened this can of worms, but O'Connell was right. Murder trumped cheating every day of the week. I just wasn't sure how to ask about the Priapus app. "How far along are you and Eve in your wedding planning?"

"Not far. We were supposed to pick out flowers Saturday, but that got postponed because of Colton."

"What about her dress?"

"What about it?"

"Does she have one?"

"Of course."

"Have you seen it?"

"No, that would be bad luck, but I paid for it."

"And your tux?"

"In my closet. What is this about?"

"I just wondered how much planning you still had to do. You're three weeks out from the big day."

"Yeah, so? Eve's a brilliant wedding planner. She's coordinated much more complicated events than this. We're just having a small, intimate gathering. Only our closest friends and relatives will be here. We're having it in the backyard. If she can throw together a launch with hundreds of people in two days, she can get our wedding off the ground in three weeks."

I'd seen his backyard. I doubted he could fit more than ten people out there. Maybe they weren't having a wedding with bridesmaids and groomsmen. "True." But I wasn't convinced.

"Why do you ask?"

"Just curious." I should have come up with a better excuse, but nothing came to mind. I blamed lack of sleep. "Do you know if Eve ever used a dating site or app before the two of you got together?"

"She did. We both did. That's how we met."

"Do you remember which site it was?"

"I don't remember the name, but it was designed for professionals."

"Do you still have an account?"

"Of course not. Why? Did you find Eve on one of those sites?"

"No, but we're looking just to make sure. So far, I've found nothing indicating she's been unfaithful." Except the Priapus app. "At Cross Security, we like to be thorough."

"I appreciate it."

"We tend to pull up a lot of old records. You know what they say. Nothing deleted from the internet is ever truly deleted, which is why I was asking. I wanted to make sure if we stumbled upon any old dating profiles we'd know immediately they were inactive. You really don't remember the name of that dating site where you met?"

"No, I don't, but it wasn't one of the big ones. It was small. It just helped people who were always bogged down at work to connect in person. I don't think it had photos or anything. It was almost like those old want ads in the paper. 'Real estate mogul looking for companion. Must be a thin brunette with a sense of adventure.' That sort of thing. Frankly, I'd be surprised if it even exists anymore. I doubt you'll find it."

"Like I said, we're thorough." I also couldn't help but think Andre and Eve first hooked up through Priapus.

THIRTY-FIVE

"The scarf's not a match." O'Connell slid a blown-up printed copy of the photo I sent him next to the image from the surveillance footage. "Those are diamond patterns. Eve's scarf has squares."

I picked up both photos and studied them closely. "You're right."

"You sound disappointed. Shouldn't you be relieved they're different?"

"I don't know. I don't know anything anymore." I put my head in my hands. "This is a mess. Why are you trying to get your case tangled up in mine? The two should have absolutely nothing to do with one another."

"Hey, you're the one crossing the streams. You told me Landau belonged to Priapus, and then you told me you saw the app on Eve's phone. I didn't do that. You did."

"I thought it might be relevant."

"I appreciate that. I'm just saying it might not matter." He rocked back in his chair. "Priapus has over three hundred users. We aren't even positive one of them is the killer or that the other three victims were members. The only thing we know for certain is Victor Landau was a member, and he was killed during or immediately after hosting a sex party. Ritch Summers verified that sex party was part of the secret underground sex club. But other than that, Ritch Summers won't talk. He won't tell us if the other victims were part of Priapus. Our perusal of the app didn't get us anywhere. So I don't know."

"The techs can't crack it?"

"I was laughed out of the lab when I asked."

I massaged my temples. "This sucks."

"I bet Landau said the same thing."

"Ugh."

"I think it's time to start over." O'Connell wheeled his chair closer to the murder board. "The first victim was an addict. We thought he died of an overdose. Police found drugs at the scene. That's a direct violation of the Priapus guidelines, which might mean he wasn't a member or didn't give a shit about the sex club's rules. Since he's dead, we can't exactly ask him about it."

"And the other two?"

"I don't know. What I do know is the two members of Priapus we've spoken to refuse to tell us anything else about the club. Summers made it sound like everything got coordinated through the app, which isn't going to get us anywhere. Locating and questioning other sex club members probably won't help. They're all too afraid of unwanted exposure and potential legal recourse for violating their NDAs. It's time we look elsewhere."

"What about Elegant Events?"

"As far as I know, they've never hosted a sex party or club retreat for Priapus, unless I missed that photospread in the portfolios we looked at."

I gave him my best withering stare. "That's not what I meant. When you left, you were following up on leads. What did you find?"

"Eve hosted events at every venue where a murder occurred, even the first, but not on the same days. Always before. I checked the hotels' security footage. I saw Eve and her assistants walk through various parts of the hotels at some point prior to and during the events and cleanups, but nothing after that. They never went near the suites that were used for the sex parties, and I can't place any of them at the hotels during the murders. Eve didn't have any rooms registered in her name or in her business's name, but with disguises and all, who knows? She could have snuck in under an alias. Didn't you say Cross told you Eve had a lot of friends in high places who might not travel under their real names?"

"Uh-huh." That didn't make me feel any better.

"Do you believe Eve's a suspect?"

"No, but one of her assistants could be. They drink green smoothies and celery juice. That's bound to make anyone homicidal."

"Does Martin have you on a health food kick again? You sound like you're projecting."

"No." Though if I'd told Martin the shrink had wanted me to avoid caffeine, he would have taken away my coffee, which might have resulted in unnecessary bloodshed. Luckily, I didn't have to worry about that happening since I'd kicked that manipulative bitch to the curb. "But the circumstances are right. Elegant Events had access to the hotels and all sorts of flowers."

"So do several other event planners, vendors, hotel suppliers, and hotel staff. I'm already looking into the possibilities."

"All right. Good."

But my mind had circled back to O'Connell's question about Eve. She had masks, questionable lingerie, and the Priapus app on her phone. More than likely, she and Andre were members or had been members. "Given Eve's clientele and Andre's connections, don't you think it's possible one of them knows the killer?"

"You think they witnessed a murder?" O'Connell asked.

"No, but someone in their circle, a business partner or client, could be the killer."

"That would explain why the killer chose to attend the sex parties in those hotels. He or she already had time to case the place." O'Connell leaned forward and scribbled a note. "I'll do what I can to get the guest lists and cross-reference them. If we're lucky, we'll find a match."

"The killer might not be on a guest list. You heard Eve. She invited us to check out the events she has planned to help us decide what we want for our wedding."

"Didn't she say she'd put us on the list?" O'Connell added more details to his note. "I might have to ask her about this if I don't find any other commonalities."

"I know." It'd blow my cover and destroy my surveillance. It'd also potentially put a chink in Andre's wedding plans. I pointed to the large question mark written beside Priapus on the murder board. "Do you think this goes back to Priapus?"

"You gave me that lead, Parker, so I dove in head first. Now I'm wondering if we jumped too soon. Cross gave you the sex club as a possible motive for Landau's murder. He led us to that, but we both know he despises helping the police. I'm thinking he might have led us on a wild goose chase for shits and giggles."

I hadn't thought of that. Would Cross do that? My brain said yes, but my gut wasn't sure. I approached the board to examine the printed pages hanging beneath a clip magnet. "What's this?"

"Landau had several dating profiles, so did the other victims. We're scouring records to see if there's any overlap. If someone in particular contacted them or spent an inordinate amount of time visiting the victims' profiles, we might have a suspect."

Flipping the pages, I found printouts from most of the major sites and several of the less popular ones. "Were all four victims on the same dating sites?"

"No, so I have to contact each company separately, get their records, check profiles, and compare user IP addresses, since plenty of people don't use identifiable photos."

"Or real photos," I said. "Maybe that's why want ads are so appealing."

"What?"

I shook my head. "That reminded me of something Andre said. I'm pretty sure he and Eve hooked up through Priapus. He called it a dating site."

"Well, most people aren't going to tell you they met their spouse in a sex club."

"Probably not. I need to figure out how to ask Eve about

it. With enough drinks, I bet she'd spill the beans." Maybe that's how I could determine if she was cheating. I'd asked several leading questions last night at Olympus, but the other women always butted in with their answers before Eve could say anything. I needed to get her alone or see what she did and where she went when she thought she was alone.

"You could try again at the party tomorrow night."

"I don't think she'll be very forthcoming, especially with Andre there."

"He's going?"

"I don't know for certain, but he goes to these types of things. Since Colton Raine has him feeling insecure, I'm guessing he'll be there." I noticed the time. "I have to get back. Eve should be finishing up at work. I'm not sure where she's going afterward, but I'm hoping it'll be somewhere exciting."

"You're just hoping to catch her cheating so you can quit that case and focus solely on mine."

"I have to before you blow it out of the water."

"I'll try not to," O'Connell promised. "Hey," he stopped me before I could depart, "I thought you didn't want to work a serial killer case."

"I don't, but if a crazy woman is killing men she dated or wanted to date, I need to stop her. It gives all women a bad name, and with Martin's reputation, he might be somewhere on that list."

"Do you honestly believe that?"

"No, but at this point, I wouldn't be surprised."

After leaving the precinct, I spent the rest of the afternoon tailing Eve. Thankfully, she stuck to her schedule and went home to Andre for movie night. As soon as they were settled, I decided it was time for me to go home too.

THIRTY-SIX

"You're getting sloppy."

"I am not," I growled.

He shoved my back into the ground. "Bang."

"Dammit." I slapped my palm against the mat. "Let's go again."

"Come on, Parker," Bruiser said, "it's an impossible situation."

"Again," I insisted.

He released his grip, and we reset our positions. This time, I tried swinging my leg higher, hoping to hook my knee around his neck. He parried with his forearm, drove my thigh down on the opposite side, pulled the prop we were using as a gun, and pressed it into my low back. "Bang."

"Fuck." I rolled onto my stomach, pounding my fist into the mat. "Again."

Bruiser leaned back, waiting for me to flip over before pinning me again. I was determined to find another way out of the hold, the one from my nightmares, the one that resulted in the hole in my thigh. So far, I'd come up with nothing. Bruiser insisted there was no feasible escape plan, but there had to be.

This time, I tried to headbutt him. The move surprised

him, and he leaned back on his haunches. But with my legs still pinned beneath him, I couldn't do much. I remembered grabbing for a broken piece of wood, but we hadn't recreated every aspect of that scene, so instead, I took a swing at his jaw. He grabbed my hand and pinned it above my head. I tried to fight him off with my other hand, and he grabbed that one two, bringing both of our arms together above me.

My heart rate skyrocketed, but I stayed present and focused. *Don't panic.* This was how Martin triggered me that night. At least this little exercise taught me something. It probably tied back to when I'd been hung by my wrists and tortured. Damn, I'd had a hell of a few years.

Predictably, I twisted and fought, but Bruiser was too strong. He pinned both of my wrists with one hand, pulled the fake gun, and aimed it at my head. "Bang."

"Fucking hell."

"It's an unwinnable scenario, Parker. You did the best you could and survived. Unscathed just isn't a possibility."

"I refuse to accept that." I flopped back against the mat. "There's always another way. I'm just not seeing it. Let's go again."

"That's enough." Martin moved away from his perch on the stairs. I didn't know how long he'd been watching us. "Bruiser, stop banging my girlfriend."

"She asked me to." Bruiser got off the ground and offered me a hand up, which I refused to take. "Repeatedly."

"That's because you're leaving her unsatisfied." Martin kept his eyes on me, the air becoming charged.

I stared back at Martin. "I'm not finished yet."

"I know, but you picked the wrong man for that. I'll make sure you finish." He put a hand on Bruiser's shoulder. "I'll take over from here. Why don't you take off for the night?"

"Yes, sir." Bruiser quietly excused himself while Martin knelt on the ground above me.

Martin picked up the fake gun we'd been using and examined the wood prop. "He used toys and still couldn't get you there?" He clucked his tongue in disapproval, tucking the gun away and getting into position. "Ready?"

"Yep."

He reached for my belt, and I twisted to the side beneath him. He moved his hands up to my shoulders, pushing me harder into the ground. This time, I brought my arms up inside of his, throwing his arms off to the side. He wobbled, and I tried to sucker-punch him.

Martin wasn't nearly as well-trained as Bruiser, but he could hold his own in a fight. He batted my hand away, my knuckle brushing against the stubble on his jaw. He lunged, grabbing both of my arms with his and holding them out to the sides, as if we were announcing a touchdown, and kissed me.

I nipped at his lip. Since he wasn't playing fair, neither was I, but that didn't deter him. Instead, he kissed me again, never releasing my hands. He knew if he did, I'd do something unexpected to cheat. He pulled back and pressed his forehead against mine.

"You survived. That's all that matters," he breathed.

"No," I turned my face away from him, "I should have been able to get away. To get the gun. To stop him."

"Alex, it was already too late. The damage was done."

"Then why didn't I stop him before?"

"You couldn't have known he'd escape from prison. You couldn't have known any of it. Deep down, you know that." He released my hands and held my face, forcing me to look at him. "You didn't come home last night, so we didn't get a chance to talk." He ran a thumb along the dark circle beneath one of my eyes. "How did your therapy session go?"

"This has nothing to do with that. Bruiser and I have been sparring for a while now."

"I know." He stroked my hair. "I'm just asking."

"Let me up."

"If I do, you'll run."

I glared at him. "I'm not going to run away. I'm going to finish my workout."

"Fine." He stood, offering me his hand.

I took it and let him pull me to my feet. I crossed to the other side of our home gym, stretched my arms over my head, and leaned over to one side and then the other. Exhaling, I placed my right hand lightly on the barre and moved into first position.

"Just so you know, I quit therapy." I did a few pliés and relevés to warm up, moving from a semi-squat to rising up onto the balls of my feet and back again.

"Wow, you made it through two whole sessions. Is that a personal best?"

"More like one and a half." I moved through the various positions before letting go of the barre and switching to a simplistic routine. My leg was stronger, but it still trembled. "Dance with me."

Martin moved closer. "I hate to disappoint, but I'm out of my depth here."

"Really? You never pranced around in a leotard?" I stood on my left leg, my right raised in a straight line behind me, and swept my body downward, lifting my leg higher as I stretched my left arm out in front of me. Slowly, I came back up, executing a little leap before switching legs. My right leg shook. "It's easy. Take my hand and don't let me fall." Martin held his hand in the air, level with mine, and I grasped his palm. He stepped back to make room as I swept forward and moved closer as I stood back up. "See, not that hard."

"What happened with the shrink?"

"I ran into Lucca in the waiting room." I gripped his palm harder as the tremor increased under the exertion. "She said it wasn't intentional, but she also told me she wasn't FBI. I know for a fact one of those isn't true. Possibly both."

"Are you okay?"

"I'm good. Relieved, actually. The last thing I wanted was for some stranger to poke around in my head. It's annoying enough when you do it. Plus, sleeping for a week has gotten rid of the hallucinations and panic attacks. I just need to take better care of myself."

"Didn't I say something along those lines?"

"Yes, but you didn't charge me three hundred dollars, so it didn't sound as impressive."

"My bill's in the mail." He lowered as I did, my face

inches from the ground as I performed a standing split. "We can find someone else."

"I don't want someone else." I looked up from the spot I'd been focused on to maintain my balance and met his eyes. "I have you. That's enough."

"What about sleeping?"

"What about it?"

"Without the pills, your nightmares will return."

"So I'll deal with them."

"We'll deal them," Martin promised, but I could tell he thought I should seek professional help. "Is this why you didn't come home last night and why you look like you haven't slept?"

"I was working." Slowly, I returned to standing and repeated the leg raise, but my thigh was cooked. Martin anticipated my fall, sliding in closer and slipping his free hand around my ribcage.

"When your legs start to shake, that usually means you're finished."

"You're right. I'm done."

He smirked. "I told you I'd get you there."

I returned his look. "I hate to break it to you, handsome, but Bruiser tired me out. If you want, we can still cuddle."

Martin snorted. "Whatever you say." He scooped me into his arms and whispered in my ear, "But we both know the truth."

THIRTY-SEVEN

"What happened with Eve last night?" O'Connell asked when I set foot inside the precinct.

"Nothing. She left work at 6:45, stopped at the grocery store for ice cream and a ton of toppings, and went to Andre's. They ordered in, ate dinner, and probably did some things with the chocolate syrup that I don't want to think about."

"They're in love."

"He loves her."

O'Connell snorted. "She's like you, Alex. Cool on the outside, a hot mess on the inside."

I glared at him. "Are you wearing that to Colton's launch party?"

"No, I have a black suit and black tie in my locker. You look nice, by the way." He examined the royal blue dress I wore. "Who's watching Eve now?"

"Lucien's keeping an eye on her. I couldn't get into Spark without arousing suspicion, but he said he'd take care of it."

"All right. I want to see what I can find out about Eve's business practices and if everyone she tells to check out her parties gets put on the guest lists. Hopefully, that'll be the end of it and I won't tip her off to your investigation. After that, I'll do some recon and see what types of people show up at this thing and if anyone looks familiar. I just spent the entire day pulling IDs of the women who looked at the victims' dating profiles. So I should be able to recognize faces."

"You seriously think the killer's going to be at Colton Raine's launch party?"

"I have no idea what to think, but it won't hurt to see how these things work. It might give me some insight into the events Eve throws. Plus, she probably uses the same caterers and cleanup crew. I might get lucky and recognize one of them from the surveillance footage from the hotels. It could lead to something."

"Aren't you optimistic?"

"One of us should be." He nodded to the empty chair near the front desk. "Give me a minute to change. We're riding together, right?"

"I hope so. I parked my car outside Spark and took a cab here. Just in case anyone's paying attention, I thought it'd be best if the happy couple arrives together."

"That would make sense."

The drive to Spark didn't take long. Unlike the last time I was here, the alley beside the club was filled with cars. Street parking was impossible to find, so we ended up parking several blocks away and walking. This had been the first time I'd worn heels since getting shot, and by the time we made it to the door, I regretted it.

"You gonna be okay?" O'Connell asked.

I gave him a look. "Martin would have carried me."

"Who are you kidding? He would have had his driver drop you off at the front door."

"True." We got in line to wait for entry. Several high-end performance vehicles were parked nearby. I recognized Colton's Lotus and Cross's Porsche. I wasn't sure about the others. They could belong to Colton's guests, or Colton parked those cars here for a potential demonstration or to build anticipation. It's the type of thing Eve would insist on.

Thankfully, we didn't have to wait long. Everything

moved like clockwork. I recognized George from my previous visit. I just hoped he wouldn't get suspicious that I was here with another man.

"Name." George stared down at the clipboard.

"Nick James and Alexandra Peters." O'Connell waited while George moved the pen down the page.

"Go on in."

"I almost called you Lola," O'Connell whispered. "You could have worn the same dress. This is a similar enough undercover assignment."

"Don't remind me."

We entered the club, which had undergone a complete makeover. The subdued music was replaced by pounding rhythms that moved with the bouncing colored lights. Reds, yellows, and greens. I wasn't entirely sure of the theme, but if I had to describe it in one word, I'd call it fast. Everything was streaked, from the lights to the linens on the tables to the shiny jumpsuits the servers wore.

"This must be what happens when you inhale too much exhaust at a race." O'Connell looked around the room. "Colton definitely has branding down."

"I'm guessing that was Eve's doing."

A server walked by with an empty tray. I watched her go. Tan-colored tights covered her long legs beneath the silver shorts of her jumpsuit, which was unzipped halfway down her chest. The name tag above her left breast had been stitched on, made to look like a mechanic's uniform if he'd cut off the sleeves and pant legs and wore the coveralls skin tight.

"Those have to be custom made," O'Connell said after she passed. He took a headcount. There were at least twenty-five servers working the room, each with a similar uniform made to look like mechanics or pit crew.

I spotted my boss at the bar. He was chatting with Andre. Could this situation get any worse?

"There's Eve." O'Connell nodded toward the woman moving swiftly around the edge of the crowded dance floor. She wore a slinky red dress that shimmered every time the light hit it, just like the highlights in her wavy hair.

Eve grabbed one of the servers by the crook of her

elbow, whispered something in her ear, and let the woman continue on her way. After greeting several of the guests, she pressed a hand to her ear, indicating she had a Bluetooth or radio clipped in, said something to whoever was on the other end, and continued to the bar.

"Should we go over there?" O'Connell asked.

"Not yet." I watched her slide into the spot beside Andre. He looped an arm around her waist. She let her elbow rest on his shoulder, leaning her head down and close to his. They looked good together. Maybe she was faithful.

Andre introduced her to Cross, and Eve smiled. I doubted either man had told her the truth. But just in case, I wanted to stay out of drink-throwing distance until I was sure it was safe.

The bartender poured a glass of white wine for Eve, and she took a sip. She gave Andre a chaste peck on the lips, nodded at Cross, and pulled away from Andre. His arm stretched to its full length, lingering on the small of her back as long as possible before she stepped out of reach.

"Do you think they told her the truth?" O'Connell asked.

At that moment, Eve spotted us. "I guess we're about to find out."

She didn't look mad or betrayed. If anything, she appeared more relaxed than I'd seen her in the last few days. Smiling, she made her way to us. "You came."

"Of course." O'Connell wrapped his arm around me and let his hand rest on my waist. "Thanks for inviting us. This is incredible."

"He's just saying that because he likes the outfits the servers are wearing."

"They're awesome, aren't they? Sexy and fun." She pointed out the centerpieces on the tables. "This is the grown-up version of every little boy's race car birthday party. At least that's how Colton described what he wanted."

"You did a wonderful job." I studied the arrangement on the table. It was such a random hodgepodge of flowers and automotive themed objects, yet it came together perfectly with bright reds, greens, and yellows. "We're already getting so many ideas." I gave O'Connell a wicked look. "But we will not be having the pit crew catering our wedding, no matter what he says."

"Gotcha." Eve waved to someone who just walked in.

"Thanks for putting us on the guest list," O'Connell said. "You said you've done this before, but I feel like a real VIP. Does every party crasher get star treatment?"

"Yes. The only party crashers I want at my events have to be the ones I approve." She looked pointedly toward two larger men dressed similarly to O'Connell but who had wireless radios clipped to their ears. "Spark's manager provided security for this event, but most venues have security. If they don't, I've hired firms in the past. Nowadays, no one can be too careful."

"Don't I know it," I muttered.

Eve glanced behind her, her eyes brightening. "Have you met Andre yet?"

"Your fiancé?" It was easy to play dumb. I just hoped Andre could act just as clueless.

"Yes, I always add him to the list." She met his eyes, her cheeks flushing a little under his adoring gaze. "He's actually speaking to a gentleman right now who runs a security company."

"Aww, that's so sweet that he's helping." I focused on the man at the bar, but he stayed cool. Cross must have coached him. "Wow, he's really buff. You're one lucky lady."

"I know." Her smile grew even brighter. The adoration had to be mutual.

"Sweetheart," O'Connell gave my side a squeeze, "I'm standing right here. Try to refrain from drooling over other men in my presence, okay?"

"Whatever you say, snook-ums."

Eve zeroed in on a photographer. "I'll check back with you later. Please, enjoy yourselves. Try the crab puffs. They're amazing." She hurried past us, leaving a trail of perfume in her wake.

We watched her make her way to a photographer and a few members of the media. I recognized one of them from his photo in a business magazine that had featured Martin on the cover last year. "She pulled out all the stops for this event. She must have some powerful people on speed dial." I scanned the room, spotting Colton Raine at the large round table in the center of the VIP area. The privacy curtains had been removed and the tables and booths rearranged. Colton's table was in the center of the raised platform, making him the main attraction. From the large gathering around him, everyone else thought so too.

"I'm going to look around, talk to some of the staff, and see if I spot any familiar faces. Depending on how that goes, I might head out," O'Connell said. "Are you going to be okay?"

"Yep. It's about time I get to work too. Thanks for the ride."

"Anytime. I'll catch you later, Alex."

O'Connell headed toward the back rooms, and I headed to the bar. Andre North and Cross continued to chat, so I ordered a lemon drop martini and took a seat beside my boss.

"Alex," Andre said, "lovely to see you."

"You too." I waited to see if he'd ask any questions, but my client had been informed of my presence and role at the club.

Andre finished his drink and placed the empty glass back on the napkin. "All right, I'm going to find Eve." He put some cash in the tip jar. "Which way did she go?"

I pointed toward the VIP area where she'd led the reporters.

"Thanks." Andre nodded to me and shook hands with Cross. "Lucien, I'm looking forward to hearing from you soon."

"Absolutely." Cross waited for Andre to walk across the dance floor before turning around to face me. "I see you're finally dressed appropriately." He gazed down at my shoes. "How's the leg?"

"Not happy with this arrangement."

He gestured to the bartender for a refill and eyed my glass. "You brought the detective here."

"You knew about that."

"I don't like it. He could jeopardize your role."

"Assuming you haven't done that already." I picked up my glass, ran the lemon wedge around the rim to pick up some of the sugar, and bit into the sour fruit.

"Since you found your own invite to the party, you don't need me here." Cross eyed the VIP section, practically salivating over his desire to speak to Colton Raine and pitch him on signing with Cross Security. As it stood, I wasn't positive he wouldn't have Elegant Events agree to put us on retainer too. However, that would complicate matters, and Cross didn't like complicated.

"In that case, why did you stay so long?" I asked.

"It'd be rude not to." He looked around before scooting his chair closer to mine. He leaned in, crowding me to block our conversation from anyone who might find it more entertaining than the party going on around us. "You didn't come back to the office last night after you left Eve with Andre."

"I had to work out my leg and catch up on some sleep. What's going on?"

"Justin found a discrepancy in Eve's travel records. Her passport wasn't scanned when she left or reentered the country on her last trip. At first, I thought it might be an oversight. She flew on a private jet. Occasionally, things are overlooked, so I did a bit more digging. I contacted her carrier and checked to see where her cell phone pinged during the two weeks she was gone." Cross glanced around. "She never left the city."

"Are you sure?"

"Positive."

"Could she have left her phone behind?"

"That's what I thought, but while I was talking to Andre, I asked, and he said that he and Eve spoke several times during her trip."

"Could she have used another phone and had the calls forwarded?"

Cross cleared his throat, growing frustrated with my questions. "No. I checked into every possibility. She was here. She never left."

"Do you know where she was?"

"I was hoping you might have some suggestions. The

other day you seemed sure she had no intention of going through with the wedding, that her relationship with Andre was one-sided, so you tell me where she might have been. It wasn't at work."

"What about her apartment?"

"I thought you searched her apartment while she was away."

"I did. She wasn't home." I thought about the empty fridge and the dying flowers. "She stayed elsewhere." I gave Cross my wide-eyed stare. "You pinged her phone. Didn't you get a location?"

"Nothing definitive. She bounced around, hitting most of the towers in the area."

"She didn't go the gym or continue with any of her normal habits. Is it possible she stayed here to coordinate her celebrity client's Dubai bash and just wanted to take a break from the rest of her life for a while?"

"You tell me."

I didn't know Eve, but I knew what it was like to want to crawl into a hole and hide from the world for days at a time. "Since she wasn't at home, work, or the gym, she must have had another place to stay."

"Uh-huh." Cross sipped his scotch, waiting for me to provide him with an answer.

"I haven't run across anything. I haven't discovered any of her real friends, not the kind who'd let her hide out for a couple of weeks anyway. I'm still not sure if she's cheating." I swallowed. "She has the Priapus app on her phone, and when I spoke to Andre, he mentioned they met on a dating app, one that didn't have profile photos or the usual method of meeting but more of a want ad type of interface."

"You think she's using the app to find a new beau?"

"I have no idea. I hoped you would. You gave me Priapus."

"For the detective's case, not yours."

"Did you know they were connected?"

Cross took another sip, his expression souring even more by the second. "No, and now isn't the time to discuss such matters."

"You're right. It's also not the time to openly discuss our client's case or his girlfriend's potential cheating." However, my mind went straight to Colton Raine. She could have been holed up with the race car driver. That would explain how she'd gotten the caterers' uniforms made so quickly. Frankly, if she hadn't known she'd need them at least a week in advance, I didn't see how she'd have been able to get so many of them custom made in less than two days. Unless Elegant Events operated its own sweatshop, that was the only reasonable answer I could come up with. "I'll check into Colton Raine in the morning, snoop around his apartment, and question his neighbors."

"Good idea."

"Uh-huh." I resisted the urge to say something snarky and instead took a sip of my martini.

Cross left to mingle, so I hung around the bar, grabbing snacks and finger foods off the freshly filled trays. When I had eaten enough to make sure the vodka didn't go to my head and my thigh had recovered from our walk to the club, I decided it'd be best to find Eve and keep an eye on her.

The private areas of Spark remained private, but since the caterers and other staff Eve hired had everything set up back there, I wandered around under the guise of collecting info for my upcoming wedding. Unfortunately, I didn't spot anyone or anything of importance. Eve wasn't having sex with a stranger, and I didn't recognize any of the staff or caterers as dead ringers for the police sketches O'Connell had made from the hotel security footage and Ritch Summers's recollection.

So I left the back rooms, wandered across the dance floor, finding the live band to be the epitome of fast, before making my way to the tables. This was like a blend of the events Martin had dragged me to mixed with the feel of a wild college party.

Eve wasn't anywhere. I checked the perimeter again and headed up to the VIP area. Colton Raine's table was empty. It had been for the last hour or so. I figured he'd gone somewhere else to speak to investors or give an interview, but his absence didn't bode well.

"Excuse me," I stepped up to a table where several attractive women were seated, "have you seen Colton?"

"He took off forty-five minutes ago," one of them said. "I'm sure he'll be back after the cigarette."

"Did he leave with someone?"

She snorted. "He's Colton Raine. The man doesn't know how to go anywhere alone."

I didn't like the sound of that. I searched the rest of the VIP area, but I didn't spot Eve either. Shit. I'd lost sight of my mark. Cross would not be pleased.

THIRTY-EIGHT

"Have you seen Andre?" I asked when I found Cross coming out of the restrooms.

"He just asked me to find Eve. She went to take care of something with the media, and when she came back, there was a problem with the ice sculpture. Andre went to get a drink while she worked, but he said that was over an hour ago. He hasn't seen her since. Where is she?"

"I don't know." I'd lost sight of everyone for a couple of hours. No Eve. No Andre. The only thing I knew for certain was O'Connell had left after he finished speaking to the caterers and staff. "Colton Raine left about an hour ago, according to the women upstairs."

"I know," Cross said. "I wanted to speak to him, but he went upstairs to the owner's loft to give an interview. When he came back down, he snuck out the back."

"Dammit." I pulled out my phone and clicked furiously, searching for the GPS signal I put on Eve's car. I'd gone back and forth over the possibility of Eve cheating, but to leave a party with the host while her fiancé waited for her was unfathomable. It never even occurred to me Eve would do anything like this. She had always appeared professional. "Her car's outside. I'll check and see if

Colton's is here, but they probably had a limo waiting. I'll find her and figure out what's going on."

"I'd expect nothing less."

Some help you are, I thought as I went out the front door.

Colton's car remained where I'd last seen it. I went over to it and felt the hood. It was cold, and no one was inside. I checked Eve's car, but it was also empty.

Returning to my car, I unlocked the doors and got behind the wheel. I'd memorized Colton's address, so I figured I'd start there. I didn't know if they'd go back to his place or pop into the nearest hotel or gas station bathroom. But they didn't strike me as the gas station bathroom types. And if what Andre had said about the sex dungeon was true, Colton and Eve might want to play rough. I should have realized Eve and Colton were sleeping together. She had the paraphernalia in her closet. Maybe Colton helped her explore her wild side.

I was halfway to his apartment when my phone rang. *O'Connell*. He'd left the party before I did. He was probably back at the precinct following up on leads.

"Hey, what's going on?" I asked.

"I just got called to the scene of another murder. No obvious signs of foul play, but it appears the victim recently had sex. I'm guessing cause of death is poison, but the ME will have to tell us for sure." He paused. "This one's different than the others. We have a big problem."

"Shit."

Cross wouldn't like it, but I detoured and headed back the way I came. When I passed Spark, my stomach did a little flip. O'Connell didn't tell me who the victim was, but the hairs on the back of my neck stood at attention. Stomping down harder on the accelerator, I went another block and screeched to a stop when I spotted the parked police cars.

Spark loomed just to our right. The crime scene was closer than the parking space O'Connell had found earlier. Oh god. I got out of the car and took a step forward on wobbly legs. The uniformed officer standing guard at the crime scene tape wouldn't budge.

"Nick," I called.

O'Connell turned from where he'd been crouched in front of the victim. "Let her through. She's consulting."

"Yes, sir." The officer lifted the tape, and I ducked beneath it.

O'Connell stood up, brushing his hands on his pants and leaving little gravel stains behind. An almost empty bottle of white wine remained on the edge of the dumpster with lipstick stains on the lip of the bottle.

"That's her calling card," I said. "Another poisoning?"

"It appears that way." O'Connell tilted his chin to the side, stretching his neck. I'd seen him do that whenever he was particularly frustrated. He exhaled and stepped out of my way, so I could see the body.

His belt was undone. The buttons on his pants remained open. His shirt was untucked and wide open. A few loose threads hung from the side as if someone had ripped open his shirt. Lipstick smears covered his chest and low abdomen. On the ground beside the body was a freshly discarded condom.

It took a good ten seconds before I brought myself to look at his face. Colton Raine. I'd seen the man alive less than two hours ago. And now he was dead. Stumbling backward, I managed to clear the crime scene tape before I heaved. This was why eating was such a bad idea.

My entire body shook so violently that every appendage trembled. Colton Raine was dead. I didn't stop it. I could have saved him. I should have saved him. O'Connell grabbed my waist to keep me from falling over while I pressed my palms against the side of the building and vomited into a bush.

"This is on me," O'Connell said in my ear.

"I missed it." I swallowed and straightened, keeping my hands against the building for support. "Eve's the killer."

"What?"

"She left the party without anyone noticing, sometime in the last two hours. She never left the city. She didn't go to Dubai. She was here when Landau was killed. I think it's her."

"If it isn't, she could be another victim." O'Connell took

the radio from the patrolman and made several requests. Units would raid Spark and question the guests. We'd find out what happened. After that, O'Connell alerted everyone to be on the lookout for Eve Wyndham. He gave them a description of what she'd been wearing and where we'd last seen her. "If she's not the killer, she must know who is. This was her party. Her friend. Possibly her lover."

"We need her DNA. We need to know for certain."

"I'll get a warrant." O'Connell made more calls.

I remained on the sidelines while the crime scene unit worked to process the evidence from the alley. The medical examiner arrived, checked the body, and found a puncture mark at the back of Colton's neck. Besides the wine bottle and condom, they didn't find anything else of interest.

"Another unit is serving the search warrant. We'll be able to pull prints and hair samples from Eve's apartment. We'll know if she's our common denominator within the hour." O'Connell rubbed a hand over his mouth as the ME carted Colton's body away.

"DNA takes longer than that."

"Prints don't." O'Connell offered me his coat, but I shook my head. "Follow me back to the station. We'll figure this out."

"Uh-huh."

As I drove past Spark, it looked like the launch party was still raging inside. I wondered what would happen to Colton Raine's new venture. Did he have a partner who'd take over the business? Would they capitalize on his murder to sell more car parts, or would this turn into entertainment news fodder? I couldn't think about any of that now. We had to find Eve.

When I arrived at the precinct, I grabbed my bag from the car and went into the women's locker room. After changing into jeans and a t-shirt, I went upstairs to major crimes and took a seat behind O'Connell's computer to see what progress the police had already made.

"Have they found her yet?" I asked when he returned from speaking to a patrolman.

"No, but the prints we found inside her apartment are a match to the set we lifted off the wine bottle in the alleyway. They also match the ones found on the wine glasses from our four other murder scenes." He grabbed Thompson's empty chair and rolled it around to his side of the desk. "You said you discovered Eve didn't leave the city. Tell me what you know."

"Not much. Cross pulled me aside after you left. We've been looking into Eve's phone records and internet history, trying to figure out if she was having an affair. Her social media posts and credit card purchases placed her in Dubai. But Cross said her cell phone pinged in the city. She never left."

"Do you know who went to Dubai in her place?"

"No." I hadn't thought about it. "I went by Elegant Events while she was supposedly away, but all of her assistants were present and accounted for." I bit my lip and stared at the computer screen, seeing nothing. "I missed it, Nick. I fucking missed it."

"So did I. This isn't your fault."

"He was right there. Colton Raine was inches away." I sucked in a shaky breath before I could start crying. No one wanted that, especially me. "We saw him with the reporters and his friends. Why couldn't I save him? Why can't I save anyone?"

"I need you to focus, Parker. Stay with me. We have to find Eve."

I nodded, not sure I'd make it through the next few minutes let alone the rest of the night. "You need to bring everyone in. Everyone from the party. Someone might have seen or heard something. The people there work for Eve. Andre's there. Someone must know where she'd go."

"It's being taken care of." He glanced around the bullpen. All hands appeared to be on deck. "You've been tailing Eve for the last two weeks. Tell me everything you know. Where would she go? Why would she change her tactics all of a sudden? What happened? What triggered her?"

"I don't know. Did she make us? Cross introduced himself as a security consultant. Maybe she knew we were on to her. I don't know."

O'Connell grasped my shoulders. "Breathe. I was there

too. I saw what you did. She seemed happy and in love. She didn't act worried. The only signs of stress she exhibited related back to the party, not to us. It's possible she was deflecting, but I missed it." He glanced toward Moretti's empty office. "I'm sure I'll catch hell for it, but none of that matters now. Evidence says she was at every murder. She had access to all sorts of flowers. She could have used them to make the poisons."

"She never left the city, which means her alibis are shot. She had tons of wine in her fridge. I should have realized that was her beverage of choice."

"Was she drinking that the night she went to Olympus?"

"No, she had a blue martini." I tried to figure out where she'd go or what she'd do next. "Still, I should have made the connection. She had the fucking app on her phone."

"Her hookup with Colton Raine didn't go through the app," O'Connell said, either to cheer me or because he was musing out loud. "We've been monitoring it ever since."

"What about the other victims? What about Landau? Did they all have the Priapus app on their phones?"

"We know Landau's a member, but the techs didn't find the application on his phone. We didn't find it on any of the victims' phones. That's why we can't make a solid connection between the killings and the sex club."

"She probably erased them to cover her tracks. She would have had time and access. While everyone else was getting it on, she could have rummaged through her target's belongings and deleted anything that would lead back to her."

"Not everything." O'Connell started typing. "Victor Landau's firm held a party two and a half months ago. I didn't put it together because it didn't appear relevant, but Elegant Events planned the corporate getaway. Landau didn't hire Eve specifically. Like I said, it came from the firm, but he was there. Everyone was there. That might have been how they first met."

"That would have been around the same time Landau scheduled a meeting with Cross. Maybe he discovered the truth about her, and Eve threatened him. But if that happened, why did he allow her into his hotel room?"

"She might have snuck in via the balcony." O'Connell glanced over at me. "That might explain the scopolamine in his system. She would have wanted him compliant and relaxed."

"Did you ever find out who rented the other rooms on that floor?"

"The hotel had a block saved, but they weren't registered to Elegant Events. It was some LLC." He pointed to a stack of files. "The info should be in there."

I scanned for a name. It was a foreign held company. From what I gathered, that company hadn't blocked off any rooms at the hotels where the previous murders took place. Nothing connected, at least not in a straight line.

"This doesn't help." I put the paper down, but I couldn't shake the feeling the name was familiar.

"I know, and it's my job to make a connection."

"Mine too." I stepped away from his desk and dialed Cross. "Colton Raine's dead. Do you know where Eve is?"

"You can't seriously believe she killed him."

"The evidence suggests otherwise." I sighed. "Where are you?"

"On my way back to the office. The police broke up the party. At least now I know why."

"And Andre?"

"I haven't seen him. They probably arrested him."

"Lucien, I'm in no mood for one of your anti-police speeches. A man was murdered. A man that drank inside a club fifty feet away from me."

"Have the police pinged Eve's phone?"

I relayed the question to O'Connell.

"It's turned off. She probably ditched it." The detective continued to type, and I repeated what he said to Cross. I knew I should have stuck the GPS tracker to Eve instead of her car.

"All right. I'll see what I can find on my end." Cross hesitated for a moment. "Do you know why she'd kill Colton Raine?"

"No, but by the time the police finish processing the DNA, I'm guessing I'll have proof she was cheating on Andre."

"Wonderful," Cross said sarcastically. "Why is it every case I give you turns into a shitshow?"

"Just lucky, I guess."

THIRTY-NINE

"Where the hell is she?" I paced back and forth beside O'Connell's desk. "What did traffic cams show?"

"Nothing. We didn't see them enter or leave the alley. We see them walking together in that direction, but that's about it. Damn blind spots." O'Connell's desk phone rang, and he picked it up. "DNA found on the condom beside Colton's body and in Landau's room is a match to the hairs we pulled off Eve's brush."

"So she's our killer?"

"It looks like it."

I swore. Gripping the back of the chair, I dug my nails into the fabric. "Any sightings?"

"No." O'Connell rocked back in his seat. "We've questioned her assistants, her friends, and every guest at the party. No one knows where she went. No one saw her leave with Colton."

"They didn't leave together. Cross saw Colton sneak out after he finished giving an interview, and Andre said Eve went to check on something in the back and never returned. Is Andre still in interrogation?"

"No," O'Connell said. "He answered our questions and left. He knows we have no reason to hold him."

"He's upset."

"Yeah. He doesn't believe Eve could do something like this. He's convinced we're mistaken." He glanced at the clock on the wall. "Even if he knows where she is, he won't help us. Units are keeping watch in case Eve shows up at his place or his office. We also have officers sitting on her apartment and Elegant Events. There's nothing else for us to do."

"The hell there isn't." I stared at the murder board. Aside from Colton, each of the victims attended a party or event by Elegant Events two to three months before their murders. Eve must have met them at the parties, pursued them, or did something to earn an invite to their sex parties, and once there, killed them. Her connection to the men hadn't been obvious until now. "She's been playing the long game. She played Andre. She played us. We have to find her."

"We will, and as soon as we do, we'll get the answers we need. You should go home and get some sleep. I'll call you as soon as we find her."

"Yeah, right."

He sighed. "Officers are everywhere. Every hotel and club. They're searching Colton's place. We've already searched Eve's apartment, but we didn't find anything. So we're keeping our eyes peeled. She won't get away. She's too high-profile to evade us indefinitely."

"Whatever you say." I grabbed my bag. I'd never be able to live with myself if Colton's killer got away when she'd been so close. So obvious. Unfortunately, even if I found Eve, I still didn't know if I'd be able to deal with the guilt of another failure.

I drove around for a while, checking the shops and hotels I'd seen Eve visit. But it was five a.m. The shops were closed, and the hotels hadn't seen her. I checked my copy of her schedule. Before she canceled everything for Colton's launch party and press luncheon, she and Andre had plans to pick out flowers for their wedding. That wouldn't be happening now.

Unsure what else to do, I went to the office. Since I couldn't find her and the police were having no luck, perhaps Cross's resources could shed some light on the problem. The high-rise was quiet at this time of morning. Reception was empty, and I passed my colleagues vacant offices on my way to the break room.

With coffee in hand, I opened my door and flipped on the light. Now what? The computer held little appeal since I wasn't sure where to search or what to do. The police were combing through Eve's social media presence for clues.

I paced in front of the couch for a moment while I sipped the hot beverage. I needed a plan. Actually, I needed a miracle. Too bad Martin Technologies wasn't working on a time machine.

How did Eve trick us? Deciding that standing here feeling sorry for myself wasn't a good use of my time, I went behind the computer. Her business credit card indicated she had gone to the UAE, but her phone records and the evidence found in Victor Landau's hotel room said otherwise. How did she pull that off?

I checked her financials again, but she hadn't used any of her cards, corporate or personal, since yesterday. I scanned the list of charges. The foreign charges included a hotel room, restaurant charges, deposits for catering, linens, the whole shebang. Who was the client?

Once I found his name, I picked up the phone. Her celebrity-influencer client didn't speak to me, but his assistant did. "Eve Wyndham," I repeated.

"Yes, I know Ms. Wyndham."

"When was the last time you or your boss saw her?"

"A month ago. She introduced us to an intern she hired. The service we received and the party she planned were excellent. At first, we were concerned, but since Ms. Wyndham's been busy planning her own wedding, we reluctantly allowed her protégé to take over."

"Do you have a name?"

"Margaret Gillman."

That sounded vaguely familiar, so I did a search, realizing the intern in question was Eve's cousin. "I'm going to e-mail you a photo. Can you verify this is the same woman?"

"Yes, that's her."

"Thanks." I hung up, phoned the precinct, and told them to bring Eve's cousin in for questioning. I doubted they'd bothered to send units there. But if Eve had her cousin cover for her in the UAE, she might have swapped places and hid out at her house during the Dubai trip. Hell, Eve might be hiding out at her house right now while she came up with a better escape plan.

With nothing else to do but wait, I took the elevator up to see if Cross or Justin might be in. It was almost six a.m. So the chances were pretty good.

The elevator doors opened, and I stepped out. Justin wasn't at his desk. Most of the lights were off, but I saw a faint glow coming from inside Cross's office. I moved closer and peered inside. Seated on the couch was a distraught Eve Wyndham.

"You son of a bitch." I rested my hand on my gun as I moved into the room. "What do you think you're doing?"

Cross looked up at me from behind his computer. "Alex, please."

"The police are searching for her. You're harboring a fugitive. This is illegal. She's a killer." Except with the mascara streaks running down her face and her trembling bottom lip, she didn't look much like a killer. She looked terrified.

"Alex?" she gulped, confused. "What are you doing here?"

"I work here." I stared at her. "And I'm working for the police as a consultant."

"I didn't kill anyone," she insisted.

"So who did?" I blocked the door and scanned the room for something to restrain her until the police arrived. I'd seen a roll of duct tape on Justin's desk the other day. Was it still there?

"That's what I'm trying to figure out," Cross muttered.

"Colton Raine is dead." I inched back the way I came, keeping my eye on Eve and Cross. At the moment, I didn't necessarily trust either of them. "We found your lipstick on the wine bottle and your DNA on the condom beside his body."

"I didn't kill Colton." She wiped at her eyes with trembling hands. "We had sex, but I didn't kill him."

"What about Victor Landau? Did you have sex with him too?"

She started to cry harder and pressed a hand against her mouth. She looked up at me. "Not Victor, but someone else. I don't know his name. I just met him that one time at Victor's party. He dressed like the Lone Ranger, mask and all."

"Alex, this isn't helping," Cross warned.

"What about the other three? Or are there more?"

She squeezed her eyes closed. "I made a mistake."

"Oh, I'd say so." I didn't see the tape, so I stood in the doorway and reached for my phone. "I'm calling this in." I glanced at Cross. "We don't conduct murder investigations, remember?"

Before either of them could say anything to the contrary, Cross's phone rang. He hit the speaker button. "Yes? Did you find it yet?"

"No, sir. Something else came up. We have an emergency situation with the Clayborn case."

"Clayborn?" he asked, reaching into his desk drawer and removing his gun.

"Yes, sir. You need to come down here now."

"All right. Take it easy. I'll be right there."

Cross tucked the gun behind his back. "Alex, you're right. The police will sort this out. You should take Eve to the station. I don't trust the cops to do it. Go now. Straight to the lobby and out. Don't stop for anything."

"What?" Eve gasped. "You promised."

"Things change." Cross met my eyes. "Go. I have other business to handle." He didn't wait for me to answer before he stormed out of his office and down the stairs, leaving the elevator for my use.

Eve tried to run past me, but I shoved her back onto the couch and closed the door. Then I called O'Connell and told him I had Eve.

"You can't do this. I'm innocent," she insisted.

"Prisons are full of innocent people. I'm sure you'll fit right in." But Cross's abrupt exit and strange behavior had triggered that nagging itch in the back of my brain. Something else was going on here. "Why did you come to Lucien for help?"

"Andre said he'd protect me."

"So Andre knows you're here?"

She nodded, looking even more frightened than before. She didn't look at all like the in-control, work-focused, blushing bride-to-be that I'd been tailing for the last two weeks. "He told me to come here."

"You called him? When? Tell me what happened tonight?" None of it was admissible in court, but I wasn't a cop. And whatever she said to me right now would only further their investigation.

"Colton." She sniffled, fidgeting with the strands of her hair.

"You cheated on your fiancé?"

"Yes. No. I don't know. I had sex with Colton. I'm supposed to be getting married in three weeks. That's why. I just snapped. I'll never get to be touched by another man or adored or loved. No one will look at me like they want me and actually get me. I just…I wanted to feel wanted. To have that rush. That new thing that only happens with someone the first time."

"But this isn't the first time you've cheated."

"No, it's the second. I didn't plan on doing it again. I thought I'd gotten it out of my system, but Colton was just so persuasive."

"Who was the first? The Lone Ranger?"

"Yes."

"At Victor Landau's sex party?"

She bit her lip. "Yes."

"He's dead too. Did you know that?"

"I saw it on the news, but I didn't kill Victor either. I didn't even have sex with him."

"What about the other sex parties you attended?"

"I didn't participate. I just watched. I was curious."

"And when the festivities were over, you thought you should kill the man of the hour for the hell of it?"

The blood drained from her face. "No. I've never killed anyone. I don't even like squishing bugs."

"The wine glasses link you to at least four sex parties, including Landau's. Each one resulted in murder, just like Colton Raine's murder tonight. Don't tell me that isn't on you."

"It isn't."

The scary part was I believed her, but she'd fooled me before. I didn't trust my gut or my judgment. I'd been screwing up too much lately. "If that's true, you must know who the killer is. You were at all five scenes. You're the only person we can place with the victim around the time of the murder. So if it isn't you, you have to give me something."

"It wasn't me. I swear to god, but I don't know who it could be. No one else was there. Not tonight. Not with Colton. That was just us." She sniffed, fighting to control herself. Her entire body shook as if she wanted to run but couldn't. She wasn't faking the fear. I just didn't know if it was fear of being caught or of being wrongfully accused. "Colton convinced me to sneak out with him. It'd be fun. We could be bad. He teased that we might get caught. That turned him on, but it freaked me out. I love Andre. I do. I never wanted to hurt him. I just didn't want to regret marrying him. That's how this whole thing started. Colton and I met outside Spark. We went into the alley. I've never done anything like that before. It was exhilarating. When we were finished, he was very much alive."

"Then what happened?"

"I pulled down my dress and left him to put himself back together. But he never came back to Spark. I found Andre and asked if he'd seen Colton, but Andre told me the police had been asking the guests who were leaving about Colton's whereabouts and he heard one of them say he'd been killed. I freaked. That's when Andre snuck me out the back, put me in a cab, and sent me here."

"What time was that?"

"I don't know? Around one or two. I didn't notice the time."

Her story didn't make sense. And what made even less sense was my boss leaving his office with a gun to go talk to the guy's downstairs in the lab. I checked his computer screen, finding the paper trail on several LLCs and other shell companies that had rented out room blocks in the hotels at the times and dates where the murders occurred. Now I knew why the name had sounded so familiar.

"Shit." I went through Cross's drawers until I found some cable ties. I wasn't sure what was going on, but I was done screwing up. I bound Eve to the filing cabinet and locked Cross's door. Grabbing my gun, I got into the elevator, wondering if this was one of my wackier nightmares because the world wasn't usually this insane.

FORTY

The elevator doors slid open, and I peered out. The thirty-first floor was empty. Overnight, it usually ran on a skeleton crew. One medic, one computer tech, and one forensic expert. But I didn't see anyone, not even Cross.

I stepped off the elevator, moving down the corridor and checking the different labs and rooms as I went. The tech on the phone told Cross there was an emergency, so where were they?

The large computer lab was vacant, so I shut the door and moved on to the rooms used to recreate crime scenes. Empty. I continued toward the medical area in the back. I'd just passed the restroom when the door behind me creaked.

Before I could turn around, the barrel of a tactical shotgun pressed into the back of my head. "Hands up. Face forward. Don't turn around." He reached around and took my gun from my hand and tossed it down the corridor. It slid to a stop behind the front desk.

Exhaling, I slowly brought my hands up to shoulder height. "Do you want to tell me what's going on? Ballistics is the third door on your left."

"You're still funny."

"One of us ought to be amused, and it sure as hell isn't me. What are you doing, Andre? What's going on?"

"Move." He pressed the gun more forcefully into the back of my head to encourage me to walk forward.

"No problem." I bit my lip, contemplating the best way to disarm him. He was close enough that I should be able to wrestle the gun from him. But if he pulled the trigger, at this range, my brains and blood would make a mess all over the floor. The janitors would be picking bits of me off the tile for weeks.

He forced me down the hall and grabbed my shoulder, stopping me in the doorway to one of the rooms. The three techs cowered in the corner. One of them had been injured, and the medic hovered over her. I couldn't tell the extent of her injuries, but it was enough to convince the rest of the lab rats to play nice. Cross remained near the door. He caught my eye, anger and concern boiling up to the surface.

"Lucien, you told me no one else was working this early," Andre said. "Didn't I warn you what would happen if you lied to me again?"

"He didn't lie." I stared into Cross's eyes, hoping to communicate a plan. Andre was outnumbered five to one. We could take him. It shouldn't be that hard. "I just got here. I wanted to do some research and figure out what happened outside Spark."

I shifted my weight to my left leg, my stronger leg, and turned my right foot out.

Cross shook his head ever so slightly. "Alex is the most insubordinate employee I have. I never know where she is or what she's doing."

"You expect me to believe that?" Andre prodded me to move deeper into the room, but this was the ideal spot. Any farther and I'd risk a wild shot hitting the techs.

"It's the truth. She never listens." Cross stared at me. "For once in your life, do as you're told."

But I couldn't let anyone else get hurt. I spun, knocking the barrel of the shotgun away from me with my right forearm. It knocked against the doorjamb, and I rushed forward with my left shoulder. With the way Andre North was built, I would have had better luck running straight into a brick wall. I hit solid muscle.

Andre cracked me across the face with the butt of the

shotgun, and I went down. He put his foot on my back and the barrel against my cheek. Blood dripped down from the laceration and ran into my mouth.

"Stop." Cross stepped forward. "You want my files. You want everything I have on you. But you won't get them without my cooperation, and if you kill her, I won't give you a damn thing."

I huffed against the tile, tasting salty, metallic blood. I wasn't sure exactly what was happening or why Andre North wanted Cross's files or me dead, but it was safe to assume it had to do with the string of murders.

Andre held me in place with his foot. "You better hurry before any more of your employees show up. You wouldn't want anyone else to get hurt."

Cross nodded and went to the nearest computer terminal. "How did you subvert the surveillance cameras at the hotels? No one saw you enter or leave. That was brilliant. I've been in this business a long time and have never seen anyone move so stealthily, especially a man of your size."

Andre chuckled, sounding like the pleasant man I'd met a few weeks ago. "Years of doing home renovations has taught me a few things. After Eve would return from having her naughty little adventures, I'd use my rope ladder and drop down from the floor above, take care of business, and climb back up. No one was ever the wiser."

"You knew she was cheating on you?" I asked.

Andre looked down, releasing some of the pressure from the gun barrel. "Not at first, but I suspected. She'd host events and invite me. And I'd watch her, the way she flirted, the way they flirted back. I told myself it was harmless. Until she started sneaking out. She'd say she had to go out of town to set something up for a client, but she'd sneak away. Once, she even told me she was staying at her cousin's, but I had the app too. I knew about the sex parties, the locations, everything. She'd rent rooms under her clients' names and accounts, so I wouldn't find out. But I did."

"So you followed her?"

Andre shook his head. "No, I knew ahead of time where

they'd be, so I checked in under my company or one of my partner's corporations. I was so sure that I was wrong. Except I stayed out on the balcony, the one diagonally above the room, and watched the love of my life climb over the railing and knock on the door. I could barely recognize her, dressed up and disguised, but it was always Eve. The way she moves, laughs, and fixes her hair, I know my Eve. She was so afraid of getting caught or so embarrassed by what she was doing, she literally snuck in the back."

"So you poisoned them?" I asked.

"With whatever flowers she'd bring home from the events or whatever was growing around my properties." He rubbed a hand over his face and backed off so I could get off the ground. He jerked the gun toward the end of the desk, so I crawled over to it and took a seat. Keeping my hands where he could see them. The longer we kept him talking, the better off we'd be. I glanced back at the injured tech, but her injuries didn't appear to be life-threatening. "I always knew when she met someone. She'd keep tabs on them. She'd say it was for business, but she'd check their social media pages and follow their businesses. It drove me crazy." He narrowed his eyes. "She used to do that with me. When we first met. I don't know what happened. Did she get bored? Is that it?"

"No," I said, "she loves you. She just wants to have more experiences before she commits to you for the rest of her life."

"Really?" Andre asked, seeming more unstable by the second.

"Yes," Cross said.

Andre shook his head. "I don't know. How did you find any of this out? Didn't you see what she was like? What she was doing?"

"She was careful," I said. "We didn't see anything."

Suddenly, his mood shifted. "Oh really? I'm having a hard time believing that. I need to know what you have on me." He kept the gun aimed in my direction but turned his focus to Cross. "Victor Landau was another of Eve's playthings. She threw that party for his firm, and she met him for coffee once or twice afterward. I warned him to back off, and the next day, he came running straight to you. What did he tell you? What did you tell the cops?" He jerked his chin toward me. "This bitch is working for them."

"Consulting, not working," I said, hoping to confuse or distract him long enough for Cross to do something.

"It's the same fucking thing." Andre kept his attention on my boss.

"Victor Landau didn't tell me anything. He took a call in the middle of the meeting and left," Cross said. "I didn't open a file on you until you came to me."

"Sure, that's why he still had your card in his wallet the day he fucked my fiancée." Andre took a step toward Cross. "I asked the sniveling architect about it. I even forced some truth serum down his throat, but he wouldn't fess up."

That explained the scopolamine. "He wasn't lying," I said. "Eve didn't have sex with him."

Andre turned on me. For a moment, I thought he might squeeze the trigger out of anger. "How would you know?"

"Eve told me."

He scoffed. "You expect me to believe that?" He turned back to Cross. "You said you had evidence and files. Now you say you don't. Which is it? Because if you don't have anything, I don't need any of you."

"We have intel on you now," I said. "We were piecing it together. We couldn't figure out how you got into the rooms, but we knew you did. We knew about the poison, about Eve's involvement."

"She didn't kill them," Andre said. "She didn't even know they were dead. I kept that away from her. I told her Colton was dead, but she doesn't know I killed him. She fucked him. God, I listened to her moans, hating every moment. As soon as she walked away, I..." Andre shook his head. "Colton Raine is lucky I didn't rip his head off and spit down the hole in his throat. But he's gone now. They're all gone now. Eve's mine. I won. We're getting married. We'll be together. Everything will be okay from now on, just as soon as you give me what you have, so I can destroy your files." He took a step closer to me, holding the gun level at my head. "I don't know what you and Lucien have going on, but it's obviously something special. So you better hurry it up, Lucien."

The elevator chime sounded, and Andre turned to look into the hallway. Without wasting a moment, Cross ran at Andre, leapt into the air, and tackled him to the ground. Scrambling to my feet, I ran to the cabinet in the back of the office, threw it open, and entered the code to unlock the gun safe. One of the techs had the same idea, picked up the metal IV pole, and crashed it down on top of Andre, who now had Cross pinned to the floor and was pressing the barrel of the shotgun horizontally across my boss's neck.

"Freeze," I yelled at the same time as O'Connell, who'd just burst through the doorway.

Andre pushed down harder, choking Cross, who was now turning purple.

"Police. Drop the gun." O'Connell aimed.

But I pulled the trigger. I didn't shoot to kill despite the fact every cell in my body told me to eliminate the threat for good. Andre was crazy. And having a crazed killer who'd already demonstrated he was hell-bent on revenge turn his sights on me wasn't on my to-do list when I woke up this morning. But neither was taking a life.

The bullet went into Andre's right shoulder blade and got lodged somewhere inside. That gave Cross enough leverage to shove Andre off of him. With the killer sprawled on his back, O'Connell kicked the gun away.

"Andre North, you're under arrest for the murder of Colton Raine." O'Connell flipped him over, handcuffed him, and called for backup units and ambulances. Then he read him the rest of his rights.

"Are you okay, Lucien?" I asked as my boss coughed a few times and rubbed his neck.

He nodded. "I thought you were a better shot."

"She is," O'Connell said. "That's why you're not dead. If she'd shot him in the head, it probably would have gone through you too."

"He killed all of them." I stared at Andre who looked just as intimidating even as he bled through his shirt and remained handcuffed on his stomach with three guns pointed at him.

"I have some files for you, Detective O'Connell," Cross offered, "but first, I have to take care of my people." He went to the back of the room and knelt down beside the injured tech. She'd taken a hit to the ribs from Andre's shotgun. The medic had been afraid her lung might collapse. But once backup and the ambulances arrived, everyone was squared away.

"I thought you said Eve was here," O'Connell said to me as we watched four uniformed officers escort Andre out of the building and to a waiting cop car.

"She is. I chained her to the filing cabinet in Cross's office."

"Eve's here?" Andre turned to look at us while one of the cops opened the back door on the patrol car. "Can I see her? I want her to know this is over. That I forgive her. That we can be together now."

"Take him away," O'Connell said. Once the door closed, he turned to me, just as the EMT taped the bandage to my face. "I'm going to need you to explain all of this to me, starting with why Cross is suddenly being so cooperative."

"I'll do my best. But you might not believe it. I'm not sure I believe it."

*   *   *

By the time I finished at the precinct and Eve explained her side of things which mirrored what she'd already said and what Andre had told us, O'Connell had a strong case against Andre. Eve, despite her flip-out and adulterous behavior, wasn't a killer. If anything, her freaking out over their wedding had been much less of a freak out than the possessive behavior Andre had exhibited.

"She's better off without him." I signed the last of the paperwork and glanced into the conference room where Cross was filling out an official statement.

"He would have killed her," O'Connell said. "Eventually, she would have done something to set him off and he would have turned that rage on her."

"She loved him but had no idea how dangerous and unstable he was. I'm guessing that's why she freaked out at the idea of marriage and committing herself to him and that's actually why she acted out. Subconsciously, she might have been looking for an out."

"I think you're right." O'Connell rocked back in his chair. "Do you think you might have picked up on something subconsciously too and that's why you hallucinated him killing her?"

I'd told O'Connell about my PTSD episode after Andre had been booked. "You give me a lot more credit than I deserve."

"It's called the benefit of the doubt."

"Too bad Andre hadn't done the same with Eve. It's also a shame she hadn't acted out in a healthier and safer manner."

"How? By talking to him?"

"I don't know. Maybe."

"He would have killed her. This way, he was able to blame other people for their relationship problems and take it out on them. It's probably the only thing that kept her safe."

"You're probably right. This could have gone bad a thousand different ways. The body count could have been much greater, but no matter what I tell myself, five people are still dead. One of them I should have saved. Instead, I let the psycho live."

"A life is still a life."

"What if he gets out and comes for one of us? Then what?"

"He won't," O'Connell promised. "The case is airtight. Even your boss made sure of that. Andre won't get off. He killed them. It's up to a judge and jury to decide what happens next."

"Yeah, but—"

"Andre won't hurt anyone else, Alex. I promise you that." He jerked his chin toward the exit. "Go home. I'm sure Martin's waiting for you."

"Great, now I have to explain this to him." I gestured at the bandage on my face. "Any ideas?"

"I'll take care of the big stuff. You can handle that on your own."

"Fine." I got out of the chair and put on my jacket. "Damn, on top of everything, I owe Jablonsky twenty bucks since he was right."

"So do I." O'Connell pulled the money out of his wallet and handed it to me. "Give this to him the next time you see him."

"Sure thing, Nick. And from now on, keep your cases away from mine."

"I'll try, but I can't make any promises."

Don't miss the next Alexis Parker novel, *Past Crimes*.

Eight years ago, Lucien Cross covered up a murder. Now Alexis Parker has to prove he didn't do it. Except, she's not convinced he isn't guilty.

Ever since Alex went to work for Lucien Cross, nothing's been the same. She's always been wary of him. Now, she finally knows why.

The police discovered a body and enough evidence to put Cross in a cell for the rest of his life. He won't offer an explanation. He hasn't even said he's innocent. The only thing he wants is Alex to work the case and clear his name. But how can she do that when every bit of evidence points to the contrary?

Available in print and ebook.

Warning Signs

ABOUT THE AUTHOR

G.K. Parks is the author of the Alexis Parker series. The first novel, *Likely Suspects,* tells the story of Alexis' first foray into the private sector.

G.K. Parks received a Bachelor of Arts in Political Science and History. After spending some time in law school, G.K. changed paths and earned a Master of Arts in Criminology/Criminal Justice. Now all that education is being put to use creating a fictional world based upon years of study and research.

You can find additional information on G.K. Parks and the Alexis Parker series by visiting our website at
www.alexisparkerseries.com

Made in United States
Orlando, FL
27 June 2024

48366992R00186